THE GOLD TRAIL

MORE WILDSIDE CLASSICS

THE GOLD TRAIL

HAROLD BINDLOSS

WILDSIDE PRESS

THE GOLD TRAIL

CHAPTER I

BOTTOMLESS SWAMP

It was Construction Foreman Cassidy who gave the place its name when he answered his employer's laconic telegram. Stirling, the great contractor, frequently expressed himself with forcible terseness; but when he flung the message across to his secretary as he sat one morning in his private room in an Ottawa hotel, the latter raised his eyebrows questioningly. He knew his employer in all his moods; and he was not in the least afraid of him. There was, though most of those who did business with him failed to perceive it, a vein of almost extravagant generosity in Stirling's character.

"Well," said the latter, "isn't the thing plain enough?"

The secretary smiled.

"Oh, yes," he said. "Still, I'm not sure they'll send it over the wires in quite that form."

His employer agreed to the modification he suggested, and the message as despatched to Cassidy read simply, "Why are you stopping?"

After that the famous contractor busied himself about other matters until he got the answer, "No bottom to this swamp."

Then his indignation boiled over, as it sometimes did, for Stirling was a thick-necked, red-faced man with a fiery temper and an indomitable will. He had undertaken a good deal of difficult railroad work in western Canada and never yet had been beaten. What was more to the purpose, he had no intention of being beaten now, or even delayed, by a swamp that had no bottom. He had grappled with hard rock and sliding snow, had overcome professional rivals, and had made his influence felt by politicians; and, though he had left middle-age behind, he still retained his full vigor of body and freedom of speech. When he had explained what he thought of Cassidy he turned again to his secretary.

"Arrange for a private car," he said. "I'll go along to-morrow and make them jump."

The secretary, who fancied there would be trouble in the construction camp during the next few days, felt inclined to be sorry for Cassidy as he went out to make the necessary arrangements for his employer's journey west.

Stirling had spent a busy morning when he met his daughter Ida and her friends at lunch. He did not belong to Ottawa. His offices were in Montreal; but as Ottawa is the seat of the government he had visited it at the request of certain railroad potentates and other magnates of political influence. With him he had brought his daughter and three of her English friends, for Ida had desired to show them the capital. He had no great opinion of the man and the two women in question. He said that they made him tired, and sometimes in confidence to his secretary he went rather further than that; but at the same time he was willing to bear with them, if the fact that he did so afforded Ida any pleasure. Ida Stirling was an unusually fortunate young woman, in so far, at least, as that she had only to mention any desire that it was in her father's power to gratify. He was a strenuous man, whose work was his life; subtle where that work was concerned when force, which he preferred, was not advisable, but crudely direct and simple as regards almost everything else.

"I'm going west across the Rockies to-morrow," he said. "We'll have a private car on the Pacific express. You'd better bring these folk along and show them the Mountain Province."

Ida was pleased with the idea; and Stirling and his party started west on the morrow.

In the meanwhile, Construction Foreman Cassidy was spending an anxious time. He was red-haired and irascible, Canadian by adoption and Hibernian by descent, a man of no ideas beyond those connected with railroad building, which was, however, very much what one would have expected, for the chief attribute of the men who are building up the western Dominion is their power of concentration. Though there were greater men above Cassidy who would get the credit, it was due chiefly to his grim persistency that the branch road had been blasted out of the mountainside, made secure from sliding snow, and flung on dizzy trestles over thundering rivers, until at last it reached the swamp which, in his own simple words, had no bottom.

There are other places like it in the Mountain Province of British Columbia. Giant ranges, whose peaks glimmer with the cold gleam of never-melting snow, shut in the valley. Great pine forests clothe their lower slopes, and a green-stained river leaps roaring out of the midst of them. The new track wound through their shadow, a double riband of steel, until it broke off abruptly where a creek that poured out of the hills had spread itself among the trees. The latter dwindled and rotted, and black depths of mire lay among their crawling roots, forming what is known in that country as a muskeg. There was a deep, blue lake on the one hand, and on the other scarped slopes of rock that the tract could not surmount; and for a time Cassidy and his men had floundered knee-deep, and often deeper, among the roots while they plied the ax and saw. Then they dumped in carload after carload of rock and gravel; but the muskeg absorbed it and waited for more. It was apparently insatiable; and, for Cassidy drove them savagely, the men's tempers grew shorter under the strain, until some, who had drawn a sufficient proportion of their wages to warrant it, rolled up their blankets and walked out reviling him. Still, most of them stayed with the task and toiled on sullenly in the mire under a scorching heat, for it was summer in the wilderness.

Affairs were in this condition when Clarence Weston crawled out of the swamp one evening and sat down on a cedar log before he followed his comrades up the track, though he supposed that supper would shortly be laid out in the sleeping-shanty. The sunlight that flung lurid flecks of color upon the western side of the fir trunks beat upon his dripping face, which, though a little worn and grim just then, was otherwise a pleasant face of the fair English type. In fact, though he had been some years in the country, Englishman was unmistakably stamped upon him. He was attired scantily and simply in a very old blue shirt, and trousers, which also had once been blue, of duck; and just then he was very weary, and more than a little lame.

He had cut himself about the ankle when chopping a week earlier, and though the wound had partly healed his foot was still painful. There were also a good many other scars and bruises upon his body, for the cost of building a western railroad is usually heavy. Still, he had an excellent constitution, and was, while not particularly brilliant as a rule, at least whimsically contented in mind. His comrades called him the Kid, or the English Kid, perhaps on account of a certain delicacy of manner and expression which he had somehow contrived to retain, though he had spent several years in logging camps, and his age was close onto twenty-five.

While he sat there with the shovel that had worn his hands hard lying at his feet, Cassidy, who had not recovered from the interview he had had with Stirling that morning, strode by, hot and out of temper, and then stopped and swung round on him.

"Too stiff to get up hustle before the mosquitoes eat you, when supper's ready?" he said.

Weston glanced down at his foot.

"I was on the gravel bank all afternoon. It's steep. Seemed to wrench the cut."

"Well," said Cassidy, "I've no kind of use for a man who doesn't know enough to keep himself from getting hurt. You have got to get that foot better right away or get out."

He shook a big, hard fist at the swamp.

"How'm I going to fill up that pit with a crowd of stiffs and deadbeats like those I'm driving now? You make me tired!"

He did not wait for an answer to the query, but plodded away; and Weston sat still a few minutes longer, with a wry smile in his eyes. He resented being over-driven, though he was more or less used to it, and now and then he found his superior's vitriolic comments upon his efforts almost intolerably galling. Still he had sense enough to realize that the remedy open to him was a somewhat hazardous one, because, while it would be easy to walk out of the construction camp, industrial activity just then was unusually slack in the Mountain Province. Besides, he was willing to admit that there were excuses for Cassidy, and there was a certain quiet tenacity in him. He was also aware that the man with little money has generally a good deal to bear, for Weston was one who could learn by experience, though that faculty was not one that hitherto had characterized the family from which he sprang.

None of the Westons had ever been remarkable for genius—a fact of which they were rather proud than otherwise. They had for several generations been content to be men of local importance in a secluded nook of rural England, which is not the kind of life that is conducive to original thought or enterprising action. They had chosen wives like themselves from among their neighbors, and it was perhaps in several respects not altogether fortunate for Clarence Weston that his mother had been ultraconservative in her respect for traditions, since he had inherited one side of her nature. Still, in her case, at least, the respect had been idealistic, and the traditions of the highest; and though she had died when he was eighteen she had instilled into him a certain delicacy of sentiment and a simple, chivalrous code that had somewhat hampered him in the rough life he had led in the Canadian Dominion.

As a very young man he had quarreled with his father over a matter trifling in itself, but each had clung to his opinions with the obstinacy of men who have few ideas to spare, and Clarence had gone out to seek his fortune in western Canada. He had naturally failed to find it, and the first discovery that there was apparently nobody in that wide country who was ready to appraise either his mental attainments or his bodily activity at the value of his board was a painful shock to the sanguine lad. That first year was a bad one to him, but he set his teeth and quietly bore all that befell him; the odd, brutal task, paid for at half the usual wages, the frequent rebuffs, the long nights spent shelterless in the bush, utter weariness, and often downright hunger. It was a hard school, but it taught him much, and he graduated as a man, strong and comely of body, and resolute of mind. What was more, he had, though he scarcely realized it, after all, only left behind in England a cramped life embittered by a steady shrinkage in the rent roll and as steady an increase in taxation and expenses. His present life was clean, and governed by a code of crude and austere simplicity. His mother's spirit was in him, and, being what he was, there were things he could not do. He did not attempt to reason about them. The knowledge was borne in upon him instinctively.

He rose, by and by, and, for he was hungry, limped on to the sleeping-shanty of the construction gang. It was built of logs and roofed with rough cedar shingles hand-split on the spot. The sun beat hot upon them, and they diffused a faint aromatic fragrance, refreshing as the scent of vinegar, into the long, unfloored room, which certainly needed something of the kind. It reeked with stale tobacco-smoke, the smell of cookery, and the odors of frowsy clothes. A row of bunks, filled with spruce twigs and old brown blankets, ran down one side of it, a very rude table down the other, and a double row of men with bronzed faces, in dusty garments, sat about the latter, eating voraciously. Fifteen minutes was, at the outside, the longest time they ever wasted on a meal.

That evening, however, they were singularly short of temper, for Cassidy had driven them mercilessly all day, and, though not usually fastidious, the supper was not to their liking. The hash was burnt; the venison, for one of them had shot a deer, had been hung too long; while the dessert, a great pie of desiccated fruits, had been baked to a flinty hardness. That was the last straw; for in the Mountain Province the lumber and railroad gangs as a rule work hard and live well; and when the cans of green tea had been emptied the growls culminated in a call for the cook.

He came forward and stood before them, a little, shaky, gray-haired wreck of a man, with the signs of indulgence plain upon him. Whisky is scarce in that country, but it is obtainable, and Grenfell generally procured a good deal of it. The man was evidently in a state of apprehension, and he shrank back a little when a big, grim-faced chopper ladled out a great plateful of the burnt stew from a vessel on the stove.

"Now," he said, "you've been spoiling supper too often lately, and I guess we've got to teach you plain, cookery. Sit right down and get that hash inside you."

The man protested that he had had his supper before they came in; whereupon the other seized him by the shoulders and thrust him down roughly into a seat at the table.

"Well," he said, "you've got to have a little more. If it's good enough for us, boys, it's not going to hurt him."

There was a murmur of concurrence when he looked around at the rest; and the cook, seeing no help for it, made a valiant attempt to eat a little of the greasy mess. Then he revolted from it and glanced at his companions supplicatingly.

"I can't do it, boys. You'll let me off?" he pleaded.

None of the rest showed any sign of relenting. They were inclined to be pitiless then, and the rude justice of the chopper's idea appealed to them.

"When you've cleaned up that plate," said one.

The victim made a second futile attempt, and, after waiting some minutes for him to proceed, they decided that it was too hot in the shed, so, conveying him outside, they seated him on a great fir stump sawed off several feet above the ground, with the plate beside him. Then they took out their pipes and sat around to enjoy the spectacle. As a rule there is very little cruelty in men of their kind; but they were very human, and the cook had robbed them of a meal somewhat frequently of late. Besides, they had smarted all day under Cassidy's bitter tongue, and they felt that they must retaliate upon somebody. No one said anything for several minutes, and then the big chopper once more approached his victim.

"Now," he said, "since you have to go through with it, you may as well start in. If you don't, I'll put the blame stuff down your throat."

It was, perhaps, no more than justice, for the cook was paid well; but there was one man in the assembly to whom this did not altogether appeal. The victim was frail and helpless, a watery-eyed, limp bundle of nerves, with, nevertheless, a pitiful suggestion of outward dignity still clinging to him, though his persecutors would have described him aptly as a whisky tank. The former fact was sufficient for Weston, who did not stop to think out the matter, but rose and strode quietly toward the fir stump.

"I think this thing has gone far enough, boys. You'll have to let him off," he said.

"No, sir," said the big chopper. "He's going right through. Anyway, it's not your trouble. Light out before we rope you in too."

Weston did not move until three or four more strode forward hastily, when he stooped for an ax that lay handy and swung it round his head. It came down with a crash on the plate, and the hash was scattered over the withered redwood twigs. Then, while a growl expressive of astonishment as well as anger went up, the chopper scraped up part of the stew with red soil and fir twigs mixed in it.

"He has got to eat it, and then I'll tend to you. You'll see that they don't get away, boys," he said.

Weston clearly had no intention of attempting to do so, and the cook would have found it hopeless, for the rest closed round the stump in a contracting ring. While they knew that Cassidy had been summoned to Stirling's car, they were unaware that there were other spectators of the little drama. Two young women had, however, just emerged from among the towering firs that hemmed in the muskeg. One was attired elaborately in light garments and a big hat that appeared very much out of place in that aisle of tremendous forest, but there was a difference between her and her companion. The latter knew the bush, and was dressed simply in a close-fitting robe of gray. She held herself well, and there was something that suggested quiet imperiousness in her attitude and expression. This was, perhaps, not altogether unnatural, for hitherto when Ida Stirling desired anything that her father's money could obtain her wish was gratified. She laid her hand warningly on her companion's arm, and drew her back into the shadow of the firs.

"I really don't think we need go away," she said. "They won't notice us, and you will probably see something that is supposed to be characteristically western, though I'm not sure that it really is."

The meaning of the scene was tolerably plain to both of them. The little cleared space formed a natural amphitheater walled in by somber ranks of pines; and, standing higher, they could see over the heads of the clustering men. There was no difficulty in identifying the victim, the persecutor and the champion, for Weston stood stripped to blue shirt and trousers, with the big ax in his hand and his head thrown back a trifle, gazing with curiously steady eyes at the expectant faces before him. Then as two or three of the men drew in closer he raised his free hand.

"This thing lies between Jake and me, and I'm open to deal with him," he said. "Still, I've got the ax here if more of you stand in."

The man scarcely raised his voice, but it was clear that he was quietly and dangerously resolute. Indeed, his attitude rather pleased some of the rest, for there was a fresh murmuring, and a cry of, "Give the Kid a show!"

Then, and nobody was afterward quite certain who struck first, the trial by combat suddenly commenced. There are very few rules attached to it in that country, where men do not fight by formula but with the one purpose of deciding the matter in the quickest way possible; and in another moment the two had clinched. They fell against the tree stump and reeled clear again, swaying, gasping, and striking when they could. It is probable that the Canadian was the stronger man, but, as it happened, his antagonist had been born among the dales of northern England, where wrestling is still held as an art. In a few minutes he hurled the chopper off his feet, and a hoarse clamor went up, through which there broke a shout:

"The Kid has him!"

Then the two men went down together, heavily, and rolled over and over, until Cassidy came running down the track and burst through the ring of onlookers. In one hand he carried a peevie, a big wooden lever with an iron hook on it, such as men use in rolling fir logs. He belabored the pair with it impartially, and it was evident that he was not in the least particular as to whether he hurt them or not. Loosing their hold on each other they staggered to their feet with the red dust thick on their flushed faces.

Cassidy flourished the peevie.

"Now," he cried, "is it fighting ye want?"

There was a burst of laughter; and the assembly broke up when Cassidy hustled the chopper off the field. The cook, with commendable discretion, had slipped away quietly in the meanwhile, and the two young women, whom nobody had noticed, turned back among the firs. The girl in the elaborate draperies laughed.

"I suppose it was a little brutal, and we shouldn't have stayed," she said. "Still, in a sense the attitude of the one they called the Kid was rather fine. I could have made quite a striking sketch of him."

Ida Stirling made no direct reply to this, but, as she found afterward, the scene had fixed itself on her memory. Still it was not the intent men or the stately clustering pines that she recalled most clearly; it was the dominant central figure, standing almost statuesque, with head tilted slightly backward, and both hands clenched on the big ax haft.

"The man they were tormenting must have done something to vex them. They really are not quarrelsome," she said.

CHAPTER II

THE PACKER

Weston was engaged with several others flinging gravel into a flat car with a long-hafted shovel the next morning when Cassidy strode up the track; and, though the men already had been working hard, they quickened the pace a little when they saw him. He could tell at a glance whether a man were doing his utmost, and nothing less would satisfy him. He knew also exactly how many cubic yards of soil or gravel could be handled by any particular gang. If the quantity fell short, there was usually trouble. However, he said nothing to the others that morning, but beckoned Weston aside, and stood a moment or two looking at him, with a grimly whimsical twinkle in his eyes.

Weston had not suffered greatly during the struggle of the previous evening, but there was a discolored bruise on one of his cheeks and a big lump on his forehead. He was glad to stand still a moment, for he had been shoveling gravel for several hours, and that is an occupation that conduces to an unpleasant stiffness about the waist. He was, however, somewhat puzzled by the red-haired Cassidy's sardonic grin.

"Well," said the latter, with an air of reflection, "I guess you might do if you got a piece of raw steak from the cook and tied it around your face."

"For what?" asked Weston, sharply.

"For a packer. The boss's friends are going camping in the bush."

Weston did not answer immediately, for in that country, where roads are still singularly scarce, packing usually means the transporting of heavy loads upon one's back. The smaller ranchers are as a rule adept at it, and when it is necessary, as it sometimes is, will cheerfully walk over a mountain range with a big sack of flour or other sundries bound upon their shoulders. Four or five leagues is not considered too great a distance to pack a bushel or two of seed potatoes, or even a table for the ranch, and Weston, who had reasons for being aware that work of the kind is at least as arduous as shoveling gravel, did not feel greatly tempted by the offer. Cassidy seemed to guess what he was thinking.

"It's a soft thing I'm putting you on to, as a special favor," he explained. "It will be up-river most of the way, and I've got a couple of Siwash to pole the canoes. All you have to do is the cooking, make camp, and tend to Miss Stirling's friends when they go fishing." He waved his hand, and added, as though to clinch the argument, "I've known people of that kind to give a man that pleased them ten dollars."

Weston's face flushed a little, but he said he would go; and the next day the party started up-river in two Indian canoes. Besides Weston and the dark-skinned Siwash packers, it consisted of four: a tall, elderly man called Kinnaird, with the stamp of a military training plain upon him; his little, quiet wife; his daughter, who was somewhat elaborately dressed; and Ida Stirling. Kinnaird and his daughter traveled in the larger canoe with the Indians and the camp gear, and Mrs. Kinnaird and Miss Stirling with Weston in the other.

Though Weston was more or less accustomed to the work, he found the first few hours sufficiently arduous. It is not an easy matter to propel a loaded canoe against a strong stream with a single paddle, and it is almost as difficult to pole her alone; while there were two long portages to make, when the craft and everything in them had to be hauled painfully over a stretch of very rough boulders. Kinnaird took his share in it, and Weston was quite willing to permit him to do so; but the latter was floundering toward the canoes alone, with a heavy load on his shoulders, when he came to a sharply sloped and slippery ledge of rock. It was very hot in the deep valley, and the white stones and flashing river flung up a blaze of light into his eyes; while he limped a little under his burden, for his foot was still painful. He had no idea that anybody was watching him; and, when he slipped and, falling heavily, rolled down part of the slope, scattering the packages about him, he relieved his feelings with a few vitriolic comments upon the luxurious habits of the people who had compelled him to carry so many of their superfluous comforts through the bush. Then he set about gathering up the sundries he had dropped. First of all he came upon a lady's parasol, white outside and lined with green. He regarded it with a rueful smile when he had tried and failed to open it.

"Trouble ahead," he commented. "It cost eight or nine dollars anyway, and now it's broken."

Then he came to a rather big valise, which swung open and poured out part of its contents when he lifted it by the handle. They seemed to consist of voluminous folds of delicate fabric and lace, and he was gazing at them and wondering how they were to be got back into the bag when he heard a voice behind him.

"Will you kindly put that down?" it said.

Weston dropped the bag in his astonishment; and, swinging around suddenly, he saw Miss Stirling standing in the shadow of a great cedar. He had been too busy during the journey up the river to pay much attention to her; but now it occurred to him that she was not only pretty but very much in harmony with her surroundings. The simple, close-fitting gray dress which, though he did not know this, had cost a good many dollars, displayed a pretty and not over-slender figure, and fitted in with the neutral tinting of the towering fir trunks and the sunlit boulders, while the plain white hat with bent-down brim formed an appropriate setting for the delicately-colored face beneath it. Still, Weston scarcely noticed any particular points in Miss Stirling's appearance just then, for he was subconsciously impressed by her personality as a whole. There was something in her dress and manner that he would have described vaguely as style, though it was a style he had not often come across in the west, where he had for the most part lived in the bush. She was evidently a little younger than himself, but she had the quiet air of one accustomed to command, which, as a matter of fact, was the case.

Then he wondered with a slight uneasiness whether she had heard all that he said when he fell down. He fancied that she had, for there was the faintest trace of amusement in her eyes. They met his own steadily, though he was not sure whether they were gray or blue, or a very light brown. Indeed, he was never quite sure of this, for they changed curiously with the light.

Then she came toward him and looked at the valise.

"It was locked when I gave it to you," she said, with a trace of severity.

"Well," answered Weston, "it doesn't seem to be locked now. I think I remember noticing that you left the key in it; but it's gone. It must have fallen out. I'll look for it."

He looked for some time, and, failing to find it, walked back to the girl.

"I'm afraid it's in the river," he said. "Still, you see, the bag is open."

"That," replied Miss Stirling, "is unfortunately evident. I want it shut."

Weston glanced at the protruding garments with which she seemed to be busy.

"I'm very sorry," he said. "I dare say I could squeeze these things back into it."

He was going to do so when Miss Stirling took the bag away from him.

"No," she said a trifle quickly, "I don't think you could."

Then it occurred to Weston that his offer had, perhaps, not been altogether tactful, and he was sensible of a certain confusion, at which he was slightly astonished. He did not remember having been readily subject to fits of embarrassment when in England, though there he had never served as porter to people of his own walk in life. Turning away, he collected a waterproof carry-all, a big rubber ground sheet, another parasol, a sketching stool, and a collapsible easel, which also appeared to be damaged. Then as he knelt down and roped them and the valise together he looked at the girl.

"I'm afraid Miss Kinnaird will be a little angry, for I think that easel thing won't open out," he said. "I'm awfully sorry."

Now "awfully sorry" is not a western colloquialism, and the girl looked at him attentively. She liked his voice, and she rather liked his face, which, since he had not been called the Kid for nothing, was ingenuous. She laughed a little. Then she remembered something she had noticed.

"Well," she observed, "I suppose you couldn't help it. That load was too heavy; and aren't you a little lame?"

"Not always," said Weston. "I cut my foot a little while ago. If it hadn't been for that I shouldn't have fallen down and broken Miss Kinnaird's things."

"And mine!"

"And yours," admitted Weston. "As I said, I'm particularly sorry. Still, if you will let me have the bag afterward I can, perhaps, mend the lock. You see, I assisted a general jobbing mechanic."

Ida Stirling flashed a quick glance at him. He had certainly a pleasant voice, and his manner was whimsically deferential.

"Why didn't you stay with him?" she asked. "Mending plows and wagons must have been easier than track-grading."

Weston's eyes twinkled.

"He said I made him tired; and the fact is I mended a clock. That is, I tried—it was rather a good one when I got hold of it."

The girl laughed, and the laugh set them on good terms with each other. Then she said:

"That load is far too heavy for you to climb over these boulders with when you have an injured foot. You can give me the valise, at least."

"No," said Weston, resolutely, "this is a good deal easier than shoveling gravel, as well as pleasanter; and the foot really doesn't trouble me very much. Besides, if I hadn't cut it, Cassidy wouldn't have sent me here."

He was, however, mistaken in supposing that the construction foreman had been influenced only by a desire to get rid of a man who was to some extent incapacitated. As a matter of fact, Miss Stirling, who had been rather pleased with the part he had played two days ago, had, when her father insisted on her taking a white man as well as the Indians, given Cassidy instructions that he should be sent. Still, she naturally did not mention this, and indeed said nothing of any account while they went on to the canoes.

It was slacker water above the rapid; and all afternoon they slid slowly up on deep, winding reaches of the still, green river. Sometimes it flashed under dazzling sunshine, but at least as often they moved through the dim shadow of towering pines that rolled, rank on rank, somber and stately, up the steep hillside, while high above them all rose tremendous ramparts of eternal snow. Then, as the sun dipped behind the great mountain wall, the clean, aromatic fragrance of pine and fir and cedar crept into the cooling air, and a stillness so deep that it became almost oppressive descended upon the lonely valley. The splash of pole or paddle broke through it with a startling distinctness, and the faint gurgle at the bows became curiously intensified. The pines grew slower, blacker and more solemn; filmy trails of mist crawled out from among the hollows of the hills; and the still air was charged with an elixir-like quality when Weston ran his canoe ashore.

While he and the Indians set about erecting a couple of tents, he saw Miss Kinnaird standing near him and gazing up across the misty pines toward the green transparency that still hung above the blue-white gleam of snow.

"This," she said to Miss Stirling, "is really wonderful. One can't get hold of it at once. It's tremendous."

The smallest of the pines rose two hundred feet above her; and they ran up until they dwindled to insignificance far aloft at the foot of a great scarp of rock that rose beyond them for a thousand feet or so and then gave place in turn to climbing fields of snow.

The girl, who was an artist, drew in her breath.

"Switzerland and Norway. It's like them both—and yet it grips you harder than either," she added. "I suppose it's because there are no hotels, or steamers. Probably very few white people have ever been here before."

"I really don't think many have," said Ida Stirling.

Then Miss Kinnaird laughed softly as she glanced at her attire.

"I must take off these fripperies. They're out of key," she said. "One ought to wear deerskins, or something of that kind here."

Weston heard nothing further, and remembered that, after all, the girl's sentiments were no concern of his. It was his business to prepare the supper and wait on the party; and he set about it. Darkness had descended upon the valley when he laid the plates of indurated ware on a strip of clean white shingle, and then drawing back a few yards sat down beneath the first of the pines in case they needed anything further. A fire blazed and crackled between two small logs felled for the purpose and rolled close together, and its flickering light fell upon him and those who sat at supper, except at times when it faded suddenly and the shadows closed in again. He was then attired picturesquely in a fringed deerskin jacket dressed by some of the Blackfeet across the Rockies. Kinnaird, who had once or twice glanced in his direction, gazed hard at him.

"Have you ever been in India?" he asked.

"No, sir," said Weston in a formal manner, though "sir" is not often used deferentially in western Canada.

Kinnaird appeared thoughtful.

"Well," he said, "I can't help thinking that I have come across you somewhere before. I have a good memory for faces, and yours is familiar."

"I have never seen you until to-day," said Weston. "I don't remember your name, either."

"The curious thing," persisted Kinnaird, "is that while I can't quite locate you I am almost sure I am right. What makes me feel more certain is that, though you were younger then, you have grown into the man I should have expected you to." Then he laughed. "Anyway, it's clear that you don't remember me."

He turned to the others, and Miss Kinnaird asked for more coffee, after which Weston, who brought it, sat still again to wait until he could take away the plates. It was evident that his presence placed no restraint on the conversation. At length he became suddenly intent. Kinnaird was contrasting Canada and England for Miss Stirling's benefit.

"Of course," he said, "we have nothing like this, but in the north, at least, we have odd bits of rugged grandeur where the wildness of the hills about one is emphasized by the green fertility of the valleys. There is a typical place where we spent a few months last year that I should like you to see. If you come back with us, as you half promised, we will take you there."

Weston leaned forward a little, for he had still a curious tenderness for the land of the fells and dales in which he had been born. He did not know that Ida Stirling, who had watched him closely when Kinnaird addressed him, had now fixed her eyes on him again. The latter turned to her as he proceeded.

"The old house," he said, "would make a picture in itself with its little stone-ribbed windows, and the much older square tower and curtain wall that form one wing. There is a terraced garden in front, and a stream comes frothing out of a wooded ghyll at the foot of it."

Weston started, for there was no doubt that the house Kinnaird described was the one in which he had been born. As it happened, the firelight fell upon his intent face as he waited for the answer, when Miss Stirling, who had missed his start, asked a question:

"The people who owned it were friends of yours?"

"No," said Kinnaird, "I never saw them. I took the place through an agency for the rough shooting and as a change from London. They had to let it and live in a neighboring town. The result of slack management and agricultural depression, I believe."

Weston set his lips. He had written home once rejecting a proposition made him, and his people had afterward apparently forgotten him. He had made up his mind that he would not trouble them again, at least while he toiled as a track-grader or a hired man; but now, when it seemed that trouble had come upon them, he regretted many things.

Kinnaird signed to him that he might take away the plates, and he gathered them up, scarcely conscious of what he was doing, and then stumbled and dropped the pile of them. Though made of indurated fiber, they fell with a startling clatter, and Kinnaird looked at him sharply as he picked them up; but in another few moments he had vanished beyond the range of the firelight into the shadows of the bush.

Ida Stirling had, however, noticed enough to arouse a young woman's curiosity, especially as there was a suggestion of romance in it, and before she went to sleep she thought a good deal about the man she had never seen until two days ago.

CHAPTER III

THE MODEL

The morning broke clear and still across the scented bush, and Miss Kinnaird and Ida Stirling, who had been awakened early by the wonderful freshness in the mountain air, strolled some distance out of camp. For a time they wandered through shadowy aisles between the tremendous trunks, breathing in sweet resinous odors, and then, soon after the first sunrays came slanting across a mountain shoulder, they came out upon a head of rock above the river. A hemlock had fallen athwart it, and they sat down where they could look out upon a majestic panorama of towering rock and snow.

Arabella Kinnaird gazed at it intently when she had shaken some of the dew from the frills and folds of her rather bedraggled skirt.

"It will never be quite the same again," she observed, evidently in reference to the latter, and then waved one hand as though to indicate the panorama, for she was usually voluble and disconnected in her conversation. "This, as I said last night, is wonderful—in fact, it almost oppresses one. It makes one feel so little, and I'm not sure that I like that, though no doubt it does one good."

Her companion smiled.

"Aren't you going to paint it?" she asked.

Miss Kinnaird pursed up her face, which was a trick she had.

"Oh," she said, "I don't know. After all, portraiture is my specialty, and this silent grandeur is a little beyond my interpretation."

She paused, and added the next few words in an authoritative manner, as though she had a truth of some consequence to deliver:

"The difficulty is that you really can't interpret anything until you are quite sure what it means. You see, I'm feverishly restless by temperament, and accustomed to indulge in all kinds of petty, purposeless activities. They are petty, though the major calls them duties—social duties—and being, I'm afraid, a rather frivolous person in spite of my love of art, they appeal to me."

Ida said nothing. It was not necessary, and as a rule not advisable, to encourage Arabella Kinnaird when she commenced, as she sometimes described it, to talk seriously; and she rattled on:

"My dear, I'm all appreciation, and graciously pleased with the wonders that you are showing me; but still this valley strikes me as being short of something. It's too calm and quiet. Even Eden was not complete until man appeared in it, though, as usual, he made trouble shortly afterward. It is a thing he has kept on doing ever since."

Ida laughed.

"I'm not sure you're sticking to historical facts," she said.

"Facts," returned her companion, "don't count for much with me. I deal in impressions; and sometimes I feel full of them. I could astonish everybody if I could get them out; but that, of course, is the difficulty.

Feeling, unfortunately, isn't quite the same thing as power of expression. Still, you asked me what I thought about these mountains, and I'm trying to tell you. You have brought it on yourself, you see. The key-tone of this place is an almost overwhelming tranquillity. One rather shrinks from that kind of thing when one is not used to it, and longs to do something to disturb it. It's a natural impulse. When you see a smooth sheet of ice you generally look for a big stone with which to smash it."

She swung around and favored her companion with a glance of critical scrutiny; and there was no reason why Ida Stirling should shrink from it. She sat leaning forward, looking out at the mountains with steady eyes that had a half-smile in them. Her attitude was reposeful and her face quiet; but there was something in both that faintly suggested a decided character.

"I don't think I'm readily disturbed," she said.

"No," answered her companion reflectively, "but the disturbance will no doubt come. You're in harmony with the key-tone of this valley; but too much serenity isn't good for me; and it's probable that nobody ever retains it very long. There's always the disturbing element in a world that's full of men. It was, as I remarked, man who brought trouble into Paradise."

Miss Kinnaird was addicted to talking a good deal of nonsense, and she frequently wearied her listeners; but there was a certain shrewdness in her, and at times she got near the truth. Indeed, her companion afterward decided that she had done so in this case. Ida Stirling had met many rising young men, and some who had made their mark, but none of them had aroused in her the faintest thrill of unrest or passion. So far, the depths of her nature had remained wholly unstirred. One could almost have told it from her laugh as she answered her companion's last observation.

"I thought it was woman's curiosity," she said; and then remembered suddenly that on the previous evening she had certainly been a trifle curious about the strange packer from the railroad gang.

Miss Kinnaird made no reply to this; but in a moment she stretched out a pointing hand.

"Now," she said, "the disturbing element is obtruding itself."

Farther down the river there was a flash of something white amidst the pale green shimmer of the flood. Ida rose, but her companion beckoned her to sit down again.

"Oh," she said, a trifle impatiently, "don't be prudish. He's ever so far off, and I've never had an opportunity to study anybody swimming."

It was, of course, Weston, who supposed himself far enough from camp not to be troubled by spectators, swimming with a powerful side-stroke upstream. Ida sat down again, and both of them watched him as he drew a little nearer. So many times every minute his left arm swept out into the sunlight as he flung it forward with far-stretched palm. It fell with the faintest splash, and there was a little puff of spray as his head dipped and the water washed across his lips. Then the white limbs flashed amidst the green shining of the river, and the long, lithe form contracted, gleaming as a salmon gleams when it breaks the surface with the straining line. The still river rippled, and a sun-bronzed face shot half-clear again. Miss Kinnaird watched the swimmer's progress with open appreciation.

"Dancing," she said didactically, "isn't to be compared with that! It's the essence of rhythmic movement! I must certainly study swimming. I wish he'd come right on."

Ida was not sure that she agreed with her; and, just then, Weston, swinging suddenly around, went down into the green depths, and, shooting up with white shoulders high above the water, swept away again down-stream. Miss Kinnaird rose as he did so, and turned back toward the camp.

"That packer is rather fine, considered as a muscular animal," she said.

Ida smiled at this, somewhat sardonically.

"In your country you wouldn't think of regarding him as anything else. Doesn't being an artist emancipate one from the conventional point of view?"

"No," replied Miss Kinnaird reflectively, "it doesn't, that is, when you do not paint for your living—which, of course, alters everything."

Then her eyes twinkled as she favored her companion with a passable imitation of her father's didactic tone and manner.

"As the major says, social distinctions are necessary safeguards, and cannot lightly be disregarded. If they were not, they could not have existed as long as they have."

She laughed.

"In the case of a man who has inherited his station and his possessions," she added, "it is a very natural and comfortable creed."

"Ah," said Ida, "my father worked in a sawmill."

She spoke quietly, but there was something in her voice that warned her companion that there were subjects upon which they might have a clash of opinion. In the east there is pride of possession; but the pride of achievement, which is, perhaps, more logical, is more common in the west.

It was an hour later when Weston laid breakfast before them; and Ida, who regarded him unobtrusively with careful attention, decided that Arabella Kinnaird was right. The packer, with his lean, symmetrical litheness, his pleasant English face, his clear eyes, and his clean, bronzed skin, was certainly well-favored physically, and she began to wonder whether her companion could not have gone further in her comments; until she remembered again that the commencement of a good many troubles is probably woman's curiosity.

The canoes were launched after breakfast, and it was afternoon when they pitched camp beside a still, blue lake. Then Major Kinnaird strolled away with a trout-rod to a neighboring rapid, and Mrs. Kinnaird went to sleep in a hammock. Her daughter got out her sketch-book, and sitting down among the boulders bade Ida summon Weston. He came, and stood looking at them inquiringly, picturesque in his wide hat and his fringed deerskin jacket. Miss Kinnaird pursed up her face.

"I want to make a sketch of you. You have rather a good head," she said.

Weston gazed at her a moment in astonishment, and then a twinkle crept into his eyes. Her matter-of-fact brusqueness, which made it perfectly plain that his views in the matter did not count, might have roused a sense of opposition in some men, but he had acquired a wide toleration in western Canada.

"Shall I stand here, miss?" he asked.

"No," said the girl, "a little farther to the right, where the sunlight falls upon the trunks behind you; but you mustn't look wooden. That will do. Still, you'll have to take off that jacket. It's frippery."

The suspicion of a flush crept into Weston's face; but, after all, a loose blue shirt and duck trousers are considered dress enough in the bush of the Pacific Slope, and he discarded the offending jacket. Miss Kinnaird, however, was not quite satisfied.

"Can't you take up that ax and look as if you were ready to use it?" she said. "Oh, no! That is far too much like a waxwork! Hold up your head a little! Now, don't move any more than you can help! I think that will do."

Weston stood as he was for the best part of an hour. He felt inclined to wonder why he did it, as he had not found shoveling gravel anything like so difficult. Then Miss Kinnaird informed him that, as she desired to make a study of the background, she would not keep him any longer; and he strolled away to the waterside, where, after stretching himself wearily, he lay down and took out his pipe. He had not been there long when Ida, who came out from among the trees, sat down on one of the boulders not far from him.

"You must have been horribly cramped, but it didn't strike Miss Kinnaird, or she wouldn't have kept you there so long," she said.

"No," answered Weston, reflectively, "I don't think it would strike Miss Kinnaird. She's English, isn't she?"

"Of course. But aren't you English, too?"

Weston's eyes twinkled.

"I am. Still, I don't want you to think that it's merely because Miss Kinnaird comes from the same country that I do that I didn't expect her to realize that to stand posed for an hour or so is apt to cramp one."

Ida laughed. It evidently was clear to him that Miss Kinnaird regarded him as a packer and nothing else, and had decided that he had probably grown used to physical discomfort. Ida was, however, rather pleased to see that he accepted the fact good-humoredly and did not resent it. She was in no way astonished that he should answer her as he had, for, in the west, a man may speak naturally to any young woman who addresses him, without feeling called on to remember the distinctions of caste.

"I wonder," she said, "whether you would tell me what caused the trouble you were mixed up in two or three nights ago."

Weston's face grew slightly flushed, for he was still in certain respects somewhat ingenuous; but he told her simply what had led up to the affray.

"After all you could hardly blame the boys," he added. "They had had a hard day, and it was not the first time Grenfell had done them out of their supper."

"Still, he had spoiled your supper, too," said Ida. "If you couldn't blame them, why did you interfere?"

It was rather a difficult question. Weston could not very well tell her, even had he quite realized it, that there was in him a vein of rudimentary chivalry that had been carefully fostered by his mother. The males of the Weston line had clung to traditions, but they had for the most part been those of the Georgian days, when very little refinement of sentiment was expected from the country gentleman. The traditions Agnes Weston had held by, however, went back to an earlier age. She had been High Church and imaginative, a woman of impracticable as well as somewhat uncomfortable ideals, and finding her husband proof against them she had done what she could with her son. The result was a somewhat happy one, for in the Kid, as his comrades termed him, her fantasies and extravagances had been toned down by the very prosaic common sense of the Weston male line. They were full-fleshed, hard-riding Englishmen who lived on beef and beer. Though Weston was naturally not aware of it, there were respects in which Ida Stirling was like his mother. Ida, however, usually kept her deeper thoughts to herself, which Mrs. Weston had seldom done, but she shaped her life by them, and they were wholesome.

"Well," he said diffidently, "it was quite a humiliating situation for the old man. He was a person of some consequence once—a rather famous assayer and mineralogist—and I think he felt it."

"That is not what I asked you," said Ida, with a trace of dryness.

Weston spread out his hands as though to excuse himself.

"Then," he said, "they were all against him, and I think Jake—I mean the big chopper—would have forced the stuff down his throat. It was horribly burnt. There are," and he hesitated, "things one really has to do."

His companion nodded. She liked his diffidence, which, while very evident, was wholly genuine, and the faint color in his face gave him an appearance of boyish candor.

"Even when the odds against you are quite steep?" she said. "In the case we are discussing the result was no doubt that bruise on your face." Then she changed the subject. "If he was a famous mineralogist, why is he cooking in a railroad camp?"

"Everybody knows," said Weston. "The usual trouble—whisky."

The girl made a little gesture of comprehension that had in it also a hint of disgust, and then seeing that he would say nothing further until she gave him a lead she spoke again.

"What brought you out here?" she inquired.

Weston had been asked the same question several times before, and had never answered it. In fact, he did not know why he did so now.

"I quarreled with my people. In one respect, anyway, I don't regret it. It's rather a beautiful country."

He sat, with his wide hat tilted back and the sun on his face, looking out upon the blue lake between the towering pines. Their shadows floated in it, and tremendous slopes of rock ran up toward the gleaming snow on the farther side. The bush lay very silent under the scorching sun, and it was filled with the heavy odors of the firs, in which there was a clogging, honey-like sweetness.

"It's a little difficult to understand why you seem to be content with track-grading. One would fancy it to be unusually hard work," said the girl.

"Oh, yes," agreed Weston, laughing. "Still, you see, I don't intend to remain a track-grader indefinitely."

"No?" said Ida, inquiringly. "What do you mean to do?"

Weston saw that she was interested, and he was still young enough to be willing to discuss his own plans and projects—though for that matter one comes across older men who can talk of nothing else.

"This country is full of gold and silver," he said. "Other men strike it now and then, and I really don't see why I shouldn't."

"When they do, haven't they usually to sell it for almost nothing to somebody who gets up a company? Besides, do you know anything about prospecting?"

Weston laughed.

"A little. It's my one dissipation; and it's rather an expensive one. You have to work for months to save enough to buy a camp outfit and provisions, and if you mean to stay any time in the ranges you have to hire a horse. Then you come back in rags with a bagful of specimens that prove to be of no use at all; and you go to work again."

"You have done that often?"

"Three or four times."

"Then," asked Ida, "isn't it foolish to go back again?"

Weston looked at her a moment hesitatingly, and then made a little gesture of deprecation.

"It sounds absurd, of course, but I have a fancy that if I keep it up long enough I shall strike gold. You see I'm a water-finder, anyway."

"A water-finder?"

Weston nodded.

"It's an old English idea. Water evidently used to be scarcer there, and even now there are places where good wells aren't plentiful. You go along with a hazel twig, and it dips when you cross water running under-ground. That is, if you have the gift in you. Anybody can't do it. You think that quite foolish, don't you?"

Ida really did, though she did not seem to admit it.

"Have you ever tried the gift out here?" she asked.

"On the prairie, quite often. A good deal of it is burnt up and dry. I generally found water."

"You turned the—power—to account? I mean—you made—money out of it?"

There was a sudden change in Weston's face.

"No," he said, "I never took a cent."

"But why?"

"Well," replied the man slowly, "my mother had some old-world belief, and she said it was a special gift. She knew I had it. She said a thing of that kind should never be used for money."

"But haven't all those who claimed special powers—priests, magicians, medicine-men—always been willing to sell them?"

Her companion's eyes twinkled.

"Well, I dare say they have. Still, you see, it's possible that they never really had the gifts they claimed at all. Now I—can—find water, and I have a notion that I can find the precious metals too. Quite absurd, isn't it?"

Ida thought it was, but the quiet confidence behind his whimsical manner appealed to her. He was, it seemed, a man of simple character and few ideas, but she knew that he had nerve and vigor, and, after all, the western Dominion is the land of strenuous, all-daring, simple men. Besides, she had watched the resolution flash into his young face when he stood facing the angry crowd of track-graders with the ax in his hand, and she had seen very much the same tenacity and steadfastness stamped on the faces of successful men. Her father was one, and he was a man who had scarcely been educated, and was certainly devoid of any complexity of character. Stirling had made his mark by smashing down opposition, and, when that was not possible, grimly holding on and bearing the blows dealt him. There was, as she recognized, something to be said in favor of that kind of man.

Then Kinnaird came up through the bush with his rod and a few troutlings, dry-shod and immaculate in a jacket that fitted him like a uniform, and Ida went back to camp with him. She fancied, however, that her father or Weston, who sat still and filled his pipe again, would have come back with a heavy fish, or at least thorn-rent and dripping wet.

CHAPTER IV

IDA'S FIRST ASCENT

The party had spent another day or two beside the lake when, one drowsy afternoon, Kinnaird, who sat on the hot, white shingle by the water's edge, with a pair of glasses in his hand, sent for Weston. Miss Kinnaird and Ida Stirling were seated among the boulders not far away.

"I understand that the river bends around the range, and the crest of the first rise seems no great height," he said. "There is evidently—a bench I think you call it—before you come to the snow, and the ascent should be practicable for a lady. Take these glasses and look at it."

Weston, who took the glasses, swept them along the hillside across the lake. It rose very steeply from the water's edge, but the slope was uniform, and as a good deal of it consisted apparently of lightly-covered rock and gravel the pines were thinner, and there was less undergrowth than usual. Far above him the smooth ascent broke off abruptly, and, though he could not see beyond the edge, there certainly appeared to be a plateau between it and the farther wall of rock and snow.

"I think one could get up so far without very much trouble, sir," he said.

"That," replied Kinnaird, "is how it strikes me. My daughter is rather a good mountaineer, and Miss Stirling is just as anxious to make the ascent. I may say that we have had some experience in Switzerland, not to mention the hills among the English lakes. Do you know anything about climbing?"

"No, sir," said Weston; "not as it is understood in Switzerland, anyway. I don't suppose there's an ice-ax in the country, and I never saw a party roped. Still, I have been up seven or eight thousand feet several times."

"What were you doing?" asked Miss Kinnaird.

Weston saw the faint twinkle in Ida Stirling's eyes, and fancied that he understood it. Very few of the inhabitants of that country climb for pleasure, and it is difficult to obtain any of the regulation mountaineering paraphernalia there; but when the wandering prospector finds a snow-crested range in his way he usually scrambles over it and carries his provisions and blankets along with him. The fact that there are no routes mapped out, and no chalets or club shelters to sleep in, does not trouble men of that kind.

"Once or twice we were on the gold trail," he said. "Another time I packed for a couple of Englishmen who were looking for mountain goats."

"Get any?" Kinnaird asked sharply.

"No, sir. We didn't even see one," said Weston; and again he noticed Miss Stirling's smile.

"Well," said Kinnaird, "we are breaking camp tomorrow, and my idea is that Mrs. Kinnaird should go on with the baggage in the canoes.

The rest of us will follow the bench, and after working around the head of the big spur yonder come down again to the water by the other slope. You are, of course, willing to make the ascent with us?"

"I am under your orders," said Weston. "Still, I shouldn't advise it."

"Why?"

It was rather difficult to answer. Weston could not tell the major that he considered him a little too old for that work, or that he was dubious about his daughter's stamina and courage. He had seen self-confident strangers come down from those mountains dressed in rags, with their boots torn off their bleeding feet. Besides, he felt reasonably sure that, as he was not a professional guide, any advice that he might feel it wise to offer would not be heeded.

"I have heard that there is thick timber on the other slope," he said. "It's generally rather bad to get through."

Kinnaird, who never had been in really thick timber, dismissed the matter with a smile.

"We will start at six to-morrow, and endeavor to get down to camp again on the other side in the afternoon. You will arrange about provisions."

Weston said that he would do so, but he was not exactly pleased when he watched the major climb the hillside immediately behind them, with his glasses, to plot out the route. It seemed very probable that once he had fixed on one he would adhere to it at any cost, and, perhaps, the more persistently if the course in question appeared inadvisable to his companions. Weston did not pretend to be a great judge of character, but Kinnaird, who, it seemed, had held command in India, struck him as that kind of man. His wife was a little, placid lady, whose bodily vigor and any resolution of character she might once have possessed had apparently evaporated under the Indian sun, and, as far as Weston had noticed, she invariably agreed with whatever was said. When he waited on them at supper their talk was of the easier ascents in Switzerland, and in the mountains of his own land, whose names rang like music in his ears—the Striding Edge, the Great Gable Needle, and Saddleback Crags. The Needle was certainly difficult to climb, but the Striding Edge on a still day was a secure promenade compared with some of the ledges along which he had seen western prospectors struggle with a month's supplies.

Supper, which as usual was prepared about six o'clock, had been over an hour or two, when, after waiting for an opportunity, he found Ida alone beside the lake.

"Can't you persuade these people not to go, Miss Stirling?" he asked.

The girl smiled.

"No," she said, "I think you ought to recognize that."

"Then can't you make some excuse, for stopping behind with Mrs. Kinnaird?"

"Why?"

Weston made a little gesture.

"It will probably be a tough climb. I'd rather you didn't go."

Dusk was creeping up the hillside, but there was still a little light among the misty pines, and the girl flashed a quick glance at him. He seemed diffident, but it was evident that he did not wish her to go, and once more she felt that he aroused her curiosity.

"That," she observed, "is not exactly an answer. Why should I stay below?"

Weston was relieved at this, for it seemed preferable to him that she should be the one to raise the personal side of the question.

"Well," he said, "for one thing my employer is your father."

It occurred to the girl that the qualification might as well have been left out. It was too suggestive, since it conveyed the impression that the fact he had mentioned was not the only one that influenced him; but she had noticed already that Weston was not a finished diplomatist. She became more curious as to why he was especially concerned about her safety, though, as a matter of fact, he could not have told her, because he did not know.

"Major and Miss Kinnaird are his guests," she observed.

Weston recognized the reproof in this, and stood silent a moment or two until she spoke again.

"Are you afraid my nerve may not prove equal to Miss Kinnaird's?" she asked.

Weston smiled and answered without reflection.

"No," he said, "that certainly wasn't troubling me. When the pinch comes you could be relied on."

He was conscious that he had gone too far, and, as often happens in such cases, immediately went further.

"There is something about you that makes me sure of it."

"Well," said Ida, coldly, "it is very probable that the pinch won't come at all."

She turned away and left him; and Weston frowned at the supper dishes he had carried down to the lake.

"I dare say that looked very much like a gratuitous impertinence from—the packer," he observed.

He awakened at four the next morning; and the mists were steaming among the pines when the Indians ferried the party across the lake. Then for a couple of hours they went up steadily, between apparently endless ranks of climbing pines, with odd streams of loose gravel sliding down beneath their feet. Kinnaird led the way; the girls came behind him climbing well; and Weston brought up the rear with an ample supply of provisions and a couple of big blankets strapped on his shoulders. He explained that the blankets would do to sit on, but, knowing a little about those mountains, he was somewhat dubious about their getting down again that afternoon. The load was heavy, and by and by his injured foot commenced to grow painful.

Then they left the last of the dwindling pines behind, and pushed on along a slope that was strewn with shattered rock and debris which made walking arduous. Then they reached a scarp of rock ground smooth by the slipping down of melting snow, and when they had crossed that their difficulties began. The scarp broke off on the verge of an almost precipitous rift, and a torrent that seemed drawn out into silk-like threads roared in the depths of it. A few pines were sprinkled about the slopes of the gully, and one or two of them which had fallen lay athwart the creek.

They stopped for a few minutes upon a dizzy ledge of rock, from which they looked far down across battalions of somber trees upon the gleaming lake below. Here Weston was guilty of an indiscretion. He admitted afterward that he ought to have known that a man used to command in India, who claimed some acquaintance with Alpine climbing, was not likely to be advised by him.

"I believe we could get down, sir, and there are several logs across the creek," he said. "We must get over it somehow, and the gully will probably run into a canon lower down."

"That," remarked Kinnaird, dryly, "is perfectly evident. It is, however, my intention to follow up the gully."

Weston was conscious that Ida Stirling was glancing at him, but his face remained expressionless; and as he suggested nothing further, they went on again. The mountain slope had been steadily growing steeper beneath them, and they had not yet reached the bench. They went up for another hour, and then came out upon the expected strip of plateau in the midst of which the gully died out. The plateau, however, lay on the northern side of a great peak, and was covered with slushy snow. Kinnaird looked somewhat dubiously at the latter, which seemed deep in the hollows.

"The snow will have gone once we get around the western shoulders," he said. "It must be almost as near to get down from that side, and the canoes will have gone on by now. Still, it's rather a long time since breakfast."

He glanced at the girls, and appeared relieved when Ida said:

"I think we would better push on a little further before we stop for lunch."

They plunged into a snow-drift to the knees, and when they had floundered through it for thirty yards or so Weston sank suddenly well over his waist. He flung himself forward, and with the help of Kinnaird wriggled clear, but when they looked down there was empty blackness beneath the hole he had made.

"It's a snow-bridge, I think, sir," he said. "The creek's running under it. Anyway, I didn't touch anything solid with my feet."

Kinnaird's face grew graver.

"If you're right," he observed, "it would be wiser to work around."

They spent an hour doing it, and then, crossing knee-deep, they sat down on a ledge of jutting rock while Weston laid out a simple meal. It was very cold in the shadow of the peak, and a bitter wind that seemed to be gathering strength whistled eerily about the desolation of rock and snow. They were wet to the knees, and Weston fancied that the girls' cheerfulness was a trifle forced. He was ready to admit that he was somewhat stiff and weary, for he had carried the provisions and the heavy blankets that the girls had now tucked round them.

The latter commenced to flag when they started again; and, as it happened, the strip of bench they followed rapidly narrowed in and grew rougher until it became little more than a sloping ledge with the hillside dropping almost sheer away from it. It was strewn with great fragments that had fallen from the wall of rock above, and banks of snow lay packed between them in the hollows. Every now and then one or another of the party sank deep on stepping down from some ledge of slippery stone. They were on the northern side of a spur of the higher range, though they were approaching the angle where it broke off and fell in a steep declivity facing west. This point they had to turn before they reached the spot from which Kinnaird purposed descending to the river. They made very slow progress, while the shadow of the peaks grew blacker and longer across the hills. At length, when they had almost reached the corner, Kinnaird stopped to consider, and the girls sat down with evident alacrity. This time he looked at Weston, and his manner implied that he was willing to consider any views that he or the others might express.

"I'm afraid that I have been a little at fault," he admitted. "In fact, I quite expected that we would be down again by this time. It is now well on in the afternoon, and, as we have probably covered about two-thirds of the distance, it would not be advisable to go back as we came up."

"That," said Arabella Kinnaird decisively, "is unthinkable."

She turned to Weston, who nodded.

"Anyway, the canoes have gone on, which means that there would be nothing to eat until we came up with them," he said. "It must be eight or nine miles, by water, from our last camp to where they are to wait for us, and the ladies couldn't go so far through the thick timber in the valley."

Kinnaird looked beneath him.

"Well, I don't think anybody could get straight down from here," he said.

It was clearly beyond the power of those who were with him, as they quite realized. A few yards away, the hillside fell almost precipitously for perhaps a thousand feet to the tops of the pines below. Part of it was smooth rock, but long banks of gravel lay resting in the hollows at so steep a slope that it was evident that a footstep would be sufficient to dislodge them. Indeed, without that, every now and then some of them broke away and plunged down into the valley. Close behind the party a wall of crags rose sheer for a hundred feet at least. Kinnaird glanced up at them with a frown.

"I fancy we should find another level strip above," he said; "but since we can't get up the only thing to do is to push on. From what I saw through my glasses when I went up the lake, there is certainly an easier slope once we get around the corner."

They went on, wearily, with the wall of rock creeping out nearer and nearer to the edge of the declivity, and it became quite clear to Weston that the girls' strength was rapidly failing. Still, he quietly urged them on, for it was now becoming a somewhat momentous question whether they could get down before darkness fell; and as a rule the white mists settle heavily upon those ranges with the dusk. Then the margin between rock and declivity almost disappeared, and Weston, looking down on the somber tree-tops, felt reasonably certain that there was now another wall of crags between the foot of the slope and them.

"I suppose you are quite sure, sir, that the face of the hill is less steep around the corner in front of us?" he asked.

"I am," replied Kinnaird. "I traced out the route with my glasses from the head of the lake. Where I was wrong was in not heading for higher level. The bench I intended to follow is clearly above us."

Weston glanced at Ida, and noticed that her face was very weary and a trifle gray, but she smiled at him reassuringly; and they floundered on until the wall of rock pushed them right out to the edge of the declivity. They clung to it here and there with their hands while they felt for a foothold among the banks of gravel. Suddenly, Ida slipped and clutched at Weston. Her hand fell upon the package of provisions that he had slung behind his shoulders with a strip of deerhide, and, for she was of full stature and not particularly slender, it broke away. Then there was a roar of sliding stones, and Weston, dropping on his knees, flung an arm about the girl. She fell as he did it, and they slid down together a yard or so before he drove one foot deep into the gravel and brought himself up. Then he risked a glance at her.

"Don't look down!" he commanded sharply.

Her face was set and white, but she met his gaze, and in her eyes there was something that suggested confidence in him. He felt that he could be sure of her nerve, but whether her strength or his would suffice for the scramble back was another matter, and he was horribly afraid. Kinnaird, lying flat down, held out his hand, and in a moment or two Weston and the girl stood with the others close beneath the rock. He did not know how they got there. He was quivering all through, and the perspiration of tense effort dripped from him. While he stood there gasping, the packet of provisions, which had apparently rested for a few moments among the gravel dislodged by his efforts to climb up, rolled down the slope, and he watched it rush downward until he turned his eyes away. It was too horribly suggestive; but his gaze was drawn back again against his will, and he saw the package vanish suddenly. That made it quite clear that the slope ended in another wall of crags.

He did not remember whether Ida or the others said anything to him; but they crept on again, almost immediately, clinging to the rock, and scarcely venturing to glance down at the climbing forest which now appeared to lie straight beneath them but very far away. A cold wind stung their faces, the rocks above rose higher, but there was, at least, no snow beneath their feet, and they moved on yard by yard, scarcely daring to breathe at times, until at length Kinnaird cried out in a voice that was hoarse with exultation:

"We are over the worst!"

Then Weston gasped with sincere relief, for it was clear that they had crept around the perilous corner. The wall of rock receded, and the slope became less steep in front of them. It was, however, strewn with massy fragments and debris carried down by the snow, and the sun that flung a warm light upon it hung just clear of the peaks across the valley. There was no doubt that his companions were worn out, and he fancied that the girls could scarcely drag themselves along, but they had now no provisions and it was clearly advisable to get down, at least as far as the timber, where one could make a fire, before darkness fell; and they pushed on. Arabella Kinnaird, scrambling over a pile of ragged stones, came down heavily. She cried out as she did so, and then rising with some difficulty, immediately sat down again with her face awry.

"It's my knee," she said faintly.

Kinnaird scrambled toward her, but she waved him back.

"Go on with the packer," she said.

Kinnaird and Weston proceeded a little farther down the slope, which was practicable, though very steep; and when Ida called them back, Arabella smiled ruefully.

"It's horribly bruised, and I'm afraid I've twisted a ligament or something of that kind," she said. "At least, I can't put any weight on it."

There was an expressive silence for the next few moments, and Kinnaird gazed down into the valley with consternation in his eyes. The sun had dipped behind the peaks by this time, and the great hollow was growing dim and hazy. The river was blotted out, and even the climbing forest seemed indistinct.

"Could you get along on my arm?" he asked.

"No," said Arabella sharply, "I don't think I could put my foot on the ground."

Weston said nothing, though he realized that the situation was becoming serious. They had had no more than one hasty meal since early morning, and they were worn out. It was also, as he knew, very cold up on the hills at night. While he considered the matter, Kinnaird stretched out a pointing hand.

"Look!" he said.

A trail of filmy vapor crawled out athwart the lower pines and covered them as it rolled rapidly upward. While they watched it the depths of the valley were filled and became a dim white plain that extended its borders as it ascended. Long billows of vapor rolled out from its edges and slid up the hollows, blotting out the somber ranks of climbing pines one by one until all had gone and rock scarp and rugged peak rose isolated from a vast sweep of mist. It crawled up the slope where they sat, and then stopped and came no higher, leaving the rampart of rock and snow behind them to glimmer coldly blue and gray against the clear green radiance of the evening sky. Kinnaird looked at Weston as if willing to entertain any suggestion.

"It's clear that we can't get down," he said.

Weston nodded.

"I fancy that I could reach the timber, sir," he said. "I'll bring up a load of branches to make a fire."

He loosed the blankets from his shoulders, and floundering down the slope was lost in the vapor.

CHAPTER V

IDA'S CONFIDENCE

An hour passed, and it was growing dark when Weston scrambled up the hillside empty-handed.

"There's a slope between us and the timber, sir, that's too steep to get down," he announced. "I worked along the edge of it until the light failed me and the mist got very thick."

"You did quite right to come back," said Kinnaird. "We shall have to stay here. What do you suggest?"

Weston looked around him carefully.

"There's a little hollow under the ledge yonder. You should keep fairly warm there close together with the blankets over you."

Kinnaird demurred to this, but Weston, drawing him aside, spoke forcibly, and at length he made a sign of acquiescence.

"Well," he said, "no doubt you're right. After all, the great thing is to keep the warmth in us. Where are you going?"

"I'll find a burrow somewhere within call," said Weston quietly.

He was busy for some little time scraping stones out from the hollow beneath the ledge, and then he built a rough wall of the larger ones on two sides of it. After that they got Miss Kinnaird there with some difficulty, and when she and the others had crept into the shelter and wrapped the blankets round them, he turned away and stretched himself out beneath the largest stone he could find. For an hour he lay there smoking, and then put his pipe away. He had not much tobacco, and it occurred to him that he might want the little that remained on the morrow.

In the meanwhile it had grown bitterly cold, and one never feels the cold so much as when a day's arduous exertion has exhausted the natural heat of the body. Weston was also very hungry, and after beating his numbed hands he thrust them inside his deerskin jacket. They had probably reached no great height, but summer was only commencing, and it was evidently freezing. Indeed, the nights had been cold enough when he lay well wrapped up in the sheltered valley. Still, the mist, at least, climbed no higher. The stars were twinkling frostily, and opposite him across the valley a great gray-white rampart ran far up into the dusky blue. He watched it for a while, and then it seemed to grow indistinct and hazy, and when some time afterward he opened his eyes again he saw that there was no mist about the slopes beneath.

Then, as he looked about him, stiff with cold, he noticed that a half-moon had sailed up above the peaks. Its elusive light lay upon the slope, but ledge and stone seemed less distinct than their shadows, which were black as ebony. After that he commenced a struggle with himself, for, numbed as he was, he did not want to move, which is one of the insidious effects of cold. It cramps its victim's volition as well as his body, and makes him shrink from any attempt at the muscular effort which would make it easier for him to resist it. After all, the endurance of bitter frost is rather a question of moral than physical strength, as every prospector who has crossed the snow-bound altitudes on the gold trail knows.

He forced himself to get up, and stood still, shivering in every limb, while a bitter wind struck through him as he gathered his resolution together. Then, stripping off his deerskin jacket, he flung it over one arm as he turned toward his companions' shelter. Kinnaird was awake, and his daughter cried out drowsily when Weston stood looking down at him.

"It's clearing, and I think I could get down," he said. "It would be better if Miss Stirling came with me."

"Yes," said Kinnaird reflectively, "I think she ought to go."

There was, however, a difficulty when Ida rose to her feet, and stood looking about her half awake. She could not speak distinctly, but she seemed bent on staying. Then Kinnaird made a sign to Weston, who quietly slipped his arm within the girl's and drew her away. She went with him some little distance, too dazed to resist, and then, snatching her arm free, turned upon him white with cold and anger.

"What right have you or Major Kinnaird——" she began, but Weston checked her with a little forceful gesture.

"I, at least, have none at all," he admitted. "In a way, however, I suppose I'm responsible for the safety of the whole party. Could you have done Miss Kinnaird any good by staying?"

Cold and half dazed as she was, a moment's reflection convinced Ida that she could have done very little beyond helping to keep her companion warm. Weston, who did not wait for her answer, went on:

"Now," he said severely, "do you feel as comfortable as usual, or are you almost too cold to move?"

The girl admitted that the latter was the case, and Weston spread out his hands.

"Well," he said, "it will be at least another six hours before the first sunlight falls on that ledge. Besides, as you may remember, you have had only one meal since early yesterday morning, and I shall be especially fortunate if I can get back here with the Indians by noon. Major Kinnaird and his daughter must stay, but that doesn't apply to you. Are you still quite sure you have any cause to be angry with me?"

Ida looked at him with a little flash in her eyes.

"Oh," she said, "I suppose you're right. Still, is it necessary to make the thing so very plain?"

Weston laughed.

"I just want you to realize that you are in my hands until we reach level ground," he replied. "In the meanwhile I should like you to put on this jacket."

He held out the warm deerhide garment, and the girl flashed a covert glance at him. He stood close by her in loose blue shirt and thin duck trousers, and, as far as she could see by the moonlight, his face was pinched and blue with cold.

"I won't," she said.

Weston pursed up his face whimsically. He seldom shone where diplomacy was advisable. As a rule, he endeavored to bring about the end he had in view by the most direct means available. In the present instance he felt very compassionate toward his companion, and recognized only the necessity of getting her back to camp, where there was food and shelter, as soon as possible. Still, it not infrequently happened that his severely simple procedure proved successful.

"Well," he said, "since I don't intend to wear it we'll leave it here. I'll leave you for a minute or two while I prospect for an easier route than the one by which I came up."

He flung down the jacket, and, striding away, disappeared, while Ida shivered as she glanced about her. She could no longer see the shelter she had left, and she stood alone in the midst of a tremendous desolation of rock and snow, with the valley yawning, a vast dusky pit, beneath her feet. It was appallingly lonely, and she was numb with cold, while, since she was sure that she could not climb back to her companions unassisted, there was only one person on whom she could rely, and that was the packer, who had insisted on her doing what he thought fit. When he came back she had put on the jacket, but he had sense enough to make no sign of having noticed it.

"I can see our way for the next few hundred feet," he said.

The way did not prove an easy one, but they went down, with the gravel sliding beneath them, and now and then a mass of debris they had loosened rushing past. It occurred to Ida that Weston limped somewhat awkwardly, and once or twice she fancied that she saw his face contract as they scrambled over some shelf of jutting stone; but they pushed on cautiously until they came to a precipitous descent. Ida sat down gasping, when her companion stopped, and gazed with an instinctive shrinking into the gulf below. She could now see the climbing pines, black beneath the moon, and the river shining far away in the midst of them, but they seemed to go straight down. She was very weary, and scarcely felt able to get up again, but in a minute or two Weston held out his hand.

"I fancy that this ridge dies out somewhere to the left. We'll follow the crest of it until we can get around the end," he said.

They went on very cautiously, though there were times when Ida held her breath and was glad of the firm grasp that her companion laid on her arm. She would not look down into the valley, and when she glanced aside at all it was up at the gleaming snow on the opposite side of it. She seemed to be walking in mid-air, cut off from the comfortable security of the solid earth below, and she found the clamor of falling water that came faintly up to her vaguely reassuring. There had been an almost appalling silence where she had left her companions beneath the frozen peaks, but now one could hear the hoarse fret of a rapid on the river, and this was a familiar sound that she welcomed.

Still her weariness gained on her, and her limbs grew heavier, until she could scarcely drag herself along. Weston's limp became more perceptible too, but he went on with an almost cruel persistency, and forced her forward with his hand on her arm. Sometimes he spoke to her, and, though his voice was strained, his words were cheering and compassionate.

At length, the descent they skirted became less steep, and scrambling down over a broken slope they presently reached the timber—straggling juniper, and little scattered firs that by and by grew taller and closer together; and, though the peril was over, it was then that their real difficulties commenced. The slope was so steep that they could scarcely keep a footing, and now and then they fell into the trees. There were places where these grew so close together that they could scarcely force a passage through, and others where they had gone down before a screaming gale and lay piled in a tangled chaos over which it was almost impossible to flounder. It was dark in the timber, and they could not see the broken ends of the branches that rent their clothing; but they went on somehow, down and down, until, when they reached a clearer space where the moonlight shone through, Ida sank down limply on a fallen tree. Her skirt was rent to tatters, and one shoe had been torn almost to pieces.

"I simply can't go on," she said.

Weston leaned against a neighboring fir, looking down at her very compassionately, though she noticed that his face, on which the moonlight fell, was somewhat drawn and gray.

"Try to think," he said.

"I can't," replied Ida, "I only want to sleep."

Her companion moved forward and quietly laid his hand on her arm as though to urge her to rise.

"Don't you understand how it is? Your friends are up yonder in the frost with nothing to eat. I have to take the Indians back for them."

"Then you must go on," the girl said faintly.

Weston shook his head.

"No," he declared, "not without you. That's out of the question. If there were no other reason, we should have to come back here for you, and I expect that in the daylight we shall find a shorter way up. It will be noon anyway before we get there, and you wouldn't wish to keep your friends waiting longer."

Ida rose with an effort, and clung heavily to his arm when they crept downward again; but the light grew a little clearer as they proceeded, and the sound of the river rang louder in their ears. Then, in the gray of the morning, they staggered out upon the bank of the river. Walking, half awake, Ida floundered among the boulders and through a horrible maze of whitened driftwood cast up by the stream. Farther on they fortunately found stretches of smooth sand, and they plodded over these and through little pools, though she afterward fancied that Weston carried her across some of the deeper ones.

The sun was high when they saw the two canoes drawn up on the bank, and a few moments later Mrs. Kinnaird appeared among the firs. She ran toward them, stumbling in a ludicrous fashion amidst the boulders, and then stopped a few yards away and gazed at Ida. The girl could scarcely stand from weariness, and her dress clung about her, wet with the river-water and rent to tatters. There was fear in the little lady's eyes.

"Where are they?" she asked.

Weston stepped forward limping, and his face was set and gray.

"Up yonder, and quite safe," he said. "Miss Kinnaird has hurt her knee. Nothing serious, but it hurts her to walk. I came for the Indians to help her down again."

He raised his hand restrainingly.

"There is no cause for alarm. Get Miss Stirling something to eat, and leave the rest to me."

He turned away abruptly, and limped past them toward the camp. When Mrs. Kinnaird and Ida reached it, he was hastily getting together provisions, and the Indians were already hewing down two slender firs. When they stood waiting, each with a stout fir pole on his shoulder, he turned to the anxious lady, who seemed bent on going with him.

"It's quite out of the question for you to undertake that climb. We'll be back again in a few hours with the major and Miss Kinnaird," he said.

Ida went up to him and touched his arm, and, for no very evident reason, the color crept into her face when he looked at her inquiringly.

"Can't the Indians find the way themselves?" she asked. "You are scarcely fit to go."

Weston shook his head.

"I must manage it somehow," he said. "They have nothing to eat up yonder, and the Indians might not find them until it's dark again."

He broke off for a moment with a forced smile.

"Try to reassure Mrs. Kinnaird, and then go to sleep as soon as you can."

In another minute he had limped away, and Mrs. Kinnaird found the girl looking down with a very curious expression at a little smear of blood on a smooth white stone. There were further red spots on the shingle, and they led forward in the direction in which the rescue party had gone.

"Oh," she said, "he told me he had cut his foot, and he couldn't have waited long enough to eat anything."

Then she gasped once or twice, for she was worn out to the verge of a break-down, and Mrs. Kinnaird, who saw how white her face was growing, slipped an arm about her and led her back toward the tent.

The afternoon passed very slowly with the little, anxious lady, and every now and then she crept softly out of the tent and gazed expectantly up the steep hillside. Still, each time she did it, there was nothing that she could see except the long ranks of somber firs, and the oppressive silence was broken only by the sound of the river.

Then she slipped back quietly into the tent where Ida lay in a restless sleep. Now and then the girl moved a little, and once or twice she murmured unintelligibly. It was very hot, for the sunrays struck down upon the canvas between the firs, whose clogging, honey-like sweetness was heavy in the air.

By and by, however, it grew a little cooler, as the shadow of the great dark branches crept across the tent. Then they moved out upon the dazzling river and slowly covered it. Mrs. Kinnaird, rising once more in an agony of impatience, stumbled against one of the tent supports. The crutch and ridge-poles rattled, and Ida opened her eyes.

"Oh," she said drowsily, "you needn't be anxious. He is quite sure to bring them back."

She apparently tried to rouse herself, and, failing, went to sleep again; but she left Mrs. Kinnaird a little comforted. The latter was observant, and she felt that Ida Stirling had a reason for her confidence which, she fancied, was not lightly given.

The sunlight had, however, faded off the valley when she rose for the last time from the seat she had found outside the tent, for there was no doubt now that a faint patter of feet on stones mingled with the clamor of the river. Almost as she did so, a few plodding figures appeared beneath the firs, and she saw that two of them carried a litter between them. Then she saw her husband walking very wearily, and she ran forward with a little cry. She grasped one of the poles between which a sagging blanket hung, and Weston, who held the ends of them, looked at her.

"Miss Kinnaird isn't hurt much," he said harshly. "Don't stop us now!"

Then she heard her daughter's voice bearing out this assurance, and she went back with the plodding men, while her husband stumbled along wearily at her side. In a minute or two Weston, calling to one of the Indians, laid down his end of the poles, and, staggering away, sat down heavily. None of them troubled themselves about him, and Ida, who had risen when she heard their voices, helped to convey Miss Kinnaird into the tent. In the meanwhile one of the Indians growled to his comrade when he found the fire out, and stolidly proceeded to relight it, while Weston lay with his back against a fir and watched him with half-closed eyes. The Siwash, however, proved that he was capable of preparing a meal, and when it was finished, Arabella, who appeared much fresher than the major, proceeded to relate her adventures to Ida and her mother.

"It was rather horrible up on the range, and I was almost afraid they wouldn't get me down," she said. "I don't know how they did it, I'm sure. Parts of the way were simply awful. They had to cut the little trees down for yards at a time to get my blanket litter through, and there were places so steep that they could scarcely crawl down. The Indians, of course, had to be relieved now and then, and my father and the packer took turns with them."

She looked at the major with a smile.

"When it was especially steep, I preferred an Indian and the packer. Once, you know, you dropped me; but nothing seemed to disconcert that young man. He must have been horribly worn out, for he had been up twice, but he was so steady and reassuringly quiet. I suppose a man of his kind would appreciate twenty dollars. He really deserves it."

Ida frowned, and remembered the trail of blood on the white stones when the packer had started. Kinnaird made a little abrupt movement.

"I'm afraid that I was forgetting all about the man in my relief at getting you safely down," he said. "We owe him a good deal, and I'll go out presently and thank him; but there's another matter. Your knee ought to be attended to."

That commenced a discussion, but Arabella persisted that she would get over the injury if she didn't walk for a few days.

Then Kinnaird summoned one of the Indians to clear away the meal. The brown-skinned, dark-haired man appeared in the entrance of the tent and spoke haltingly in English.

"They wait," he said, pointing to the supper plates. "Want piece shirt—handkerchief. Packer man's boot full of blood."

Those he addressed looked at one another, and Kinnaird, rising, went out hastily.

CHAPTER VI

KINNAIRD STRIKES CAMP

It was about the middle of the next afternoon when Ida Stirling, walking slowly along the river-bank, came upon Weston sitting with his back to a tree. He wore no boot on one foot which was wrapped in bandages, and when he would have risen Ida checked him with a sign, and sat down not far away.

"Is it too hot in the tent?" he asked.

Ida flashed a swift glance at him. He seemed perfectly contented, and very much at his ease, and it was a little difficult to believe that this was the sharp-voiced mart who had ordered her to put on his jacket early on the previous morning. Now he was smiling languidly, and there was a graceful carelessness that was almost boyish in his manner, which made it a little easier to understand why his comrades had called him the Kid. She was rather pleased with it.

"No," she said. "At least that was not what brought me out. The major has gone fishing; Mrs. Kinnaird has gone to sleep; and Arabella appears a little cross."

Weston nodded.

"It's excusable," he said. "How is Miss Kinnaird's knee?"

"I don't think it's very bad. How is your foot? It doesn't seem to have affected your temper."

Weston laughed.

"I'd forgotten all about it. In some respects I feel a little obliged to it. You see, for once in a while, it's rather nice to have nothing to do, and know that one's wages won't immediately stop. Besides, to be waited on is a pleasant change."

Ida's eyebrows straightened a trifle as they sometimes did when she was not exactly pleased. It is by no means an unusual thing in the west for a packer or a ranch hand to converse with his employers or their friends on familiar terms, and it occurred to her that it was a trifle superfluous for him to insist on reminding her of his status when she was willing to forget it. Still, she was quite aware that this man had not always been a packer, and she was conscious of an increasing curiosity concerning his past.

"That is an unusual experience with you?" she asked.

"Oh, yes," said Weston. "Anyway, during the last few years."

She was foiled again, for she could not press the question more closely; and, sitting still in the shadow, she looked up between the dark fir branches at the line of gleaming snow and the great rock rampart beneath which they had crept.

"Were you ever up so high before?" she ventured.

"Yes," said Weston. "I believe so; but never for pleasure. In fact, I think some of the ranges we crossed on the gold trail must have been considerably higher. I told you that prospecting is one of my weaknesses."

"You did," agreed Ida. "It's one I could never understand, though I have spent some time, in this province. Every now and then it seems that the rancher must leave his clearing and wander off into the bush. As you admitted, he generally comes home dressed in rags, and very seldom brings anything with him. Why do you do it?"

Weston laughed in a rather curious fashion.

"Oh," he said, "don't you know? Did you never feel, even in winter in Montreal, when you had skating-rinks, toboggan-slides, snow-shoe meets, and sleigh-rides to keep you amused, that it was all growing tiresome and very stale? Haven't you felt that you wanted something—something you hadn't got and couldn't define—though you might recognize it when you found it?"

Once more Ida's eyebrows straightened. He was going rather deeper than she had supposed him capable, though she was not altogether unacquainted with the restlessness he had described. Weston glanced at her face, and nodded.

"Well," he said, "that's very much what happens to the rancher and the track-grader every now and then; and when it does he goes up into the bush—prospecting. Still, I think you were wrong when you said that we seldom bring back anything. Did you bring nothing down with you from the quiet and the glimmering moonlight up yonder above the timber line?"

His companion looked up across the climbing forest to the desolation of rock and snow through which she had wandered with him a little while ago. It had been her first ascent, and she now felt the thrill of achievement and remembered how she had come down that apparently endless slope in the darkness. The feat looked almost impossible, by daylight. Then she remembered also how her nerves had tingled, and the curious sense of exaltation that had come over her as she crept along the dizzy edge of the great rock scarp in the moonlight, far above the unsubstantial ghosts of climbing trees. For the time being, it had proved stronger than weariness or the sense of personal danger, and she had a vague fancy that the memory of it would always cling to her.

"Yes," she said, "I think I brought down something, or rather it attached itself to me. What is it?"

Weston spread out his hands with a boyish laugh.

"How should I know? Its glamour and mystery, perhaps. Still, though the prospector knows it, everybody can't feel it. One must have sympathy. It would make itself felt by you."

The girl's face checked him. She felt that there was a subtle bond of mutual comprehension between her and this stranger; but she was not prepared to admit it to him; and he recognized that he had, perhaps, gone further than was advisable.

"Still," he continued, "though it's plainest up on the high peaks, the bush is full of it. You can recognize it everywhere. Listen!"

Ida did so. She heard the hoarse fret of the river, and the faint elfin sighing high up in the top of the firs.

It was the old earth music, and it drowned the recollection of social conventions and caste distinctions. It was the same to camp-packer and rich contractor's daughter. As Ida listened it seemed to stir the primitive impulses of her human nature. She took alarm and stopped her ears to it.

"Is it wise to listen?" she asked. "It leads to nothing but restlessness."

"It seldom leads to any material benefit," Weston admitted. "After all, I think, one has to be a vagabond before one can properly appreciate it."

"You seem sure of that?" Ida's curiosity to know more of him would not permit her to avoid the personal application.

"I'm afraid there must be a little of the vagabond in me," said Weston, with a smile. "Once I walked into Winnipeg without a dollar, and was fortunate in hiring myself to add up figures in a big flour-mill. The people for whom I worked seemed quite pleased with the way I did it, and paid me reasonably. I lived in a big boarding-house like a rabbit-warren. Through the thin partitions I could hear the people all about me stirring in their sleep at night. I went to the mill in a crowded car every morning, and up to the office in an elevator. I stayed with it just a month, and then I broke out."

"Broke out?" said Ida.

"Threw the flour-mill people's pens across the office. You see, I was getting sick for room and air. I presented the concern with my last week's stipend, and a man at the boarding-house with my city clothes."

"What did you do then?"

"Took the trail. There was limitless prairie straight on in front of me. I walked for days, and slept at night wherever I could find a bluff. I could hear the little grasses whispering when I lay half-awake, and it was comforting to know that there were leagues and leagues of them between me and the city. I drove a team for a farmer most of that season. Then I went on to a track that they were strengthening and straightening in this province. It ran between the rock and the river, and the snow hadn't gone. We worked waist-deep in it part of the time, and thawed out every stick of giant-powder at the fire. The construction boss was a hustler, and he drove us mercilessly. We toiled raw-handed, worn-out and savage, and he drove us all the harder when one of the boys tried to brain him."

"And you never longed to be back in the office at the flour-mill?"

Weston laughed.

"Didn't you find those sleigh-rides, skating-rinks, and even the trips west in your father's private car, grow exceedingly tame?"

"Ah," said Ida, "you must remember that I have never known anything else."

"Then you have only to wait a little. It's quite certain that you won't be able to say that some day."

It seemed to Ida inadvisable to pursue the subject further, though she was not sure that he wished to do so.

"How did you expend your energy after you left the track?" she asked.

"I don't quite remember. Drove horses, went about with a thrashing outfit, hewed logs for bridges—but haven't I talked too long about myself? You have told me nothing of—Montreal."

Ida risked a chance shot.

"Don't you know that kind of life? It must be very much the same as the one your people lead in England. It doesn't count that their amusements are slightly different."

Weston foiled her again.

"Well," he said, with an air of reflection, "I don't quite think it is; but perhaps I'm prejudiced. I wheeled scrap-iron at the rolling-mills when I was in Montreal."

He leaned farther back against the tree, with a little whimsical smile. It was pleasant to appear as a modern Ulysses in the eyes of a very pretty girl, but he had, as she was quick to recognize, taken up the role unconsciously.

"Where are you going next?" she asked.

"I shall probably go off prospecting if I can raise the money. That is partly why I hope that Major Kinnaird will keep me as long as he camps out in the bush."

Ida laughed.

"I think you may count on that. He is rather pleased with you. In fact, I heard him say that if he'd had you in India he would have made a capable sergeant of you."

She saw a shadow creep into his face, and wondered what had brought it there, for she did not know that in his younger days he had thought of Sandhurst. Then, seeing that he did not answer, she rose.

"Well," she said, "Arabella is probably wanting me."

He watched her move away among the great fir trunks, and then took out his pipe with a little sigh. Still he had, or so he fancied, sense enough to refrain from allowing his thoughts to wander in her direction too frequently, and, soothed by the murmur of the river, he presently went to sleep. When he awakened it was time to see that the Indians got supper ready.

During the evening, Stirling reached the camp; and when the Siwash who had poled his canoe up the river had drawn it out, they sat down somewhat limply on the shingle, for he had as usual traveled with feverish haste. He stayed until the next day, which was rather longer than any of them expected; and it was not by accident that he came upon Weston alone before he went away. The latter was then engaged in lighting a fire, and his employer sat down on a fir branch and quietly looked him over.

"Foot getting better?" he asked.

"I think it is," said Weston.

Stirling nodded.

"I understand that you have been of some service to these people; and they're my daughter's friends," he said. "Is there anything I can do for you?"

"No," replied Weston, "I don't think there is."

The contractor looked at him steadily for a moment or two.

"Well," he said, "if anything strikes you, there's no reason why you shouldn't let me know. Feeling anxious to get back to the track?"

Weston's eyes twinkled.

"I don't think I am."

"Then you may stay right where you are, and take care of my daughter. If she wants to climb mountains or shoot rapids, it's to be done; but you'll fix things so it can be done safely. You're in charge of this outfit, and not that major man."

Stirling was never addicted to mincing matters, but Weston could not quite repress a grin.

"It would make things a little difficult if Major Kinnaird understands that," he said.

"Then you must see that he doesn't. You can fix it somehow. It's up to you."

He rose, as if there were nothing more to be said, and then as he moved away he turned and waved his hand.

"I'll have you moved up a grade on the pay-roll."

He started down the river in another half-hour, and left Weston thoughtful. He had never seen his employer before; but it was evident that the latter had made a few inquiries concerning him, and had been favorably informed.

For another fortnight Weston tactfully carried out his somewhat difficult task; and then it was with a curious sense of regret that he stood one evening in a little roadside station. Major Kinnaird was apparently counting the pile of baggage some little distance away, his wife and daughter were in the station-room, and Ida and Weston stood alone where the track came winding out of the misty pines. She glanced from him to the forest, and there was just a perceptible hint of regret in her voice.

"It has been very pleasant, and in one way I'm almost sorry we are going to Vancouver," she said. "This"—and she indicated the wall of hillside and the shadowy bush—"grows on one."

Weston nodded gravely.

"It does," he said. "You have been up among the high peaks, and you'll never quite forget them, even in the cities. Now and then you'll feel them drawing you back again."

The girl laughed, perhaps because she realized that the memory of the last few weeks would remain with her. She also remembered that he had said that the stillness among the white peaks and in the scented bush was filled with a glamour that seized on one.

"Well," she confessed, "I may come back with other friends some day; and in that case we shall certainly ask for you as guide. I want to say, as Major Kinnaird did, that we owe a good deal to you. I am only sorry that the trip is over."

Then her tone changed a little, and Weston supposed that she was unwilling to make too great an admission.

"There are so many little discomforts you have saved us."

"Yes," he agreed, a trifle dryly, "I suppose there are. However, I shall probably have gone away when you come back again."

He broke off for a moment, and then turned toward her quietly.

"Still," he said, "I seem to feel that I shall see you again some day."

His voice was perfectly steady, but, though the light was fading fast, Ida saw the glint in his eyes, and she answered conventionally.

"Of course," she said, "that would be a pleasure."

Then she spoiled it by a laugh when she saw the smile creep into her companion's eyes; for it was clear to both of them that the formal expression was in their case somewhat out of place. They realized that there was more that might have been said; and it was a slight relief when the shriek of a whistle came ringing down the track and a roar of wheels grew louder among the shadowy pines. Then the great mountain locomotive and the dusty cars came clanking into the station, stopped a few moments, and rolled away again; and Weston was left with the vision of a white-robed figure in a fluttering dress that leaned out from a car platform looking back at the gleaming snow and then turned a moment to wave a hand to him.

It was an hour later, and the big nickeled lamps were lighted, when Arabella Kinnaird looked up at her companion as she sat in a lurching car while the great train swept furiously down the Fraser gorge.

"Now," she exclaimed, "I remember! That packer has been puzzling me. His face was familiar. The same thing struck the major, as you heard him say."

"Well?" inquired Ida, a little too indifferently.

Her companion laughed.

"You overdo it. It would be wiser to admit that you are curious. The major said he'd seen him somewhere, and so he has, in a way. You remember his talking about the old North Country Hall he took for the shooting? Well, the owners had left that young man's photograph among some other odds and ends in what they probably called the library."

Ida had no doubt upon the matter, for she recalled the curious intentness of Weston's face as he sat in the firelight listening to Kinnaird's description of the house in question. Still, she was not prepared to display her interest.

"Well?" she inquired again.

Arabella Kinnaird made a sign of impatience.

"Can't you see? They wouldn't have had his photograph unless he had been a friend of the family or a relative. I wonder whether he told you his real name?"

"He didn't."

"It doesn't matter," said Miss Kinnaird. "I feel tolerably sure it is Weston, and that is the name of the people who own the place. You don't appear to understand that the fact has its significance."

"How?" asked Ida.

"You haven't been in England or you'd understand. The people who live in those old places are often very poor, but a certain number of them have something that the people who have only money would give a good deal to possess. As a matter of fact, though distinctly human in most respects, they are—different."

Ida laughed.

"Oh," she said, "I've naturally heard of that. It's quite an old notion, and didn't originate with you English people. Didn't the Roman emperors claim to have the Imperial purple in their veins? Still, out here, when we speak of a man appreciatively we say his blood is—red."

"And that's the color of packer Weston's."

A faint gleam crept into Ida's eyes as she remembered the white-faced man who had limped out of camp one morning almost too weary to drag himself along.

"Well," she said, "I think you ought to know. When he went back up the range for you he left a trail of it behind him."

Her companion had no opportunity for answering, for Major Kinnaird came back from the smoking end of the car just then, and when he spoke to Ida his daughter took up a book she had laid down.

In the meanwhile, a mountain locomotive and a train of flat cars came clanking into the station where Weston waited. Swinging himself onto one he took his place among the men who sat on the rails with which the car was loaded. Then, as the big locomotive slowly pulled them out, some of his new companions vituperated the station-agent for stopping them, and one came near braining him with a deftly-flung bottle when he retaliated. There were a good many more men perched on the other cars, and Weston concluded, from the burst of hoarse laughter that reached him through the roar of wheels, that all of them were not wholly sober. They had been recruited in Vancouver, and included a few runaway sailormen. One told him that they were going into the ranges to fill up a muskeg, and he expressed his opinion of the meanness of the company for not sending them up in a Colonist train, and offered to throw Weston off the car if he did not agree with him. He explained that he had already pitched off two of his companions.

Weston endeavored to pacify him; but, failing in this and in an attempt to crawl over the couplings into the adjoining car, he reluctantly grappled with the man and succeeded in throwing him into a corner. Then one of the others rose and stood over his prostrate comrade with a big billet of firwood that had been used to wedge the rails.

"I can't sleep with all this circus going on," he said gruffly. "Make any more trouble and off you go."

The other man apparently decided to lie still, and his comrade turned to Weston.

"Guess the construction boss isn't going to find them tally out right to-morrow," he observed, "We've lost quite a few of them coming up the line."

He went to sleep again soon afterward, and Weston was left in peace. In front of him the great locomotive snorted up the climbing track, hurling clouds of sparks aloft. Misty pines went streaming by, the chill night wind rushed past, the cars banged and clanked, and now and then odd bursts of harsh laughter or discordant singing broke through the roar of wheels. It was very different from the deep tranquillity of the wilderness and the quiet composure of the people with whom he had spent the last few weeks, but, as Ida Stirling had suggested, Weston's blood was red, and he was still young enough to find pleasure in every fresh draught of the wine of life. It was something to feel himself the equal in bodily strength and animal courage of these strong-armed men who were going to fill up the muskeg.

CHAPTER VII

GRENFELL'S MINE

It was Saturday evening, and Weston sat on a ledge of the hillside above the silent construction camp, endeavoring to mend a pair of duck trousers that had been badly torn in the bush. He held several strips of a cotton flour-bag in one hand, and was considering how he could best make use of them without unduly displaying the bold lettering of the brand, though in the bush of that country it was not an unusual thing for a man to go about labeled "Early Riser," or somebody's "Excelsior." His companions had trooped off to the settlement about a league away, and a row of flat cars stood idle on the track which now led across the beaten muskeg. On the farther side of the latter, the tall pines lay strewn in rows, but beyond the strip of clearing the bush closed in again, solemn, shadowy, and almost impenetrable. There was a smell of resinous wood-smoke in the air, but save for the distant sound of the river everything was very still.

Weston looked up sharply as a patter of approaching footsteps rose out of the shadows behind him. Some of the men were evidently coming back from the settlement earlier than he had expected. In a few minutes three or four of them appeared among the trees, and he recognized them as some of his friends, small ranchers who had, as often happens on the Pacific Slope, been forced to leave their lonely, half-cleared holdings and go out to earn the money that would keep them through the winter. Two of them were apparently assisting another man along between them, and when they drew nearer Weston saw that the latter was Grenfell, the cook.

"Guess it's 'bout time somebody else took care of you," said one, when they came up. "Sit right down," he added, neatly shaking Grenfell off his feet and depositing him unceremoniously at Weston's side.

Another of the men sat down close by, and Grenfell waved his hand to the others as they moved away.

"Bless you! You're good boys," he said.

The man who remained grinned at Weston.

"We've packed the blame old deadbeat 'most three miles. If Tom hadn't promised to see him through I'd have felt tempted to dump him into the river. The boys were trying to fill him up at the Sprotson House."

Grenfell, who did not appear to hear him, thrust a hand into his pocket, and pulling out a few silver coins counted them deliberately.

"Two—four—six," he said. "Six dollars to face an unkind world with. It isn't very much."

He sighed and turned to Weston.

"You know I've got to quit?"

"That's right," interposed the other man. "Cassidy's had 'most enough of him. He never could cook, anyway, and the boys are getting thin. Last thing he did was to put the indurated plates on the stove to warm. Filled the thing right up and left them. When he came back the plates had gone."

Weston, who had been sent to work some distance from the camp that day and had not heard of this mishap, felt sorry for Grenfell. The man evidently had always been somewhat frail, and now he was past his prime; indulgence in deleterious whisky had further shaken him. He could not chop or ply the shovel, and it was with difficulty that his companions had borne his cooking, while it seemed scarcely likely that anybody would have much use for him in a country that is run by the young and strong. He sat still regarding the money ruefully.

"Six of them—and they charge you one for a meal and a drink or two," he said. "If I hadn't known where there was quartz streaked right through with wire gold I might have felt discouraged." Then he straightened himself resolutely. "Seems to me it's time I went up and looked for it again."

"How can you know where it is when you have to look for it?" the other man inquired.

Grenfell glanced at him severely.

"I'm not drunk—it's my knees," he pointed out. "Don't cast slurs on me. I was once Professor of—mineralogical chemist and famous assayer too. Biggest mining men in the country consulted me."

The track-grader nodded as he glanced at Weston.

"I guess he was," he said. "We had a man from back east on this section who had heard of him."

Then he turned to Grenfell.

"Go ahead and explain about the mine."

"I'm not sure that that's quite straight," Weston objected. "If he does know anything of the kind——"

"Oh," said his companion, "I'm not on. If he ever did know I guess he has forgotten it long ago. He has been forgetting right along whether he put salt in the hash or not, and each time he wasn't sure he did it again. That's one of the things that made the trouble."

Grenfell stopped him with a gesture.

"I'm going to talk. Don't interrupt. Mr. Weston was once or twice a good friend to me, and you have seen me through a few times lately. Now I know a quartz lead that's run through with wire gold quite rich enough to mill at a profit, but I can't go up and look for it in the bush myself. When I walk any distance my knees get shaky. Make you firm offer—even shares to come up with me."

"Where is it?"

Grenfell turned and glanced toward the dim line of snow that gleamed high up above the forests in the north.

"There's a lake—the Lake of the Shadows—Verneille called it that," he said dreamily. "It lies in a hollow of the range with the black firs all round. There's a creek at one side, with a clear pool where it bends, and I came there one day very hot and hungry with the boots worn off me. I think"—and by his tense face he seemed to be trying earnestly to remember something—"we were quite a few days crossing that range, and our provisions were running put when we hit the valley."

"Well?" prompted the track-grader when he stopped.

"I crawled down to the pool to drink. There were pebbles in it and a ledge above. There were specks in the pebbles, and specks that showed plainer in the ledge. The stones were shot with the metal when I broke one or two of those I took out."

He fumbled inside his pocket and produced a little bag from which he extracted a few broken bits of rock. Weston, to whom he passed them, could see that little threads of metal ran through them. "You're quite sure it's gold?" the other man inquired.

"Am I sure!"

Grenfell smiled compassionately.

"I was Professor—but guess I've told you that already."

"The lead?" inquired the other man.

"Outcrop, a few yards of it. Then it dips on a slight inclination, and evidently runs back toward the range. An easy drive for an adit. Stayed there two days, Verneille and I. Quite sure about that gold."

Weston's face grew intent.

"You recorded it?"

"We staked a claim, and started back; but Verneille couldn't find a deer, and when we first hit the valley provisions were running out. There was a mist in the ranges, and whichever way we headed we brought up on crags and precipices. Then we went up to look for another way across and got into the snow. I never knew how I got out—or where Verneille went, but when I struck a prospector's camp—he wasn't with me."

The track-grader nodded. He had been born among the ranges, and knew that the prospectors who went out on the gold trail did not invariably come back. He had heard of famishing men staggering along astonishing distances half-asleep or too dazed to notice where they were going. He and Weston had done so themselves, for that matter.

"You told the prospector about the lead?" Weston inquired.

"If I did he never found the mine. I was scarcely sensible when I reached his camp, and I lay there very ill until he went on and left me with half a deer he'd shot. After that I nearly gave out again making the settlements."

"Well," said the track-grader, "where's the lake?"

Grenfell spread out his hands.

"I don't know. I went up to look for it three or four times several years ago."

He broke off abruptly, and there was silence for a minute or two. Strange as the thing appeared, it was not altogether an unusual story. All the way from California to the frozen north one now and then may hear of men who struck a rich quartz or silver lead in the wilderness, and, coming down to record it, signally failed to find it again. What is stranger still, there are mines that have been discovered several times by different men, none of whom was ever afterward able to retrace his steps. At any rate, if one accomplished it, he never came back to tell of his success, for the bones of many prospectors lie unburied in the wilderness. Indeed, when the wanderers who know it best gather for the time being in noisy construction camp or beside the snapping fire where the new wagon road cleaves the silent bush, they tell tales of lost quartz-reefs and silver leads as fantastic as those of the genii-guarded treasures of the East, and the men who have been out on the gold trail generally believe them.

On the surface Grenfell's task seemed easy. He had to find a lonely lake cradled in a range; and there are, as the maps show, three great ranges running roughly north and south in the Pacific Province. Still, in practice, it is difficult to tell where one leaves off and the other begins, for that wild land has been aptly termed a sea of mountains. They seem piled on one another, peak on peak; and spur on spur, and among their hollows lie lonely lakes and frothing rivers almost without number, while valley and hill-slopes are usually shrouded in tremendous forest to the line where the dwindling pines meet the gleaming snow. Weston was, of course, aware of this, and he felt, somewhat naturally, that it complicated the question.

Then Grenfell turned to him and his companion.

"I've made you my offer—a third-share each," he said. "Are you coming?"

The track-grader shook his head.

"No," he replied, "I guess not. I'm making good wages here. So long as I can keep from riling Cassidy they're sure." Then he grinned at Weston. "It's your call."

Weston sat silent for a full minute, but his heart was beating faster than usual, and he glanced up from the piles of gravel and blackened fir stumps by the track to the gleaming snow. A sudden distaste for the monotonous toil with the shovel came upon him, and he felt the call of the wilderness. Besides, he was young enough to be sanguine, although, for that matter, older men, worn by disappointments and toilsome journeys among the hills, have set out once more on the gold trail with an optimistic faith that has led them to their death. Ambition awoke in him, and he recognized now that the week or two spent in Kinnaird's camp had rendered it impossible for him to remain a track-grader. At length he turned to Grenfell.

"Well," he said, "if you're still in the same mind to-morrow I'll come. Still, if you think better of it, you can cry off then."

His sense of fairness demanded that; for he would not bind a man whose senses were, it seemed reasonable to suppose, not particularly clear. Grenfell evidently understood him, and drew himself up with an attempt at dignity.

"My head's quite right when I'm sitting down; it's my knees," he said. "Want to put the thing through now—half-share each. We'll call it a bargain."

The track-grader nodded to Weston.

"I guess you needn't stand off," he said. "He knows what he's doing."

They shook hands on it, and then proceeded to discuss ways and means. It was clear that they might be some time in the wilderness, and would need provisions, new boots, blankets, a rifle, and a tent; and all of these things are dear in that country. They recognized that it would be advisable also to take a horse or mule. Weston did not think that any of the bush ranchers would hire them one, as horses are not always brought back from such journeys. This would render it necessary to buy one; and to meet this expenditure Grenfell had six dollars and Weston not very much more.

While they were considering what items they could leave out, two or three men came up the trail from the settlement, which led close by, and one of them threw Weston a couple of letters.

"Mail-carrier rode in before we left, and I guessed I'd bring them along," he said.

There was scarcely light enough to see by, and Weston had some little difficulty in reading the letters. One was from Stirling and ran:

"Start on Monday for Winnipeg. I want a talk with you and may make a proposition. Enclose order that will frank you over the C.P.R."

Weston gazed at it with a thoughtful face. Winnipeg was a very long way off, and it was tolerably clear that Stirling, perhaps influenced by something his daughter or Major Kinnaird had said, meant to offer him promotion. Still, though he did not know exactly why, he shrank from accepting any favor from Miss Stirling's father, and, besides that, he had already pledged himself to Grenfell. He laid down the letter and opened the second one. Out of this he took an order on one of the H.B.C. settlement stores, dated at the Vancouver station. It was marked duplicate, and read:

"To Agent, Anson's Forks station:

"Provide Mr. Weston with whatever he may require in the shape of blankets, provisions, and any sundries in your stock for a prospecting trip."

A sheet of paper had been laid beside it, and Weston's face flushed as he read, "Won't you accept this with the good wishes of your late companions?"

It was evidently from Miss Stirling, for it was a woman's writing, and he did not think an Englishwoman would have said "Won't you," as she had done. He could recognize the delicacy with which she had refrained from offering him money, or even stipulating any definite sum in the order, and it was evident that she had taken some trouble to arrange the matter with the H. B. C. agent at Vancouver. The thing had been done in kindness, and yet it hurt him. He could have accepted it more readily from anybody else. On the other hand, he remembered that she had known him only as a track-grader, and that he was, as a matter of fact, nothing else. He could not send the order back without appearing ungracious or disposed to assert that he was of her own station. Then another thought struck him.

"I don't think they knew my name. They called me Clarence," he said. "Somebody must have thought it worth while to write Cassidy."

He had forgotten his companions, and when Grenfell looked at him inquiringly, he laughed.

"It's something I was thinking of," he said, handing the order across. Grenfell gazed at it with unqualified satisfaction.

"This straightens everything out," he said.

"I'm not quite sure it does," returned Weston, dryly. "In fact in some respects it rather complicates the thing. That, however, is a point that doesn't concern you."

His companion, who appeared to concur in this, glanced with evident regret at the six dollars which still lay beside him.

"If I'd known that the order was in the mail, the boys would have had to carry me every rod of the way back to camp," he said. "It's not the first time that I've been sorry I practiced economy."

Weston left him shortly afterward, and went back with the other man toward the shanty.

"The chances seem too steep for you?" suggested Weston.

"Well, I guess he did strike that gold; but I shouldn't be too sure of it. It's quite likely that he fancied the whole thing. You can't count on the notions of that kind of man."

He broke off for a moment, and appeared to consider.

"There's another point. The old tank has no nerves left, and he's no use on his legs. Guess, you'll have to carry him over the range."

Weston fancied that this was probable, and the track-grader, who turned away to speak to another man, left him in a thoughtful mood.

CHAPTER VIII

IN THE RANGES

A month had passed when Weston stood one morning outside the tent he scarcely expected that he or his comrade would sleep in again. It was pitched beside a diminutive strip of boggy natural prairie under the towering range, though the latter was then shrouded in sliding mist out of which the climbing firs raised here and there a ragged spire or somber branch. The smoke of the cooking-fire hung in heavy blue wreaths about the tent, and a thick rain beat into the faces of the men.

The few weeks they had spent in the wilderness had made a change in them. Grenfell had clearer eyes and skin, and was steadier on his legs, for he had slaked his thirst with river-water for some time now. Weston was a little leaner, and his face was grimmer than it had been, for the whimsical carelessness had faded out of it. Both of them were dressed largely in rags, and their stout boots were rent; and they were already very wet, though that was no great matter, as they were used to it. There are a good many rivers among those ranges, and no bridges. They were then glancing at the horse which was cropping the harsh grass of the swamp. It was of the Cayuse Indian breed, and not particularly valuable, but it could be sold for something if they succeeded in taking it back to the settlements. This, however, did not appear to Weston very probable.

"Short hobbles," suggested Grenfell. "There's grass enough to last awhile, and it's likely that we'll strike this way back. It's a long way to the settlements, and there'll be quite a load of provisions and things to pack."

They had made a cache of most of their provisions the previous night, after searching in vain for a route by which they could lead the horse over the range in front of them; but Weston shook his head.

"No," he said, "we may not come back this way after all, and a horse is pretty sure to get a hobble of any kind foul round something in the bush. I can't have the beast held up to starve."

"Well," said Grenfell, "I guess you understand what leaving it loose means?"

Weston did. He recognized that if they ever regained that valley they would have to push on for the settlements through a most difficult country, under a heavy load, and even then leave behind them many things which might have ministered to their comfort. Still, he was resolute.

"The beast could find its food somehow if we left it loose, and it's quite probable that it would work down along the back trail to the settlements when the grass round here gets scarce," he said. "In any case we'll give it a chance for its life."

Grenfell made a sign of acquiescence.

"Have it your way. If we ever come back to this cache again, and I'm played out, as I probably will be, you'll have the pleasure of packing down everything we want."

Weston did not answer, but there was a little satisfied smile in his eyes as he watched the horse wander away unhampered into the rain. After this they sat down to a very simple meal. Then they strapped their packs on their shoulders—a thick blanket each, a small bag of flour, some salt pork and green tea, and, while Grenfell carried the light ax, Weston slung a frying-pan, a kettle and a pannikin about him, as well as a rifle, for there are black-tail deer in that country, and they could not be sure that their provisions would last the journey through. The prospector soon discovers how much a man can do without, and it is a good deal more than men bred in the cities would suppose. The oddments rattled and banged about Weston's shoulders as he went up the steep slope through the thick timber; and by the time they had cleared the latter, Grenfell was visibly distressed, and both of them realized that their difficulties had commenced.

Any one unaccustomed to the country would probably have considered the devious march that they already had made arduous enough, but they had, at least for the most part, followed the valleys and crossed only a few low divides, and it was evident now that their way led close up to the eternal snow. There was a rock scarp in front of them, up part of which they went on their hands and knees. When they reached the summit of this, the slightly more level strip along which they floundered was strewn with shattered rock and gravel that had come down from the heights above with the thaw in the spring; and it was with difficulty that they made a mile an hour. The gold trail is usually long and arduous; but the prospector is content to have it so, for once it is made easier the poor man's day has gone. Then the men of the cities set up their hydraulic monitors, or drive their adits, and the free-lance who disdains to work for them rolls up his old blankets and pushes out once again into the waste.

They made supper at sunset among the last of the dwindling pines; and then lay awake shivering part of the night, for a nipping wind came down from the snow, and they were very wet and cold. It rained again the next day and most of the following one. Still, they spent the two days crawling along the farther side of the range, for when they had struggled through the snow in a rift between two peaks, a great wall of rock that fell almost sheer cut them off from the next valley. Somewhat to Weston's astonishment, Grenfell now showed little sign of flagging. He seemed intent and eager; and when they stopped, gasping, where the rock fell straight down beneath their feet to the thick timber that climbed from a thread-like river, he sat down and gazed steadily below him.

"They're hemlocks along that bend?" he asked, pointing to a ridge of somber green that rose above the water.

"Yes," said Weston, "I think they are."

Grenfell straightened himself suddenly.

"My sight's not as good as yours, but I seemed to know they must be. Can you make out any Douglas firs in the thicker timber?"

"Yes," said Weston, excitedly, "there's a spire or two higher than the rest. You recognize the place?"

His companion sat still with signs of tension in his face, and it was clear that he was racking his befogged brain. The few weeks of abstinence and healthful toil had made a change in him, but one cannot in that space of time get rid of the results of years of indulgence; and under stress of excitement the man became confused and fanciful.

"I'm not sure. I'm trying to think," he said, laying a lean, trembling hand on Weston's arm. "Did you never feel that there was something you ought to recollect about a spot which you couldn't have seen before?"

Weston was in no mood to discuss questions of that kind, though the curious sensation was not altogether unfamiliar to him.

"There's only one way you could have known there was hemlock yonder," he asserted.

Grenfell looked up at him with a dry smile.

"You have to remember that I have been up in the ranges several times. Parts of them are very much alike."

After that Weston sat very still for several minutes, though he found it exceedingly difficult. He had more than once during the last few weeks doubted that Grenfell had ever found the quartz-reef at all, for it seemed quite possible that he had, as the track-grader suggested, merely fancied that he had done so, and the man's manner had borne out that supposition. Cut off from the whisky, he had now and then fallen into fits of morbid moodiness, during which he seemed very far from sure about the gold. This had naturally occasioned Weston a good deal of anxiety. He had thrown up his occupation and sunk his last dollar in the venture, and the finding of the quartz-reef would, he commenced to realize, open up to him alluring possibilities. At length his companion spoke slowly.

"If the river runs across the valley to the opposite range a mile higher, this is the way I came down when I found the gold," he said.

Weston scrambled to his feet. Floundering in haste along the edge of the crag, he stopped some sixty yards farther on, with a little quiver running through him. From that point he could see that the river ran straight across to the opposite wall of rock. He flung up his arms with an exultant shout. Then they went on eagerly when Grenfell joined him.

"Yes," said the latter, when he had glanced below, "I must have seen it the time I struck the gold. Only then I came down the valley."

They pushed on. Toward sunset a thick rain once more came down, and filmy mists wreathed themselves about the hills and by and by filled up the valley, and the strip of mountainside along which the two lonely men plodded rose isolated from a sea of woolly vapor. They held on, however, until, when the dusk commenced to creep up the white peak above them, Weston stopped with a little start. There was a curious huddled object in a crevice of the rocks not far in front of him.

"Do you see that?" he asked. "What can it be?"

Grenfell gazed at the thing steadily, and then turned to his companion.

"I think it's Verneille," he said.

They came a little nearer, and saw that he was right, for presently Grenfell stooped and picked up a discolored watch. It had fallen away from the moldering rags, but it had a solid case, and, when at length he succeeded in opening it, he recognized the dial. He gazed at it with a softening face, and then slipped it into his pocket.

"He was a good comrade. A man with long patience, and I think he had a good deal to bear from me," he said.

In the meanwhile Weston stood still, with the rain on his face and his battered hat in his hand. Verneille lay in a cleft of the rocks, where it seemed he had crawled when he broke down on his last weary march, but the sun and the rain had worked their will, and there was very little left of him. Indeed, part of the bony structure had rolled clear of the shreds of tattered rags. Grenfell gazed at him fixedly, and neither of the men said anything for the next minute or two. The peak above them was fading in the growing night, and the stillness of the great desolation seemed intensified by the soft patter of the rain. Then Weston roused himself with an effort, for there was something to be done.

"We can't leave him lying there," he said. "There is a little soil among the stones. It's a pity we didn't bring the shovel."

The shovel was in the cache with one or two other prospector's tools, which, as the reef they desired to find was uncovered in one place, they had not thought it worth while to carry over that high ridge; so they set to work in silence with the rifle butt and their naked hands. Fortunately, the stones were large, and the soil beneath them soft, and in about twenty minutes they were ready for the rest of their task. It was one from which they shrank, but they accomplished it, and Grenfell straightened himself wearily as they laid the last stone on the little mound.

"It's all we can do, but I should feel considerably better if I could get a hard drink now," he said.

Then he made a little forceful gesture.

"After all, he's well out of it. That man was white all through."

It was Verneille's only epitaph, pronounced most incongruously with the same breath that expressed his comrade's longing for whisky, but perhaps it was sufficient, for when one is called a white man it implies a good deal in that country. Nobody, it seemed, knew where he came from, or whether there was any one who belonged to him, but he had done his work, and they had found him sitting high on the lonely range to point the way. That might have been of no great service if it were only treasure to which the gold trail led, but in the unclaimed lands the prospector scouts a little ahead of the march of civilization. After him come the axmen, the ploughmen and the artisans, and orchards and mills and oatfields creep on a little farther into the wilderness. Civilization has its incidental drawbacks, but, in the west, at least, its advance provides those who need them with new homes and food; and, when one comes to think of it, in other respects it is usually the dead men who have pushed on in advance who point the way.

A part only of the significance of that fact occurred to Grenfell when the two men had plodded slowly on and left the little pile of stones behind, and that was naturally the part applicable to his particular case.

"This makes the thing quite certain," he said. "We're on the trail."

It was not astonishing that Weston had deduced as much already.

"Have you any idea where you separated?" he inquired.

"No," said Grenfell, wrinkling his forehead as though thinking hard. "I've often tried to remember. As I told you, we started out from the lake with scarcely any provisions left, and we couldn't find a deer. I was played out and half-dazed, but for a time we pushed on together. Then one day I found myself in the thick timber alone. Verneille must have kept the range, and I was in the valley. I was very sick when I struck the prospector's camp, and when I came round I had only the haziest memory of the journey."

"If we can find a spot where the valley dies out into the range, it will probably be where you left him," said Weston. "It would give us a point to work from. In the meanwhile we want a place to camp."

They went down to the first of the timber, and, spreading their blankets in a cranny of the rocks, built a great fire soon after darkness fell. Weston, who made the fire, filled the blackened kettle with water from the creek, and Grenfell, who crouched beside the snapping branches, also left him to prepare the supper. They had been on their feet since sunrise, and it was evident that he was very weary. He recovered a little when he had eaten, but he leaned back against the wet rock with a furrowed face when Weston took out his pipe.

"Abstinence has its drawbacks," he said, shivering in the bitter wind which whirled the stinging smoke about them. "With a very small measure of whisky one could be warm and content." He glanced back into the darkness that hid the towering peaks. "Verneille's to be envied—he's well out of it."

"You said that before," said Weston, in whose veins life ran hot and strong.

"I did," his companion replied, with a little hollow laugh. "You'll find out some day that I was right. He was dead when he fell to pieces in the wind and weather."

"Of course!" said Weston with a trace of impatience, for Grenfell's half-maudlin observations occasionally jarred on him; but the latter still looked at him with a curious smile.

"Keep clear of drugs and whisky. It's good advice," he said. "You may go a long way before you die."

"I'd feel a little more sure of it if we could find the mine. It would give you a lift up, too."

Grenfell shook his head.

"It could never lift me back to where I was," he said. "Could it give me the steady nerves and the brain I used to have? There was a time when scarcely a big mine was started in the west before they sent their specimens to me. What could success offer me now besides a few more years of indulgence and an opportunity for drinking myself into my grave in comfort and with comparative decency?"

Weston supposed that this was the effect of weariness; but his comrade straightened himself a little, and his uncertain gaze grew steadier.

"There's one thing it can do," he went on. "It can show those who remember him as he was that Grenfell the assayer and mineralogist can still look round a mineral basin and tell just where the gold should be."

Weston was no geologist, but he had seen enough of it to recognize that prospecting is an art. Men certainly strike a vein or alluvial placer by the merest chance now and then, but the trained man works from indication to indication until, though he is sometimes mistaken, he feels reasonably sure as to what waits to be uncovered by the blasting charge or shovel. Grenfell's previous account of the discovery had, however, not made quite plain the fact that he had adopted the latter course.

"You told me you found the quartz by accident when you went to drink at a creek," he said. "Any green hand might have done the same."

Grenfell laughed.

"The point is that I knew there was gold in the valley. I told you we stayed there until the provisions had almost run out. I wanted material proof—and I was satisfied when I found that little strip of outcrop."

"A little strip! You said the lead ran right back to the hill and one could follow it with an adit."

"It does, although I haven't seen it. The adit would dip a little. The thing's quite certain."

Weston once more became sensible of the misgivings that not infrequently had troubled him. His comrade, he believed, really had been a famous mineralogist, but now he was a frail and broken man with a half-muddled brain who could not be trusted to keep the fire going beneath the pots while he cooked a meal. He was also a prey to maudlin fancies, and it seemed quite possible that the mine was no more than a creation of his disordered imagination. There were only two things that partly warranted his belief in it-a fragment of quartz, and the presence of the dead man on the lonely range, though Weston admitted that there was a certain probability of Grenfell's having deluded Verneille too. He had, however, pledged himself to look for the lead, and that, at least, he meant to do. The search, in the meanwhile, was sufficient to occupy him, as he was one who escaped a good many troubles by confining his attention to the task in hand.

"Well," he said, dismissing the matter from his mind, "I'll turn out at sun-up, and when we've had breakfast we'll go on again."

He lay down near the snapping fire and, drawing up the blanket to keep the rain from his face, was sound asleep in a few minutes. Grenfell, however, sat awake for a long time, shivering in the whirling smoke, and now and then glancing curiously at his companion.

CHAPTER IX

A FRUITLESS SEARCH

They had wandered far through the ranges, and camped beside several lonely lakes, none of which, however, proved to be the one for which they were searching, when Weston rose one morning from his lair among the dewy fern. He did it reluctantly, for during the past week he had carried Grenfell's load as well as his own, and it would have pleased him to lie still a little longer. His shoulders were aching, and the constant pressure of the pack-straps had galled them cruelly; but in one respect it would not have troubled him if his burden had been heavier, for their provisions were running out rapidly. There was a river close by, but he no longer felt the least inclination for a morning swim, or, indeed, for any occupation that was not obviously necessary. He had lived very sparingly of late, and had contrived that Grenfell got rather more than his share of the cut-down rations. It was clear to him that the older man's strength was rapidly failing.

He kicked the embers of the fire together, and, after laying on a few resinous billets split the night before, placed an inch or two of pork in the frying-pan, and then carefully shook out a double handful of flour from the almost-empty bag. This he beat up with water and poured into the hot pan when the pork was done. He watched it until it hardened a little on one side, when he flung it up into the air and caught it in the pan again. There is an art in making palatable flapjacks out of nothing but flour and water. When the meager breakfast was ready, he awakened Grenfell, who sat up grumbling.

"It's time we made a start. This is our last day," said Weston.

Grenfell, who did not answer, made his toilet by buttoning his jacket and stretching himself, after which he blinked at his companion with watery eyes.

"There are no marble basins or delicately perfumed soaps in the bush," he said.

Weston laughed.

"I don't remember having seen them at the muskeg camp. In the meanwhile, breakfast's ready. I'm sorry there isn't a little more of it."

His companion glanced at the frying-pan.

"A scrap of rancid pork, and a very small flapjack—burnt at that! To think that human intelligence and man's force of will should be powerless without a sufficiency of such pitiable things. It's humiliating."

Then, with a grimace of disgust, he stretched out his hand for the blackened pannikin.

"Green tea is a beverage that never appealed to me, and I feel abject this morning. Now, if I had a little Bourbon whisky I could laugh at despondency and weariness. That golden liquid releases the mind from the thraldom of the worn-out body."

"It depends on one's knees," said Weston, with a trace of dryness.

"Yours have a habit of giving out unexpectedly, and I shouldn't like to carry you up this valley. Anyway, breakfast's ready, and we have to find that lake to-day or give up the search."

They set about breakfast, and again it happened that Grenfell got rather more than his share. Then Weston, who carried also the heavy rifle, strapped the double burden on his shoulders, and they started on their march, walking wearily. The valley that they followed, like most of the others, was choked with heavy timber, and they pressed on slowly through the dim shadow of great balsams, hemlocks, and Douglas firs, among which there sprang up thickets of tall green fern that were just then dripping with the dew. The stiff fronds brushed the moisture through the rags they wore and wet them to the skin; but they were used to that. It was the fallen trees that troubled them most. These lay in stupendous ruin, with their giant branches stretching far on either side, and, where tangled thickets rendered a detour inadmissible, it now and then cost them half an hour's labor with the ax to hew a passage through. Then there were soft places choked with willows where little creeks wandered among the swamp-grass in which they sank to the knees; but they pushed on resolutely, with the perspiration dripping from them, until well on in the afternoon.

Once or twice Weston wondered why he had held on so long. It was some time since they had found Verneille lying high upon the desolate range, and this was still the only thing which seemed to bear out his comrade's story. The latter had only a few very hazy recollections to guide him, and during the last week he had not come upon anything in the shape, of a mountain spur or frothing creek that appeared to fit in with them. There was, however, a vein of tenacity in Weston, and he was quietly bent on going on to the end—that is, until there were no more provisions left than would carry them back to the cache, marching on considerably less than half rations.

They had made, perhaps, two leagues with infinite difficulty, when toward the middle of the afternoon they came upon a spur of the range that ran out into the valley. Weston decided that they could probably see some distance across the timber from the crest of it, so they climbed up painfully. They were gasping when they reached a ledge of rock a little below the summit, but that was not why they sat down. Both shrank from the first momentous glimpse into the head of the valley, for if there were no lake there they had thrown away their toil and must drag themselves back to the settlements defeated and broken men. It is hard to face defeat when one is young, and, perhaps, harder still when one is old and has nothing to fall back on. Grenfell expressed part of his thoughts when he turned to his companion.

"We shall decide the thing in a few more minutes," he said. "I suppose we couldn't risk going on a little farther to-morrow?"

Weston shook his head resolutely, though he felt the same temptation. It was in one sense curious that the older man should defer to him.

"No," said Weston, "we should have turned back several days ago. It will be a tough march to reach the cache now."

Grenfell made a little gesture.

"Well," he said, "we'll go up and see."

They went up, part of the way on their hands and knees, and then, though the slope was less steep, both of them hung back when they neared the crest of the divide. There was still a faint probability that their journey had not been futile, and they clung to it desperately. Grenfell went first, and, when he reached the crest, stood stone still with his back to Weston, who held his breath as he scrambled after him. Then Grenfell, turning a little toward him, suddenly flung out a pointing hand.

The head of the valley stretched away beneath them, but there was no gleam from a lonely lake in the midst of it. From hillside to hillside the close ranks of somber firs ran unbroken.

Weston's face grew hard and grim.

"That's the end," he said hoarsely. "There is nothing for it but to take the back trail."

Then the strength seemed to melt out of Grenfell, and he sat down limply.

"It was the belief that I should find that lake some day that has kept me on my feet the last eight years," he said. "Except for that I should have gone under long ago. Now, it's hardly likely that I shall ever get back here again."

He turned and blinked at Weston with half-closed eyes.

"You can't understand. You have the world before you," he said.

Weston fancied that he could understand in part, at least. His comrade was an old and frail and friendless man for whom nobody in that country was, as they say there, likely to have any use, and the fact that he probably had himself to blame for it did not make things easier. Weston forgot that he also was a man without an occupation, and his face grew sympathetic; but in a few minutes Grenfell seemed to pull himself together.

"Well," he said, "we'll take the back trail."

They followed it for a week, but the distance that they covered diminished day by day. Grenfell would insist on sitting down for half an hour or so at regular intervals, and when they faced a steep ascent Weston had to drag him. The man seemed to have fallen to pieces now that the purpose that had sustained him had failed, and his comrade, who carried a double burden and undertook all that was necessary each time they made camp, grew more and more anxious every day, for, though they did not eat enough to keep the strength in them, their provisions were almost exhausted. Nor could he find a deer; and it became a momentous question whether they could reach the cache before the last handful of flour was gone. Still, they held on along the back trail, with the burst boots galling their bleeding feet, worn-out, haggard, and ragged, until, one day on the slope of the range, they lost the trail, and when evening was drawing in they held a consultation.

There was a valley; a creek came frothing down not far from them; a narrow, steep-sided cleft rent through stupendous rocks; and the white ridge high above it seemed familiar. Weston gazed at the latter thoughtfully.

"We could get up that way, and there'll be good moonlight to-night," he said. "If that snow-ridge lies where I think it does, there's a ravine running down through the neck of the high spur; and once we strike the big dip it's a straight trail to the cache. If we started now we ought to get there to-morrow."

He broke off for a moment, and opened the almost-empty bag.

"In fact we have to."

Grenfell made a sign of acquiescence, and by and by they rose and forced a passage through the timber into the ravine. Then they went up and up, through the creek and beside it, crawling over fallen trees, and dragging themselves across slippery shelves of rock, until, though still very steep, the way grew a trifle easier. It was Grenfell's last effort, and Weston had no courage left to cheer him on. At times he stumbled beside him, and then went on and sat down gasping to wait until his comrade came up with him again. It was a week since they had made more than half a meal, and much longer since they had eaten a sufficient one. They were famishing, worn-out, and a trifle fanciful, while the light was dying fast and a great wall of mountains, beyond which the cache lay, still rose in front of them.

Dusk crept up from the valley and overtook them as they climbed, then passed ahead and blotted out the battalions of somber pines. The little breeze that had sighed among the latter died away, and the hoarse clamor of the creek intensified the deep silence that wrapped dusky hillside and lonely valley. Then a half-moon sailed out above the dim white peaks, and its pale radiance gleamed on frothing water and dripping stone, and showed the two men still climbing. They drew their breath heavily; the sweat of effort dripped from them; but they toiled upward, with tense faces and aching limbs. The cache could not be very far away, and they realized that if once they lay down they might never commence the march again.

By and by the creek seemed to vanish, and its roar died away, while after that they wandered, still ascending, apparently for hours among dim spires of trees, until the path once more dipped sharply beneath their feet. They had traversed a wider, shallower valley between the spur and the parent range. Weston was afterward quite sure of that, for it had a great shadowy wall of rock on one hand of it.

"We are coming down upon the cache. We have crossed the neck," he said.

They blundered downward, walking now with half-closed eyes, and sometimes for a few moments with them shut altogether. At times they fell over boulders and into thickets of rotting branches that lay around fallen trees, but, though their senses had almost deserted them, they were certainly going down. The pines grew taller and thicker; withered twigs and needles crackled beneath their feet; though in places they plunged downward amidst a rush of slipping gravel. Still, half-dazed as he was, Weston was puzzled. It seemed to him that the gully they were descending was longer than it should have been. It ought to have led them, by that time, out on a plateau from which the hillside fell to the hollow where they had made the cache. He did not, however, mention this to Grenfell.

By degrees the dim black trees grew hazier and less material. They appeared unsubstantial shadows of firs and pines, and he resented the fact that they barred his passage, when he blundered into one or two of them. There was a creek somewhere, but it was elusive, flashing here and there in the uncertain moonlight and vanishing again. Once or twice he thought he had left it behind, and was astonished when shortly afterward he stumbled into it to the knees. He had a distressful stitch in his side, which, though he had been conscious of it for several hours, was growing almost insupportable. Sometimes he called to Grenfell, who seldom answered him, just to break the oppressive silence. It seemed to enfold and crush him in spite of the clamor of the creek which indeed he scarcely heard. No man, he fancied, had crept through those solitudes before; but several times he felt almost sure that he saw shadowy figures flitting among the trees, and Grenfell declared that he heard the clank of cow-bells. Weston was not astonished, though he knew that no cattle had ever crossed that range.

At last in the gray dawn they came to a little opening where the ground was soft. It seemed familiar, and both of them stopped. They certainly had seen before something very much like the slope of rock that rose in front of them. Weston, blinking about him, discovered in the quaggy mould two foot-prints half filled with water. He called to Grenfell, who leaned on his shoulder while he stooped to see them more clearly. Then he discovered two more footprints a little farther away. They were fresh, and evidently had not been made by the man who left the others. Suddenly, he straightened himself with a harsh laugh.

"That is where we went up last night. We are back again," he said.

Grenfell gazed at him stupidly.

"But we went through the valley between the range and the spur," he insisted. "I remember it. We must have done so."

Weston's face showed drawn and grim in the creeping light.

"If you went over all the range by daylight you would never find that valley again. It will have vanished altogether, like the lake."

"But I camped beside the lake."

"Well," said Weston, "we floundered through the valley, and we have come back to where we started. That's a sure thing. What do you make of it?"

Grenfell admitted that it was beyond him.

"It doesn't count for much in any case. We can't make the cache now—and I'm going to sleep," he said.

Weston let his pack drop, and, unrolling their blankets, they stretched themselves out beneath a great black pine. They had made their last effort, and their strength was spent. There was, it seemed, no escape. In the meanwhile, mind and body craved for sleep.

CHAPTER X

THE HOTEL-KEEPER

The sun was high in the heavens when Weston awakened, ravenous, with an almost intolerable stitch in his side. He rose with a stagger, and then sat down again, while his face went awry, and took out his pipe. He had still a very little tobacco left, and he fancied that it might deaden the pangs of hunger. Then he glanced at Grenfell, who lay fast asleep close by, with his blanket falling away from him. The man's face was half buried among the withered needles which were thick in his unkempt hair, and he lay huddled together, grotesque and unsightly in ragged disarray. Weston vacantly noticed the puffiness of his cheeks, and the bagginess beneath his eyes. The stamp of indulgence was very plain upon him, and the younger man, who had led a simple, strenuous life, was sensible of a certain repulsion from him.

He realized also that were he alone it was just possible that, before his strength failed him altogether, he might reach the spot where they had cached their provisions, and for several minutes he grappled with the question whether he should make the attempt. Then he brushed aside the arguments that seemed to warrant it, and admitted that in all probability Grenfell would have succumbed before he could get back again. After all, this outcast who had led him into the wilderness on a fruitless search was his comrade, and they had agreed to share and share alike. That Grenfell had at the most only a few years of indulgence still in front of him did not affect the question. The specious reasons which seemed to prove that he would be warranted in deserting his comrade would not fit in with his simple code, which, avoiding all side issues, laid down very simply the things one could not do.

Rising stiffly, he laid the flour-bag, which he had not shaken absolutely empty, by Grenfell's side; and, taking from his pocket an indelible pencil that he happened to have with him, he moistened the point of it and scrawled a message across a piece of the almost-empty package in which they had carried their tea.

"Gone to look for a deer," it read, and he laid a stone on it where Grenfell could not fail to see it.

Then he took up the repeating rifle, and lurching down-hill plunged into the forest. Both the black-tail deer and the mule-deer are to be met with in that country, but, somewhat strange to say, they are, as a rule, more plentiful round the smaller settlements than in the wilderness, and they are always singularly difficult to see. The inexperienced sportsman cannot invariably discern one when it is pointed out to him, and the bush deer very seldom stand silhouetted against the sky. Their pale tinting blends with that of the fir trunks and the tall fern, and they seem to recognize the desirability of always having something near them that breaks their continuity of outline. Besides, to hunt in the thick bush needs the keenest powers of observation of both ear and eye, and an infinite patience, of which a worn-out, famishing white man is very rarely capable. When one steps on a dry twig, or sets a thicket crackling, it is necessary to lie still for minutes, or to make a long detour before again taking up the line of approach to a likely spot; and that morning Weston blundered noisily into many an obstacle. His eyes were unusually bright and fiercely keen, but his worn-out limbs would not quite obey him.

He lay still among the undergrowth about the rocky places where the deer come out to sun themselves clear of the dew-wet fern, and crawled into quaggy swamps where the little black bear feeds, but he could find no sign of life. When he strained his ears to listen there was only the sound of falling water or the clamor of a hidden creek. Sight was of almost as little service among those endless rows of towering trunks, between which the tall fern and underbrush sprang up. There was no distance, scarcely even an alternation of light and shadow. The vision was narrowed in and confused by the unchanging sameness of the great gray colonnade.

Still, Weston persisted in his search; though it was not patience but the savageness of desperation that animated him. He would not go back empty-handed, if he struggled on until he dropped.

It was late in the afternoon before his search was rewarded. He had reached a strip of slightly clearer ground when he heard a faint rustle, and he stiffened suddenly in strung-up attention. There was, he remembered, a great hemlock close behind him, but he recognized that any movement might betray his presence, and, standing very still, he slowly swept his eyes across the glade. A curious, hard glint crept into them when they rested on one spot where something that looked very much like a slender, forked branch rose above a thicket. Then a small patch of slightly different color from the thicket appeared close beneath, and, though he knew that this might send the deer off, he sank slowly down until he could sit on his drawn-back right foot. He could not be sure of the steadiness of his hands, and he wanted a support for the rifle. Though every nerve in him seemed to thrill, it was done deliberately, and he found that he could see almost as clearly from the lower level.

Then he waited, with the rifle in his left hand, and that elbow on his knee, until there was a faint crackling, and a slightly larger patch of fur emerged from the thicket. He held his breath as he stiffened his left fingers on the barrel and dropped his cheek on the butt. There would, he knew, be only one shot, a long one, and, while it was not particularly easy to get the sight on that little patch, it was considerably handier to keep it there. Besides, he was not sure that the rear slide was high enough, for the light was puzzling. It might very well throw him a foot out in the elevation.

He crouched, haggard, ragged, savage-eyed, steadying himself with a strenuous effort, while the little bead of foresight wavered. It moved upward and back again half an inch or so while his finger slowly contracted on the trigger. Then, as it swung across the middle of the patch, he added the last trace of pressure. He saw a train of sparks leap from the jerking muzzle, and felt the butt jar upon his shoulder. Still, as is almost invariably the case with a man whose whole force of will is concentrated on holding the little sight on a living mark, he heard no detonation. He recognized, however, the unmistakable thud of the bullet smashing through soft flesh, and that was what he listened for.

As he sprang to his feet, jerking another cartridge from the magazine, there was a sharp crackling amidst the thicket and a rustling of the fern. A blurred shape that moved with incredible swiftness sailed into the air, and vanished as he fired again. The smoke blew back into his eyes, and there was a low rustling that rapidly grew fainter. He ran to the thicket, and found what he had expected—a few red splashes among the leaves. Where the deer was hit he did not know, but he braced himself for an effort, for he fancied that he could follow the trail.

It proved a long and difficult one, but as he worked along it, smashing through thickets and crawling over fallen trees, the red sprinkle still showed among the leaves, and it did not seem possible that the deer could go very far. Still, by this time the light was growing dim, and he pressed on savagely with the perspiration dripping from him in an agony of suspense. Even his weariness was forgotten, though he reeled now and then.

At length, when he reached the head of a slope, there was a crackling amidst the underbrush, and once more a half-seen shape rose out of it. The rifle went to his shoulder, and, though he had scarcely expected the shot to be successful, the object in front of him collapsed amidst the fern. He could no longer see it, but, whipping out the big knife that he carried in his belt, he ran toward the spot where it had appeared. The ground seemed to be falling sharply, and he recognized that there was a declivity not far away.

The deer rose once more, and, though only a yard or two away, he could scarcely see it. His eyes seemed clouded, and he was gasping heavily. Whether he dropped the rifle with intent or stumbled and let it slip he never knew, but in another moment he had flung himself upon the deer with the long knife in his hand. Then his feet slipped, and he and the beast rolled down a slope together. The blade he gripped struck soil and stones, but at length he knew that it had gone in to the hilt in yielding flesh, and with a tense effort he buried it again. After that he staggered clear, half-dazed, but exultant, with a broad crimson stain on the rags he wore. The beast's limbs and body quivered once or twice, and then it lay very still.

Weston took out his pipe and lay down with his back against a tree, for all the power seemed to have gone out of him, and he did not seem able to think of anything. The pipe was empty before it dawned on him that his comrade was famishing, and there was still a task in hand. He set about it, and, though it was far from heavy, he had some difficulty in getting the dressed deer upon his shoulders. How he reached camp with it he never knew, but he fell down several times before he did so, and the soft darkness had crept up from the valley when he staggered into the flickering glow of a fire. His face was drawn and gray, and there was blood and soil on his tattered clothing. He dropped the deer, and collapsed beside the fire.

"Now," he said hoarsely, "it's up to you to do the rest."

Grenfell set about it in wolfish haste, hacking off great strips of flesh with patches of hide still attached to them; and it was only when he flung them half-raw out of the frying-pan that Weston roused himself. Fresh bush venison is not a delicacy even when properly cooked, and there are probably very few civilized men who would care to consume much of it. The muscular fiber resembles cordage; and strong green tea is no doubt not the most desirable beverage to accompany it; but Grenfell and Weston ate it in lumps and were asleep within five minutes after they lay down gorged to repletion beside the sinking fire. It is generally understood that a famishing person should be supplied with nourishment sparingly, but in the wilderness the man in that condition eats as much as he conveniently can, and usually sleeps for about twelve hours afterward. In any case, the sun was high the next day when Weston awoke, feeling, except for his muscular weariness, as fresh as he had ever felt in his life. He roused Grenfell with his foot.

"Get up," he said, "we have to consider what to do."

Grenfell blinked at him, with a grin.

"Consider!" he ejaculated. "I know. The first thing is to eat breakfast. Then we'll lie down again until it's time for supper."

They did as he suggested, for there was meat enough to last until they found the cache. This they managed to do two days later. Somewhat to Weston's astonishment they found, also, the horse still feeding on the strip of natural prairie; and, as the beast and the buried camp gear it could now carry back represented their whole worldly wealth, this was a source of gratification to both of them. The man without an occupation or a dollar in his pocket does not, as a rule, find life very easy.

They made the first settlement on the railroad safely; and Weston, hearing that a new sawmill had been started in a neighboring valley, set out the next morning in search of it, leaving Grenfell to dispose, of the camp gear and the horse. The manager of the sawmill was, however, marking trees in the bush, and, as Weston had to wait some time before he learned that no more hands were wanted, it was evening before he reached the little wooden hotel where he had left his comrade. It had a veranda in front of it, and he stopped when he reached the steps, for it was evident from the hoarse clamor and bursts of laughter which came out of the open windows that something quite unusual was going on. Then a man came down the steps chuckling, and Weston, who stopped him, inquired the cause of the commotion.

"Two or three of the boys we have no great use for are going out to-night to the copper vein the Dryhurst people are opening up," said the stranger. "Your partner has been setting up the drinks for them."

Weston was not pleased at this, but the other piece of information the man gave him was interesting.

"Are they taking on men?" he asked.

"Anybody who can shovel. Sent down to Vancouver for men a day or two ago."

"Then," said Weston, "why didn't this hotel-keeper tell me, instead of sending me across to the sawmill?"

His informant laughed.

"Jake," he said, "is most too mean to live. He strikes you a dollar for your breakfast and another for supper, though anybody else would give you a square meal for a quarter. Guess that may have something to do with it."

Weston nodded.

"It's very probable," he said. "They're evidently getting angry about something inside there. What's the trouble?"

"Guess it's your partner," said the other man, with a grin. "It seems Jake bought a horse from him; but you'd better go in and see. I decided to pull out when one of them got an ax. Struck me it would be kind of safer in my shanty."

He went down the stairway; and as Weston went up a raucous voice reached him.

"The money!" it said. "The money or the horse! You hear me! Hand out the blame money!"

Weston pushed open the door and stopped just inside it. The room was big, and, as usual, crudely furnished, with uncovered walls and floor, and a stove in the midst of it. A bar ran along part of one side, and a man in a white shirt was just then engaged in hastily removing the bottles from it. Another man, in blue shirt and duck trousers, stood beside the stove, and he held a big ax which he swung suggestively. It was evident that several of the others were runaway sailormen, who have, since the days of Caribou, usually been found in the forefront when there were perilous wagon bridges or dizzy railroad trestles to be built in the Mountain Province. There was, however, nothing English in their appearance.

"He wants his horse! Oh, bring it out!" sang the man with the ax.

There was a howl of approval from the cluster of men who sat on a rough fir table; but the man behind the bar raised an expostulating hand.

"Boys," he said, "you have got to be reasonable. I bought that horse. If the deadbeat who made the deal with me wants it back, all he has to do is to produce the money."

Then Grenfell, who leaned on the table, drew himself up, and made a gesture of protest. He was as ragged and unkempt as ever.

"I've been called a deadbeat, and I want it taken back," he said. "It's slander. I'm a celebrated mineralogist and assayer. Tell you how the deep leads run; analyze you anything. For example, we'll proceed to put this hotel-keeper in the crucible, and see what we get. It's thirty parts hoggish self-sufficiency, and ten parts ignorance. Forty more rank dishonesty, and ten of insatiable avarice. Ten more of go-back-when-you-get-up-and-face-him. Can't even bluff a drunken man. I've no use for him."

There was a burst of applause, but Weston fancied that the hotel-keeper's attitude was comprehensible in view of the fact that the drunken man had a big ax in his hand. Crossing the room, he seized Grenfell's shoulder.

"Sit down," he said sternly. "Have you sold that man my horse?"

"He has, sure," said one of the others. "Set us up the drinks afterward. We like him. He's a white man."

"How much?" Weston asked.

"Twenty dollars."

Then the man with the ax, who appeared to feel that he was being left out of it, swung the heavy blade.

"We want our horse!" he said. "Trot the blame thing out!"

One of the others thereupon raised a raucous voice and commenced a ditty of the deep sea which was quite unquotable. Weston silenced him with some difficulty and turned to the rest.

"Boys," he said, "has the man yonder spent twenty dollars on drinks to-day?"

They were quite sure that he had not. He had, they admitted, set up a round or two, but they were not the boys to impose upon a stranger, and in proof of this several of them asked the hotel-keeper what he had received from them. Then Weston turned to the latter.

"Now," he said, "we'll try to straighten this thing out, but I've no intention of being victimized. It's quite clear that the boys don't seem in a humor to permit that either."

"You've got us solid," one of them assured him. "All you have to do is to sail right ahead. Burn up the blame hotel. Sling him out of the window. Anything you like."

"Well," said Weston, addressing the hotel-keeper, "while I don't know what your tariff is, it's quite evident to me, after what the others have said, that my partner couldn't very well have spent more than five or six dollars. We'll call it eight to make more certain, and I'll pacify him if you'll hand me twelve."

"Twelve dollars," sang the axman, "or the horse! Bring them out!"

"It's worse than holding up a train," complained the hotel-keeper. "Still, I'll part with it for the pleasure of getting rid of you."

He did so; and when Weston, who pocketed the money, inquired when the next east-bound train left, one of the others recollected that it was in rather less than half an hour. Some of them got up with a little difficulty, and Grenfell looked at Weston deprecatingly.

"You mustn't hurry me," he observed, "my knees have given out again."

They set out in a body, two of them assisting Grenfell, who smiled at the men assembled in the unpaved street to witness their departure. There were eight of them altogether, including the man who still carried the ax, which, it transpired later, belonged to the hotel-keeper. The soft darkness fell, and the white mists crawled up the hillside as, laughing harshly, they plodded through the little wooden town. They were wanderers and vagabonds, but they were also men who had faced the stinging frost on the ranges and the blinding snow. They had held their lives lightly as they flung the tall wooden bridges over thundering caÃ±ons, or hewed room for the steel track out of their black recesses with toil incredible. Flood and frost, falling trees, and giant-powder that exploded prematurely, had as yet failed to crush the life out of them, and, after all, it is, perhaps, men of their kind who have set the deepest mark upon the wilderness.

CHAPTER XI

IN THE MOONLIGHT

It was, as far as outward appearances went, a somewhat disreputable company that had assembled in the little station when the whistle of the Atlantic train came ringing up the track, and Weston would have been just as much pleased if the agent had provided a little less illumination. Several big lamps had just been lighted, though, there was a bright moon in the sky, and Grenfell, who was dressed for the most part in thorn-rent rags, sat on a pile of express freight amidst a cluster of his new comrades discoursing maudlin philosophy. The other man, who still clung to the hotel-keeper's ax, was recounting with dramatic force how he had once killed a panther on Vancouver Island with a similar weapon, and, when he swung the heavy blade round his head, there was a momentary scattering of the crowd of loungers, who had, as usual, gathered to see the train come in.

"Yes, sir, I split that beast right up first time," he said. "I'm a chopper. You'd have seen the pieces fly if I'd sailed into that hotel bar a little while ago."

Weston fancied that this was probable, for the man was dexterous, and there was applause when he set the bright blade whirling, and passed the haft from hand to hand. Most of the loungers could do a good deal with the ax themselves, and the lean, muscular demonstrator made rather a striking figure as he stood poised in statuesque symmetry under the lamplight with the bright steel flashing about him.

In the meantime, Weston leaned on the pile of cases and packages somewhat moodily. After paying for his ticket and Grenfell's to the station nearest the copper-mine he had about four dollars in his pocket, and he did not know what he should do if no employment were offered him when he got there. He had no doubt that he could provide for himself somehow, but Grenfell was becoming a responsibility. He felt that he could not cast the man adrift, and it seemed scarcely likely that anybody would be anxious to hire him. Still, Grenfell was his comrade, and they had borne a good deal together during their journey in the wilderness. That counted for something. There was also another matter that somewhat troubled Weston. He was not unduly careful about his personal appearance, but he had once been accustomed to the smoother side of life in England, and his clothing was now almost dropping off him. The storekeeper, whom he had interviewed that morning, had resolutely declined to part with a single garment except for money down; and, after an attempt to make at least part of the damage good with needle and thread, Weston found the effort useless and abandoned it.

Then two great locomotives came snorting out of the shadows that wrapped the climbing track, and he grasped the shoulder of his comrade, who did not appear disposed to get up. There was a little pointed badinage between those who were starting for the mine and the loungers, and in the midst of it the big cars rolled into the station. Weston started, and his face grew darkly flushed, for two white-clad figures leaned out over the guard-rail of one of the platforms, and for a moment he looked into Ida Stirling's eyes. There was no doubt that she had recognized him, and he remembered the state of his attire, and became uneasily conscious that Grenfell, who clung to his shoulder, was swaying on his feet. He knew that a man is usually judged by his company, and it was clear that nothing that she might have noticed was likely to prepossess Miss Stirling in his favor. The car, however, swept past him, and with some difficulty he got Grenfell into another farther along the train. Then, while his companions exchanged more compliments with the loungers, the big locomotives snorted and the dusty cars lurched on again.

They naturally traveled Colonist, and when Grenfell stretched himself out on a maple board it became evident that he had forgotten his blanket. Weston threw his own over him, and the old man blinked at his young companion with watery eyes.

"You stood by me. You're white," he said; and added with a little patronizing gesture, "I'm not going to desert you."

After that he apparently went to sleep, and Weston, who felt no inclination for the company of the others, went out and sat on one of the car platforms, glad for the time being to be rid of him.

There was a moon in the sky, and the silvery light streamed down on towering hillside and battalions of flitting pines. The great train swept on, clattering and clanking, and dust and fragments of ballast whirled about the lonely man. Still, the rush of the cool night wind was exhilarating, and his mind was busy, though his thoughts were not altogether pleasant. The few weeks he had spent in Ida Stirling's company had reawakened ambition in him; and that was why he had set out with Grenfell in search of the mine. Though he had not reproached his comrade, and had, indeed, only half believed in the quartz lead, the failure to find it had been a blow. There was in that country, as he knew, no great prospect of advancement for a man without a dollar; and though he realized that it had not troubled him greatly until a little while ago, he now shrank from the thought of remaining all his life a wandering railroad or ranching hand. He had also a great desire for Miss Stirling's good opinion, although he scarcely expected her to think of him, except as one who had proved a capable guide.

He knew that he could never quite forget the night they had made the hazardous descent together, and her courage and quiet composure under stress and strain had had their effect on him. The imperious anger with which she had turned on him when he forced her away from Miss Kinnaird had also stirred him curiously. He could still, when he chose, see her standing in the moonlight with a flash in her eyes, questioning his authority to prevent her from snaring her companion's peril. She was, he felt, one who would stand by her friends. He was young, and the fact that she had seen him supporting the lurching Grenfell at the station troubled him.

He had smoked his pipe out twice when he heard the vestibule door click, and he started when he looked up, for Ida Stirling stood beside him. Her light dress fluttered about her, and she stood with one hand resting on the rail. There was no doubt that she recognized him, and when he rose and took off his shapeless hat she looked at him steadily for a moment or two. He wondered whether he were right in his surmises as to why she did this; and, though his forehead grew a trifle hot, he decided that he could not blame her. Appearances had certainly been against him.

"I am going to join Mrs. Kinnaird. She is in the car behind the sleeper, and that is farther along;" she said.

Weston moved so that she might step across to the adjoining car; but she did not seem to notice this, and leaned on the rail close beside him.

"The train is very hot with the lamps lighted," she said.

Weston understood this to mean that she was disposed to stay where she was and talk to him awhile, which suggested that she was to some extent reassured about his condition.

"Yes," he returned, "it is. In fact, I felt it myself. The smell of the pines is a good deal pleasanter."

There was nothing original in the observation, and, though the roar of wheels made it a trifle difficult to hear, he was careful as to how he modulated his voice. Perhaps he was superfluously careful, for he saw a smile creep into Ida's eyes.

"You seem amused," he said, and, for they stood in the moonlight, the blood showed in his face.

"Why did you speak—like that?" his companion asked.

Weston looked at her gravely, and then made a little deprecatory gesture.

"It was very stupid, I dare say. Still, you see, you were out on the platform when the train came into the station."

There was something that puzzled him in Ida's expression.

"Well," she admitted, "I really had my fancies for a moment or two, though I blamed myself afterward. I should have known better."

It was rather a big admission, but she said nothing else, and it was Weston who broke the silence.

"I have to thank you for the prospecting outfit," he said.

The girl flashed a quick glance at him.

"It was partly Major Kinnaird's idea. You made use of it?"

Weston smiled.

"Grenfell and I did. That explains the state of my attire. You see, we have just come down from the bush."

Then, somewhat to her astonishment, he took out his watch, and pointed to the guard. It was of plain plaited leather, and had, she fancied, probably cost about twenty-five cents.

"I don't know whether this could be considered part of a prospecting outfit, but they had a bunch of them in the store," he said. "I felt I should like some trifle that I could wear to remember our trip in the ranges. I thought you wouldn't mind."

A momentary trace of embarrassment became visible in his companion's face. The man was a bush packer, and she had seen him in somewhat disreputable company, but she was ready to admit that he had aroused her curiosity. She could be honest, and she would have admitted it as readily had she never heard from Arabella Kinnaird of his connection with the old hall in England. She looked at him, with a little laugh.

"Oh," she said, "everybody likes to be remembered, and I'm no exception in that respect. There is really no reason why you shouldn't have bought the guard."

Weston, who felt that he had gone quite far enough, merely bent his head in a manner that, as she naturally noticed, the average bush packer would not have adopted. It was she who first spoke again.

"You were successful in your search?" she asked.

Weston laughed.

"Do I look like a man who has just found a goldmine?"

"Well," said the girl, with a twinkle in her eyes, "I came across two successful prospectors in Vancouver not long ago, and there was really nothing to suggest it in their appearance. So you didn't find the mine? Won't you tell me about your journey?"

"It's quite a story. Won't the others miss you?"

Ida turned toward him suddenly.

"Don't you mean more than that?"

"Well," admitted Weston slowly, "I think I did. Perhaps it was a liberty."

"It was," said Ida, and, though she laughed, there was a little flash in her eyes. "Major Kinnaird and his wife are English, and it is quite possible that they would not be pleased to hear that I had come out to talk with you on the platform of a car. Still, in Canada we have our own notions as to what is fitting, and that I consider it perfectly natural that I should do so is quite sufficient for me. I do not defer to anybody's opinion as to how I should treat my friends. Now, unless you have any more convincing excuses, you may tell me about the search for the mine."

Weston did so, and, for the mere pleasure of having her near him, he made rather a long tale of it. She stood where the vestibule of the car in front partly sheltered her from the rush of the cold night wind, swaying lightly to the jolting of the platform as the great train sped on among the pines. Still, her light dress which gleamed white in the moonlight fluttered about her and now and then flowed against her companion. The simple tale of stress and effort borne and made was one that went well with the snorting of the big locomotives toiling up the climbing track and the rhythmic roar of wheels flung back by primeval forest or towering wall of rock. The girl had imagination enough to realize it.

"Oh," she said, "one likes to hear of such things."

Then she noticed the gauntness of his bronzed face and how lean he was.

"Still," she added, "it has left its mark on you. You failed to find the mine—it wasn't your fault—what are you going to do now?"

"Some day," said Weston, "I shall go back and search again."

He had made the resolution only that moment, but she saw the sudden glint in his eyes.

"It was in the meanwhile I meant," she said.

"I am going a little way up the track with my partner to a copper-mine."

"Ah," said the girl reflectively, "I suppose you feel that you must take that man?"

"What else could I do with him?"

Ida's eyes softened curiously. After the scene at the station she fancied that she understood the responsibility that he had taken upon himself.

"And suppose they don't want you at the mine?"

"In that case we should go on again somewhere else."

"Of course your partner, who can earn nothing, will go with you."

Then she spoke almost sharply.

"How much money have you in your joint possession?"

"Three or four dollars," said Weston.

Again she turned toward him with a flush on her face.

"Now," she said, "I think you can disregard trivial conventionalities. Won't you let me lend you some?"

"No," replied Weston quietly. "I shall not forget that you offered it, but I'm afraid it's quite out of the question."

She knew that he meant it, and, though she greatly desired to lessen his difficulties, she was, for no reason that was very apparent at the moment, pleased with his answer. Then she changed the subject.

"Can your partner cook?" she asked.

"No," answered Weston, smiling, "he certainly can't. I and a good many more of the boys know that from experience."

"Ah," said Ida reflectively, "that destroys another chance. Well, I am glad that I have seen you, but I think I must join Mrs. Kinnaird now."

She held out the hand she had laid on the rail. It happened that as she did it the train swung around a curve. The car slanted sharply, and she swayed with the effort to keep her balance. In another moment Weston's arm was around her waist. Then there was empty blackness beneath them as the cars sped out upon a slender trestle, and the roar of a torrent came up from below through the clash and clatter and clamor of the wheels. There was probably no risk at all, for there were rails on either side of them, but the girl, who had almost lost her footing, was glad of the man's steadying hand, and did not draw herself away until the big loco-motives were speeding smoothly on beneath the shadowy pines again. Then she drew back a pace or two.

"Thank you," she said quietly.

Weston took off his battered hat, and, stepping across the platform, opened the door of the adjoining car. When she had passed through it, he sat down and took out his pipe, with a curious little thrill running through him and his nerves tingling.

Ida, also, felt her face grow a trifle hot, and, though she was as composed as usual when she joined Mrs. Kinnaird, her thoughts were busy for some time afterward. The man, she admitted, had done no more than was warranted, but there was no disguising the fact that his supporting grasp had had a disconcerting effect on her. Then she dismissed the thoughts of that, and remembered with compassion how lean and worn he looked. There was also something that stirred her sympathy in the idea of his saddling himself with the care of a helpless comrade who had no real claim on him, though that was, she decided, after all, the kind of thing one would expect from him. Then, recognizing that this was admitting a good deal, she endeavored to interest herself in what Mrs. Kinnaird was saying.

It was late at night when the train stopped again, and Weston did not know that when he and his companions alighted at a little desolate station among the ranges, the blind of one window in the big sleeper was drawn aside. In a few moments the train went on, but Ida Stirling did not sleep for some time afterward. She had had a momentary glimpse of a ragged man standing with the lamplight on his lean face and a hand laid reassuringly on the shoulder of his half-dazed companion.

CHAPTER XII

THE COPPER-MINE

The red sun had risen above the dusky firs on a shoulder of the range when Weston and his companions reached the copper-mine. It consisted of an opening in the forest which clothed the hillside with the black mouth of an adit in the midst of it, and a few big mounds of debris, beside which stood a rude log shanty. The men who had just come out of the latter gazed at the strangers with undemonstrative curiosity, and when, saying nothing, they, trooped away to work, the new arrivals sat down to wait until the mining captain should make his appearance. In the meanwhile one of them amused himself by throwing stones at a smaller log building with a galvanized roof which stood among the firs. He looked at the others for applause when he succeeded in hitting it.

"Let up," said a comrade. "The boss lives in there."

The man flung another stone, a larger one, which rang upon the iron roof.

"Well," he said, "I guess that ought to fetch him."

It evidently did so, for the door of the shanty opened, and a man attired in shirt and trousers came out. He was a big, lean man, somewhat hard of face, and he favored the assembly with a glance of quiet scrutiny, for he was, as it happened, acquainted with the habits of the free companions.

"Getting impatient, boys?" he asked, and his voice, which was curiously steady, had in it a certain unmistakable ring. It suggested that he was one accustomed to command. "Well, what do you want?"

"A job," said one of Weston's companions.

The man looked at him with no great favor.

"Quite sure it isn't money? You can't have one without the other here."

Then Grenfell rose and waved his hand.

"The explanation, I may observe, is unnecessary. In this country you don't get money anywhere without first doing a good deal for it. Unfortunately, it sometimes happens that you don't get it then."

"How long is it since you did anything worth counting?" asked the captain.

One of Grenfell's companions pulled him down before he had a chance to reply.

"Now you sit right down before you spoil things," he said. "You can't put up a bluff on that kind of man. You don't know enough."

The miner glanced at them again, with a little grim smile.

"Well," he said, "you may stay there until I've started the boys in the adit. Then I will come back and talk to you."

He moved away, and one of those he left relieved his feelings by hurling another stone which crashed upon the iron roof of the shanty.

"That's a hustler—a speeder-up," he said. "You can't monkey with him."

They waited for about an hour before the man came back, and, sitting down on a fir stump, called them up one by one. Weston was reassured to see that each was despatched in turn to the log building where he presumed the tools were kept; but he and Grenfell were left to the last, and he was somewhat anxious when he walked toward the stump. The man who sat there glanced at his attire.

"Been up against it lately?" he inquired.

Weston admitted that this was the case; and the other smiled dryly.

"Can you chop and shovel?" he asked.

Weston said that he could; and the miner appeared to consider.

"Well," he said, "I'll put you on at——," mentioning terms which Weston fancied were as favorable as he was likely to get. "Still, you'll have to hustle, and we charge usual tariff for board. You may start in."

Weston glanced toward Grenfell, who was still sitting where he had left him.

"You see," he said, "there's my partner. We go together."

"I can't help that. You have my offer. I can't have that kind of man on our pay-roll."

Weston stood silent for a moment or two. He had arrived at the wooden hotel too late for supper the previous evening, and, as a rule, neither blandishments nor money will secure the stranger a meal at an establishment of that kind after the appointed hour. As the result, he had eaten nothing since noon, when the sawmill hands had offered him a share of their dinner; and, having assisted Grenfell along an infamous trail most of the night, he was jaded and very hungry. Now work and food were offered him, and there was not a settlement within several leagues of the spot. He had, however, already decided that he could not cast his comrade adrift.

"Well," he said, "perhaps there's a way out of it. If you'll let him camp with the boys, I'll be responsible for his board."

"Any relation of yours?"

"No," replied Weston simply, "he's just my partner."

The other man looked at him curiously, and then made what Weston fancied was an unusual concession.

"Well," he said, "we'll fix it. You may go along and drill with the boys yonder in the open cut."

Weston did as he was bidden, and spent the rest of the morning alternately holding the jarring drill and swinging a hammer. It was strenuous work which demanded close attention, for the hammer was heavy, and it is far from easy to hit a drill neatly on the head, while the man who fails to do so runs the risk of smashing the fingers of the comrade who holds it. It was not much more pleasant when he gripped the drill in turn, for, though the other man stood on a plank inserted in a crevice, Weston had to kneel on a slippery slope of rock and twist the drill each time the hammer descended. The concussion jarred his stiffened hands and arms. The distressful stitch also was coming back into his side, and once or twice his companion cast an expostulating glance at him.

"You want to speed up," he said. "Guess that boss of ours knows just how much the most is that a man can drill, and he has to do it or get out."

Though it cost him an effort, Weston contrived to keep his companion going until the dinner hour arrived, and he found the work a little easier when he had eaten. Still, he was perplexed about Grenfell, who did not understand what arrangement he had arrived at with the mine captain. Grenfell spent the afternoon mending his own and some of Weston's clothes, which badly needed it, and the evening meal was over when the latter sat with the others outside the shanty wearing a jacket which his companion had sewed. Grenfell, however, was not with them just then. By and by the man who had desired to wreck the hotel bar turned to Weston.

"What are you going to do with your partner?" he asked.

"I don't quite know," said Weston. "In the meanwhile he'll stay here."

"How's he going to raise his board?"

"That's not quite your business," said Weston quietly.

The man laughed good-humoredly.

"Well," he replied, "in one way I guess it isn't. Still, if you pay your partner's board you're going to have mighty little money left. Mended that jacket, didn't he? Won't you take it off?"

Weston wondered a little at this request, but he complied; and the man passed the garment around to' the others, who gravely inspected the sewed-up rents and the patches inserted in it.

"Quite neat, isn't it?" he commented.

They admitted that it was; and the chopper, handing the garment back to Weston, smiled as though satisfied.

"I've an idea, boys," he announced.

His companions appeared dubious, but he nodded quietly.

"I've got one sure," he said. "Now, in a general way, if there's a store handy, I've no use for mending clothes; but you have to wash them now and then, and it never struck me as quite comfortable to put them on with half the stitching rubbed out of them. Well, washing's a thing I'm not fond of either, and it's kind of curious that when one man starts in at it everybody wants the coal-oil can."

They murmured languid concurrence, for, as he said, clothes must be washed and mended now and then, and the man who has just finished a long day's arduous toil seldom feels any great inclination for the task. It usually happens, however, that when one sets about it his companions do the same, and there is sometimes trouble as to who has the prior claim on the big kerosene can in which the garments are generally boiled.

"Well," said the chopper, "I've a proposition to make. There are quite a few of us, and a levy of thirty or forty cents a week's not going to hurt anybody while there's a man round here who can't chop or shovel. Guess he has to live, and it's a blame hard country, boys, to that kind of man. Now, it's my notion we make the fellow mender and washer to the camp."

There was a murmur of applause, for, when they own any money, which, however, is not frequently the case, the free companions are usually open-handed men, and Weston was not astonished at their readiness to do what they could for his companion. He had been in that land long enough to learn that it is the hard-handed drillers and axmen from whom the wanderer and even the outcast beyond the pale is most likely to receive a kindness. Their wide generosity is exceeded only by the light-hearted valor with which they plunge into some tremendous struggle with flood and rock and snow.

"Make it half a dollar anyway," said one of them.

Then Weston stood up, with a little flush on his face and a curious look in his eyes.

"Thank you, boys, but I have to move an objection," he said. "This is a thing that concerns me."

"Sit down," commanded one of them sharply. "It's a cold business proposition."

They silenced his objections, and sent for Grenfell, who appeared disconcerted for a moment when he heard what they had to say. Then he laughed somewhat harshly.

"Well," he said, "I'll be glad to do it, and I don't mind admitting that the offer is a relief to me."

They strolled away by and by, and Grenfell made a little grimace as he looked at Weston.

"When I can tell how the ore should pan out by a glance at the dump, and plot just how the vein should run, it's disconcerting to find that the only way I can earn a living is by washing and mending," he said. "In fact," and he spread out his hands, "the thing's humiliating."

To a certain extent Weston sympathized with him. The man, it seemed, had been a famous assayer, and now the one capability which was of any use to him was that of neatly mending holes in worn-out garments. He undertook the task cheerfully, however, and things went smoothly for a week or two. Then a stranger, who appeared to be a man of authority, arrived at the camp. He was a young man, who looked opinionative, and when he first appeared was dressed in city clothes. Soon after his arrival he strolled around the workings with the man whom Weston hitherto had regarded as the manager. When he spoke sharply to one or two of the men, the driller who worked with Weston snorted expressively.

"Colvin puts the work through, but that's the top boss," he said. "You can see it all over him. Learned all about mining back east in the cities, and couldn't sink a hole for a stick of giant-powder to save his life. Been down at Vancouver fixing up with the directors what they're going to tell the stockholders. Still, I guess he's not going to run this company's stock up very much."

"How's that?" Weston asked.

The man lowered his voice confidentially.

"Well," he said, "there's a good deal in mining that you can't learn from books, and a little you can't learn at all. It has to be given you when you're born. Colvin's a hustler, but that's 'bout all he is, and I've a kind of notion they aren't going to bottom on the richest of this vein. Anyway, it's not my call. They wouldn't listen to me."

Weston's gesture might have expressed anything. He naturally had been favored with hints of this kind while he followed other somewhat similar occupations, for it is not an uncommon thing for the men who toil with the drill and shovel to feel more or less convinced that those set over them are not going about the work in the right way. He had also more than once seen this belief proved warranted. His companion's suggestions, however, were borne out when he sat smoking with Grenfell in the bush after supper.

"I've been in the adit this afternoon," observed the latter. "Colvin sent me along to where they are putting in the heavy timbering." He laughed softly. "Well, they're throwing away most of their money."

"You're sure?" inquired Weston.

"Am I sure!" expostulated his comrade. "I need only point out that I ought to be."

"Then," said Weston, reflectively, "unless they ask your opinion, which isn't very probable, I'd say nothing about it. Some people don't take kindly to being told they're wrong. The thing doesn't affect you, anyway."

He was a little astonished at the change in his companion, for a sparkle crept into Grenfell's watery eyes, and his voice grew sharper.

"You haven't the miner's or the engineer's instinct; it's the same as the artist's," he said. "He can see the unapproachable, beautiful simplicity of perfection, and bad work hurts him. I don't know that it's a crime to throw away money, but it is to waste intelligence and effort that could accomplish a good deal properly directed. Why was man given the power to understand the structure of this material world? I may be a worn-out whisky wreck, but I could tell them how to strike the copper."

"Still," said Weston, dryly, "I'd very much rather you didn't. I don't think that it would be wise."

His companion left him shortly afterward, and it was some days later when the subject was reopened. Then Grenfell came to him with a rueful face.

"I've had an interview with the manager," he explained.

"Well," said Weston, sharply, "what did he say?"

Grenfell shrugged his shoulder.

"Told me to get out of camp right away."

Just then Colvin approached them, and his manner was for once slightly deprecatory.

"It doesn't pay to know more than the boss," he said; and then he looked at Weston. "He has to get out. What are you going to do?"

He had Weston's answer immediately.

"Ask you for my time."

"Well," said Colvin, with a gesture of expostulation, "I guess you know your own business. Still, I'm quite willing to keep you."

Weston thanked him, and then went with him to his shanty where he was handed a few bills, and in another hour he and Grenfell had once more strapped their packs upon their shoulders. He did not know where he was going, or what he would do, but he struck into the trail to the railroad, and it was dusk when they reached a little wooden settlement. He went into the post-office to make a few inquiries before he decided whether he should stay there that night, and the woman who kept it, recognizing him as a man from the mine, handed him a letter. When he opened it he saw, somewhat to his astonishment, that it was from Stirling. It was very terse, but it informed him that Miss Stirling and her friends purposed camping among the islands of one of the eastern lakes, which was then a rather favorite means of relaxation with the inhabitants of Toronto and Montreal. Stirling desired him to accompany the party, on terms which appeared very satisfactory, and added that if he were acquainted with another man likely to make an efficient camp attendant he could bring him along.

Weston started a little when he reached the last suggestion, for he fancied that it was Miss Stirling who had made it. He leaned on the counter for several minutes, thinking hard; and then, though he was not sure that he acted wisely, he started for the station to despatch a telegram, as Stirling had directed. The next morning the agent handed him tickets for himself and Grenfell, and they set out on the Atlantic train.

CHAPTER XIII

STIRLING LETS THINGS SLIDE

It was early evening when Weston swung himself down from the platform of the Colonist car in a little roadside station shut in by the pine bush of Ontario. There was a wooden hotel beside the track, and one or two stores; but that was all, and the fact that nobody except the station-agent had appeared to watch the train come in testified to the industry, or, more probably, the loneliness of the district. While Weston stood looking about him a man came out of the office, and he was somewhat astonished to find himself face to face with his employer.

The smart straw hat and light summer suit did not become the contractor. He was full-fleshed and red of face, and the artistically cut garments striped in soft colors conveyed a suggestion of ease and leisure which seemed very much out of place on him. One could not imagine this man lounging on a sunlit beach, or discoursing airily on a cool veranda.

"Got here," he said abruptly, and then swung around and looked at Grenfell. "This is the other man? Well, he can stay and bring along the baggage. There's most a freight-car full. They'll give him a wagon and team at the hotel."

He indicated a great pile of trunks and cases with a wave of his hand, and, seeing Weston's astonishment, added with a twinkle in his eyes:

"My daughter and her friends are camping. They have to have these things."

Weston understood his employer's smile. This, he recognized, was a man who could be content with essential things, and in all probability had at one time esteemed himself fortunate when he succeeded in obtaining them.

"Hadn't I better help him load them up?" he asked.

"No," said Stirling, with a curtness at which Weston could not take offense. "He can put in the evening that way if it's necessary. It will supple him, and I guess he needs it. I have a rig ready. You're coming along with me."

Weston took his place in the light, four-wheeled vehicle, and found it difficult to keep it, for the trail was villainous, and Stirling drove rapidly. Their way led between shadowy colonnades of towering firs, and the fragile, two-seated frame bounced and lurched into and out of deep ruts, and over the split trees that had been laid flat-side downward in the quaggy places—like a field gun going into action was the best comparison Weston could think of. The horses, however, kept their feet, and the wheels held fast. Once, when a jolt nearly pitched him from his seat, Stirling laughed.

"After the city it's a relief to let them out," he said. "I did this kind of thing for a living once. The mine was way back in the bush, leagues from anywhere, and I hired out as special store and despatch carrier. There was red-hot trouble unless I got through on time when the mail came in."

He drove the team furiously at an unguarded log bridge which was barely wide enough to let the wheels pass.

"It's quite a way to the lake yet, and we want to make the camp before it's dark," he explained. "Know anything about sailing a boat?"

Weston said that he did, and Stirling nodded.

"That's good," he observed somewhat dryly, "so does the major man."

Weston ventured to smile at this, and once more his employer's eyes twinkled.

"Some of you people from the old country are quite hard to amuse; though I'm open to admit that we have a few of the same kind on this side," he said. "My daughter seemed to fancy they wouldn't find a lake camp quite right without a boat, so I sent along and bought one at Toronto. Had her put on a flat car, and hired half the teams in the district to haul her to the lake. Now, I guess there are men in this country who, if they wanted a boat, would just take an ax and whipsaw and build one out of the woods."

Weston laughed. He was commencing to understand the man better, for he had met other men of Stirling's description in Canada. As a matter of fact, they are rather common in the Dominion, men who have had very little bestowed on them beyond the inestimable faculty of getting what they want at the cost of grim self-denial and tireless labor. Still, as it was in Stirling's case, some of them retain a whimsical toleration for those of weaker fiber.

"It's a bush camp?" Weston asked.

Stirling smiled good-humoredly.

"They call it that," he said. "It cost me quite a few dollars. You'll see when you get there."

Weston was somewhat relieved when they safely accomplished the first stage of the journey, and, turning the team over to a man by the waterside, paddled off to a big, half-decked boat beautifully built and fitted in Toronto. Stirling, who admitted that he knew nothing about such matters, sat down aft and lighted a cigar, while Weston proceeded to get the tall gall mainsail and big single headsail up. He was conscious that his companion was watching him closely, and when he let go the moorings and seated himself at the tiller the latter pointed up the lake.

"About a league yet—round that long point," he said.

A moderately fresh breeze came down across the pines, and when Weston, getting in the sheet, headed her close up to it, the boat, slanting sharply, leaped forward through the smooth water. He sat a little farther to windward, and the slant of deck decreased slightly when Stirling did the same.

"You can't head there straight?" the latter asked.

"No," said Weston, "not with the wind as it is. She'll lie no higher."

"Well," observed Stirling, "she's going, anyway. That pleases me. It helps one to get rid of the city. We'll have a talk, in the meanwhile. I sent for you before. Why didn't you come?"

It was somewhat difficult to answer, and Weston wrinkled his forehead, stiffening his grasp on the tiller.

"I was fortunate enough to be of some little service to Miss Stirling's friends on the range, and I fancied that because of it you meant to offer me promotion of some kind," he said.

"Well?" queried Stirling, with his eyes fixed on his companion's face.

Weston hesitated. He could not very well tell this man that a vein of probably misguided pride rendered him unwilling to accept a favor from Ida Stirling's father.

"I don't think there was any obligation, sir," he said.

"That," remarked Stirling dryly, "is a kind of feeling that may trip you up some day. Still, you came this time."

"I did," said Weston. "You see, the case was rather different. You offered to hire me to do a thing I'm accustomed to. It's my occupation."

His companion made a little sign of comprehension, though there was a faintly whimsical smile in his eyes.

"Now, you're wondering why I brought you back east all this way?"

Weston admitted it, and the contractor fixed his eyes on him.

"Well," he said, "it seems that there's fishing and sailing to be done, and I'm not quite sure about that major man. Guess he's always had people to wait on him, and that doesn't tend to smartness in any one. When my daughter and her friends go out on the lake, or up the river, you'll go along with them."

This was, perhaps, a little hard on Major Kinnaird, but Weston to some extent sympathized with his employer's point of view. The contractor was not a sportsman as the term is generally understood, but he was a man who could strip a gun, make or mend harness, or break a horse. When he had gone shooting in his younger days it was usually to get something to eat, and, as a rule, he obtained it, though he rent his clothes or got wet to the waist in the process. He could not sail a boat, but if he had been able to do so he would also in all probability have been capable of building one. Stirling was a man who had never depended very much on others, and could, if occasion arose, dispense with their services. He recognized something of the same resourcefulness in Weston, and, because of it, took kindly to him.

In the meanwhile the breeze had freshened, and the boat, slanting more sharply, commenced to throw the spray all over her as she left the shelter of the woods behind. She met the short, splashing head sea with streaming bow, and the sliding froth crept farther and farther up her lee deck as she smashed through it. Then as the water found its way over the coaming and poured down into her, Stirling glanced at his companion.

"Got all the sail she wants?" he asked. "Is she fit to stand much more of it?"

"She should be safe with another plank in, but I was thinking of taking some of the canvas off her now," said Weston.

Stirling hitched his twelve stone of flesh farther up to windward.

"Then," he said, "until she puts that plank in you can let her go."

A wisp of spray struck him in the face, but Weston, who saw the smile in his eyes, was curiously satisfied. It suggested, in the first place, an ample confidence in him, which was naturally gratifying, and in the second, that Stirling in spite of his years could take a keen pleasure in that particular form of the conflict between the great material forces and man's nerve and skill. It is a conflict that goes on everywhere in the newer lands.

For another half-hour Weston kept the staggering over-canvased craft on her feet by a quick thrust of the tiller or a slackening of the sheet, and his companion appeared oblivious of the fact that he was getting wetter and wetter. She was fast, and she went through the little curling ridges with an exhilarating rush, while the foam swirled higher up her depressed deck, and the water flung up by her streaming bows beat in between her shrouds in showers. Then, when half the deck dipped under, Weston thrust down his helm, and the craft, rising upright, lay with her big mainsail thrashing furiously above her.

For ten minutes Weston was very busy with it, and, when he had hoisted it again with a strip along the foot of it rolled up, he crouched forward in the spray struggling with the big single headsail, which was a much more difficult matter. Once or twice he went in bodily when the hove-down bowsprit put which he crawled, dipped under, but he succeeded in tying up the foot of that sail too, and scrambled aft again breathless and gasping. He noticed that his employer, who did not seem to mind it, was almost as wet as he was.

"I'm sorry, but you told me I could let her go," he apologized.

Stirling smiled somewhat dryly.

"I'm not blaming you; but you don't quite finish. Wondering why I did it, aren't you?"

Weston did not admit it, but perhaps his face betrayed him, for his companion nodded.

"Well," he said, "you told me that you could sail a boat, and I wanted to make sure of it. Seems to me anybody could hold the tiller when she's going easy in smooth water. Know how I used to choose when I wanted a chopper, in the days when I worked along with the boys? Well, I gave the man an ax, set him up in front of the biggest tree I could find, and made him chop."

There could be no doubt about the efficiency of that simple test, and Weston recognized that it was very much in keeping with his employer's character, though he fancied that it was one which, if rigorously applied everywhere, would leave a good many men without an occupation. He only laughed, however; and nothing more was said until the boat reached in shoreward on another tack. It carried her round the long point, and a deep, sheltered bay with dark pine forest creeping close down to the strip of white shingle which fringed the water's edge opened up. Then, as the trees slid past one another, a little clearing in the midst of them grew rapidly wider, and Weston was somewhat astonished to see a very pretty wooden house grow into shape. He glanced at Stirling.

"Yes," said the latter, with a suggestion of grim amusement, "that's the camp."

Once more Weston understood him, and, as their eyes met, man and master smiled. Both of them knew there were hosts of strenuous, hard-handed men growing wheat and raising cattle in that country who would have looked on that camp as a veritable mansion. They were, however, men who had virgin soil to break or stupendous forests to grapple with, tasks of which many would reap the benefit, and they very seldom troubled much about their personal comfort.

After a while, Weston, lowering the headsail, dropped the anchor over close to the beach, and Major Kinnaird paddled a canoe off gingerly. He was, as usual, immaculately neat, and Weston noticed the contrast between him and Stirling, whose garments had apparently grown smaller with the wetting. The latter pitched his valise into the canoe without waiting for Weston to see to it, and then stood up endeavoring to squeeze some of the water from his jacket.

"It's the only one I've got," he said to Kinnaird. "Anyway, I guess the thing will dry, and I've had a sail that has made me feel young again."

Then they went ashore, and Weston, who was very wet, was left shivering in the wind to straighten up the gear, until a bush rancher, who had been engaged to wait on the party until he arrived, paddled off for him. The rancher had prepared a satisfactory supper; and some time after it was over, Stirling and Mrs. Kinnaird sat together on the veranda. There was, at the time, nobody in the house. The breeze had fallen lighter, though a long ripple still lapped noisily upon the beach, and a half-moon had just sailed up above the clustering pines. Their ragged tops rose against the sky black as ebony, but the pale radiance they cut off from the beach stretched in a track of faint silvery brightness far athwart the lake.

Mrs. Kinnaird, however, was not watching the ripple flash beneath the moon, for her eyes were fixed on two dusky figures that moved through the shadow toward the water's edge. By and by there was a rattle of shingle, and presently the black shape of a canoe slid down into the moonlight. It rose and dipped with the languid ripple, and the two figures in it were silhouetted against the silvery gleam. One was a man in a wide hat who knelt and dipped the flashing paddle astern, and the other a girl. The craft crossed the strip of radiance and vanished round the point, after which Mrs. Kinnaird flashed a keen glance at her companion. He sat still, and his face, on which the moonlight fell, was almost expressionless, but Mrs. Kinnaird fancied he had noticed as much as she had, and that he had possibly grasped its significance. In case he had not done the latter, she felt it her duty to make the matter clear to him.

"I suppose that is Ida in the canoe," she said.

"It seems quite likely," replied her companion. "It couldn't have been your daughter, because she went along the beach not long ago with the major, and I don't think there's another young lady in the vicinity."

"Then the other must be—the packer."

The pause and the slight change of inflection as she said "the packer" had not quite the effect she had intended. Stirling himself had once labored with his hands, and, what was more, afterward had a good deal to bear on that account. He was not particularly vindictive, but he remembered it.

"Yes, it's Weston," he said, and his companion felt herself corrected; but she was, at least where Major Kinnaird was not concerned, in her quiet way a persistent woman. Besides, Miss Stirling, who was going with her to England, would some day come into considerable possessions, and she had a son who found it singularly difficult to live on the allowance his father made him.

"Is it altogether advisable that she should go out with him?" she asked.

Stirling smiled somewhat dryly, for there was a vein of combativeness in him, and she had stirred it.

"You mean, is it safe? Well, I guess she's quite as safe as she would be with me or the major."

"Major Kinnaird was a flag officer of a rather famous yacht club," said the lady, who, while she fancied that her companion meant to avoid the issue, could not let this pass. She was, however, mistaken in one respect, for Stirling usually was much more ready to plunge into a controversy than to back out of it.

"Well," he said reflectively, "the other man has earned his living handling sail and people, which is quite a different thing."

Then he leaned toward her, with a twinkle in his eyes.

"Madam," he added, "wouldn't you better tell me exactly what you meant?"

Mrs. Kinnaird had a certain courage, and she was endeavoring to do her duty as she understood it.

"That packer," she said, "is rather a good-looking man, and girls of Ida's age are sometimes a trifle—impressionable."

Then, somewhat to her astonishment, Stirling quietly agreed with her.

"Yes," he said, "that's so. Seems to me it was intended that they should be. It's part of the scheme."

He made a little gesture.

"We'll let that point slide. Anything strike you as being wrong with Weston?"

"No," said the somewhat startled lady, "the man is of course reliable, well-conducted, and attentive; but, after all, when one says that——"

"When you said reliable you hit it. It's a word that means a good deal; but couldn't you say a little more than well-conducted? From something your daughter learned by chance, his relatives are people of position in the old country. That counts for a little, though perhaps it shouldn't."

Once more Mrs. Kinnaird's astonishment was very evident.

"It shouldn't?"

"That's just what I meant. If a man is clean of character, and has grit and snap in him, I don't know that one could reasonably look for anything further. I can't see how the fact that his grandfather was this or that is going to affect him. The man we're talking of has grit. I offered him promotion, and he wouldn't take it."

"Ah," said his companion, "didn't that strike you as significant?"

Stirling looked thoughtful.

"Well," he admitted slowly, "as a matter of fact, it didn't; but it does now."

He sat silent for almost a minute, with wrinkled forehead, while Mrs. Kinnaird watched him covertly. Then, feeling the silence embarrassing, she made another effort.

"Supposing that my fancies concerning what might perhaps come about are justified?" she suggested.

Stirling faced the question.

"Well," he said, "whether they're justified or not is a thing we don't know yet; but I want to say this. I have never had reason to worry over my daughter, and it seems to me a sure thing that she's not going to give me cause for it now. When she chooses her husband, she'll choose the right one, and she'll have her father's money; it won't matter very much whether he's rich or not. All I ask is that he should be straight and clean of mind, and nervy, and I guess Ida will see to that. When she tells me that she is satisfied, I'll just try to make the most of him."

He broke off for a moment, and laughed softly.

"I guess it wouldn't matter if I didn't. My girl's like her mother, and she's like—me. When she comes across the right man she'll hold fast by him with everything against her, if it's necessary, as her mother did with me."

He rose and leaned against a pillar, with a curious look in his face.

"The struggle that her mother and I made has left its mark on me. The friends we left in the rut behind us looked for my failure, and it seemed then that all the men with money had leagued themselves together to stop me from going on. Somehow I beat them, one by one—big engineers, financiers, financiers' syndicates, corporations—working late and working early, sinking every dollar made in another venture, and living any way. There were no amenities in that fight until those we had against us found that it was wiser to keep clear of me."

Then, with a little forceful gesture, he took off his hat.

"What I am, in part, at least, my girl's mother made me. She's asleep at last, and because of what she bore it's up to me to make things smoother for her daughter. Madam," he added, turning to his companion with a smile, "I have to thank you for doing what you must have figured was your duty; but in the meanwhile we'll—let things slide."

He turned away and left her before she could answer, astonished but a little touched by what she had heard. Still, the gentler impression vanished, and when she informed Major Kinnaird of what had been said she was once more somewhat angry with Stirling.

"It is really useless to reason with him," she said. "The man has wholly preposterous views."

CHAPTER XIV

IDA ASSERTS HER AUTHORITY

It was a hot afternoon, and Ida, who was tired of fishing, sat carefully in the middle of a fragile birch canoe. Her rod lay unjointed beside her, and two or three big trout gleamed in the bottom of the craft, while Weston, who knelt astern, leisurely dipped the single-bladed paddle. Dusky pines hung over the river, wrapping it in grateful shadow, through which the water swirled crystal clear, and the canoe moved slowly downstream across the slack of an eddy. Farther out, the stream frothed furiously among great boulders and then leaped in a wild white rush down a rapid, though here and there a narrow strip of green water appeared in the midst of the latter. The deep roar it made broke soothingly through the drowsy heat, and Ida listened languidly while she watched the pines slide past.

"I wonder what has become of the major," she said at length, with a little laugh. "It is too hot for fine casting, and he probably has had enough of it. After all, it really doesn't matter that the fish won't rise."

She saw Weston's smile, which made it evident that he was equally content to drift quietly through the cool shadow with the sound of frothing water in his ears. Then she wondered whether that was his only cause for satisfaction, and recognized that, if this were not the case, she had given him a lead. He did not, however, seem very eager to make the most of it.

"We might get another fish in the broken water," he suggested. "Would you like to try?"

"No," said Ida, "I wouldn't."

She was a trifle displeased with him. The man, she felt, might at least have ventured to agree with her, and there was, after all, no reason why he should insist on reminding her, in one way or another, that he was merely her canoe attendant, when she was willing to overlook that fact. She had once or twice, when it was evident that he did not know that she was watching him, seen something creep into his eyes when he glanced in her direction. He was, however, for the most part, almost unduly cautious in his conversation, and she now and then wondered whether his reticence cost him anything.

"It's a pity it isn't always summer afternoon," she said.

Weston looked at her rather curiously, though for the next few moments his lips remained set. There was a good deal he could have said in that connection, but he suppressed it, as he had done more than once already when similarly tempted. He felt that if he once allowed his sentiments audible expression they might run away with him.

"Oh, yes," he said, "I suppose it is."

Ida wondered whether he was quite insensible to temptation, or absurdly diffident, for she had now given him two openings, and he had answered with only the tritest of remarks. She knew he was not stupid, but there were times when, for no apparent reason, he seemed suddenly to retire into his shell. She did not know that on these occasions he had laid a somewhat stern restraint upon himself.

"This land is not quite as grand as British Columbia, but I think I almost like it better," she said. "Still, we spent a very pleasant time in the ranges."

"Those ranges could hardly be beaten," said Weston.

He paddled a little more strenuously after this, and Ida abandoned the attempt to extract any expression of opinion from him. She had made sufficient advances, and she would go no further.

"Well," she said, "I don't care to fish any longer. Can't we shoot that rapid?"

Weston's answer was given without hesitation. It requires nerve and judgment to shoot a frothing rapid. Just then, however, the task promised to be a relief to him. His companion was very alluring, and very gracious now and then, and that afternoon he found it remarkably difficult to remember that she was the daughter of his employer, and that there were a good many barriers between her and himself.

"Yes," he said, "I think it would be safe enough if you'll sit quite still."

Three or four strokes of the paddle drove the canoe out into the stream, and after that, all he had to do was to hold her straight. This was, however, not particularly easy, for the mad rush of water deflected by the boulders swung her here and there, and the channel was studded with foam-lapped masses of stone. Gazing forward, intent and strung-up, he checked her now and then with a feathering backstroke of the paddle, while the boulders flashed up toward her out of the spray, and the pines ashore reeled by. The foam stood high about the hollowed, upswept bow, and at times boiled a handbreadth above the depressed waist, but, while the canoe swept on like a toboggan, none came in. There was more than a spice of risk in it, and Ida, who knew what the result would be if her companion's nerve momentarily deserted him, now and then glanced over her shoulder. When she did so, he smiled reassuringly, leaning forward with wet hands clenched hard on the flashing paddle. She felt that he was to be relied on.

Then she abandoned herself to the exhilaration of the furious descent, watching boulder and eddy stream by, while the spray that whirled about her brought the crimson to her face. At length the pace grew a little slacker, and Weston drove the canoe into an eddy where a short rapid divided them from the smooth green strip of water that poured over what could almost be called a fall. Then she turned toward him with glowing face.

"That was splendid!" she exclaimed. "Can't we go right on down the fall?"

Weston ran the canoe in upon the shingle before he answered her.

"No," he said, though it cost him an effort not to do as she wished, "I'm sorry I can't take you down."

Ida glanced at the slide of silky green water that leaped out over a shelf of rock and fell through a haze of spray into a whirling pool. It did not look altogether attractive, and now that she could see it more clearly she rather shrank from it; but she was accustomed to having exactly what she wished, and her companion had not shown himself quite as ready to meet her views that day as she would have liked. An impulse that she did not altogether understand impelled her to persist.

"The Indians go down now and then," she said.

"Yes," admitted Weston, "I believe they do."

"Then why can't you?"

Weston appeared a trifle embarrassed.

"It wouldn't be quite safe."

"You mean to you?"

The man's face flushed a little. He had done a good deal of river work, and none of his companions had accused him of lack of nerve, but, though he had an excellent reason for knowing that the thing was possible, he had no intention of shooting the fall.

"Well," he said, "if you like to look at it in that way."

Ida rose and stepped ashore without taking his proffered hand. Then she leaned on a boulder while Weston sat still in the canoe, and for a moment or two they looked at each other. The situation was a somewhat novel one to the girl, for, in spite of the fact that she desired it, the packer evidently did not mean to go. This alone was sufficient to vex her, but there was another cause, which she subconsciously recognized, that made her resentment deeper. It was that this particular man should prove so unwilling to do her bidding.

"It is quite a long way to the lake, and the trail is very rough," she said.

"It is," admitted Weston, who was glad to find a point on which he could agree with her. "In fact it's a particularly wretched trail. Still, you have managed it several times, and we have generally left the canoe here."

"This time," said Ida, "we will take it down to the lake. I may want it to-morrow. You will have a difficult portage unless you go down the fall."

Weston recognized that this was correct enough, for the river was shut in by low crags for the next half-mile at least, and he remembered the trouble he had had dragging the canoe when he brought it up. He had also had Grenfell with him then.

"Well," he said, "if you would rather not walk back, it must be managed."

"I told you I wanted the canoe on the lake tomorrow," said the girl.

Weston was quite aware that there was another canoe which would serve any reasonable purpose already on the beach, but he merely made a little sign of comprehension and waited for her to go. Somewhat to his annoyance, however, she stood still, and he proceeded to drag out the canoe. The craft was not particularly heavy, but it was long, and he had trouble when he endeavored to get it upon his back. He had more than once carried the Siwash river-canoes over a portage in this fashion, but there is a trick in it, and the birch craft was larger and of a different shape. He felt that he could have managed it had there been nobody to watch him, but to do it while the girl noticed every movement with a kind of sardonic amusement was quite a different matter. He was very hot when, after a struggle of several minutes, he got the craft upon his shoulders; and then, after staggering a few paces, he rammed the bow of it into a tree. The shock was too much for him, and he went down head-foremost, with the canoe upon him, and it felt quite heavy enough then. As the man who attempts the feat has his hands spread out above him, that fall is, as a rule, a very awkward one. It was a moment or two before he crawled out from under the craft, gasping, red in face, and somewhat out of temper, and he was not consoled by his companion's laugh.

"I am sorry you fell down, but you looked absurdly like a tortoise," she observed.

Weston glanced at the canoe disgustedly.

"Miss Stirling," he said, "I can't carry this thing while you stand there watching me. Do you mind walking on into the bush?"

Ida was not in a very complaisant mood, and she glanced at him coldly.

"If my presence annoys you, I can, of course, go on," she said.

She felt that it was a little paltry when she walked on into the bush, but her action had been dictated at least as much by curiosity as by petulance. She fancied that she had set the man a task that was almost beyond his strength, and, knowing that she could release him from it at any time, she was anxious to see what he would do. She walked on some distance, and then sat down to wait until he came up with her, and when half an hour had slipped by and he failed to appear, she strolled toward the edge of the wall of rock.

The river swept furiously down a long declivity just there, and the strip of deeper water flown which one could run a canoe was on the opposite shore. It would, she fancied, be almost impossible to reach it from the foot of the rock on which she stood. Then, to her astonishment, she saw Weston letting the canoe drive down before him close beneath the rock. There was a short rope made fast to it, and he alternately floundered almost waist-deep through the pools behind the craft and dragged it over some thinly-covered ledge. He was very wet, and looked savage, for his face was set, while by the way he moved she fancied for the first time that he had hurt himself in his fall. She could not understand how he had got the canoe down to the river; and for that matter Weston, who had attempted it in a fit of anger, was never very sure. Then she became conscious of a certain compunction. The thing, she felt, had gone quite far enough, and when he drew level with her she called to him.

"You needn't take any more trouble. I can go on by the trail, after all," she said.

Weston looked up.

"There's no reason why you should do that," he replied. "I can't leave the canoe here, anyway, and I can take you in a little lower down."

He went on without waiting for an answer, and though the trail was very rough she had no difficulty in keeping abreast of him along the bank. Indeed, she felt that when he reached the spot where she could join him, he would have gone quite far enough, in view of the progress he was making. Once or twice he floundered furiously as the stream swept his feet from under him, and there were times when it seemed to require all his strength to prevent the canoe from being rolled over in the white rush of water that poured across some slippery ledge; but he slowly plodded on, and, though she did not know why, she was glad that he did so. It was, she was conscious, not altogether because he was executing her command.

At length she joined him where the river flowed deep and smooth beneath the pines again; and, when she had taken her place and he dipped the paddle, she turned to him.

"How did you get the canoe down to the water? The rock is very steep."

"I'm not quite sure," answered Weston. "I think I let it slide. Anyway, I shoved it over the edge. It went down too quickly for me to remember exactly what it did. I'm afraid there are a few rather big scratches on it."

"But how did you get down?"

The man smiled dryly.

"I believe I slid with it."

It occurred to Ida, who was commencing to feel a little ashamed of having exerted her authority in such a manner, that she could afford to be generous.

"I'm sorry I put you to so much trouble," she said. "But why didn't you tell me it would be difficult?"

Weston ceased paddling a moment, and looked at her steadily.

"It's my place to do what I'm told. Besides, you said that you didn't want to go back by the trail."

A slight flush crept into Ida's face.

"Wouldn't it have been better if you had done as I wanted, and shot the fall?"

"No," said Weston resolutely, "it wouldn't have been safe."

There was silence for a minute or two, and then Ida spoke again.

"I must admit that I knew the portage would be a little difficult when you were by yourself, but I didn't think it would give you quite as much trouble as it has," she said. "Still, I think you should have told me. After all"—and she seemed to have some difficulty in finding the right words— "we have never asked you to do anything unreasonable."

Weston understood that what she meant was that she, at least, had not treated him as a mere camp-packer, and, as she was quick to notice, the blood crept into his face. Her manner, which was not conciliatory, had, also, an unsteadying effect on him.

"Well," he said, with a little laugh, "there are naturally two or three of my duties which I don't find particularly agreeable, but that's a very common thing, and you wouldn't expect me to point it out. They're all in the bargain—and the others make up for them."

She noticed his swift change of expression, and did not urge him to explain what he meant.

"Anyway, what I have to do is a good deal nicer than handling heavy rails," he added, with a rather grim smile.

Ida fancied that this was a clumsy attempt to qualify his previous statement, and she said nothing further until they reached the camp. Mrs. Kinnaird kept her occupied for the next hour or two; and that evening when she was sitting on the veranda she heard Grenfell speaking to his comrade not far away.

"Why did you bring that canoe down?" he asked.

"Miss Stirling wanted it," said Weston.

"What did she want with it, anyway?"

It was evident from Weston's voice that he was not anxious to pursue that subject.

"I don't know," he said. "It paddles easier than the other one."

"Well," said Grenfell, "you and I are going to have trouble taking the blame thing up the river again. It's quite different from coming down. I suppose you shot the fall?"

"I didn't."

Grenfell's tone suggested astonishment.

"You hauled the canoe over the portage! What made you do that, when you have twice come down the fall?"

Ida started at this, and leaned forward eagerly to catch Weston's answer.

"I fancied there might be a little risk in it, and I had Miss Stirling with me."

Ida felt her face grow warm as she remembered that she had twitted him with having less nerve than the Indians; but Grenfell apparently was not yet satisfied.

"You could have sent the girl on, and then have shot the fall," he said. "It would have saved you quite a lot of trouble."

"Oh, yes," agreed Weston, who appeared to resent his curiosity. "Still, I didn't."

Grenfell moved away, and Ida recognized now that, in spite of a good deal of provocation, Weston had acted with laudable delicacy. It was clear that his obduracy in the matter of taking her down the fall had been due to a regard for her safety. He had also saddled himself with a laborious task to prevent this fact from becoming apparent. She fancied that, had she been in his place, she could have arranged the thing more neatly; but, after all, that did not detract from the delicacy of his purpose, and she sat very still, with a rather curious expression in her face, until Grenfell came to announce that supper was ready.

CHAPTER XV

THE ROCK POOL

Ida was quietly gracious to Weston during the week that followed his opposition to her wishes at the portage. This was not so much because she knew she had been wrong in insisting on his taking her down the fall, for, after all, that matter was a trifling one, but it was more because she was pleased by the part that he had played. The man, it seemed, had preferred to face her anger rather than to allow her to run any personal risk, and afterward had undertaken a very laborious task to prevent her from discovering why he had borne it. This was as far as she would go, though she was aware that it left something to be explained.

In any case, there was a subtle change in her manner toward Weston. She had never attempted to patronize him, but now she placed him almost on the footing of an intimate acquaintance. It was done tactfully and naturally, but Mrs. Kinnaird noticed it, and took alarm. Why she should do so was not very clear, for Stirling certainly had not encouraged her to put herself to any trouble on his daughter's account, but perhaps it was because Ida was going to England, and she had a well-favored son. It is also possible that, being a lady of conventional ideas, she acted instinctively and could not help herself. That a young woman of extensive possessions should encourage a camp-packer was, from her point of view, unthinkable.

For this reason, perhaps, it was not astonishing that there was for some little time a quiet battle between the two. When Ida desired to go fishing, Mrs. Kinnaird suggested something else, or contrived that the packer should be busy. Failing this, she patiently bore discomforts from which she usually shrank, and put her companions to a good deal of trouble by favoring them with her company. The major naturally did not notice what was going on, and she did not enlighten him; nor did Weston, for that matter; while Arabella stood aside and looked on with quiet amusement. It is probable that had Ida stooped to diplomacy, she would have been beaten, but, as it was, her uncompromising imperiousness stood her in good stead.

In any case, she went up the river alone with Weston on several occasions, in spite of Mrs. Kinnaird, and one morning the two sat together among the boulders beside a pool not far above the fall. There had been heavy rain, and the stream, which had risen, swirled in an angry eddy along the rock that rose close in front of them from that side of the pool. A great drift-log, peeled white, with only stumps of branches left, had jammed its thinner top on a half-submerged ledge, and the great butt, which was water borne, every now and then smote against the rock. The pines along the river were still wet, and the wilderness was steeped in ambrosial odors. Ida sat with thoughtful eyes regarding the endless rows of trunks, through which here and there a ray of dazzling sunlight struck; but her whole attention was not occupied with that great colonnade.

"I think you were right when you said that the bush gets hold of one," she said. "I sometimes feel that I don't want to go back to the cities at all."

Weston smiled, though there was something curious in his manner. It seemed to suggest that he was trying to face an unpleasant fact.

"Well," he said, "I told you that would probably be the case. In one way it's unfortunate, because I suppose you will have to go. You belong to civilization, and it will certainly claim you."

"And don't you?"

Weston made a little whimsical gesture.

"In the meanwhile, I don't quite know where I belong. It's perplexing."

Ida noticed the "in the meanwhile." It had, she fancied, a certain significance, and hinted that by and by he expected to be more sure of his station.

"You don't wish to go back?" she asked.

"No," said Weston decisively. "Anyway, not to the packed boarding-house and the flour-mill. Even in winter, when these rivers are frozen hard and the pines stand white and motionless under the Arctic frost, this is a good deal nicer."

"You're getting away from the point," said Ida, laughing. "I meant to England."

Weston leaned forward a little, looking at her with a curious expression in his eyes.

"For three or four months in the year England is the most beautiful country in the world," he said. "We haven't your great pines and foaming rivers, but, even in the land from which I come in the rugged north, every valley is a garden. It's all so smooth and green and well cared for. One could fancy that somebody loved every inch of it—once you get outside the towns. I said the dales were gardens—in summer they're more like Paradise."

It was evident that the exile's longing for the old land was awake within him, and Ida nodded sympathetically.

"Won't you go on?" she begged.

"Ah!" said Weston. "If I could make you see them—the wonderful green of the larch woods, the bronze of the opening oaks, and the smooth velvet pastures between the little river and the gleaming limestone at the foot of the towering fell! All is trimmed and clipped and cared for, down to the level hedgerows and the sod on the roadside banks, and every here and there white hamlets, with little old-world churches, nestle among the trees. You see, it has grown ripe and mellow, while your settlements are crude and new."

The girl sat silent a brief space. She had read of the old country, and seen pictures of it, and it seemed to her that his term, a garden, described parts, at least, of it rather efficiently.

Then, though he had already assured her that he meant to stay in the bush, she wondered whether he never longed to gather a flower of that trim garden. In fact, it suddenly became a question of some moment to her.

"You will go back to it some day?"

"No," said Weston, with a little wry smile; "I don't think so. After all, why should I?"

Ida was sensible of a certain satisfaction, but she desired to make more sure.

"There must be somebody you would wish to see, or somebody who would care to see you?"

"Ah," said Weston, "the failures are soon forgotten over yonder. Perhaps it's fortunate that it happens so."

A shadow crept into his face.

"No," he added, "unless it is as a successful man, it is scarcely likely that I shall go back again."

Ida glanced at him covertly, with thoughtful eyes. Though his attire was neater than it had been when she had seen him on other occasions, he still wore the bush packer's usual dress. There was, however, a subtle grace in his manner, and, though he was by no means a brilliant conversationalist, there was something in his voice and the half-whimsical tricks of fancy which now and then characterized him that made a wide distinction between him and the general hired hand. Once more it seemed to her that when he had called the old country a garden it was a somewhat apt description, for this man had evidently been subjected to careful training and pruning in his youth. He was, she felt, one who had grown up under a watchful eye.

"Well," she said, with a little laugh, "perhaps you are wise. One could almost fancy that the old land is overcrowded, and even on the richest soil one needs light and air."

Weston's smile showed that he could understand her train of thought.

"I certainly think that some of us are hardier for transplanting," he replied. "It is easier to make a vigorous growth out in the open, in the wind and the sun. Besides, over yonder every one is pinched and trimmed back to the same conventional pattern. They sacrifice too much for uniformity."

"Still," said Ida, once more harping on the idea that troubled her, "there are only wild flowers in the wilderness. One understands that we have nothing like your peerless English blooms."

Weston looked at her with a little gleam in his eyes.

"Oh," he said, "one must be honest, and even for the credit of the old land I can't admit that. It couldn't be, when you have your sunlight and your crystal skies. It always seems to me that strength is essential to perfect grace, and one finds both, and sweetness unexcelled, out here in Canada."

He rose, and, taking up the rod, straightened the gut trace.

"There is a big trout rising in the slack," he said. "I think you could cast from the bank."

Ida took the rod from him, and a little thrill of satisfaction ran through her as she poised herself upon a jutting stone at the water's edge. He had spoken vaguely, and she would have resented any undue explicitness, but she had watched his face, and it had set her doubts at rest. If any English girl had ever looked upon this man with favor, which seemed probable, it was evident that he had long ago forgotten her; and she fancied that if he had once been stirred to passion he was not a man who would lightly forget. Then she set about casting for the trout, which rose again; for, in view of her encounters with Mrs. Kinnaird, it seemed advisable to take a few fish back with her, if only to show how she had spent the time.

At the third cast there was a splash and a sudden silvery gleam, and a tightening of the line. Then the reel clinked furiously, a bright shape flashed through the froth of the eddy, and went down, after which the line ripped athwart the surface of the pool. Weston, who whipped up the net, waded in knee-deep.

"Keep the butt down!" he called. "Reel in! Take up every inch of slack."

The fish broke the surface and went down again, and a flush of crimson crept into Ida's face as she stood quivering while the line went round the pool. Then the strain eased a little, and she spun the reel, until the fish, showing a gleaming side in the swing of the eddy, made a rush again.

"Hold on this time," said Weston. "It's making for the drift-log. There are branches under it."

The rod bent, but the moving line led straight toward the drift-log, until, in a moment, it stopped suddenly. Ida turned to the man with a gasp.

"It's in under those branches," she said.

Weston, glancing at the line, threw down the net, for, though he scarcely had expected this, the fish evidently had not snapped the gut trace, which was now entangled among the broken branches.

"Give me some slack when I call," he said.

It was rather a long jump, but he managed to reach the butt of the log, and he scrambled along it toward its thinner top, which stretched out along the side of the rock. There was deep water under it, and the eddy swung fiercely toward the rapid which swept on to the fall; but the trunk provided a tolerably safe pathway to one accustomed to the bush, and he reached a spot where a snapped-off branch projected into the river. Then, stripping off his jacket, he lay down and crawled along the branch. As he lowered one arm and shoulder into the water, it seemed to Ida that the log rolled a little, and when he raised himself again, with the water dripping from him, she called out to warn him.

"The log's not safe," she said.

It was not evident that Weston heard her through the roar of the short rapid above the fall, for he lowered himself once more. Ida was quite sure that the trunk tilted a little now, but when he turned a wet face toward her, in her eagerness she forgot that the thing might be perilous. Weston did not notice that he was disturbing the equilibrium of the tree.

"Let your reel run!" he cried.

He groped around among the branches, with a good deal of the upper part of his body under water, and when at length he emerged there was a big, gleaming fish in one hand. Ida saw him jerk its head back, with his fingers in its gills, and then, standing upright, he hurled it toward her.

"It beats the major's largest one!" he announced.

Ida laid down her rod and scrambled toward the fish; but there was a splashing sound as she bent over it, and when she looked around sharply she saw the big pine slide out into the stream. Weston stood with his back toward her, apparently gazing at the rock, until he suddenly leaped forward and clutched at it. She could not see what he clung to, but the surface was uneven, and he evidently had found a foothold. Then, while a thrill of horror ran through her, she glanced at the pine and saw it whirl out into the rapid. Twice the top of it, which swung clear, came down with a splash, and then it plunged wildly into spray about the fall. She did not care to watch what became of it, and she clenched her hands hard as she looked around again.

Weston was clinging to the rock, and his face, which was turned partly toward her, was set and grim. In a moment he moved forward a little, feeling with outstretched hand for a fresh hold, while one foot splashed in the swirling water. Ida held her breath as she watched him. He swung suddenly forward a yard or so, and then, with a wild scramble, found a foothold. Ida, who was conscious that her heart was beating painfully fast, wondered what kept him from falling. There was not a crevice or a cranny that she could see; but she could not see anything very well, except the tense figure stretched against the stone and the set, white face. Dark pines and foaming water had faded into insignificance.

He moved again, and crept forward with agonizing slowness, until at length he stopped and gazed at the wall of rock still in front of him. That part of it was very smooth and overhung a little between where he was and the steeply sloping strip of shingle on which the girl stood. The stream swirled past furiously, and it was evident to Ida that if he lost his hold it must sweep him down the rapid and over the fall.

She was never sure how long he clung there, but his white face and the poise of his strung-up figure impressed themselves indelibly on her memory. Strain was expressed in every line of his body and in his clutching hands. Then the strength and decision that was in her asserted itself, and she overcame the numbing horror that had held her powerless. Snatching up her rod, she turned to him resolutely.

"You must jump!" she called.

Weston looked at the slender point of the rod she held out, and somewhat naturally hesitated. It was some distance from him, but in another moment the girl was wading out from the shingle. Her skirt trailed in the water which swirled by her, but, though the shingle dropped steeply, it afforded her a foothold, and she stretched out the rod a little farther.

"Jump!" she cried commandingly. "Jump right now!"

The man flung up his hands. As a matter of fact, there was not room for him to jump at all. Ida braced herself for an effort as he lurched down from the rock. There was a great splash and a wrench that almost dragged her off her feet; then he was close beside her, waist-deep in the stream. He did not stop, but clutched her by the shoulder and drove her before him up the shingle. Then he sat down, gasping, while the water ran from him; and she moved back a pace or two and leaned on a boulder, with her face almost as white as his.

"You must be very wet. I thought the river had us both," he said.

Ida laughed, a rather harsh and foolish laugh, for now that the tension had slackened she felt curiously shaken. The man turned and looked back at the pool.

"No," he said, "I don't think I ever could have got out of there alone."

Then he scrambled in a half-dazed fashion to his feet, and raised a hand to where his hat should have been. The hat was, however, a long way down the river by this time; and when Ida noticed his astonishment at not finding it on his head, she once more broke into strained laughter. After that she pulled herself together with an effort.

"You won't mind? I can't help it," she said. "Didn't you know your hat was gone?"

Weston looked at her more steadily than perhaps he should have done. There was something in her face that suggested that the last few moments had almost unnerved her. This, as he could realize, was not altogether unnatural; and then a sudden thrill that set his nerves tingling ran through him, as their eyes met. The events of the past minute had shown them, in part, at least, how they stood toward each other, and for the moment they could not hide it. Then Weston recovered the self-command that was rapidly deserting him.

"I don't think that matters," he said, apparently referring to the hat. "I want to thank you, Miss Stirling. It's quite clear that I owe a good deal to your quickness and nerve."

There were signs that his formal tone had cost him an effort, but the fact that, slightly dazed as he was, he had forced himself to make it, and had called her Miss Stirling, was significant, and Ida fell in with the course he had adopted. It was difficult for both of them, but she recognized that the matter must be passed over as lightly and as speedily as possible.

"You shouldn't have gone out on that log at all," she said. "You must have seen it wasn't safe."

Weston laughed, though the signs of struggle were still on his face.

"Did you notice that?" he asked.

"I didn't," said Ida, and then a curious little thrill of anger ran through her. The man's attitude was only what should be expected of him in view of the difference between their stations, but, after all, it seemed to her that he had almost too much self-control.

"That is, not at first," she added. "Afterward I did notice it, and I called to you. You didn't hear?"

"No," said Weston, "I didn't hear you."

He looked at her steadily; and the girl, who felt the impulsive desire to wound him too strong for her, made a little gesture.

"I am rather ashamed of it, but the next moment I quite forgot that there was any danger," she said. "You see I was so intent upon the fish."

"Then," said Weston, very quietly, "I don't think you could blame me."

He stooped, and, picking up the rod, set about taking it to pieces with a curious deliberation. Then he glanced at the girl.

"I can only offer you my thanks, Miss Stirling, but they're very sincere," he said. "Don't you think it would be better if we went back to camp?"

Ida rose and returned with him through the scented bush, but neither said anything further, for the same restraint was upon both of them.

CHAPTER XVI

ON THE LAKE

It was rather late that night when Weston and Grenfell sat smoking beside the dying fire. The breeze that came off the lake was colder than usual, and the rest of the party had retired indoors, but one window of the little wooden house stood open, and Miss Kinnaird's voice drifted softly out of it. She was evidently singing a selection from an opera. Grenfell, who lay with his back against one of the hearth-logs, appeared to be listening critically.

"It's pretty and nothing more," he said. "That girl's too diffuse—she spreads herself. She might have painted if she'd been poor; though that's not a sure thing either."

"Why isn't it?" asked Weston, who had, however, no great interest in the matter.

"She has too level a head," Grenfell said. "It's as fatal in art as it is in some professions. You have to concentrate, hang on to the one thing, and give yourself to it. Miss Kinnaird couldn't do that. She must stop and count the cost. To make anything of this life one now and then must shut one's eyes to that. There generally has to be a sacrifice."

He broke off, and looked at his companion rather curiously.

"The other girl could make it. She wouldn't ask whether it were worth while."

Weston was a trifle startled. He had that very day seen something in Ida Stirling's eyes that seemed to bear out what his comrade suggested. It had been there for only a moment, which he felt might have been fateful to both of them, and he knew that it was beyond his power to analyze all the qualities that the look had suggested. It had, however, hinted at a courage sufficient to set at defiance conventions and the opinions of her friends, and at the capacity to make a costly sacrifice.

"You seem sure of that?"

"Well," said Grenfell, reflectively, "I think I am. You see in one or two respects I'm like Miss Stirling."

"You like Miss Stirling!"

There was an indignant protest in Weston's voice which brought a twinkle into Grenfell's watery eyes.

"Just so," he said. "When I know what I want the most, I set about getting it. I guess that's sense—sense that's way beyond prudence. What one wants is, in a general way, what one likes, which is a very different thing from what's good for one. It's very seldom that one finds the latter nice. Get these distinctions?"

"I can't see the drift of them," said Weston, impatiently.

"It may strike you as we proceed. If you stop to consider whether it's judicious to reach out for the thing you want, you generally end by not getting it or anything else. Isn't it better to clutch with courage, even if you have to face the cost?"

"I'm not sure," said Weston, dryly. "Is it quite impossible to like a thing it is desirable that you should have?"

"One doesn't often like it," explained Grenfell, with a grin. "Even when one does, the same principle applies. As a rule, one can't get it without a sacrifice."

"That's the principle you acted on?"

Grenfell spread out his hands.

"I guess it is," he said. "In my case the thing I wanted wasn't good for me. I had to choose between my profession and whisky, and I did. Anyway, I've had the whisky."

Weston sat thoughtfully silent a minute or two. It seemed to him that while the result of the course his comrade advocated might well prove to be disastrous, as it had certainly done in his particular case, there was a warranty for it. If it were true that practically nothing could be obtained without cost, it was clear that the excess of prudence which shrank from incurring the latter could lead only to aridity of life. The thoughtless courage which snatched at what was offered seemed a much more fruitful thing, though one might afterward bear the smart as well as enjoy the sweet. To accomplish or obtain anything one must at least face a risk. He remembered how, when he clung hesitating to the slippery rock, Ida Stirling had bidden him jump. He was, however, not a moralist, but a man with a simple code which, a few hours ago, had proved singularly difficult to adhere to. He had then seen something in Ida Stirling's eyes that set his nerves tingling, but he could not take advantage of the momentary reaction of relief at his escape. He wondered, though, why Grenfell had spoken as he had, until the latter turned to him again.

"You mentioned that you nearly pulled Miss Stirling in when she held out that rod," he said. "You didn't notice that she showed any signs of letting it go?"

"I don't think she did."

"You don't think so!" laughed Grenfell. "That girl would have gone right down the fall before she let you go. She's the kind that sees things through. I wonder whether she said anything in particular afterward?"

Weston's face hardened as he looked at him out of half-closed eyes.

"She did not. What makes you suggest it?"

"Well," said Grenfell, reflectively, "she's flesh and blood like the rest of us. She's also a girl with courage enough not to hesitate. I'm not sure"—and he spread out his hands—"that I couldn't have made better use of your opportunities."

Weston said nothing, though he was hot with anger; and just then Kinnaird, who appeared in the lighted doorway of the house, moved in their direction. He stopped close beside them.

"I think I would better tell you now that we have decided to leave this place early next week," he said. "You can see about getting the surplus stores and some of the baggage down the lake to-morrow."

Weston fancied that he looked at him rather hard; but, though the unexpected news had filled him with dismay, he sat very still until Kinnaird, who said nothing further, turned away. Then Grenfell looked up with a smile.

"The major," he said, "has perhaps had sufficient fishing, or his precipitation may be due to the fact that Mrs. Kinnaird is not in some respects a friend of yours. I'm rather surprised that Miss Stirling, who must have known it, mentioned the other little matter. Anyway, as you may feel inclined to point out, that's not my business. The question is what we're going to do now."

"Look again for that mine of yours," said Weston, quietly.

Grenfell made a little sign of comprehension.

"Well," he said, "we'll go. What's more, I know that one of us is going to locate that quartz some day."

He spoke as with conviction, and then, lighting his pipe, slowly strolled away; but Weston sat beside the sinking fire for another hour or so. It was clear to him that he must find Grenfell's lost mine.

It was two days later when he next had any speech with Ida Stirling, and then, though he did not know that Mrs. Kinnaird had done her utmost to prevent it, they were crossing the lake alone in the sailboat. The boat was running smoothly before a little favoring breeze, and Ida sat at the tiller, looking out upon the shining water. They had not spoken since they left the beach, but by and by she turned toward Weston.

"I am glad it is so fine an evening since it's scarcely likely that I shall have another sail," she said. "We have decided to leave early on Monday."

Weston nodded. It was the first time she had mentioned their departure to him, and he recognized that unless he were cautious it might prove a dangerous subject.

"You are going to Montreal?" he inquired.

"In the first place. However, we are going to England in a week or two."

Though he was on his guard, she saw him start, but he stooped and coiled up one of the halyards before he answered her.

"You will, of course, be there some time?"

"Six months at least, perhaps longer."

She watched him quietly, but he sat very still with the rope in his hand.

"Well," he said, "I think you will like it. You will be in London, I suppose?"

Ida felt vaguely sorry for him. Though he had said it was scarcely probable that he would go back to it, she knew that he had not forgotten the land from which he was exiled. Indeed, a certain wistfulness in his eyes suggested that he still thought of it with the exile's usual tenderness. She was going to take her place in the world to which she felt reasonably certain he had once belonged, while he swung the ax or plied the shovel beside some western railroad track; though she did not mean for him to do the latter if she could help it, of which, however, she was far from sure.

"Yes," she said. "Still we shall spend some time at the house in the north of England you once heard Major Kinnaird mention."

There was no doubt that this shot had reached its mark, for she saw his little abrupt movement. Then he turned toward her fully, which he had not done for the last minute or two.

"Miss Stirling," he said, with a faint flush in his face, "I am going to ask you a rather curious thing. If you meet any of the people about there, I should rather you did not mention my name, though, of course, it is scarcely likely that you would find any reason to do so."

He broke off, and hesitated a moment.

"You see, I know the place."

"Ah," said Ida, with no sign of surprise. "What were you doing there?"

The man smiled rather bitterly.

"I was something similar to head gamekeeper. It wasn't an occupation I cared much about."

"You got tired of it?"

"Anyway, that wasn't why I gave it up. I was turned out. Fired, they call it in this country."

Ida for a moment was almost angry with him. She felt, simply because he had said it, that this must be correct as far as it went, but she was equally sure that he could have gone a good deal further. She was, of course, aware that there were a good many men in Canada whose absence from the old country was not regretted by their friends, and she was a little hurt that he did not seem to shrink from the possibility of her setting him down as one of them. She could not know that he was in a very bitter mood just then.

"Well," she said, "as you say, it is not likely that I shall have any occasion to mention you, and I certainly won't do it casually. You must, however, be content with that."

"Yes," said Weston. "After all, it really doesn't matter very much anyway."

Ida let the matter drop, for she had something else to say, and it had been in her mind rather often lately.

"When we leave here you will be without an occupation, won't you?" she asked; and then proceeded somewhat hastily without waiting for him to answer. "Now, you have done a good deal to make the time pass pleasantly both here and in British Columbia."

"It did pass pleasantly?"

The question was suggestively abrupt, and Ida saw that, as happened now and then, the man was for the moment off his guard. This, however, did not displease her.

"Of course," she said. "For that matter it couldn't have been very burdensome to you."

Weston laughed in a rather curious fashion, and she saw the blood creep into his face.

"I'm glad you have enjoyed it," he said. "It seems unfortunately certain that I shall not have another time like this."

Ida was aware, of course, that the real man had spoken then, but in another moment he once more, as she sometimes described it to herself, drew back into his shell.

"I interrupted what you were going to say," he observed, with a deprecatory gesture.

"It's very simple," said the girl. "If my father or any one else makes you an offer, I should like you to take it. In one sense, chopping trees and shoveling gravel on the track leads to nothing."

The flush Ida had already noticed grew a little plainer in the man's face, but he smiled.

"I'm afraid I can't promise to do that," he said. "You see," and he seemed to search for words, "there is a good deal of the vagabond in me. I never could stand the cities, and that ought to be comprehensible to you when you have seen the wilderness."

"In summer," said the girl dryly. "Isn't it very different during the rest of the year?"

"Oh," declared Weston, "it's always good in the bush, even when the pines are gleaming spires of white, and you haul the great logs out with the plodding oxen over the down-trodden snow. There is nothing the cities can give one to compare with the warmth of the log shack at night when you lie, aching a little, about the stove, telling stories with the boys, while the shingles snap and crackle under the frost. Perhaps it's finer still to stand by with the peevie, while the great trunks go crashing down the rapids with the freshets of the spring; and then there's the still, hot summer, when the morning air's like wine, and you can hear the clink-clink of the drills through the sound of running water in the honey-scented shade, and watch the new wagon road wind on into the pines. You have seen the big white peaks gleam against the creeping night."

It was evident that he was endeavoring to find cause for contentment with the life before him, but Ida fancied that he wished to avoid the question she had raised.

"You forget to mention the raw hands and the galled shoulders, as well as the snow-slush and the rain. However, that's not quite the point. As I said, all that leads to nothing. Are you too proud to take a trifling favor because it comes through me?"

Weston met her gaze, and there was a grave forcefulness in his manner which almost astonished her. He evidently for once had suffered his usual self-restraint to relax, and she felt it was almost a pity that he had not done so more frequently.

"Miss Stirling," he said, "you are, as it happens, one of the few people from whom I could not take a favor of that kind."

She understood him, and for a moment a flicker of color crept into her cheek. It was, she felt, a clean pride that had impelled him to the speech. There were, she admitted, no benefits within her command that she would not gladly have thrust upon him; but, for all that, she would not have had him quietly acquiesce in them. Perhaps she was singular in this, but her forebears had laid the foundations of a new land's future with ax and drill, clearing forest and breaking prairie with stubborn valor and toil incredible. They had flung their wagon roads over thundering rivers and grappled with stubborn rock, and among them the soft-handed man who sought advancement through a woman's favor was, as a rule, regarded with quiet scorn. She said nothing, however, and it was a few moments before Weston looked at her again.

"Anyway," he said, "I couldn't do what you suggest. I am going back into the ranges with Grenfell to look for the mine."

"Ah," said Ida, "you haven't given up that notion yet?"

The man smiled grimly.

"I am keener about it than ever. Perhaps it's somewhat curious, but I seem certain that we shall strike that quartz lead one of these days."

Ida was glad to let the conversation take this new turn, for she understood his eagerness now, and she had felt that they were skirting a crisis each time she had talked with him of late. She had the courage to make a sacrifice, and, indeed, had the occasion arisen, would probably have considered none too costly; but it seemed due to him as well as to her that he should at least make some strenuous effort to pull down the barriers between them.

"Well," she said quietly, "it is very curious that you discovered no trace of it. You said you found Grenfell's partner lying dead upon the range, and, as their provisions were running out when he left the lake, he could not have gone very far. Was it a big lake?"

"It couldn't have been. Grenfell said he walked round it in a couple of hours."

Ida looked thoughtful.

"Still, when you had the spot where you came upon Verneille to work from, you should have seen it from one of the spurs of the range."

"Yes," admitted Weston, "that seems reasonably evident, though we certainly saw no sign of it." He broke off and laughed. "The whole thing sounds crazy, doesn't it? Still, as I said, I believe we are going to be successful."

He turned away and busied himself with some of the gear; and neither of them said anything further until they ran into the bay before the house. Three or four days later Weston conveyed the party down the lake to the carriage that was waiting to take them to the station; and Ida laid her hand in his for only a moment before she drove away.

CHAPTER XVII

SCARTHWAITE-IN-THE-FOREST

Ida Stirling had spent some time in England when, one autumn evening, she descended the wide oak staircase of Scarthwaite Hall at Scarthwaite-in-the-Forest. There was no forest in the vicinity, though long ago a certain militant bishop had held by kingly favor the right of venery over the surrounding moors, and now odd wisps of straggling firs wound up the hollows that seamed them here and there. Nobody seemed to know who first built Scarthwaite Hall, though many a dalesman had patched it afterward and pulled portions of it down. It was one of the ancient houses, half farm and half stronghold, which may still be found in the north country. They were, until a few decades ago, usually in possession of the Statesmen who worked their own land. The Statesmen have gone—economic changes vanquished them—but the houses they inherited from the men who bore pike and bow at Bannockburn and Flodden are for the most part standing yet. They have made no great mark in history, but their stout walls have time and again been engirdled by Scottish spears, and after such occasions there was not infrequently lamentation by Esk and Liddell.

It was clear that Scarthwaite Hall had been built in those days of foray, for one little, ruined, half-round tower rose from the brink of a ravine whose sides the hardiest of moss-troopers could scarcely have climbed. A partly filled-in moat led past the other, and in between stretched the curtain wall which now formed the facade of the house itself. Its arrow slits had been enlarged subsequently into narrow, stone-ribbed windows, and a new entrance made, while the ancient courtyard was girt with decrepit stables and barns. Most of the deep, winding dale still belonged to it, but the last Weston had signally failed to make a living out of it, or to meet his debts. He lived in a little town not far away, and let Scarthwaite for the shooting when he could, which explains how Major Kinnaird had taken it.

Ida looked about her as she came down the stairway. It led into a dark-paneled, stone-arched hall, which, since habitable space was rather scarce at Scarthwaite, served as general living-room. A fire was burning in the big, ancient hearth, and a handful of people were scattered here and there, waiting for dinner, which should have been ready a few minutes earlier. Kinnaird, who appeared a trifle impatient, was standing near his wife and a couple of shooting men, and his daughter was talking to one or two of his neighbors. Ida smiled as one of the latter glanced up at her, and she moved toward him when she reached the foot of the stairway. Ainslie, the owner of some quarries in the vicinity, was a middle-aged man whom she had met once or twice before.

When she had greeted him, she stood still a moment or two, listening to the murmurs of general conversation. Then she saw Kinnaird, who was standing not far from her, take out his watch.

"It's a little too bad of Weston. I shouldn't have waited for anybody else," he said. "As it is, I suppose we'll have to give him a minute or two longer."

The remark was evidently overheard, as perhaps Kinnaird intended. One of the others laughed.

"Ralph Weston was never punctual in his life," he said.

"Considering everything," observed one of the women standing near Ida, "it is rather curious that Weston should have promised to come at all. It must be a trifle embarrassing to dine at one's own place as another man's guest."

"Oh," said the man beside her, "Weston would go anywhere for a good dinner and a good glass of wine."

Ida, as it happened, had not heard what guests Mrs. Kinnaird had expected, and she started at the name. It was a moment or two later when she turned to her companion.

"This house belongs to the man they seem to be waiting for?" she asked.

Ainslie nodded.

"Yes," he said, "I suppose it does."

"Then why doesn't he live in it?"

"It takes a good deal to keep up a place of this kind, and, until Major Kinnaird came, it's some time since anybody seriously attempted it."

"Ah!" said Ida. "Mr. Weston's means are insufficient?"

"It's a tolerably open secret. There are a good many people similarly situated. A small and badly-kept estate is not a lucrative possession."

"Then why don't they keep it up efficiently?"

"Now," said Ainslie, "you're getting at the root of the matter. In my opinion it's largely a question of character. In fact, after the glimpses I've had of the wheat-growers in Dakota, Minnesota, and western Canada, it seems to me that if our people were content to live and work at home as they do out yonder they would acquire at least a moderate prosperity. Still, I'm rather afraid that wouldn't appeal to some of them. As it is, their wants are increasing, and the means of gratifying them steadily going down."

"All this applies to Mr. Weston in particular?"

"I don't think it would be a breach of confidence if I admitted that it does. Perhaps, however, I'm a little prejudiced. Weston doesn't like me. He blames me for encouraging his son in what he calls his 'iconoclastic' notions."

Ida, who was becoming interested, smiled.

"After all," she said, "the comparison isn't very unfavorable to the son. I believe the original iconoclasts were the image-breakers in Byzantium."

"Were they? I didn't know it," said Ainslie. "It's a moral certainty that Weston didn't, either. In fact, I've no doubt he fancies that Darwin and Bradlaugh, and he'd certainly include Cobden, invented them. Anyway, the lad wasn't very much of an iconoclast. He believed in his images, which were not the same as those his father worshiped; and all he wanted was to see them work. I think it hurt him when they didn't, or, at least, when they didn't appear to."

"Ah," said Ida, "that's rather too involved for me."

"Well," returned her companion, "we'll leave Weston out. I'm not sure about what he believes in, and it's probable that, he doesn't know himself, except that it's everything as it used to be. His wife was High Church, with altruistic notions, and it's no secret that she made things rather uncomfortable for her husband; but when she took the lad in hand she succeeded perhaps too well. You see, he wanted to apply her principles; and altruism leads to trouble when its possessor comes across formulas that don't stand for anything."

Just then there was a rattle of wheels outside, and a minute or two later a little full-fleshed man, with a heavy face, in conventional dress, entered the hall. He greeted those who stood about, when he had shaken hands with Kinnaird.

"Sorry I'm a little behind," he apologized. "Had to post over. I told Walters at the George to keep me the black mare. Instead, he let that waterworks chief navvy fellow have her. The horse he gave me would hardly face Scarside Rise."

One or two of the guests smiled, for the navvy in question was a rather famous engineer who had had a difference of opinion with Weston over certain gravel he desired to quarry on the Scarthwaite estate. Then Mrs. Kinnaird stepped forward, and they went in to dinner.

It was not yet dark outside, but the table was lighted; and Ida, who sat not far from Weston, watched him closely. She had at first been startled by the likeness between him and the man she had met in Canada, but she was now conscious of an increasing dissimilarity. There was a suggestion of grossness in the face of Major Kinnaird's guest, which had certainly not been a characteristic of Weston the packer. The older man's expression was petulant and arrogant; that of the one who had served her as camp attendant had been, as a rule, good-humoredly whimsical. Nor did she like the half-contemptuous inattention that Weston displayed when one or two of the others addressed him. In several cases he merely looked up and went on with his dinner as though it were too much trouble to answer. Ida felt reasonably sure that his manners would not have been tolerated in most of the primitive logging camps of western Canada. It became evident, however, that there were topics in which he took some interest, when a man who sat near turned to him.

"We were in the meadows by Ghyllfoot this afternoon, and they were looking very sour and rushy," he said. "They were drained once, weren't they?"

"They were," replied Weston, sharply. "It's stiff land. In my father's time, Little used to grow good wheat there. Still, even tile drains won't last forever. The soil gets in."

"You're correct about the wheat," said another man. "Little's nephew still talks about it. They used to grind it at the Ramside mills. Wouldn't it be worth while to have the meadows redrained, if only for the grass?"

Ida, who was watching him, fancied that this was a sore point with Weston, for he momentarily forgot his dinner.

"No," he answered curtly. "I took some trouble to make young Little understand it when he came to me with a nonsensical proposition not long ago. Like the rest of them, he's always wanting something. I asked him where he thought the money was coming from."

Ida was not surprised at this, though she knew that in western Canada the smaller settlers as a rule stripped themselves of every comfort, and lived in the most grim simplicity, that they might have more to give the land.

Then, as the man did not answer, Weston solemnly laid down his fork, with the manner of one making a painful sacrifice.

"There is a good deal of nonsense talked about farming in these days," he observed authoritatively. "You can put a fortune into drains and fences and buildings, but it's quite another matter to get two or three per cent, upon it back. In the old days I hadn't a horse in the stables worth less than sixty guineas, and my father thought nothing of giving twice as much. The other things were to match." He looked down the table with a flush of indignation in his heavy face. "Now, Walters at the George gives a navvy the horse I hired. Still, what can you expect when they pile up the taxes on us, and open new doors continually to the foreigners? We grew wheat at Scarthwaite, and it was ground at Ramside mill. The last time I looked in, Harvey had his stores full of flour from Minneapolis and Winnipeg. I asked him whether he didn't feel ashamed of having any hand in that kind of thing."

Ida could not check a smile. In Weston's case, at least, the reason why western wheat had displaced the local product was tolerably plain. This full-fleshed man differed, she fancied, in most essentials from the lean farmers who drove the half-mile furrows, or ripped up their patches of virgin sod with plodding oxen on the vast expanses of the prairie. While he indulged his senses and bought sixty-guinea horses, they rose at four or earlier, and, living on pork and flour and green tea, worked in grim earnest until it was dark. Blizzard and hail and harvest frost brought them to the verge of ruin now and then but could not drive them over it. They set their lips, cut down the grocery bill, and, working still harder, went on again. A good many of them had, as she knew, come from England.

Then Weston appeared to remember his dinner, and made a little vague gesture which seemed to indicate that there was no more to be said.

"I don't want to hear about drains and deeper tillage while we let every foreigner pour his wheat and chilled beef into our market. It's nonsense," he asserted.

Some one started another topic; and an hour or so later most of the little party strolled out on the terrace in front of the house. It was almost dark now, but the evening was no more than pleasantly cool, and Ida sat down on an old stone seat.

Scarthwaite faced toward the west, and she looked out across a deep, green valley toward the sweep of upland and heather moor that cut black and solemn against a paling saffron glow. It was very still, though now and then a bleating of sheep rang sharply out of the wisps of mist that streaked the lower meadows. Perhaps it was the stillness or the scent of the firs that climbed the hollow of the ghyll behind the house that reminded Ida of the man who had strolled with her through the shadow of the giant redwoods of the Pacific Slope. In any case, she was thinking of him when Arabella Kinnaird stopped for a moment at her side and glanced toward Weston, who stood not far away.

"You heard that man's name. Did you notice a resemblance to anybody we have met?" she inquired.

"Yes," said Ida. "Of course, it may be accidental."

Her companion laughed.

"I don't think it is. In view of what I once told you on the subject, it's a matter I mean to investigate."

She moved away; but it was Ida who first was afforded an opportunity of deciding the question, for a few minutes later Ainslie strolled toward her. When he sat down beside her, she indicated the waste, of climbing pasture, which ran up, interspersed with gorse bushes and clumps of heather, to the dusky moor.

"Not a sign of cultivation," she said. "I suppose that grass is never broken up? How much foundation is there for Mr. Weston's views?"

Ainslie laughed.

"I'm afraid I'm hardly competent to decide, but there are people who agree with him. Still, I think it's reasonably certain that a good deal of the higher land that now carries a few head of sheep would grow oats and other things. It's largely a question of economics. Somebody would have to spend a good deal of money and labor on it first, and the result, which wouldn't be very apparent for two or three years, would be a little uncertain then. It depends on how much the man who undertook it wanted back to make the thing worth while."

"They are content with food, and sometimes very indifferent shelter, in western Canada."

"There," said Ainslie, "you have the thing in a nutshell. You have, no doubt, formed some idea of Weston's wants, which are rather numerous. In fact, some of us seem to consider it the correct thing to cultivate them. The more wants you have the greater man you are."

Ida smiled a little as she remembered a man of considerable importance in the wheat-lands of Assiniboia, whom she had last seen sitting, clad in blue shirt and very old trousers, on a huge machine which a double span of reeking horses hauled through the splendid grain. He had driven it since sunrise, and it was dusk of evening then, and his wants were, as she knew, remarkably simple. He bore his share of the burden under a burning sun, but it seemed to her that, had Weston been in his place, he would have ridden around that farm with a gloved hand on his hip, and would have raised it only now and then, imperiously, to direct the toilers. Then she thought of another man, who was like him in some respects, and was then, in all probability, plodding through the lonely bush.

"You mentioned a son," she said. "What became of him?"

"He went out to Canada. Quarreled with his father. As I believe I suggested, the lad was at heart a rebel." Ainslie smiled rather dryly. "A good many of us are. He wouldn't see that his mother's ideas were apt to get him into trouble when he tried to apply them."

Ida sat silent for a few moments. There was no longer any doubt in her mind that Weston who had turned his back on Scarthwaite was identical with Weston the camp-packer.

"Do you remember what they quarreled over?" she asked at length.

"Yes," said Ainslie, who was inclined to wonder at her interest in the subject, "it was water-finding. It's a thing of which you probably have never heard."

"I have," said Ida. "Won't you go on?"

"Well," continued Ainslie, "there was a tenant on this estate who was rather more badly off than the rest of them. He had a piece of upland with rock under it, and in a dry season—though we don't often get one—it was with the greatest trouble he got water enough for his stock. He asked young Weston to find him a likely spot to drive a well. The lad was walking over one parched meadow with the hazel twig in his hand, when his father came upon the procession—everybody belonging to the farm was out with him. Weston, I heard, went purple when he saw what was going on, and, from his point of view, his indignation was perhaps comprehensible. His son was openly, before one of the tenants and a parcel of farm-hands, making use of a superstitious device in which no sane person could believe. Weston, as I remember it, compared him to a gipsy fortune-teller, and went on through the gamut of impostor, mountebank and charlatan, before he commanded him to desist on the moment. I don't quite know what came next, though something was said about a lifted riding-crop, but within the week Clarence started for Canada."

"He abandoned the attempt to find water?"

Ainslie smiled.

"The farmer dug a well in that meadow, and I believe he uses it still. He held a lease, and Weston couldn't get rid of him."

He looked rather hard at Ida, and was slightly astonished at the sparkle in her eyes.

"I'm afraid I've been somewhat talkative," he said.

"No," Ida assured him, and he saw that she was stirred. "Thank you for telling me."

He moved away; and by and by Arabella Kinnaird and one of the other women approached the seat. Arabella left her companion a moment, and made a little whimsical gesture as she met Ida's gaze.

"I've been throwing away a good many blandishments on Weston," she observed. "He appears prudently reticent on the subject of his relations, and if he has any in Canada, it's evident that he isn't proud of them. Still, I haven't abandoned the amiable intention of extorting a little more information from him."

CHAPTER XVIII

WESTON'S ADVOCATE

A week had passed when Weston, who apparently had some business with Kinnaird, drove over to Scarthwaite again. This time he brought a daughter, who, it appeared, lived for the most part with some more prosperous members of the family. Arriving a little before lunch, they remained until the evening. As it happened, Miss Weston displayed what she evidently considered a kindly interest in Ida, and graciously patronized her as a stranger and a Colonial, who was necessarily ignorant of a good many of the little amenities of life in the old country.

Her intentions were no doubt laudable, but the methods she adopted to set the stranger at her ease were not those most likely to endear the insular English to their cousins across the Atlantic. Ida, to begin with, had not only a spice of temper but also no great reverence for forms and formulas, and the people that she was accustomed to meeting were those who had set their mark upon wide belts of forest and long leagues of prairie. At first she was quietly amused by the patronage of a woman whose right to bestow it consisted apparently in an acquaintance with English people of station, and some proficiency at bridge; but by and by her condescension grew wearisome, and finally exasperating. Miss Weston, however, could not have been expected to recognize this. She was a tall, pale woman, with a coldly formal manner and some taste in dress.

There were several other guests in the house, and the party spent most of the hot afternoon about the tennis net and lounging under the shadow of a big copper beech on the lawn. Once when Miss Weston left her to play in a set at tennis, Arabella Kinnaird leaned over the back of Ida's chair.

"You seem to have made rather a favorable impression upon Julia Weston, and, as a rule, she's unapproachable," she said, with a mischievous smile.

Ida's eyebrows straightened, which, to those acquainted with her, was a rather ominous sign.

"Won't you keep that woman away from me?" she begged. "I don't want to be rude, but if I see very much more of her, I may not be able to help it. In one way, I'm sorry I met her. You're not all like that."

"Well," said Arabella, "perhaps it is a pity. There really are some of us to whom you could talk without having your pet illusions about the old country shattered. In fact, I can think of one or two women about here who would strengthen them. Can't you, Mr. Ainslie?"

Ainslie, who was standing near them, smiled.

"Oh, yes," he said. "Unfortunately, however, they are, as a rule, retiring. It's the other kind that is usually in evidence. Do you feel very badly disappointed with us, Miss Stirling?"

"No," replied Ida, with a thoughtfulness which brought the smile more plainly into his eyes. "In fact, I want to think well of you. It's a thing we wouldn't quite admit, but at bottom I believe we all do."

Then she turned to Arabella.

"By the way, what has become of Mr. Weston?"

"He is shut up with my father in the library; and there are reasons for supposing that his business requires the consumption of a considerable quantity of soda and whisky. The major, I am afraid, will be a trifle difficult to get on with this evening. As a matter of fact, he isn't used to it, though he was, one understands, rather popular at the mess table. That's a trifle significant, considering what is said about us, isn't it, Mr. Ainslie?"

"Ah," said Ainslie, "we're a maligned people; and the pity of it is that it's our own people who give us away. You don't believe in doing that in the Colonies?"

"No," laughed Ida, "we are rather fond of making it clear that we are quite above the average as a people. However, it's excusable, perhaps, for, after all, there's a germ of truth in it. I think Miss Kinnaird will agree with that."

Arabella leaned a little farther over her chair.

"I'll leave you to talk it out with Mr. Ainslie. But there's another matter. Does Miss Weston recall to you anybody we have met?"

"No," said Ida, with a somewhat incautious decisiveness. "If you mean our camp-packer, she certainly does not."

Arabella understood this to mean that any comparison of the kind suggested would be derogatory to the packer, which was somewhat significant.

"Well," she said, "there is at least a physical resemblance, and though I haven't probed the matter very deeply, yet I've not abandoned it."

Then she laughed and turned to Ainslie.

"You and Miss Stirling can thrash out the question."

She strolled away, and Ainslie watched Ida, whose eyes were following Miss Weston at the tennis net.

"Yes," he remarked, "we play these games rather well; and, after all, is there any reason why we shouldn't? There are a good many people in this country who don't consider them as of the first importance."

"Oh," said Ida, "I'm really not looking for faults. Why should you suspect me of such an unpleasant attitude?"

"Well," observed her companion reflectively, "I can't help thinking that we now and then give our visitors wrong impressions by showing them the wrong things. Personally, I should recommend an inspection of our mines and mills and factories. Besides, one has rather a fancy that some of our young men, who were brought up, we'll say, to play tennis well, have shown that they can do rather more than that in western Canada."

Ida's eyes softened a little as she recalled a weary, gray-faced man limping back up the hillside one eventful morning; but the turn that the conversation had taken had its effect on her, and that effect was to have its result. Like others born in the newer lands, she believed first of all in practical efficiency, and she had learned during journeys made with her father that the man with few wants and many abilities, or indeed the man with only one of the latter strenuously applied to a useful purpose, is the type in most favor in western Canada. Graces do not count for much in the west, nor does the assumption of ability carry a man as far as it sometimes does in older communities. As Stirling had once said, when they want a chopper in that country they make him chop, and facility in posing is of very little service when one is called on to grapple with virgin forest or stubborn rock.

Young as Ida was, she had a grip of essential things, and a dislike of shams. It generally happened, too, that, when she felt strongly on any subject, she sooner or later expressed her thoughts in forcible words; and before that afternoon was over she and Arabella Kinnaird between them disturbed the composure of more than one of Mrs. Kinnaird's guests.

Tea was being laid out on a little table beneath the beech when Weston strolled across the lawn. He was redder in face than when Ida had last seen him, and a trifle heavier of expression. Pushing unceremoniously past two of the women, he dropped into a basket-chair, which bent under him, and glanced around at the others with coldly, assertive eyes. Ida, watching him, became conscious of a sense of repulsion and indignation. This arrogant, indulgent, useless man had, it seemed, not the manners of a western ranch-hand. He accepted a cup of tea from Mrs. Kinnaird with an ungraciousness which aroused Ida to downright anger; and shortly afterward he contrived to spill a quantity of the liquid upon Arabella's dress, for which he offered no excuses, though he blamed the narrow-bottomed cup. Then some one, who of course could not foresee the result, asked Arabella if she would show them some of her Canadian sketches.

Miss Kinnaird made no objection, and when, soon after the tea was cleared away, the easel she sent for had been set up in the shadow of the beech, she displayed on it several small canvases and water-color drawings. There were vistas of snow mountains, stretches of frothing rivers, and colonnades of towering firs, until at last she laid a canvas on the easel.

"This," she said, "is, I think, the best figure drawing I ever did."

Ida, leaning forward in her chair, felt the blood creep into her face. There was no doubt that the sketch was striking. It showed a man standing tensely poised, with a big, glinting ax in his hand. He was lean and lithely muscular, and his face was brown and very grim; but the artist had succeeded in fixing in its expression the elusive but recognizable something which is born of restraint, clean living, and arduous physical toil. It is to be seen in the eyes of those who, living in Spartan simplicity, make long marches with the dog-sledges in the Arctic frost, drive the logs down roaring rivers, or toil sixteen hours daily under a blazing sun in the western harvest field. In all probability it was as plainly stamped on the honest countenance of many an unconsidered English Tommy who plodded doggedly forward with the relief columns across the dusty veldt. Drivers of great expresses, miners, quarrymen, now and then wear that look. Springing, as it does, not from strength of body, but from the subjugation of the latter and all fleshy shrinking and weariness, it links man with the greatness of the unseen.

There was only the one figure silhouetted against long rows of dusky pines, but the meaning of the way in which the hard, scarred hands were clenched on the big ax was very plain, and Ida could fill in from memory the form of the big chopper and the clusters of expectant men.

"Excellent!" said one of the guests. "That fellow means to fight. He's in hard training, too, and that has now and then a much bigger effect than the toughening of his muscles upon the man who submits himself to it. Is it a portrait or a type?"

The speaker was from the metropolis, and while Arabella hesitated, Ida answered him with a suggestive ring in her voice.

"It's both, one should like to think," she said. "The man came from England; and if you can send us out more of that type we shall be satisfied."

Then she and the questioner became conscious of the awkward silence that had fallen upon the rest. They belonged to the dales, and they glanced covertly at Weston, who was gazing at the picture, purple in face, and with a very hard look in his eyes. Ida guessed that it was the scarred workman's hands and the track-grader's old blue shirt and tattered duck that had hurt his very curious pride. Still, it was evident that he could face the situation.

"Yes," he said, a trifle hoarsely, "it's a portrait—an excellent one. In fact, as some of you are quite aware, it's my son."

He rose, and crossing a strip of lawn sat down heavily near Ida. The latter, looking around, saw Arabella's satisfied smile suddenly subside; but the next moment Weston, leaning forward, laid his hand roughly on her arm.

"Why Clarence permitted that portrait to be painted I don't quite understand, though he was fond of flying in the face of all ideas of decency," he said. "You must have met him out yonder. What was he doing?"

"Shoveling gravel on a railroad that my father was grading," said Ida, with rather grim amusement, for she was determined that the man should face the plain reality, even if it hurt him.

"Shoveling gravel!" said Weston. "But he is my son."

"I'm afraid that doesn't count out yonder. In any case, he's in one sense in reasonably good company. Did you send your son to Sandhurst or an English university?"

"I didn't," said the man, gazing at her with hot, confused anger in his eyes. "For one thing, he hadn't brains enough, and, for another, there were too many charges on the property. What do you mean by good company?"

"Just a moment before I answer. Why did you turn him out?"

"That does not describe it. He went. We had a difference of opinion. He would hear no reason."

"Exactly," said Miss Weston, who now appeared close by. "Since you seem to have heard a little about the matter, I feel I must say that my brother deliberately left us at a time when his father had expected him to be of service to him."

Ida did not know whether the others could hear what was being said, as there was a strip of lawn between them and where she sat, but she felt that it did not greatly matter. She had no pity for this man or his daughter, who preferred to malign the absent rather than to admit an unpleasant fact. She would strip them of any solace they might find in shams, after which there was a little more to be said.

"The difference of opinion was, I believe, decided with a riding-crop," she said. "Still, that is a side issue, and I will tell you what I meant by good company. We have quite a few of your graduates out yonder laying railroad ties, as well as lawyers who have got into trouble over trust money, and army men who couldn't meet their turf debts or were a little too smart at cards. Some of them are of unexceptionable family—at least from your point of view. As a rule, they sleep packed like cattle in reeking redwood shacks, and either dress in rags or mend their own clothes. Among their companions are ranchers who can't live all the year on the produce of their half-cleared land, absconders from half the Pacific Slope cities, and runaway sailormen. The task set before them every morning would kill most of you."

Weston, who had winced once or twice, glanced apprehensively toward the rest. They were sitting very still, and their appearance suggested that, whether warrantable or not, they were listening.

"His insane folly has brought him down to that?" he asked.

Ida straightened herself a little, with a sparkle in her eyes.

"I don't think there has been any very great descent," she went on. "You must try to realize that those men are not wastrels now, however they may have lived in England, Montreal, or the cities down Puget Sound. They're rending new roads through the mountains to let in progress and civilization, and making fast the foundations of the future greatness of a wide and prosperous land. Already, because of what they and their kind have done, you can travel through it without seeing a ragged, slatternly woman, or a broken-down, desperate man. Besides, many of them, and certainly most of the small bush ranchers, lead lives characterized by the old heroic virtues that seem to have gone out of fashion in the cities, though you'll find some of them held up for emulation in the Pauline epistles."

Weston gazed at her in blank astonishment. She made a little, half-contemptuous gesture.

"You can't understand that? Well, one really couldn't expect you to. You have never starved your body, or forced it day after day to a task that was crushing you. Those men work in icy water, keep the trail with bleeding feet, and sleep in melting snow. They bear these things cheerfully, and I think there are no men on this earth who can match their wide charity. The free companions never turn away the ragged stranger. What is theirs is his, from the choicest of their provisions to the softest spruce-twig bed."

She laughed, and then continued:

"That's in a general way. To be particular, I'll try to tell you what

Clarence Weston has done. It's worth hearing."

She had spoken more clearly the last few moments, and it became evident at length that she had secured the attention of everybody. With an impulsive gesture she invited them all to listen.

"I'll tell you what that picture leaves out," she said. "There was an old man in the railroad camp, played-out and useless. The boys were handling him roughly because he'd spoiled their supper rather often, when Clarence Weston stepped in. The old man, you must understand, hadn't a shadow of a claim on him. Now, those are not nice men to make trouble with when they have a genuine grievance, and there were three or four of them quite ready to lay hands on Weston, while there was nobody who sympathized with him. He stood facing them, one man against an angry crowd, and held them off from the stranger who had no claim on him. Have you heard of anything finer?

"Again, when Arabella lamed herself up on a great snow range—he'd carried our food and blankets since sunrise—he went down to bring help in the darkness, through the timber and along the edge of horrible crags. The man had badly cut his foot, and the wound opened on the march, but when he made the camp, almost too weary to crawl, he went back right away, so that the Indians he took up might get there a little quicker."

She broke off for a moment, with a flush in her face and a curious little laugh.

"Now," she said, "I think I've made the thing quite plain, and I'm glad I did."

There was an expressive silence for a moment or two, and then Major Kinnaird looked at the others.

"I know nothing about the first incident, but I think that Miss Stirling could have gone a little further when she described the last one," he said. "My daughter, who was badly injured, would probably have been left another day on the range, without food or any attention, if it had not been for the courage and endurance the man displayed. I wish to say, however, that I had no idea he was any connection of Mr. Weston's until this moment."

Ida's heart warmed toward Kinnaird. Reserved and formal as he was, the man could be honest, and it was evident that his few quiet words had made almost as deep an impression as the outbreak to which she had been impelled. There was another rather awkward silence; and then Weston, who seemed to have forgotten the others, made a little abrupt movement.

"What had my son to do with you?" he asked.

The question was flung at Kinnaird, but Ida saw that it was a relief to him when she answered it.

"My father hired him. He was our camp-packer, the man who set up the tents, made the fires, and poled the canoes," she said.

Weston stood up and, looking hard at Kinnaird, straightened himself. His face was an unpleasant red, and there was badly-suppressed anger in his eyes.

"Time is getting on, and we have rather a long drive," he said. "I may ask Miss Stirling's leave to call on her later. In the meanwhile, if Mrs. Kinnaird will excuse us——"

His hostess made no attempt to keep him; and, as he moved away, his daughter stopped for a moment beside Ida's chair.

"I don't know whether what you have done was excusable or not, but you have, at least, succeeded in making the breach between Clarence and his father wider than ever," she said. "That was probably what you intended?"

Ida was momentarily puzzled.

"Intended?" she said. "If either of you had done your brother justice, I don't think I should have mentioned him at all."

Miss Weston smiled scornfully and moved away, but the blood crept into the face of the girl she left. That she had outraged these people's sense of their importance she felt reasonably sure, and their resentment, which she admitted was, perhaps, more or less warranted, did not trouble her, but the drift of Miss Weston's last observation filled her with anger. They evidently regarded her as a raw Colonial, endued with no sense of what was fitting, who could not expect to be countenanced by an insolvent land-owning family. This was amusing; but the suggestion that she recognized the fact, and because of it had endeavored to alienate Clarence Weston from his relatives, who had apparently been very glad to get rid of him, was a very different matter. However, she recovered her composure with an effort, and succeeded in taking a part in the general conversation which broke out when Weston drove away.

CHAPTER XIX

ILLUMINATION

It was three or four months later when Ida was carried swiftly westward through the London streets toward twelve o'clock one night. The motor purred and clicked smoothly, slinging bright beams of light in front of it as it twisted eel-like through the traffic. The glass that would have sheltered Ida from the cool night breeze was down, but she scarcely noticed the roar of the city or the presence of Arabella and Mrs. Kinnaird.

She was thinking of that afternoon at Scarthwaite, and wondering, as she had done somewhat frequently since then, what had impelled her to speak in that impulsive fashion. It had not been, as she now recognized, merely a desire to justify Clarence Weston in the eyes of his English relatives, for she had felt reasonably sure that this was a thing beyond accomplishment while he remained a railroad-hand or a bush chopper. The other explanation was that she had spoken to reassure herself; but that, as she would have admitted, seemed scarcely necessary, for in this respect he did not need an advocate. There was the third alternative, that the attitude of Weston and his daughter toward the absent man had fanned her dislike of shams into a blaze of downright rage, and that she had merely ridden a somewhat reckless tilt against her pet aversions.

One thing, at least, was certain. Weston had not called on her, to ask for any further information about his son; and, for that matter, she would have been astonished had he done so. She realized now that there was truth in what Clarence Weston said when he told her that the failures were soon forgotten. That, however, was a matter that depended largely on one's point of view, and she could not regard him as a failure.

There was in Ida Stirling a vein of wholesome simplicity which made for clearness of vision, and she seldom shrank from looking even an unwelcome truth squarely in the face. That Clarence Weston was probably shoveling railroad gravel did not count with her, but she was reasonably sure that the fact that she was a young woman with extensive possessions would have a deterrent effect on him. She once or twice had felt a curious compelling tenderness for him when in his presence, but reflection had come later, and she could not be sure that she loved him well enough to marry him, should he offer her the opportunity. During the last few months she had become more uncertain on this point, for her English visit was having an effect on her that she had not expected.

In the meanwhile the insistent clamor of the city was forcing itself on her attention, until at length she became engrossed by it. The theaters had just been closed, and the streets resounded with the humming of motors, the drumming of hoofs and the rattle of wheels. They also were flooded with what seemed to her garish light, for she had swept through many a wooden town lying wrapped in darkness beside its railroad track. The hansoms and motors came up in battalions, and in most of them she could see men of leisure in conventional white and black and lavishly dressed women, while the sidewalks streamed with a further host of pleasure-seekers. She wondered when these people slept, or when they worked, if indeed in one sense some of them worked at all. Even in the winter they had nothing like this in Montreal, and the contrast between it and the strenuous, grimly practical activity of the Canadian railroad camp or the lonely western ranch was more striking still. There men rose to toil with the dawn, and slept when the soft dusk crept up across solemn pines or silent prairie. These men, however, saw and handled the results of their toil, great freight-trains speeding over the trestles they had built, vast bands of cattle, and leagues of splendid wheat. After all, the genius of London is administrative and not constructive, and it is the latter that appeals most directly to the Colonial. One can see the forests go down or the great rocks rent, but the results that merely figure in the balance-sheet are less apparent.

There was another matter that claimed Ida's attention. She would meet Gregory Kinnaird at the dance, and she had seen a good deal of him during the last few months. He was not formal like his father, and in most respects she liked the man; and there was no doubt whatever that he neglected no opportunity for enjoying her company. Indeed, he had of late drawn rather close to her, and she wondered a little uneasily how far this approachment was to go. London, she was conscious, was getting hold of her, and there was, after all, a good deal it had to offer that strongly appealed to her.

By and by the motor stopped before a house with balconies and ponderous pillars, and she and her companions went up the ample stairway and into several uncomfortably crowded, flower-bedecked rooms. Ida, however, was getting used to the lights and the music, the gleam of gems, the confused hum of voices, and the rustle of costly draperies, and, though she admitted that she liked it all, they no longer had the same exhilarating effect on her. She danced with one or two men, and then, as she sat alone for a moment, Gregory Kinnaird crossed the room toward her. His face was a little more serious than usual. As a rule, he took things lightly.

"I think this is mine," he said, as the orchestra recommenced. "Still, perhaps you have had enough? I can find you a nice cool place where we can talk."

She went with him, because it certainly was uncomfortably warm where she was, and, besides, she was impelled by a certain curiosity to ascertain just how they stood. He passed through one supper-room into another, and then drew back a heavy curtain from an open window.

"It's quiet, anyway," he said, and they passed out on to a little balcony where, late in the year as it was, a row of potted shrubs cut them off from view.

Below, there were dusky, leafless trees, among which a few big lights gleamed, and the roar of the city came up across them brokenly. Ida sat down, and a ray of light fell upon her companion, who leaned against the rails. Gregory Kinnaird was well-favored physically, and bore the stamp of a military training. He was, she understood, captain of a rather famous regiment, and she liked his direct gaze, which did not detract from his easy suavity of manner. However, he appeared somewhat unusually diffident that evening.

"You like all this?" he asked, with a little wave of his hand which, she fancied, was intended to indicate the distant roar of the city as well as the music and dancing in the rooms behind her.

"Yes," she said with a smile, for he appeared to take it for granted, as others had done, that they had no brilliant social functions in Montreal. "I think I do; but when you have so much of it, the thing seems a little aimless, doesn't it?"

"Aimless?" inquired Kinnaird, who appeared to ponder over this until a light broke in on him. "Well," he admitted, "I suppose it is. Still, what else could half of them do?"

Ida laughed good-humoredly; and the man made a little expostulatory gesture.

"I generally avoid any discussions of that kind. They never lead to anything," he said. "I was wondering whether you could learn to like London as well as Montreal?"

"I don't know," replied Ida, in her most matter-of-fact manner.

"Oh," said her companion, "it seems a senseless question, but I want to explain. I have been offered an opportunity to go away—to do something—very soon. I should be away two years, at least; and as the notice is a short one, I have practically to make up my mind to-night."

It almost appeared that he had expected Ida to show some sign of interest, or, perhaps, concern, but none was perceptible.

"Where are you going?" she asked.

"To a colony in tropical Africa. They want somebody to hammer a native levy into shape and keep the niggers in some kind of order."

"Don't they have fever there?"

"I believe it isn't a particularly salubrious place," said Kinnaird, smiling, "but that kind of thing affects only some constitutions, and it makes promotion quicker."

Ida, who had perused a good many works of travel, knew a little about the fevers that afflict the country in question. In fact, she fancied that she knew more than the man did; but his careless indifference to the personal hazard pleased her. She noticed that he had spoken naturally, as he felt, without any idea of producing an effect on her.

"What is the result of that kind of work?" she asked.

"The result?" queried Kinnaird, with a puzzled air. "A battalion of thick-headed niggers with some slight knowledge of civilized drill, and, perhaps, a few stockades blown up in the bush."

Then, as he saw the half-veiled amusement in her eyes, a light seemed to break in on him.

"If one managed the thing efficiently, it would, perhaps, lead to the offer of a second-rate semi-administrative post somewhere else in the tropics, though I believe the emoluments are not what one could call liberal."

"That is all?"

"Yes," said Kinnaird. "I'm afraid one couldn't expect anything further."

Ida smiled rather curiously. She liked the man, but it was clear that his mental capacity had its limits. Though she would not have had him expatiate on the fact, she had expected him to realize that his mission was to uphold the white man's supremacy, and establish tranquillity, commerce and civilization in a barbarous land. It was, however, evident that he did not understand this. He was going out, as he said, to drill thick-headed niggers, and would, in all probability, content himself with doing that.

Then he turned toward her again.

"What it leads to doesn't matter very much. I've been getting away from the point," he said. "You see, I don't know whether I'm going at all, at the moment. It depends a good deal on what you have to say to me."

Ida started a little, though she had expected something of this kind. Still, she recovered her serenity quickly, and in a moment she looked at him inquiringly with calm eyes.

"I didn't mean to say anything for some while yet, but this thing has forced my hand," he said. "You see, I must let them know during the next day or two whether I'm going."

He broke off for a moment, and his manner became diffident.

"Miss Stirling," he added, "I think I fell in love with you the second or third time I saw you, if not the first, and as I have seen you rather often since then, you can, perhaps, imagine what I feel now. I'm afraid there is no very strong reason why you should look kindly on such a man as I am, but I came here to-night to ask if you would marry me."

Ida quietly met his gaze. The man was well-favored physically, honest, courteous and considerate, and in many ways she liked him. Indeed, she wondered with a certain uneasiness how far she had allowed the latter fact to become apparent, for it was quite another matter to marry him, as she now realized.

"Is this offer quite spontaneous?" she asked.

Kinnaird flushed a little, but she thought the more of him for the candor with which he answered her.

"In the first place, I believe my mother put the thing into my head," he admitted. "After that, it got hold of me—and I was rather glad that my people were apparently satisfied that it did. It promised to save trouble, for I should naturally have gone on with it if they had done their utmost to thwart me."

He broke off abruptly, and Ida met his gaze.

"Thank you," she said. "The honesty of that admission would have counted a good deal in your favor had the thing been possible."

The man straightened himself and clenched one hand.

"Ah!" he said. "Then it's quite out of the question?"

Ida saw the blood rise into his face, and noticed the sudden hardness in his eyes. Her answer evidently had hurt him more than she expected, and she felt sorry for him. The man's quietness and control and the absence of any dramatic protestation had a favorable effect on her, and she was almost certain that she could have married him had she met him a year earlier. In the meanwhile, however, she had met another man, dressed in old blue duck, with hands hard and scarred; and the well-groomed soldier became of less account as she recalled the man she had left in the mountains. Then Kinnaird turned to her again.

"Can't you give me a chance?" he said. "If it's necessary, I'll wait; and in the meanwhile I may do something worth while out yonder, if that's any inducement."

"I'm very sorry," replied Ida. "I'm afraid it wouldn't be."

She looked him steadily in the eyes, and he had sense enough to recognize that no words of his would move her. Though it was not an easy matter, he retained his self-control.

"Well," he admitted, "it hurts, but I must bear it. And I want to say that I'm glad in several ways that I met you." Then the blood crept into his face again. "I should, at least, like you to think kindly of me, and I'm rather afraid appearances are against me. Because that is so, there's a thing that I should like you to understand. I'd have been proud to marry you had you been a beggar."

"Thank you," said Ida, who saw that he meant it. "I'm more sorry than ever, but the thing is—out of the question."

Kinnaird gravely held out his arm, but she intimated by a little sign that she did not wish to go back with him, and in a moment the curtains swung to behind him, and he had gone.

Ida became conscious that she was growing cold; but she sat quite still for at least five minutes, thinking hard, and wondering why she felt so sorry to give up Gregory Kinnaird. It was a somewhat perplexing thing that one could be really fond of an eligible man and yet shrink from marrying him, and there was no doubt whatever that the one she had just sent away had in several respects a good deal to offer her.

She admitted that London was, as she expressed it, getting hold of her. She supposed that its influence was insidious, for she no longer looked on its frivolities with half-amused contempt, as she had at first. She realized the vast control that that city had over so much of the rest of the world, and that when some of the men with whom she had lightly laughed and chatted pulled the strings, new industries sprang up far away in the scorching tropics or on the desolate prairie, and new laws were made for hosts of dusky people. It was certainly a legitimate bargain Kinnaird had suggested. She had wealth sufficient for them both, and he could offer her the entry into a world where wealth well directed meant power, and this she undoubtedly desired to possess. There was a vein of ambition in this girl whose father had risen to affluence from a very humble origin, and while she listened to Gregory Kinnaird she had felt that she could rise further still.

She knew that she had will and charm enough to secure, with the aid of her father's money, almost what place she would, and for a few moments she saw before her dazzling possibilities, and then, with the resolution that was part of her nature, she turned her eyes away. After all, though a high position with the power and pride of leading was a thing to be desired, life, she felt, had as much to offer in different ways; and she recalled a very weary man limping, gray in face, up the steep range. The picture was very plainly before her as she sat there shivering a little, and her heart grew soft toward the wanderer. She knew at last why nothing that Kinnaird could have said or offered would have moved her, and she looked down at the lamps that blinked among the leafless boughs with a great tenderness shining in her eyes. The stir of the city fell faintly on unheeding ears, and she was conscious only of a longing for the stillness of the vast pine forest through which she had wandered with Weston at her side.

Then she rose abruptly and went back into the lighted room. Though she danced once or twice, and talked to a number of people who, perhaps fortunately, did not seem to expect her to say anything very intelligent, she was glad when Mrs. Kinnaird sent for her, and they and Arabella drove away together. The elder lady troubled her with no questions; but soon after they reached home she came into the room where Ida sat, and as she left the door open the girl saw Gregory go down the stairway with a letter in his hand. He met his sister near the foot of it, and his voice, which seemed a trifle strained, came up to Ida clearly.

"I'll just run out and post this. I've told those people that I'll go as soon as they like," he said.

Then Mrs. Kinnaird quietly closed the door before she crossed the room and sat down near the girl.

"It's rather hard to bear," she said. "Perhaps I feel it the more because Arabella will leave me soon."

The woman's quietness troubled Ida, and her eyes grew hazy.

"Oh," she said, "though it isn't quite my fault, how you must blame me. It's most inadequate, but I can only say that I'm very sorry."

"I suppose what you told Gregory is quite irrevocable?" inquired her companion.

Ida saw the tense anxiety in the woman's eyes, and her answer cost her an effort.

"Yes, quite," she said. "I wish I could say anything else."

"I can't blame you, my dear. I blame only myself," said Mrs. Kinnaird. "I'm afraid I brought this trouble on Gregory, and it makes my share of it harder to bear. Still, there is something to be said. I wanted Gregory to marry you because I wanted him near me, but I can't have you think that I would have tried to bring about a match between him and any girl with money. My dear," and she leaned forward toward her companion, "I am fond of you."

Ida made a gesture of comprehension and sympathy, and the little quiet lady went on again.

"There is just another thing," she said. "Gregory will have very little—a few hundred a year—but it would not have been a dreadfully one-sided bargain. He had, after all, a good deal to offer."

Ida raised a hand in protest.

"Oh," she said, "I know."

"Still," continued Mrs. Kinnaird, "I want you to feel quite sure that he loved you. Without that nothing else would have counted. You will believe it, won't you? It is due to my son."

She rose with a little sigh.

"Things never go as one would wish them to."

Ida was very sorry for her, but there was so little that could be said.

"I shall always think well of Gregory," she answered. "You will try to forgive me?"

Then an impulsive restless longing came over her with the knowledge that she had brought this woman bitter sorrow.

"I will go home," she broke out. "It will hurt you to see me near you when Gregory has gone away. There are friends of ours—Mrs. Claridge and her daughter, you met them—leaving for Paris on Wednesday, and they sail for New York in a week or two."

It was a relief to both of them to discuss a matter of this kind, and, before Mrs. Kinnaird left her, all had been arranged. Still, it was not Montreal and its winter amusements that Ida thought of then, but the shadowy bush, and the green river that stole out from among the somber pines.

CHAPTER XX

IDA CLAIMS AN ACQUAINTANCE

It was early on a fine spring evening when Clarence Weston lay somewhat moodily on the wooded slope of the mountain that rises behind Montreal. It is not very much of a mountain, though it forms a remarkably fine natural park, and from where Weston lay he could look down upon a vast sweep of country and the city clustering round the towers of Notre Dame. It is, from almost any point of view, a beautiful city, for its merchants and financiers of English and Scottish extraction have emulated the love of artistic symmetry displayed by the old French Canadian religious orders, as well as their lavish expenditure, in the buildings they have raised. Churches, hospitals, banks and offices delight the eye, and no pall of coal-smoke floats over Montreal. It lies clean and sightly between its mountain and the river under the clear Canadian sky.

On the evening in question the faintest trace of thin blue vapor etherealized its clustering roofs and stately towers, and the great river, spanned by its famous bridge, gleamed athwart the flat champaign, a wide silver highway to the distant sea. Beyond it, stretches of rolling country ran back league after league into the vast blue distance where Vermont lay. Still, Weston, who was jaded and cast down, frowned at the city and felt that he had a grievance against it. During the last week or two he had, for the most part vainly, endeavored to interview men of importance connected with finance and company promoting. Very few of them would see him at all, and those with whom he gained audience listened to what he had to say with open impatience, or with a half-amused toleration that was almost as difficult to bear. Perhaps this was not astonishing, as most of them already had had somewhat costly experiences with what they called wild-cat mining schemes.

There was, however, a certain vein of dogged persistency in Clarence Weston; and, almost intolerably galling as he-found it, he would still have continued to obtrude his presence on gentlemen who had no desire whatever to be favored with it, and to waylay them in the hotels, but for the fact that the little money he had brought with him was rapidly running out. One can, in case of stern necessity, put one's pride in one's pocket, though the operation is occasionally painful, but one cannot dispense with food and shelter, and the latter are not, as a rule, to be obtained in a Canadian city except in exchange for money. Weston, who had had no lunch that day, took out the little roll of bills still left in his wallet, and, when he had flicked them over, it became unpleasantly clear that he could not prosecute the campaign more than a very few days longer. Then he took out his pipe, and, filling it carefully, broke off a sulphur match from the block in his pocket. He felt that this was an extravagance, but he was in need just then of consolation. He had wandered up on the mountain, past the reservoir and the M'Gill University, after a singularly discouraging afternoon, to wait until supper should be ready at his boarding-house.

One or two groups of loungers, young men and daintily dressed women, strolled by; and then he started suddenly at the sound of a voice that sent a thrill through him. He would have recognized it and the laugh that followed it, anywhere. He sprang to his feet as a group of three people came out from a winding path among the trees. For a moment or two a wholly absurd and illogical impulse almost impelled him to bolt. He knew it was quite unreasonable, especially as he had thought of the girl every day since he had last seen her; but he remembered that she was a rich man's daughter and he a wandering packer of no account, with an apparently unrealizable project in his mind, and in his pocket no more money than would last a week. While he hesitated, she saw him. He stood perfectly still, perhaps a little straighter than was absolutely necessary, and not looking directly toward her. If she preferred to go by without noticing him, he meant to afford her the opportunity.

She turned toward her father and said something that Weston could not hear, but he felt his heart beat almost unpleasantly fast when, a moment later, she moved on quietly straight toward him. She looked what she was, a lady of station, and her companion's attire suggested the same thing, while, though Weston now wore city clothes, he was morbidly afraid that the stamp of defeat and failure was upon him. Much as he had longed for her it would almost have been a relief to him if she had passed. Ida, however, did nothing of the kind. She stopped and held out her hand while she looked at him with gracious composure. It was impossible for him to know that this had cost her a certain effort.

"Where have you come from? We certainly didn't expect to see you here," she said.

"From Winnipeg. That is, immediately," said Weston, and added, "I hired out to bring a draft of cattle."

Ida, who was quite aware that the tending of cattle on trains was not a well-paid occupation, and was usually adopted only by those who desired to save the cost of a ticket, fancied that she understood why he mentioned this, and was not sure that she was pleased. It was, as she recognized, the man's unreasonable pride which impelled him to thrust facts of that kind into the foreground. Just then, however, her father, who had waited a moment or two, stepped forward and shook hands with him.

"Where are you staying in the city?" he asked.

"At Lemoine's boarding-house," answered Weston, mentioning a street in the French Canadian quarter, from which any one acquainted with the locality could deduce that he found it desirable to study economy.

"Doing anything here?" asked Stirling.

Weston said that he had some mining business in hand; and he looked down at his clothes, when Stirling 'suggested that he should come' home with them to supper, though, from his previous acquaintance with the man, he was not astonished at the invitation. Stirling laughed.

"That's quite right," he said. "We call it supper, and that's how I dress. I don't worry about the little men when I bring them along, and the big ones don't mind."

Weston glanced at Ida, and when he saw that she seconded the invitation, he said that he would run around to his boarding-house first to see whether there were any letters or messages for him. Stirling made a sign of comprehension, for this was a thing he could understand. There had been a time when he had watched and waited for the commissions which very seldom came.

"Then you can come straight across as soon as you have called there," said Ida.

She presented him to her companion, who, it appeared, came from Toronto; and then she explained that they had climbed the mountain so that her friend might see the surroundings of the city. They walked back together until they reached a spot where two roads led downhill, and Weston left them.

It was some little time later when he reached Stirling's house, and was left to wait a few minutes in a very artistically-furnished room. Its floor was of polished parquetry with a few fine skins from British Columbia spread upon it here and there, and the dainty, spindle-legged chairs, the little tables, the cabinets and the Watteau figures were, he fancied, either of old French manufacture or excellent copies. The big basement heater had apparently been extinguished, but a snapping wood-fire blazed upon the English pattern hearth, and, for the light was fading outside, it flung an uncertain, flickering radiance about the room. Weston, sitting down, contrasted its luxury with the grim bareness of his match-boarded cubicle in the boarding-house, and with the log shanties of the railroad and logging camps. He frowned as he did so, for all that his eyes rested on made unpleasantly plain the distinction between himself and the girl whose room it evidently was.

Then he rose as she came in, attired in a long, trailing dress that rustled as she moved. It seemed to become her wonderfully, and he became conscious of a faint embarrassment. He had not seen her dressed in that fashion before, and, after the years that he had spent in lonely bush and noisy railroad camp, her beauty and daintiness had an almost disconcerting effect on him. She drew a low chair a little nearer the hearth, and, sinking into it, motioned to him to be seated.

"My father is busy, and Nellie Farquhar will not be down for a little while," she said. "We shall probably have half an hour to ourselves, and I want you to tell me all that you have been doing since we left you."

Weston understood that she meant to resume their acquaintance—though he was not sure that was quite the correct word for it—at the point at which it had been broken off, and he was rather glad that she asked him what he had been doing. It was a safe topic and naturally one on which he could converse, and he felt that any silence or sign of constraint would have been inadmissible.

"Oh," he said, "we went up to look for the mine again."

"You were not successful?"

"No," said Weston. "It was winter, and we had rather a rough time in the ranges. In fact, I got one foot frost-bitten, and was lame for some while afterward. It was the one I cut, which probably made it more susceptible."

His face hardened a trifle as he recalled the agony of the march back through the snowy wilderness, and the weeks he had afterward spent, unable to set his foot to the ground, in the comfortless log hotel of a little desolate settlement.

"Wasn't it rather foolish to go up into the ranges in winter?" Ida asked.

"It was," admitted Weston, with a faint, dry smile. "Still, you see, I couldn't stay away. The thing has become an obsession."

Ida fancied that she understood. He had on several occasions revealed to her his stubborn pride, and she knew that, whatever he thought of her, he would keep it to himself unless he found that mine. She also had some idea of what one would have to face floundering over the snow-barred passes into the great desolation in winter time.

"Well," she asked quietly, "what did you do then?"

"We worked in a logging camp until spring, and then I went down to Vancouver to raise money for the next campaign. Nobody seemed inclined to let me have any, for which one couldn't very well blame them. After all," and Weston laughed softly, "the thing looks uncommonly crazy. Later on, we got a pass to do some track-grading back east, on one of the prairie lines, and when we'd saved a few dollars I started to try my luck in Montreal."

Ida said nothing for a few moments. She could fill in most of what he left untold, and it seemed to her that one who knew how men lived in the lonely logging camps through the iron winter, or drove the new track across the prairie through the thaw slush in spring, could make an epic of such a theme. It was toil that taxed man's utmost strength of body and mind, under the Arctic frost, and, what was even worse to bear, in half-thawed mire. She had once seen the track-graders trooping back, wet to the skin, worn out, and clogged with soil to the knees, to the reeking shanty which was filled with the foul steam of drying clothes. As the result of it all, Weston had, perhaps, saved less money than she often spent on one gown. She felt very compassionate toward him, and he was troubled by the softness in her eyes. He felt that if he watched her too closely he might lose his head.

"I tried to study a few works on trigonometry and surveying during the winter, but it was a little difficult," he said. "For one thing, if you sat near the stove in the logging shack the light was dim, and you couldn't very well read anywhere else in the frost we had. Besides that, the boys generally insisted on everybody's playing cards, and if any one refused they had a playful trick of throwing things at him."

The girl, who had imagination, could picture the dimly-lighted shanty and the bronzed and ragged men flinging their long boots, as well as very pointed badinage, at the comrade who tried to read. It would, she admitted, certainly be a little difficult to study trigonometry in such surroundings.

"You see, I wanted to go into the thing systematically," continued

Weston, who felt that he was safest when he kept on talking. "We have decided that Verneille couldn't have made more than forty miles from the lake, and, as he was heading south, that gives us at most a sweep of about a hundred and twenty miles to search, though the whole of it is practically a nest of mountains. As I wasn't able to read up the subject quite as much as I should have liked, we have thought of hiring a professional surveyor and raising money enough to spend the whole summer over the thing, even if we have to let the men who help us take a share in the mine."

"I wonder whether you would be very much offended if some of your friends were to offer to bear part of the expense?" Ida asked quietly.

"I'm afraid I couldn't permit it." The man's face flushed. "They probably would never get their money back. After all, it's only a wild-cat scheme."

"That doesn't sound very convincing," said Ida. "Haven't you another reason?"

She had expected to find the suggestion useless when she made it, for she understood his attitude. He would not take her money, and that, of course, was in one respect just as she would have had it; but, on the other hand, there were so many difficulties, and probably hazards, that she could save him.

"Well," he said quietly, "it's the only reason I can offer."

There was silence for almost half a minute, and Ida felt that it was becoming singularly uncomfortable. So much could have been said by both of them that their conversation up to this point had suggested to her the crossing of a river on very thin ice. On the surface it was smooth, but the stream ran strong below, and there was the possibility that at any moment one of them might plunge through. Pride forbade her making any deliberate attempt to break the ice, but she would not have been very sorry had it suddenly given way. The man evidently was holding himself in hand, and she felt that she must emulate his reticence. She clung to the safe topic, in which she really was interested, as he had done.

"Won't you go on?" she asked. "You were not successful in Vancouver, and you tried to raise the money in Montreal. It's a little difficult, isn't it?"

"Oh, yes," said Weston, laughing, "as I'm situated, it certainly is. Of course, a good deal depends on how you set about this kind of thing, and the correct way would have been to come in on a Pullman instead of a cattle-car, and then engage a suite of rooms at the biggest hotel. Financiers and company jobbers seem rather shy of a man who gives Lemoine's boarding-house as his address, and some of them are not quite civil when they hear what he has to say to them. In fact, I'm afraid that I shall have to give them up in a day or two."

It was evident that he took his defeat quietly; but Ida thought that she knew what that quietness cost.

"How are you going to get back?" she asked.

She felt that it was rather a cruel question, for this was not the man to give up while he had a dollar in hand, and she was sure that he was going back to search for the mine again. Still, in one respect, she was a little vexed with him. His self-control was excellent, but there was rather too much of it.

"That," he said, with a whimsical twinkle in his eyes, "is a point that will require rather careful consideration."

Ida liked his smile, but the desire to startle him out of his reticence in one way or another became suddenly irresistible, and she changed the subject abruptly.

"I told you I was going to England," she said. "I wonder whether you would be surprised to hear that I spent a month or two at Scarthwaite Hall?"

Weston did not seem exactly astonished, but he was clearly disconcerted and off his guard.

"I heard that you did," he said.

"Then you know that I met your father and sister and didn't keep my promise, or, at least, that I didn't do what you wanted me to?"

"Yes," said Weston simply.

His quietness was too obvious, and she felt that it covered a good deal.

"One of them wrote you?" she asked.

"Yes," admitted Weston, "my father indulged in a few reproaches. He didn't seem to like the notion of my having served as your camp-packer. After that, you were in London?"

He was at fault on two points, for, though compelled to answer her, he should not have volunteered any information as to what was in the letter, nor should he have attempted to change the subject, for this made it clear to Ida that things had been said which he did not wish her to suspect. There would, of course, be reproaches, but it seemed probable that there would be a word or two of half-contemptuous advice as well, and she felt reasonably sure what this would be. Weston of Scarthwaite had, no doubt, suggested that the man of whom she had spoken so favorably would be a fool if he did not marry her. A trace of color crept into her face, and, seeing that there was a certain diffidence in her companion's manner, she felt that she hated Weston of Scarthwaite. It was, however, evident that silence would be too suggestive just then.

"I didn't make a promise, after all," she said. "Are you afraid that I gave your people a wrong impression about you?"

"No," replied Weston quietly, looking her in the eyes. "I know you would say nothing that was not kind of me. Still, the only thing that would affect my people would be the fact that I haven't succeeded at anything yet." He smiled rather grimly. "I'm not sure it wouldn't please them, in a way. You see, they probably expected it."

On the whole, both of them were glad that Miss Farquhar came in just then; and in a few more minutes Stirling appeared, and they went in to dinner. It was not a very elaborate meal, for the contractor, who had once toiled much as Weston had done, was, like a good many others of his kind, in some respects a simple and frugal man. Still, when Ida and Miss Farquhar left them, he laid a cigar-box on the table and filled Weston's glass with wine.

"Now," he said, "if you have no objections, you can tell me what you're doing in Montreal."

Weston supplied him with a brief account of his business, and Stirling, who asked one or two very shrewd questions, sat apparently reflecting for a minute or two.

"You struck nobody in Vancouver who seemed inclined to take a hand in it?"

"Only one concern, and they seemed very doubtful. Anyway, their terms were practically prohibitive."

"Grafton?"

"No. Norris & Lander."

"Well," said Stirling, "before you could expect to do anything here, you'd want to locate the reef and get some big mining man to visit it and give you a certificate that it was a promising property. If you had that, and a bag of specimens of high-grade milling ore, people would listen to you."

"The trouble is that I can't get them."

"Then," observed Stirling, "I guess you'll have to fall back on your friends."

"I'm afraid that none of my friends have any money to invest; and, in any case, I'd rather deal with strangers," said Weston.

His host glanced at him very keenly.

"Seems to me you have got to let the thing go," he said.

"No," declared Weston. "In some respects, it's a crazy project; but I'm going on."

Stirling quietly turned the conversation into another channel, but when Western took his departure he called up his secretary on the telephone.

"I want you to write Norris & Lander, Vancouver, the first thing in the morning, and get it off by the Pacific express," he said. "Tell them they can let a young man named Weston, with whom they've been in communication, have the money he asks for, to count as stock when he starts his company, at the biggest discount they can get. They can charge me usual brokerage, but they're to keep my name out of it."

The secretary said it should be done, and Stirling sat down to his cigar with a smile. He was inclined to fancy that Weston would find Norris & Lander much more amenable after that. It was an hour later when Ida came into the room, and he looked at her thoughtfully.

"There's some grit in that young man, and I guess it's just as well," he observed. "He's up against quite a big proposition."

He saw the faint gleam in Ida's eyes.

"If he has taken hold, I think he will put it through," she said.

She turned away the next moment, and moved a glass on the table; but, when she looked around again, she saw Stirling's smile.

"Well," he said, "considering everything, it's quite likely."

After this, he carefully picked out another cigar, and Ida left him, wondering what he could have meant.

CHAPTER XXI

THE BRÛLÉE

Stirling, who hitherto, like a wise man, had carefully avoided wild-cat mining schemes, and, indeed, ventures of any kind outside his own profession, had for once thrust his prudence into the background and done what he could to further Weston's project, for a reason which he would not have admitted to anybody else. He was not famous as a charitable person, but he had, for all that, unobtrusively held out a helping hand to a good many struggling men in need of it during his career, and there were now certain conjectures and suspicions lying half-formulated at the back of his mind. He had acted on them with the impulsive promptness which usually characterized him, and it was not his fault that his efforts proved fruitless, for Weston, as it happened, neither revisited Vancouver nor communicated with Norris & Lander.

A week after he left Montreal, Weston met Grenfell in a little British Columbian settlement shut in by towering ranges and leagues of shadowy bush, where they were fortunate enough to find a storekeeper who seemed inclined to place more credence in their story than any of the company promoters had done. What was more to the purpose, he offered to provide them with a horse, camp-gear and provisions, in exchange for a certain share in the mine should their search prove successful. The share was rather a large one, but, as the man pointed out, it was very probable that they might not strike the lode at all. They also made the acquaintance of a young surveyor who had set up in the wooden settlement several months earlier and had done very little business since. He was quite willing to give them the benefit of his professional services on somewhat similar terms to those the storekeeper had made.

The result of this was that early one morning they set out once more on the gold trail. When they made their first camp at sunset in a grove of towering pines they held a council. It was almost dark amidst the serried rows of tremendous trunks, but the light of the snapping fire fell upon their faces, which were all a trifle grave. In the case of two of the party, at least, their faces were stamped with a certain quiet resolution and a hint of the forcefulness which comes of rigid and continuous self-denial. Men discover in the bush that abstention from most of the little comforts and amenities of life not infrequently tends to vigor of body and clarity of mind. This, however, is a fact that has been accepted long ago, for it is not, as a rule, the full-fleshed, self-indulgent man who does anything worth while. Their skin was clear and bronzed, their nerves steady, and, though Grenfell differed from them in these respects, their eyes were very keen, with a snap in the depths of them. They were eyes that could look peril and defeat squarely in the face without flinching.

Devine, the young surveyor, laughed as he flung his empty enameled plate aside.

"It's quite a long time since I had a meal of that kind," he said. "After all, there is a certain satisfaction in the feeling that you couldn't eat very much more even if you had it, though that's an opportunity to which I've not been accustomed lately. I've made my supper rather frequently on half of a stale flapjack, and had the other half for breakfast the next day. Having admitted that, suppose we turn our attention to the proposition in front of us. You were heading south when you separated from Verneille, Grenfell?"

"About south. I can't be sure."

"That," observed the surveyor, "may mean anything between southeast and southwest; and if we take the spot where you found your partner afterward, and make a sweep with a forty-mile radius, which is what we've concluded was the distance he probably covered, it gives us quite a big tract of country to search. Still, we ought to find a lake that's a mile or two across."

Weston laughed softly.

"It's my third attempt, and I don't know how often Grenfell has tried. One could almost fancy that the lake has vanished. That sounds a little absurd, doesn't it?"

"Well," said Devine, with an air of reflection, "we won't admit that it's an impossibility. If you can take that for granted, it simplifies the thing."

Grenfell, who lay with his back against a fir trunk, roused himself suddenly.

"I never thought of it in that way," he said. "Still, lakes as big as that one don't vanish."

"Anyway, mines seem to do so. The woods are full of them, if all one hears is true."

"It isn't," said Weston dryly, "though I've no doubt there are a few lost mines. Are you sure you haven't done a crazy thing in joining us in the hunt for this one? Of course, I've tried to put that aspect of the matter squarely before you already."

Devine, who was a young man, flushed slightly.

"The cold fact is that I was only afraid you wouldn't take me. It's a big inducement to know that one has a reasonable supply of provisions in hand."

"You've evidently been up against it, like the rest of us," Grenfell suggested.

"I've lived for three months on the proceeds of the only job I got; and it's quite likely I shouldn't have held out if I hadn't been broken into the thing while I got through with my studies in Toronto. I don't quite know now how I did that, but I had to hire out between whiles, teaming and dredging up building stone from the lake, to make my fees, and now and then I lived on one meal a day to spin out the money. It would have been easier at the settlement, but I had a lesson soon after I put up my sign. Two city men sent up by a syndicate to look for a pulp-mill site and timber rights came along one hot day and found me splitting cedar shingles, with mighty few clothes on. The result was that while I might have made a small pile of money out of them, they sent back to Vancouver for another man and paid him twice as much, though they didn't locate the mill. I felt I had to tell you this."

It was not at all an uncommon story in that country, and when Weston looked at Grenfell with a smile, the latter waved his hand.

"Oh," he said, "we're a most worshipful company of broken dead-beats, fed on credit, and out on a forlorn hope; but it seems to me that the storekeeper who supplied us with provisions is the craziest of all the crowd."

"It was the broken men who made this country," said Devine.

There was a certain truth in this observation, as the rest of them knew, for, after all, it was the outcast and the desperate who first pushed grimly on into the wilderness, up tremendous defiles and over passes choked with snow, and afterward played a leading part in the Titanic struggle with nature in the strongholds where she had ruled supreme. The wilderness is merciless; the beaten men died, but the rest held on, indomitable; and now those who from the security of a railroad observation-car gaze upon orchard and oat-field, awful gorge and roaring torrent, can dimly realize what the making of that province cost the pioneers who marched into it with famine-worn faces and bleeding feet. That the valor of that army has not yet abated all are sure who know what the vanguard of the last host had to face on the trail to Klondyke a few years ago.

It is unpleasant to sleep in half-thawed slush around a sulky fire, or to grip canoe pole or paddle until one's swollen fingers will not straighten and the palms are raw. There is an exhilaration in plunging down a roaring rapid through a haze of spray, but it loses something of its charm when each movement required to keep the canoe straight causes the man who holds the paddle agony from the wounds the floor of the craft has rubbed on his knees; and a portage through tangled brushwood and over slippery rock around a fall forms a tolerably arduous task when he is stiff from constant immersion in very cold water and has had little to eat for a week or so. It is a little difficult to convey a clear impression of the sensation experienced during the execution of these and similar tasks, though they are undertaken somewhat frequently in that country, and, as it happens, the men most qualified to speak are not as a rule gifted with descriptive powers.

In any case, nobody answered Devine, and instead of moralizing they presently went to sleep. They were up at sunrise the next day, and started soon afterward on a march that led them through tangled pine bush, the tall grass of natural swamp prairies, rotting muskegs, and over stony hill-slopes. It was repeated with no great variation for several weeks, except that now and then they swam or ferried themselves on logs over very cold and rapid rivers. Still, thanks to the surveyor's professional skill, they were quartering the country systematically, and, though now and then they had to leave the horse at a base camp under Grenfell's charge, they had to grapple with no insuperable difficulty.

A good many leagues of range and forest had been traversed when they reached a tract where they had trouble in finding water. There was snow above them, but it either soaked down through the strata, or the drainage from it descended on the other side of the divide. It was also, though not quite summer yet, unusually hot weather, and the season had been exceptionally dry, and they had contented themselves for a week with the little muddy fluid they scraped up here and there from oozy pools that were lined with pine needles and rotting leaves, when they came to a big brûlée.

It filled a deep valley that was hemmed in by almost precipitous crags, and though charred logs and branches lay here and there, most of the burned forest was still standing. As a matter of fact, a fire in this region very seldom brings the trees down. It merely strips them. As the men pushed wearily on, endless ranks of blackened trunks moved steadily back before them. There was not a branch left. The trees were tremendous, half-calcined columns, and, for it was evident that any wild wind seldom entered the deep hollow, they might have stood in that condition a year or more. The trouble in traversing a brûlée is that one cannot tell when, from some cause or other, one of them may come down.

It was about noon, and they had with some difficulty dined on grindstone bread and canned stuff without a drink of any kind, when Weston, who was leading the horse, pulled it up suddenly. He was thirsty and short of temper, and in a mood that would have made it easier for him to smash through an obstacle instead of stopping, but he fancied that he saw a great blackened trunk close in front of him lean over a trifle. He was sure of it in another moment, and he urged the horse aside, for the towering column swayed and oscillated as though it strove to recover its equipoise, and then suddenly rushed earthward. He felt the wind it made strike cold upon his cheek, and then there was a deafening crash, and a cloud of fine black dust rose up. It whirled and eddied about him like the smoke of a great gun, and the powder that settled thick upon him clogged his eyelashes and filled his nostrils. The horse plunged viciously and came near dragging him off his feet.

After that there was for a few seconds a silence that seemed oppressive by contrast, until it was suddenly broken by another startling crash. It was repeated here and there, as though when each tree fell the concussion brought down another, and the brûlée was filled with shocks of sound that rang in tremendous reverberations along the steep rocks. In the meanwhile the men stood fast with tense, blackened faces peering at the eddying dust out of half-blinded eyes, until the crashes grew less frequent and there was deep silence again.

Then Weston, who patted the trembling horse, sat down and pointed to the great, shapeless pile of half-burned wood and charcoal close in front of him.

"A near thing. I think I'll have a smoke," he said.

"A smoke!" gasped Grenfell. "With your mouth and tongue like an ash-pit! I'd much sooner have a sherry cobbler, as they used to make it with a big lump of ice swimming in it, at the—it's the club, I mean. That is," he added, with a sigh, "if I could get it."

"You can't," observed Devine, dryly. "I'd be content with water. But didn't you break off rather suddenly in one place?"

"You're young," said Grenfell, looking at him solemnly. "If you weren't, I should regard that observation as an impertinence. I said the club, which is sufficient. They used to make you really excellent sherry cobblers there."

"Well," said Devine, with his eyes twinkling, "I guess it is, and the name was half out when you stopped. I was naturally never inside the place in question, but I've been in Montreal. It's kind of curious, isn't it, to find a man who talks about such things leading a forlorn hope, as you call it?"

"No," said Grenfell, "it isn't curious at all. There are cases in which a fondness for sherry cobblers provides a sufficient explanation for greater incongruities."

It was apparently a relief to talk of something, for there was no doubt that all of them had felt the tension of the last few minutes; but Weston cut short the discussion.

"We must get water to-morrow, anyway," he said. "Had you any trouble about it, Grenfell, the time you struck the lake?"

Grenfell sat down on a fragment of the charred log and seemed to consider.

"No," he said slowly. "That is, we didn't quite run out of it, though once or twice for several days we came across only a small creek or two. There were signs that in some seasons it would be a dry country."

He broke off and looked up at the range, while the faces of the others grew intent as they watched him.

"In a way all that's familiar," he said; "but I've felt the same thing in other places, and I can't be sure."

"Anyway," remarked Weston, "if there was a lake up yonder, the creek would naturally flow through the valley. It must have an outlet, and we're going up-grade."

"The creek," said Grenfell, sharply, "went down the other side. The lake lies just over a low divide."

Weston started a little and put away his pipe.

"Boys," he said, "we'll get on again."

They went on, and the memory of that afternoon long remained with them. They were grimed with black dust and ashes, and the ranks of charred trunks cast only thin strips of shade, while a scorching sun poured down an almost intolerable heat into the deep valley. The ground was ankle-deep in dust and charcoal, and, as they floundered through it, feathery ash rose in clouds. Their clothing grew crusted with it, and it worked through and irritated their heated skin; while every now and then one of them was compelled to stop and splutter. Their throats, as Grenfell remarked, certainly felt very much like ash-heaps. None of them had drunk anything since supper the night before, and then only a very little water that tasted alkaline.

Still, except for the loose deposit that made walking difficult, the ground was comparatively clear, and they pushed on, making a detour only now and then around a fallen tree, or waiting for Grenfell, who lagged behind and limped, until the slanting rays beat pitilessly into their faces and their aching eyes were dazzled by the burning glow. Then Grenfell sat down rather frequently.

"We're going northwest," said Weston once, while they waited for him. "You said that was how you headed the day before you struck the lake."

"Yes," said Grenfell, with an air of trying to recall something. "It was summer, and at sunset the light was in our eyes. There was a very rugged strip on the range—not unlike that one yonder. Still, I can't be sure."

Nothing more was said. It was quite clear that Grenfell's memory was not to be trusted, and they were in no mood for talking. They went on a little more slowly, but Grenfell lagged again, and it was a vast relief to all of them when the glare that hurt their eyes died out suddenly as the red sun dipped behind a wall of rock. Half an hour later the heat of the brûlée seemed to dissipate, and a wondrous invigorating coolness crept in with the dusk, when they made their camp and picketed the jaded horse. It did not seem worth while to light a fire, as they had no water to use for tea; and, after eating a little grindstone bread and salt pork cooked the previous day, they lay down rolled in their blankets.

CHAPTER XXII

GRENFELL GOES ON

Weston, tired as he was, did not sleep well that night. Although they had a pack-horse he had carried two blankets and a bag of flour, and when a man has marched from sunrise until dusk under a heavy burden, his shoulders, as a rule, ache distressfully. In addition to this discomfort, Grenfell's manner throughout that day's march had roused an unsettling sense of expectation in his comrades. The man had limped wearily and continually lagged behind, but he had, in spite of it, resolutely insisted on their pushing on as fast as possible. He had also looked about him with a certain suggestive curiosity every now and then, and though he had once or twice admitted that he could not positively identify anything he saw, his air of restrained eagerness had made its impression on Weston.

A half-moon had sailed up into the eastern sky when the latter wakened and raised himself drowsily on one elbow. All round him the great burned pines towered in black and shadowy columns against the silvery light, and a stillness that was almost oppressive brooded over the valley. No sound of running water came out of it, and there was not a breath of wind. It was cool, however, and Weston drew his dusty blanket higher about his shoulders as he glanced round the camp. Devine lay close by sleeping like a log; but Grenfell was huddled at the foot of a tree, and it became evident to his comrade that he, at least, was wide awake.

"Haven't you done enough to make you sleep?" Weston asked.

Grenfell laughed softly.

"I haven't closed my eyes. I can't keep them off the range in front of us."

Weston looked up and saw a huge black rampart cutting sharp and clear against the blueness of the night.

"Don't tell me that you recognize it," he said.

"Three nicks," replied Grenfell. "After the third one, a rounded peak. I can't tell whether I remember it from another time, but that description came to me as if I'd used it, and I think I must have done so. Anyway, you can see them yonder."

He broke off for a moment, and when he went on again his manner was deprecatory.

"Since sunrise I've been troubled with a haunting sense of the familiar, though when I found the lake with Verneille we marched through no brûlée."

"That's years ago, and this brûlée is probably not more than twelve months old—I mean as a brûlée," said Weston, impatiently, for the strain of the long march was telling on him. "Anyway, you've been half-recognizing places ever since we started on this search, and I'd rather you didn't make half sure of anything else. In fact, I can't stand much more of it."

Grenfell, who showed no sign of resentment, laughed again.

"As I think I told you, I've been troubled with memories that seem half dreams. I'm not sure that's quite unusual in the case of a man who has consumed as much whisky as I have. Besides, it's a little difficult to distinguish between dreams and what we look upon as realities, since the latter exist only in the perception of our senses, which may be deceptive. They agree on that point, don't they, in places as dissimilar as India and Germany?"

"Are you sure you didn't dream about the lead?" Weston asked bluntly. "It's a point that has been troubling me for a considerable time."

"Then why did you come up with me to search for the lake?"

"I was once or twice told at home that I was a persistent imbecile. That may account for it."

"Well," said Grenfell, reflectively, "your action on one or two occasions seems to warrant the observation—I mean when you stood the boys off me after I'd spoiled their supper, and the other time when you decided on my account not to stay on at the copper-mine. Still, I want to say that while I seem to know I will not make another journey on the gold trail, I've had a subconscious feeling of certainty since sunrise yesterday that the lake lies just ahead of us. I know nothing definite that justifies it, but we'll probably find out to-morrow. There's just another thing. If I leave my bones up here my share falls to you."

He seemed disinclined for any further conversation, and Weston went to sleep again. When he awakened the moon had sunk behind the range, and a faint gray light was filtering down beneath the blackened pines. It showed the pack-horse standing close by, and Devine stretched out beneath his blanket, a shadowy, shapeless figure, but there was, as far as Weston could see, no sign of Grenfell anywhere. He called out sharply as soon as he was sure of this, and his voice rang hollowly up the valley, but there was no answer until Devine slowly shook clear of his blankets.

"What's the matter?" he asked.

"Grenfell's gone."

"Gone!" Devine was on his feet in a moment.

"It looks like it," said Weston, sharply. "Can you see him?"

Devine gazed into the shadows, but he saw nothing beyond the rows of dusky trunks.

"Where's he gone?"

"That," said Weston, "is naturally just what I don't know. It's up to us to find out."

Then he briefly related his conversation with Grenfell, and the two looked at each other. There was just light enough to show the anxiety in their faces.

"Well," said Devine, "it's quite clear to me that he's on the trail; and it's fortunate in one way that he's left a plain trail behind him. Whether the whole thing's a delusion on his part, or whether he did strike that lode, I don't know, but I didn't like the man's looks yesterday. He seemed badly played out, and it kind of struck me he was just holding on." He turned toward the pack-horse and pulled up the picket. "Anyway, we'll get upon his trail."

They both were men of action, and inside of five minutes they had lashed their packs together and started without breakfast. Weston led the horse, while Devine picked up Grenfell's trail. Weston was a little astonished at the ease with which his companion did this.

"It's quite simple," said the surveyor, when the other stopped a moment where the footprints seemed to break off, and questioned his decision. "He's heading straight on, and not walking like a man with much strength in him. I wish I knew just how far he is ahead of us." Then he added in explanation: "I went east for a while, but I was raised in this country, and this is 'way easier than trailing a deer."

They went on a little faster after that, for Devine had promptly picked up the trail again, and by the time the red sun had cleared the range it led them out of the brûlée and into a waste of rock and gravel, where there were smaller firs and strips of tangled undergrowth. Here and there Devine stopped for a few minutes, but he found the trail again, though it led them through thickets, and now and then they floundered among half-rotten fallen trunks and branches. Fortunately, the horse was a Cayuse and used to that kind of work.

It rapidly grew hotter, until the perspiration streamed from them, and Weston, who had eaten very little the previous evening, became conscious of an unpleasant stitch in his side; but they pushed on without flagging, urged by a growing anxiety. At length the ground, which was a little clearer, rose sharply in front of them. Weston pulled up the pack-horse and looked significantly at Devine, who nodded.

"Yes," he assented, "he said a low divide. The lake lay just beyond it."

Then he cast about with his eyes fixed on the loose gravel over which they had scrambled, until he came to a spot where a wide patch of half-rotted needles lay beneath another belt of pines.

"He stopped here and sat down," he commented. "Seemed to have had some trouble in pulling out again. I don't like those footsteps. You and I don't walk like that."

"Get on," said Weston, sharply, and, turning, struck the horse.

The sun was overhead when they scrambled, gasping, over the crest of the divide and looked down into another long, winding hollow. Then they stopped again and looked hard at each other, for the hollow seemed filled with forest, and there was nowhere any shimmer of shining water.

"He can't be far ahead. Went through those vines in front of you," said Devine.

Then ensued an hour's wild scramble through undergrowth in shade, until they broke out, dripping with perspiration, from the gloom among the pines into a comparatively open space on the edge of a wide belt of willows. They left the horse tethered on the outskirts of the latter; and twenty minutes afterward Devine, who had scrambled up and down among the undergrowth, stopped suddenly.

"Come here," he cried with a suggestive hoarseness. "We're through with this trail."

He was standing waist-deep among the tangled brushwood, and it was a minute before Weston smashed through it to his side. Then he, too, stopped and started, for he saw a huddled object in tattered duck lying face downward at his comrade's feet. The latter made a little gesture when he met Weston's eyes.

"We'll make sure," he said quietly. "Still, you see how he's lying."

Weston dropped on his knees, and with some difficulty turned the prostrate figure over. Then he took off his battered hat and looked up at Devine with it in his hand. The latter nodded.

"Yes," he said, "he has pulled out once for all. Started two or three hours ago on a trail we can't pick up yet."

They drew back a little and sat down heavily on a ledge of stone, for the sight of the huddled figure in the tattered duck troubled them. It was a minute or two before either of them spoke.

"Heart trouble of some kind," said the surveyor. "If not, it isn't going to matter."

He looked around at his companion with a little wave of his hand which seemed to deprecate the mention of the subject.

"He can't tell us now where that lode is."

Weston said nothing for a minute. After all, there was so little that could be said. Then he stretched himself wearily.

"There is something to be done, but I don't feel quite equal to it yet, and I'm parched with thirst. Willows grow only where there's water."

"These," said Devine, "look kind of sickly. You can see quite a few of them have dried up; but it's a sure thing they had water to start them. Wish I knew how to strike it. It's most three days since I had what one could call a drink."

"Did you ever hear of water-finding?"

"Yes," answered Devine. "I've read a little about the old country. Kind of old English charlatanry, isn't it?"

"Well," said Weston, simply, "I could find water once upon a time. I know that, because I've done it."

"Don't you need a hazel fork? You can't get one here."

"I don't think the hazel matters. The power is in the man. I can cut a fork out of something."

Devine made a little gesture which seemed expressive of resignation.

"Well," he said, "whether we go on or go back we have to have a drink. That's a sure thing; and I feel, like you, that I want it before we set about the work that's awaiting us."

After that they both sat still again. They had to decide whether they would go back or go on, and both of them realized what the decision would be. Their guide had left them, and the last expectation of finding the lead had melted away. At first the sight of his dead comrade had driven all other thoughts from Weston's mind, but now he was compelled to admit that he had wasted time and money on a delusion. That perhaps was no great matter in itself, but it made it clear that all he could look for was to earn food and shelter as a packer, logging-hand, or wandering laborer. Impassable barriers divided Ida Stirling from a man of that kind, and he dare no longer dream of the possibility of tearing them down. At last, and the knowledge was very bitter, he was face to face with defeat. He forgot for the moment that Grenfell lay just beyond the tangled undergrowth. He gazed straight in front of him, with a hard hand clenched and a look in his wavering eyes that puzzled his companion. At length he raised himself wearily to his feet. After all, the needs of the body would not be denied, and, as Devine had said, before they set about the task that awaited them they must drink.

"Well," he said hoarsely, "I'm going to cut a fork."

He smashed back through the undergrowth toward the pines, unlashed the ax from the horse's back, and, though he was never afterward sure whether he cut it from a young fir or a bush of juniper, Devine came upon him some time later trimming a forked twig with a short stem where the two slender branches united. The surveyor glanced at it and smiled.

"Any water that ran into this hollow must have come from the range," he said. "We'll try close beneath it and give the thing a show."

They did as he suggested, and his expression was sardonically incredulous when Weston proceeded along the foot of the hillside, where the ground was a little clearer, with a branch of the fork clutched in each hand. The pointed stem was directed almost horizontally in front of him, and it remained in that position for about twenty minutes, when he lowered it with a gesture of discouragement.

"Felt nothing yet?" Devine inquired eagerly. "There's a kind of hollow yonder running into the thicket."

Weston made no answer, but he turned in among the willows, and for half an hour or so they stumbled and floundered among the clinging branches. Still there was no deflection of the fork, and when at length they stopped again, gasping and dripping with perspiration, Devine laughed rather grimly.

"Oh, give it a rest; I guess that's what it wants," he said. "I'll hang on for another half-hour, and then I'm going prospecting on my own account. We've got to strike water."

That, at least, was evident. They were parched with thirst and it was very hot. No breath of air seemed to enter that dense thicket, and a cloud of tormenting flies hung about them. Weston's head was throbbing with the heat, and his sight seemed dazed. Both of them were dusty, ragged, grim of face, and worn with travel, and the longing for even a few drops of muddy liquid was becoming almost insupportable.

It was only by a strenuous effort that Weston went on again. He felt scarcely capable of further exertion, but he could not overcome the horrible bodily craving that seemed to grow stronger with every pulsation of his fevered blood, and he plodded on into the thicket very wearily. At length Devine saw the twig bend downward for a moment in his hands,

"You did that?" he asked sharply.

"No," said Weston in a strained voice, "I certainly did not."

"Let me take hold," said Devine, and when Weston handed the fork to him he walked back a few paces and crossed the same spot again. The fork, however, pointed straight in front of him. He threw it down and said nothing, but Weston looked at him with a little grim smile.

"I've heard it said that anybody could do it, but that's not my experience," he observed.

Devine's gesture might have expressed anything.

"Oh, we were both crazy when we started with Grenfell," he said.

Weston moved forward with the fork, and, while Devine looked on, the stem once more inclined. It wavered, tilted downward a little farther, and then slowly swung back to rest again. Still, Weston held on, and when there was a further inclination it became clear that his companion was convinced.

"The thing's picking up the trail!" he exclaimed.

For a time they wandered up and down the thicket, Weston apparently directing his course by the spasmodic movements of the fork, which now and then would lie still altogether. At length it commenced to jerk sharply, and Devine looked at his companion in a curious manner.

"It's heading right back for Grenfell," he said in a hoarse whisper.

They went on until they almost reached the spot which they had left more than an hour ago. Then the fork suddenly pointed straight downward, and Weston stopped. His face was flushed, and his voice was sharp and strained.

"Go and bring the shovel!" he said.

Devine strode into the bush, and Weston struggled through the undergrowth to where Grenfell lay, scarcely a stone's throw away. Stripping off his jacket, he laid it over the dead man to keep off the flies. Then he went back and sat down with a dazed look in his eyes until the surveyor broke out from among the trees with the shovel.

"Sit still," said Devine, "I'll go down the first foot or two, anyway."

Weary as he was he plied the shovel savagely, flinging out the mould in showers, but he was knee-deep in the hole before there was a clink as the blade struck stones.

"Gravel. The water would work right through that," he said.

He toiled on until the hole was a yard in depth, but the gravel he flung out was dry, and at length he stopped and sat on the side of the excavation, gasping.

"Nothing yet," he said. "You're sure you struck it?"

"Yes," replied Weston, quietly, "I'm sure."

Once more Devine seized the shovel, but in a moment he flung it down suddenly, with a sharp, glad cry.

"It's sluicing out!"

Weston rose and strode to the edge of the hole. There was a little water in the bottom of it, and this spread rapidly until it crept up about his comrade's boots. In one place he could see a frothing, bubbling patch with an edge that was crystal clear. Then Devine stooped and, filling his wide hat, held it up to him dripping.

"We're through with one trouble, anyway," he announced exultantly.

CHAPTER XXIII

THE LODE

Weston, sitting down on the pile of gravel, took the hat from his comrade, and the trickle from the brim of it splashed refreshingly upon his hot and grimy face when he tilted it to drink. It was shapeless, greasy, and thick with dust, and few men who fare daintily in the cities would have considered it a tempting cup. That, however, did not occur to Weston, but another thought flashed into his mind as he glanced toward the undergrowth behind which the man who had led them there lay. He lowered the hat a moment and rose wearily.

"A few drops of this might have saved our partner," he said. "Now he has gone on; may the trail he has taken be a smooth and easy one."

Then he drank, standing, a deep, invigorating draught, which seemed to cool his fevered blood and put new life in him. He gasped for a moment or so, and drank again, and then, flinging wide the splashes upon hot earth and leaves, sat down heavily. As he fumbled for his pipe, Devine, who had drunk in the meanwhile, turned to him.

"No," he said reflectively, "I don't quite think you're right. It wasn't thirst that brought Grenfell to his end. He had more water than either of us—you saw to that—and, though it wouldn't have been pleasant, you and I could have held out another day."

"What was it then?" asked Weston.

"The strain of the journey on a played-out constitution, and, as I think I suggested, the effect of excitement on a diseased heart. The man was under a high tension the last day or two. It's a sure thing he had something on his mind. After all, I guess it was a delusion."

Weston said nothing, but lay still with his pipe in his hand. There was before him a task from which he shrank, but he was worn-out and could not nerve himself to undertake it yet, and in the meanwhile he thought of his dead comrade with a certain regretful tenderness. The man had had no claim on him, and there had been much that was dissimilar in their natures, but they had, after all, borne many hardships together, and that counted for a good deal. Still, in one way he could not be sorry that Grenfell had gone on, for life, as he had said, had very little to offer this outcast. It was clear that the same thing held true in his own case, and he remembered with a little wry smile that Grenfell had said his share was to go to him if they found the mine. They had not found it, and there was no prospect of their doing so, for his faith in the project had vanished now that Grenfell was dead. It remained for them only to go back to the settlements, defeated.

At length Devine broke in upon his reflections.

"I don't know whether you remember that we've had nothing since supper last night," he said. "Anyway, I don't feel equal to undertaking what's before us as I am. Seems to me the pack-horse would like a drink, too."

Weston felt a little guilty, for the events of the past hour had driven all thought of the beast out of his mind. Going back for it, he led it to the water, after which they made a simple meal. When it was over, Devine stood up resolutely.

"Now," he said, "there's a thing that must be done."

They set about it, and in another hour had laid to rest the man who had brought them there. Then Devine put down his shovel and turned to Weston.

"This thing has had its effect on me, and I guess you feel it too. He was your partner quite a while," he said. "We want to get a move on and work this depression out of us. Well, you can make camp—a little farther back—while I crawl along between the willows and the range. I want to see what's back of them. There's an idea in my mind."

Weston, who did not ask him what it was, fell in with the suggestion, and, when his comrade floundered away through the willows, proceeded to pitch the camp and build a fire ready for lighting among a few straggling firs a little back from the water. Then he went to sleep, and when the horse awakened him as it strove to pull out its picket to get another drink, he was a little astonished to see that the sun now hung low down above one range, and that Devine had not come back. He lay still, however, in the blissful content that only the worn-out know when, for a few hours, they can cease from toil. Presently he heard the willows rustle, and, though it cost him an effort, he stood up when Devine strode into camp. The latter glanced toward the hole they had dug to reach the water.

"You've let the horse break the sides down and stand in it," he said. "We'll clean it down to the gravel and pitch the soil out."

"Is it worth while?" Weston asked.

"Yes," said Devine, dryly, "as we'll probably be here a day or two, I guess it is. I'll tell you about it when we get supper."

Weston might have noticed that there was something curious in his manner, but he was very weary, and his mind was a little hazy then. He took the shovel, and toiled for some few minutes before a strip of stone he was endeavoring to wrench out broke beneath the blade. He flung the fragments out of the hole, and one of them caught Devine's eye.

"Pitch me up that big round stone," he said sharply.

Weston did as he was bidden, and his comrade, falling upon his knee, smashed the fragments into little lumps, and then, clutching some of them tight in one hand, stood up with a hoarse, exultant laugh.

"We've struck the lode!" he exclaimed.

Weston was beside him in a moment, and Devine poured the crushed fragments into his hand.

"Look!" he said.

Weston did so, and while his heart thumped painfully the blood crept to his face. The little lumps he gazed at were milky white, and through them ran what seemed to be very fine yellow threads.

"That is wire gold?"

"It is," said Devine. "A sure thing."

Then the surveyor swept off his battered hat and swung round toward the willows, a grotesque ragged figure with his hands spread out.

"You weren't crazy, partner. You brought us up out of the swamps and sloos of poverty, and planked us down right on to the lode," he said.

Weston said nothing. After all, he was English, and to some extent reticent, but he felt that his comrade's dramatic utterance was more or less warranted, for the irony and pathos of the situation was clear to him. Grenfell had found the mine at last, but the gold he had sought so persistently was not for him. Men great in the mining world had smiled compassionately at his story, others with money to invest had coldly turned their backs on him, and it had been given to a railroad hand and a surveyor, who had longed for an opportunity for splitting roofing shingles in return for enough to eat, to prove that, after all, the skill he had once been proud of had not deserted him. He had patiently borne defeat, and now the thrill of the long-deferred triumph had crushed him out of existence.

In a moment or two Devine spoke again in a different tone.

"Well, we'll get supper. You want to cool off and quiet down."

Weston felt that this was true, and it was a relief to start the fire and prepare the meal, for he had found the rush of emotion which had swept over him almost overwhelming. It was, however, not until the meal was ready that he was quite master of himself, and they ate it before they said anything further about the matter. Then Devine took out his pipe, and lying with his back against a fir, turned to his comrade as the soft dusk settled.

"Whether Grenfell knew where he was going when he started out last night, or was led by some blind impulse or subconscious memory, is more than I can tell, and, anyway, it's not a point that greatly matters now," he said. "The cold fact is that you struck the water on the creek where, as he told you, he once got a drink."

"But things don't fit in," objected Weston.

"Oh," said his companion, "you let me talk. You've been in this country a few years. I was raised in it. He said that a creek ran from the range, and, though there's mighty little water in it, I guess it does that now. There's rock, milling rock shot with gold, under it, and a small flow of water will filter a long way through gravel."

"But he described it as an ordinary open creek," persisted Weston.

"That's easy," said Devine. "It was, quite a while ago, and nature handles these mountains mighty roughly, as you ought to know. She sweeps them with cloudbursts that wash half a hillside into the valleys, and now and then with snowslides and tremendous falls of rock. One of them filled up that creek, and, as far as I can figure, it did rather more. It filled up the gully through which the creek flowed high up on the range, and, while a little water still creeps through, most of the melted snow goes down another creek. As I took the trouble to ascertain, it splits right through the lower slopes and comes out most a league away."

This seemed reasonable. Most of the streams among those ranges originate, as Weston knew, in the melting snow, but there was still a point his comrade had left unexplained.

"Then where's the lake?" he asked.

Devine laughed.

"You're sitting right beside it now."

Weston gazed at him in blank astonishment, and then a light broke in on him.

"The willows?" he said. "The water in that creek would no doubt spread underground, and this is evidently an unusually dry season. Still, Grenfell spoke of a mile or two of water. Where has it gone?"

"That," explained Devine, "seems the simplest thing of all. Anyway, I'll give you my theory. When I crawled along the edge of the willows this afternoon, I found the outlet of an old creek and a beaver-dam. Now we're assuming that the creek I've mentioned once ran into the lake just here, that is, before a snowslide filled up the ravine with debris and diverted the creek into the other gully, the mouth of which is—below—the beaver-dam."

"You have explained how the water got here, not how it got away," said Weston, impatiently.

"No," replied Devine. "I haven't explained either of them yet; but we'll get on a little. Once, and I don't think it was very long ago, there was a little water with a creek flowing out of it in this hollow. A colony of beavers came along and put up their dam across that creek, and that backed the water up a foot or two. If you'd skirted this hollow you'd have seen that it's tolerably level, and a foot rise would spread the water quite a way. I want to say that it was probably a swamp with only grass on it when the creek ran through it. Well, the beavers liked the place, and piled up their dam, while the water went farther and farther back across the swamp. Finally, the beavers either died off or something drove them out. It was probably after that that the dam broke down and the water ran off. Then the snowslide cut off the creek, and as the hollow dried out the willows spread across it."

Weston could find no fault with this train of reasoning, which made comparatively plain Grenfell's long and unsuccessful search.

"Yes," he admitted, "it's logical, and I think it's correct. I believe, from what Grenfell once said, that he crossed the range to the east of us, not far away, some years ago with another man, and he must have noticed this valley. Further, I now feel reasonably sure that he and I once stood on the shoulder of the big peak in the southwest and looked right up the hollow." He smiled rather grimly. "We naturally saw nothing. We were looking for a lake that had dried out."

He lay still for a minute or two, and then broached the subject that both had held in abeyance.

"Well," he said, "what's to be done?"

"Stay here two days," advised Devine. "Gather up a load of specimens and try to trace the vein. Then we'll put in our stakes, and start right off for the settlement, to record as many feet of frontage as the law will allow us. After that, you, as holding the larger share, will see what can be done about handing it over to a company, while I come back with provisions and get the assessment work put in. You're going to have mighty little trouble about raising the money when people see those specimens."

He broke off for a moment and glanced back toward the willows.

"In a way," he added, "it's rough on Grenfell."

"Ah," said Weston, quietly, "neither you nor I can be sure of that."

After that there was silence, and it seemed to both of them that the shadows crept in closer about their flickering fire, and that the little wind which sighed among the pine-tops had grown colder. The camp seemed strangely empty, and, glancing around from force of habit once or twice, they realized with a little start that there was now no third figure sitting beside the blaze. The man who had made that weary march with them had taken the unmarked trail.

It was two days later when they started south. Reaching a little desolate settlement in due time, without misadventure, they limped into it, ragged and dusty, leading the pack-horse, which was very lame. They stopped outside a little wooden store which had a kind of rude veranda in front of it, where the loungers sat on hot afternoons, and a man in a white shirt and store trousers came out and leaned on the railing. He had a hard face, and it grew a trifle more grim as he looked at them, for the light had not quite gone, although it was late in the evening.

"Where's Grenfell?" he asked.

"Dead," said Weston.

The man made a gesture of resignation. He had acquired his money with some difficulty, and there was no great trade in that neighborhood, while it not infrequently happened that his customers failed to pay him when the Government became economical and voted no money for the making of roads, which is the small bush rancher's chief source of support.

"Well," he said, "I'm sorry. You're broke?"

They certainly looked it, and for a moment Weston said nothing. He was aware that there was a spice of cruelty in this, but he was curious to see what the man would do. It became evident that he could, at least, face an unpleasant situation with equanimity.

"Anyway," he said, "you can come right in, and I'll get you some supper. You can put the horse in Musgrave's stable yonder."

Then, while Devine laughed softly, Weston strode up to the veranda and thrust a heavy bag into the storekeeper's hand.

"Get a light," he said, "and look at them."

It was ten minutes later when they sat around a little table in the back store, which smelt unpleasantly of salt pork and coffee. A big kerosene lamp hung above their heads, and the storekeeper gazed with almost incredulous eyes at the litter of broken stones in front of him.

"Oh, yes," he said, "it's high-grade milling ore. You'll say nothing to the boys, and get your record in to-morrow. Then what's your program?"

"I'll go on to Vancouver and see about getting a well-known mining man to go up and certify my statements," said Weston. "Then I'll try to raise sufficient money to make a start with. I ought to get it there or in Victoria."

"No," said the storekeeper, "you go on to Montreal. They've more money yonder, and it's good policy to strike for the place you're likely to get the most."

"One understands that it's difficult for the little man who has a claim to sell to get much for it anywhere," said Weston, with a smile.

The storekeeper straightened himself resolutely in his chair.

"That's a cold fact, but in this case it has to be done. I got my money hard." In proof of it he held up one hand from which three fingers were missing. "That was the result of working sixteen hours right off in a one-horse sawmill. We had one light above the bench, and when I was too played out to see quite what I was doing I got my hand drawn in. I made the rest of my pile—it's a mighty little one—much the same way, and now I'm holding tight to what is mine. I provided your outfit, for, crazy as it seemed, I believed Grenfell's tale, and I figured that you were straight men; but I know what generally happens when the little man goes around the city with a mine to sell."

He brought his hand down upon the table with a bang.

"You're going right into Montreal—I'll find the money—and you'll stand off just as long as it seems advisable for the biggest figure. When this thing's floated, we're going to get our share."

Weston, who sat on a packing-case because there was only one chair, glanced around the store. Its walls were of undressed pine logs, and it was roofed with cedar shingles hand-split. There were a few dozen bags of somebody's "Early Riser" flour standing upon what appeared to be kegs of nails, and across the room odd cases of canned goods, lumps of salt pork, and a few bags of sugar apparently had been flung together any way. Building and stock were of the crudest description, and there was certainly nothing about either that suggested any degree of prosperity. Then he glanced at his companions: the storekeeper, dressed in shirt and trousers of a kind that no fastidious man would think of wearing, and Devine, who had worn-out boots and was suggestively ragged and lean. They did not look the kind of men who were likely to pit themselves successfully against opulent financiers and stock-jobbers in Montreal, but something in their grim faces suggested that at least they meant to fight.

"Well," he said, "I'll start to-morrow, and do what I can. It's quite likely that before we put the thing through we'll have trouble."

CHAPTER XXIV

A QUALIFIED SUCCESS

Ida Stirling was sitting by an open window of a very artistically-furnished room, with an English newspaper lying on the little table beside her, and *The Colonist*, which is published in British Columbia, on her knee. She fancied from the writing on the wrapper that Arabella Kinnaird had sent her the former, and there was a paragraph in it which had interested her more than a little.

Trouble, it seemed, had broken out up a muddy African river, and a white officer lying sick of fever at the time had forthwith set off for the scene of it, with a handful of half-drilled black soldiery. They had vanished into the steamy bush, and for several weeks nothing had been heard of them; then, when those acquainted with the country had decided that the little detachment had probably been cut off to a man, half of them had unexpectedly appeared again. They now carried their leader in a hammock, as he had been wounded by several pieces of cast-iron fired out of a gaspipe gun; but they also brought back the dusky gentlemen who had been responsible for the abortive rising. Gregory Kinnaird had, it transpired, blundered into a couple of ambushes, but that, and the fact that he had marched straight through them, did not astonish Ida, who was more or less acquainted with his character. He was, the paper stated, recovering from his injuries, though it judiciously refrained from mentioning whether the authorities applauded or censured him.

It was not an uncommon story in connection with the country in question, but it sent a little thrill through the girl as she read it. The rising from the sick-bed and the blundering into the ambuscades were so characteristic of the man. He had recognized what was expected of him, and had immediately set about doing it, without any consideration for his safety, or, indeed, for that of his men. Gregory Kinnaird was not a man of marked ability, but he was, at least, one who could be relied on to attempt the carrying out of a duty he had undertaken, at any cost to himself, and this is, after all, a good deal to say in the favor of any man.

Ida had thought of him with a certain tenderness during the last half-hour. She liked these simple, downright men, and fancied that the absence of ostentation which usually characterized them was essentially English, though she had certainly met a few in that country who came under quite a different category. They were continually posing; men who could not afford to be natural lest they should give themselves away. Though she liked him, Gregory Kinnaird had, however, passed out of her life. There was a good deal he could have offered her, but, after all, she had almost as much already in Canada, and it had become suddenly clear to her, outside of a London ballroom one evening, that to like the man one would have to live with was by no means going far enough. She also admitted that she could have gone considerably further in the case of the man on whose account she had been somewhat anxiously turning over

The Colonist, which she had done regularly during the last few weeks, without, she fancied, her father, who purchased a good many provincial papers, becoming aware of it.

There was, however, once more nothing whatever in it about the adventures of any prospectors, though the paper in question now and then detailed such things at length; and she laid it down with a little sigh of weariness, for two men, in one of whom she was interested, had gone up into the wilderness some time earlier, and nothing apparently had been heard of them since. Gregory Kinnaird had, it seemed, won credit as well as blame, serving the Empire under arms in steamy Africa; but it was, she felt, a sterner and longer fight the men who were up against it—and she liked the expressive phrase—made with savage nature in the west.

After all, the rush on a rebel stockade was soon over, while it seemed to her that the march through the black pine forest, half-fed, with provisions running out, the sleeping in dripping fern or slushy snow, and the staggering along the rangeside under a crushing load for days together, with galled feet and shoulders that bled beneath the pack-straps, was a much more difficult matter. Weston, her camp attendant, had done all these things, and, as very frequently happened, had so far gained nothing by them. She was glad that he had done them, for the pride of a colonizing people was strong in her, but, after all, that was not why she loved him. Indeed, it was rather hard to find a reason for the latter fact. The only thing that mattered was that she admitted it, and now she was wondering, with an almost torturing anxiety, whether there would be any news of him in the next issue of *The Colonist*.

Laying aside the paper, she looked out on the city, which stretched away before her, with its roofs and spires and towers clear in the evening light, toward the great gleaming river; but, fair as the prospect was, her thoughts sped back to the shadowy forests and towering ranges of the Pacific Slope. As they did so, her eyes grew curiously soft, for when she had last looked upon those snow-barred heights the camp-packer had been at her side. Then she turned with a sudden start and a swift rush of blood to her face as a maid announced, "Mr. Weston."

It was, however, a moment or two before the man came in, and she was then mistress of herself, and it was reassuring to know that if there was anything dramatic in his appearance at that particular time he was evidently unaware of it. In fact, he entered the room as though he had left it just on the previous day, and, taking her hand, merely held it for perhaps a second longer than was absolutely necessary. Then he sat down and inquired after her health and Stirling's, at which Ida, who could not help it, laughed. She did not like effusiveness, but this conventional formality seemed to her singularly out of place, until she remembered that she had once or twice already found the matter-of-fact quietness with which the man made his appearance and went away again almost disconcerting. If this had been the result of affectation it would have been provocative, but, as Ida was aware, it seldom occurred to the man that anybody else was greatly interested in his doings. She felt, however, that he might have made an exception of her.

"Where have you come from now?" she asked.

Weston named a hotel of repute in that city, and, though this was not the information Ida had desired, she favored him, unobserved, with a glance of careful scrutiny. He was attired for once like a prosperous man, in garments that became him, and, as she had noticed already, he possessed the knack of wearing anything just as it should be worn, which, as far as her observation went, was the particular characteristic of some Englishmen.

"Then you are not at Lemoine's this time?"

"No," said Weston, with a whimsical twinkle in his eyes. "You see, we have at last succeeded in finding the mine."

Ida started. She regretted this, but she was human, and she knew that the man loved her. It seemed only reasonable to expect that he would proceed to make that fact clear to her now that he had found the mine, but she was a little puzzled about his smile. It indicated rather too much self-possession for a man on the verge of a proposal, and she did not know that since he entered the house he had been endeavoring to impose a due restraint upon himself.

"Oh," she said hastily, "I'm very glad. You found the mine?"

"No," replied Weston, gravely, "Grenfell found it."

"Where is he? Have you brought him with you?"

"I haven't," said Weston, and she noticed the sudden dropping of his voice, "Grenfell's dead. He—went on—the night before we struck the lode up there in the bush."

"Before you struck the lode? But you said he found it."

"Yes," admitted Weston, quietly, "I think he did."

He told her the story in a few forceful words, and when he had finished, her eyes grew a trifle hazy. She had sympathy and intuition, and the thought of the worn-out man lying still forever beside the gold he so long had sought affected her curiously. Weston, who felt his heart throb painfully fast as he watched her, nodded.

"Yes," he said, "it was rather pitiful, and there was a certain ghastly irony in the situation; but, after all, as he once admitted, there was very little that gold could have given him."

Ida sat silent a moment or two. She was sorry for Grenfell, but he had, as his comrade said, gone on, and she was more concerned about the results of his discovery to those who were left behind.

"The lode," Weston added, "is all that he described it."

It cost Ida an effort to sit perfectly calm while she waited for his next observation. It was, as she recognized, only his stubborn British pride which had prevented him from declaring what he felt for her earlier, and now the obstacle that had counted for most with him had suddenly been removed. As it happened, however, he said absolutely nothing.

"Then you and Devine and that storekeeper are prosperous men?" she asked.

Weston laughed in a rather curious fashion, and when he spoke it was as if he felt that an explanation of his attitude were due from him.

"No," he said, "not yet. In fact, so far we're nothing more than three remarkably rash adventurers—little men of no account—who have set ourselves up against the big professional company jobbers. We have won the first round, but that was fought with nature. It's comparatively easy to face weariness and wet and frost when one is used to it, but to fence with the money handler is quite a different matter. To cry our wares in the market is a thing to which we're wholly new."

He had said all that was required to make the situation reasonably clear to a girl of her understanding. The battle was less than half won, and it seemed that he would not claim her unless he came out victor, which was, in some respects, as she would have it. Though she now and then chafed at it, she loved the man's pride, and what he could win by force she would not have him purchase with the money that she could give him. She fancied, however, that if she chose to exert her strength she could sweep away all the resolutions he had formed; and she made a little of her power felt as she turned and looked at him.

"You feel that you must fight this thing out with such weapons as you have?" she asked. "I suppose you wouldn't allow your friends to provide you with more efficient ones? I know I have suggested as much already, and you would not listen, but it would make success so much easier."

It was not remarkably explicit, but Weston, to some extent at least, understood what she had implied, and he gazed at her with a curious kindling in his eyes. She leaned forward in her chair, wonderfully alluring, with a suggestive softness in her face, and he felt his resolution deserting him. It was clear to the girl, who watched every change of his expression, that the issue of the moment was in her hands, and had he told her that the rest of the struggle he was engaged in would be fought out in the snow-bound ranges where men not infrequently died, she would have exerted all her strength. As it was, however, and because of her pride in him, she suddenly determined that she would let him win his spurs. Though it was beyond defining, there was a subtle change in her manner when she leaned back in her chair.

"I think," said Weston, "the first course you mentioned is the only one open to me."

The words did not cost him as great an effort as they would have a moment or two earlier. He felt that in the meanwhile something had snapped and the tension had suddenly slackened. This was a vast relief to him, and he had recovered a good deal of his composure when the girl spoke again.

"Still," she said, "you evidently have no great liking for the market-place."

"I'm afraid I haven't," admitted Weston, with a little laugh. "After all, when one has seen how some of these mining syndicates and mortgage companies get in their work, a certain prejudice against such things isn't quite unnatural."

"Ah," said Ida, who had now decided that the conversation must be kept within safe limits, "you don't, however, mind using the shovel."

Weston was quite ready to follow the lead she had given him.

"What are we to do when we come out here?" he asked, with an air of whimsical reflection. "Half of us have no professions, and we haven't a trade. They bring us up to take life easily, and then, when some accident pitches us out into the Colonies, it's rather a shock to discover that nobody seems to have any use for us. As a matter of fact, I don't blame your sawmill bosses, your railroad men and your ranchers, considering that it takes several years to learn how to chop a tree, and that to keep pace with an average construction gang is a liberal education."

Ida laughed. The further they got away from the crisis now the better she would be pleased.

"I fancy there's still a notion in the old country that the well-brought-up young Englishman excels at anything he cares to undertake, even if it's only manual labor," she said.

"Oh, yes," laughed Weston, "I've heard it. Let them keep such notions over yonder if it pleases them. One naturally likes to think we're as good as the rest, and perhaps we're warranted, but it seems to me that the man of equal muscle raised to swing the ax and shovel is going to beat the one who's new to it every time."

"But the pride of caste!" said Ida. "Doesn't that count? Doesn't success even at such things as track-laying or chopping trees depend on moral *as* well as physical strength?"

"I think with most of us courage is largely a matter of experience," said Weston. "We learn to know what can't hurt us and to avoid the things that can. As to the other kind, the man who hazards his life and limbs in half-propped wild-cat adits, or running logs down the rapids, is hardly likely to be less cool in a tight place than the one who has never been accustomed to anything of the kind."

He was evidently expatiating on this subject merely because he felt that it was safe ground, but Ida, who partly agreed with what he said, felt that, after all, there was probably something in the insular English notion that he was too proud to uphold. This man, at least, possessed a courage that made him willing to carry the fight into the market-place with wholly unaccustomed weapons, and a pride that impelled him to lay a stern restraint upon his passion. She fancied that there were men in Canada who would not have been deterred by her money had they wished to marry her, and, for that matter, one or two in England had delicately permitted the fact to become apparent. In the meanwhile she had decided that he should have his wish. It would perhaps be possible to offer support in some shape later on, if it became apparent that he was badly beaten.

"I suppose it is not a very easy matter to dispose of an undeveloped mine?" she inquired.

Weston smiled rather dryly.

"It can be done without much trouble if you're content to give the thing away, but it's rather different if you wish to sell it. In fact, until the last week I'd no idea how hard the latter was."

"Then you have been here a week?"

There was a hint of reproach in her tone, and Weston, who understood her to mean that she was a little astonished that he had not presented himself earlier, realized that here was an opportunity that he might have profited by had he only succeeded in selling the mine. As it was, he let it pass, for he felt that if once he let himself go he would probably say a good deal more than was advisable.

"Yes," he said, with a laugh. "Still, at the rate I'm progressing, several months will hardly see me through."

Ida had formed a reasonably accurate notion of what was in his mind, and she was half vexed with him and half pleased. He was, at least, consistent, and meant to persist in the attitude he had adopted; but it was significant that he evidently was afraid to venture an inch outside his defenses. After all, she decided that it was probably advisable that he should remain behind them in the meanwhile. It was, however, more or less of a relief to her when her father came in. He did not appear in the least astonished to see Weston, and shook hands with him as though it were the most natural thing to find him sitting there.

"Business in this city?" he asked.

"Yes," said Weston, "I've been endeavoring to sell a mine."

"Then you struck the lode?"

"I've been abusing Miss Stirling's good-nature with an account of how we did it."

Stirling made a little gesture that might have meant anything, but Ida was pleased with the fact that he expressed no astonishment. It seemed to her that he had expected Weston to succeed, and she knew that he was very seldom wrong in his estimate of any man's character. She made some excuse and left them together; and when the door closed behind her Stirling turned to Weston.

"If you'll come along to my room I'll give you a cigar," he said. "Then, if you feel like it, you can tell me about the thing."

CHAPTER XXV
STIRLING GIVES ADVICE

The contractor lay back in an easy-chair when he had lighted a cigar, and watched Weston, who glanced with evident interest around the room. Its furniture consisted of very little besides a roll-top desk and a couple of chairs, but the walls were hung with drawings of machines and large-scale maps, which had projected railroad routes traced across them. An Englishman, as a rule, endeavors, with a success which varies in accordance with his temperament, to leave his business behind him when he goes home, but across the Atlantic the man of affairs usually thinks and talks of nothing else. As one result of this he has very little time to discuss the concerns of other people, which is apt to become a habit of those who have very few of their own. Stirling was, however, for private reasons willing to make an exception of Weston in this respect, and when he noticed how the latter's eyes rested on two or three models of machines which stood on a shelf near him, he took down one of them.

"I bought up the patent rights of that thing," he said. "As you see, it's a power excavator, and, while it works all right in loose stuff and gravel, the two I have on the Mule Deer road have been giving me trouble."

Weston, who was deeply interested, laid the machine on his knee and spun it round once or twice.

"The elevator buckets are the weak point," he said. "They won't deliver stiff, wet spoil freely."

Stirling's nod was very expressive, in that it suggested that he had expected his companion to locate the cause of trouble.

"You've hit it," he said, and opening the desk took out a little model of an excavator bucket, beautifully made in burnished copper, and another one more rudely fashioned out of bent card. He handed Weston the former.

"That's a rather famous man's idea," he added, with a little dry smile. "I had to leave the thing to my secretary when I was west. I've tried it on the Mule Deer road, and I'm not quite satisfied. The other's one that I've been thinking over."

Weston looked at both the models, and then, taking up the card one, unfolded it, and, after paring part of it away with his knife, bent it into a slightly different shape.

"I think that should meet the purpose. I once worked under the engineer of a very similar machine for a month or two," he said.

Stirling picked up the model and examined it carefully before he replaced it in the roll-top desk, which he shut with a snap.

"Do you feel like taking a hundred dollars for the notion?" he asked.

"I'd rather make you a present of it," said Weston, quietly.

"Well," laughed Stirling, "I'll take it. My secretary paid the other man a good deal more than that for the copper one, and it won't do quite what is wanted. If that man had run an excavator in the mud and rain I guess he'd have made it different. He sits tight in a smart office, and tries to remember what they taught him twenty years ago in the erecting shop."

It seemed to Weston that there was a good deal to be said for this point of view, though it was a matter which did not concern him. His companion's manner was friendly, and to some extent familiar, but Weston had already had an uneasy feeling in his presence that he was being carefully weighed, or measured, by an astonishingly accurate standard. His only defense, he decided, was to be perfectly natural, and in this he was judicious, as the assumption of any knowledge or qualities he did not possess would in all probability have been promptly detected. He said nothing, which is a very excellent rule when one does not know what to say, and Stirling changed the subject when he spoke again.

"So you have found the mine and come here to sell it," he observed. "I guess you have had the usual experience?"

"I don't quite know what is usual," said Weston, with a smile. "Still, I've been round this city with a bag of what people admit are rather promising specimens of milling ore, and I certainly haven't succeeded in selling the mine yet."

"The trouble is that the specimens might have been obtained from anywhere," said Stirling, dryly.

"There's one concern anyway in whose case the objection does not apply. I got a telegram from my partner, the storekeeper, to the effect that the Hogarth Combine had sent up Van Staten from Vancouver to inspect the lode. I gather that one of the boys spotted him, though he meant to do it quietly. The fact that he didn't announce his name is rather suggestive. You can read the message."

He took it from his pocket and handed it to Stirling, who wrinkled his brows.

"Well," he observed, "what Van Staten says goes. Very few of the big concerns would hesitate to purchase when he was satisfied with the thing. That storekeeper seems quite a smart man. The Hogarth people have, no doubt, made you an offer since then?"

"Four thousand dollars, all rights, and they'll meet expenses while I put in the assessment work and do all that's necessary to get title from the Crown. They were kind enough to say that it was rather a hazardous venture, but they wanted another workable reef to round up their mineral properties. The reason seemed a little vague."

Stirling smiled rather grimly. "They want everything they can get their hands on in the shape of a mineral property, as long as it costs them 'most nothing. What did you tell them?"

"That they'd have to go up six times, anyway, before I considered the thing, and then I'd want half payment in ordinary stock. They asked if I meant to stick to that, and I said I did."

"Then," asserted Stirling, "you're going to have some trouble in keeping that mine. The Hogarth people have frozen out more than one little man who didn't want to part with his property. They're said to be quite smart at it, and there are various ways of getting hold of you."

He studied Weston's face and saw it harden, which, as a matter of fact, rather pleased him. The stubbornness which had sent this young man back up the range, aching in every limb, with one boot full of blood—and Stirling had heard that story—was now, it seemed, impelling him into a struggle with a group of remarkably clever and powerful mining financiers. The successful contractor appreciated ability, especially when it was of the practical order, but perhaps he was right in rating character higher.

"Yes," said Weston quietly, "I quite expect that will be the case."

"Have you had any other offer?"

"Wannop made me a conditional one. Pending investigation, he talks of floating a company here or in London. After the success of the Hazleton and Long Divide concern, he says they're disposed to regard British Columbian ventures favorably yonder. If it goes through, I'd have to take most of the vendor's payment in shares, which I'm quite ready to do. That's a rough sketch of the scheme, sir, but in the meanwhile it's only tentative."

Stirling perused the paper handed him with close attention; and before he answered he lighted another cigar.

"Wannop's straight, but he and his friends are little men," he said at length. "You'd have the Hogarth Combine right on to you in London. One or two of their subsidiary concerns are registered there. Now, I don't know whether they really want your mine, but supposing they do, and you won't sell out to them, I guess you have some idea of what their game would be?"

"I'm afraid I haven't, sir."

"Well," said Stirling, "you'll be fortunate if you get half your authorized capital applied for, and it would be quite an easy thing for the Hogarth people to send somebody on to the market to sell your stock down. That would freeze off any other investors from coming in, and scare those who had applied for stock into selling. You can't put up a crushing and reducing plant without a pile of money, and dams and flumes for water-power would cost 'most as much; but you'd have to have them, for you could never pack your ore out to a smelter through the kind of country you have described to me. Now, unless you could get money enough to start clear with, the concern is bound to cave in. Then somebody acting for the Combine would quietly buy it up."

He broke off for a moment and looked hard at Weston.

"Suppose those people let you feel their hand and then make you a rather higher offer? What are you going to do?"

"Disregard it," said Weston, quietly.

Stirling nodded in a manner which suggested that this was what he had expected.

"Well," he said, "I guess that's the course most likely to appeal to a man constituted as you seem to be. But the question is, are you tough enough to see it through? It's one that may cost you a good deal."

"I don't know," said Weston. "I can only find out by trying."

It appeared from his companion's manner that the answer pleased him.

"Now," he said, "are you open to take advice or help from me?"

Weston met his gaze, which was now unpleasantly steady.

"Advice, sir," he answered. "I'm afraid I couldn't take help."

"From me?" said Stirling, dryly, with an emphasis on the last word which brought the blood to Weston's cheek. "Well, you can come for the advice on any matter of detail when you feel like it. In a general way I can only throw out one suggestion now, and it's at variance with the views you seem to hold. Go over to the Hogarth people, and make the most reasonable terms you can with them."

"That's what you would do in my place?" Weston asked, with a twinkle in his eyes.

"I've been a blame fool once or twice in my time," Stirling admitted. "It's curious that it didn't cost me quite as much as most people expected. Still, what I've given you is excellent advice."

He waved his hand as though to indicate that he had closed the subject, but when Weston took his departure half an hour later the contractor looked remarkably thoughtful.

"If he weren't up against the Hogarth Combine he and Wannop might put that scheme through," he mused. "As it is, I guess one way or another I've got to help him out."

Then he rose and descended to the room where his daughter was.

"I've had an interesting talk with Mr. Weston," he said indifferently. "That's quite a smart young man, but I guess one could call him a little obstinate."

Ida smiled at this, though she suspected her father's observation was not quite as casual as it seemed.

"Yes," she said, "in some respects I think he is. But how has he made that clear to you?"

Stirling, sitting down opposite her, laughed.

"He's had an offer for his mine that most of the bush prospectors would have jumped at, and if he'd played his cards judiciously the people who made it would no doubt have doubled it. I suggested that course to him, but it wasn't any use. Mr. Weston is one of the men who can't make a compromise."

"Isn't that a reasonable attitude? He presumably wants his rights."

"The little man," observed Stirling, "has no rights that he isn't prepared to hold on to in a rather uneven fight. With Weston it's all or nothing, and just now I don't quite know which he'll get. He and his partners will have to stake everything they own on a very uncertain game."

"Hasn't everybody who goes into business speculations to do that now and then?"

"No," said Stirling, reflectively, "I don't think they have. Quite often the people who deal with them have to face part of the hazard. In a general way they've something to fall back on if they're men of position: the money they've settled on their wives, a name that would get them credit on the market, or friends who'd give them a lift if they came down with a bang. Now, that young man has nothing. If he fails, he won't have a dollar to get out of this city with, for the mine won't count. He can't even hold it unless he puts in his assessment work on it, and he couldn't do that without something to live on in the meanwhile. He hasn't a friend in Canada from whom he could borrow a dollar."

Ida said nothing, and Stirling added, as if in explanation:

"I might be willing to give him a lift if it were absolutely necessary, but it seems that he's quite determined not to take a favor from me. He didn't offer me any reason for adopting that attitude."

He looked at the girl rather curiously, and she noticed the significance of his last sentence. Stirling had not said that he was unacquainted with Weston's reason, but he seemed to be waiting for her to make a suggestion, and she found the situation embarrassing.

"Well," she said, "he probably has one that seems sufficient to him."

Stirling said nothing further on the subject, and presently went out and left her; but her expression changed when he had done so, and she sat very still, with one hand tightly closed, for she now realized what the cost of her lover's defeat might be. In his case it would not mean a grapple with temporary difficulties, or a curtailing of unnecessary luxuries, but disaster complete and irretrievable, perhaps for years. If he failed, he would vanish out of her life; and it was becoming rapidly clear that, however hard pressed he might be, there was, after all, no way in which she could help him. The unyielding pride or stubbornness which animated him at length appeared an almost hateful thing.

Ida did not sleep particularly well that night, and when she went down to breakfast rather late the next morning there was a letter beside her plate. She looked up at her father when she had opened it.

"Susan Frisingham is coming here from Toronto for a day or two before she goes back to New York," she said. "She suggests taking me back with her."

"Ah!" said Stirling, with a barely perceptible trace of dryness. "You don't want to go just now?"

Ida flashed another glance at him, and noticed the faint twinkle in his eyes. She felt almost disconcerted, for it suggested comprehension, and she certainly did not want to go. She could, it seemed, do nothing to help the man she loved, and, for that matter, she could scarcely encourage or sympathize with him openly, but she would not seek pleasure elsewhere while he fought out the unequal struggle alone.

"No," she said, "I should much rather stay here."

"As you like," said Stirling, who shortly afterward departed for the city.

Mrs. Frisingham was a rich widow and a distant connection of Stirling's. She arrived that day, and on the following day contrived to spend a few minutes alone with Stirling when he came home from business.

"I wanted to take Ida back with me, and I'm a little astonished that she won't hear of it," she said.

"In that case, I'm afraid the notion can't be carried out," said Stirling.

"Isn't it rather a pity?" suggested the lady.

Stirling seemed to consider this. The two were old friends, in spite of the fact that Mrs. Frisingham, who now and then spent a few weeks in Montreal, had made several determined attempts to regulate the contractor's domestic affairs. She described him to her friends as pig-headed, and added that if it had not been for his daughter she would have given up all idea of making him listen to reason. Stirling, on his part, said that she no doubt had excellent intentions, but so had a good many people who contrived to make a considerable amount of unnecessary trouble.

"I wonder why you want her at New York?" he asked.

He had, as his companion was aware, a somewhat Unpleasant habit of going straight to the point, but on this occasion she was disposed to meet him.

"Do you mind telling me what you mean to do with the girl?"

"No," said Stirling. "I want to keep her with me just as long as she's willing to stay; but I suppose I can stand it if she marries somebody by and by."

"That," said the lady, "is just the point. You would naturally prefer him to be an eligible person. Now, if you let me have her for a while I could promise that she would meet nobody who didn't answer that description."

Stirling laughed. He had suspected her intention all along, and surmised that her offer was prompted partly by good-nature and partly by a recognition of the fact that the presence of a young woman of considerable wealth, who was beautiful as well as otherwise gifted, would increase the popularity of the receptions over which she was fond of presiding.

"I'm not quite sure her views and yours would coincide," he said. "Anyway, she has been in New York before—and in England, for that matter."

Mrs. Frisingham adroitly shifted her point of attack, and it almost appeared, though Stirling could not tell how, that she had heard of the camp-packer.

"Don't you think there's a certain danger of her going through the wood and choosing the crooked stick after all?" she asked.

Stirling smiled. "I don't know that you could call New York or London a wood. A hothouse would be nearer it," he said with an air of reflection. "Still, to fall in with the simile, there are no doubt plenty of sticks in both places, just as there are right here in this city. In fact," and his eyes twinkled suspiciously, "I'm not quite sure that isn't an excellent name for them. Quite a few are nicely varnished, and in a general way they've hall-marked gold or silver tops. The hallmark, however, guarantees only the trimmings, and from one or two specimens that I've come across I've a suspicion that in some cases the timber's rotten. When you choose a stick you want a sound one—one that you can lean on when you face a hill, and I guess that's a thing my girl will have to do now and then."

His tone had grown a trifle graver as he went on, but his companion waited, feeling that he had a little more to say, and that he might offer her a hint of some kind, as, in fact, he presently did.

"The sound sticks don't grow in stove-warmed houses, but out in the wind and sun," he said.

That was sufficient for Mrs. Frisingham, who had rather more than a suspicion that Stirling already had in his mind somebody who had not been bred in the city. An unknown man who built new railroad bridges in the wilderness, or a bush rancher, it seemed most probable.

"Well," she said, "I might perhaps warn you that the right choice is a rather serious matter, and that, after all, it's wiser to consider the opinions—call them prejudices if you like—of your own order."

"When my daughter chooses," said the contractor, smiling, "she'll choose wisely, and I'm going to be satisfied. I've had the pleasure of reassuring another lady on that point already. As to the other matter, the opinions of people of the station to which I now belong don't count for much with me. For quite a long while they were dead against my getting here at all; but I did work that this country wanted done, and I'm where I am. You don't expect me to alter my views out of deference to them?"

He broke off for a moment, and nodded to her pleasantly as he went on again.

"We're old friends, Susan, and I guess you mean to be kind; but I've been warned before, and it didn't affect me much," he said. "If Ida wants to go back with you she may, but we'll leave it at that."

He turned away, and, strolling into his own room, he took out the card model of the excavator bucket which Weston had altered, and examined it critically.

"Yes," he said, "it will do its work. I guess that's characteristic of the man."

CHAPTER XXVI

THE JUMPERS

Saunders, the storekeeper, lay outside the little tent, with the pungent pine-wood smoke drifting past him and his feet toward the fire, while dusk crept up the range and a wonderful stillness settled down upon the lonely valley. His hands were badly blistered, and he was aching in every limb, while some of his knuckles had the flesh torn off them, for Devine had brought a heavy hammer down on them several times that day instead of on the drill. For all that, he lay beside the fire in the drowsy state of physical content which is not infrequently experienced by those who have just enjoyed an ample meal after a long day of strenuous labor in the open air. However, as Saunders had reasons for believing that the result of the latter would in due time prove to be eminently satisfactory, the sensation was in his case perhaps a little more pronounced than usual.

He was not more than healthfully weary, and there was an exhilarating quality in the sweet, cool air, which was heavy with the smell of the firs, while the wonderful green transparency generally to be seen after sunset among the mountains of that land still glimmered behind the peaks on one side of the valley. The rest of the hollow was wrapped in creeping shadow against which the nearest pines stood out in dusky ranks. Saunders raised himself on one elbow and gazed at them reflectively before he turned to Devine, who was sitting near him. They had been hard at work on the mineral claims of the Grenfell Consolidated for the last few days.

"This camping in the woods would be quite nice if one could prowl round with the rifle instead of pounding the drill," he said, and then paused to glance ruefully at one of his battered hands. "Anyway, I don't know that I shouldn't just as soon do that as to hold it."

"Sorry," said Devine. "Still, you've done some shooting. We brought up a box of cartridges and now we haven't one. What you want is a single-shot rifle, or a deer that will stand still."

Saunders turned and pointed to the dismembered carcass that hung from a fir branch close at hand.

"I got that one on the run, and there was a time when I'd have had one for every ca'tridge, instead of plugging Marlin bullets into trees. It was a sport I was meant for." He paused and sighed. "I've had to be a saw-mill hand and a storekeeper."

Devine grinned at this.

"Well," he said, "you've raked more money out of pork and sugar than I have out of surveying. For that matter, you've got most of mine; and you're better off than I am, because the store's still running."

"Oh, yes," said his companion, with a sardonic smile, "it's being run by Jim from Okanagan, and he'll have the boys round in the back store evenings sampling cheese and eating crackers while they help him. They're kind of curious insects, and it's a blame pity I never remembered to put those Vancouver invoices where they wouldn't lay hands on them, for there'll sure be trouble when I get back again. You have got to strike people for full prices when they don't always meet their bills. Anyway, the man who spreads himself out on jobs that don't strictly belong to him is bound to find it cost him something."

It was significant that he spoke of going back; but both he and Devine admitted that possibility. The mine was theirs, and they certainly meant to keep it if they could, though they recognized that this might be difficult. As a matter of fact, a reef or lode mine is of almost as much immediate use to a poor man as a sewing-machine would be to a naked savage. He cannot get out the ore without sinking a shaft or driving an adit, which, in the general way, means the hiring of labor and the purchase of costly machines. Then, when that is done, he must put up a stamp-mill and reducing plant, or arrange for transport by pack-horse to somebody who has one, which is a very expensive matter in a mountainous land where roads have still to be cut. As the result of this, he must in the first place go round and beg the assistance of men with money to spare; and the latter, as a rule, insist on his handing over the mine before parting with any of their money. There are also means of putting pressure on the reluctant seller, and the usual code of morals does not seem to be considered as strictly applicable to a mining deal.

"Well," said Devine, at length, "we have still a good deal of drilling to do, and unless you're smarter with the hammer than I am we'll want new hands before we're through."

"We hold three claims, and that means quite a lot of assessment work for you and me to put in," Saunders said. "Besides, you'll have to go down and straighten up things with the Gold Commissioner."

Devine made a sign of concurrence. When he had staked off the claims with Weston he had been more concerned about tracing the lode than anything else, and it had not occurred to him that they might be contested, as it certainly should have done. As the result of this, he had neglected one or two usual precautions, and when he filed his record he had not been as exact as was advisable in supplying bearings that would fix the precise limits of the holdings.

"Yes," he said, "now that I've made a second survey, I'll take the back trail in a day or two. The stakes are planted just where they should be, but the description I gave the Commissioner wasn't quite as precise as I should have made it; and, as the thing stands, I'm not sure we'd have much to go upon if anybody pulled up our stakes and swung our claim a little off the lode. Anyway, I don't quite see why the Commissioner shouldn't pass my survey to count for assessment work."

The firelight fell on Saunders' face, and he looked thoughtful. Though the thing is by no means common, claims have been jumped in that country—that is, occupied by men who surreptitiously or forcibly oust the rightful owner on the ground that he has not done the work required by law, or has been inaccurate in his record.

"I guess you'd better go down to-morrow when the boys come up," he said. "It's a fact that Van Staten went over to Cedar to see the Gold

Commissioner, and from what one of the boys told me he had quite a long talk with him. Van Staten's straight, but it would be part of his duty to examine our record and mention it to the people who sent him up to investigate." He paused and spread out his hands. "I wouldn't stake my last dollar on the honesty of any of them."

"The boys would start when they got the news you sent them," said Devine.

Saunders smiled ruefully. He felt reasonably certain that every man in the settlement would abandon his occupation when he heard the message they had sent by an Indian they met on the trail soon after they started. Saunders, it must be admitted, had not sent it until Devine insisted on his doing so, for, as he shrewdly said, there was not a great deal of the lode that could be economically worked available, and he wanted to make quite sure that the Grenfell properties were on the richest of it, while the boys would be better employed working on their ranches and buying things from him than worrying over profitless claims. He added that if the latter broke them he would in all probability never recover what they owed him.

"They'll be here, sure, bringing as much of my pork and flour as they can pack along," he said. "It's quite likely Jim won't have raised thirty dollars among the crowd of them."

"Well," said Devine, "if I'm to take the trail tomorrow I'm going right under my blanket now."

He rolled it round him and lay down on a pile of spruce twigs outside the tent. The dew was rather heavy, but he was young and strong, and it is a luxury to sleep in the open in that elixir-like mountain air. He went to sleep at once, and it was evidently early morning when Saunders awakened him, for the moon, which had not cleared the eastern peaks when he lay down, was now high in the heavens. He sprang to his feet, and stood a moment or two shivering a little as he looked about him. It was very cold, and the little open space where the tent stood was flooded with silvery light, though here and there the shadows of the firs fell athwart it black as ink and sharp as a fretwork cut in ebony. Then he saw Saunders close beside him, fumbling with the magazine of his repeating-rifle.

"Not a blame ca'tridge left! You'd better take the ax along," he said.

"The ax?" queried Devine, who was a little startled as well as puzzled.

Saunders pointed to the shadowy bush.

"Sure," he said. "It's jumpers!"

That was enough for Devine. He flashed a glance at his companion. Saunders possessed the huckster's heart, and took pleasure in selling indifferent pork and third-grade flour at the highest prices he could possibly extort. The clink of the dollar was music to him; but it was perfectly clear that he could hold his own, on occasion, with a very tenacious hand. The man was resolutely quiet and evidently quite ready to meet the jumpers with an empty rifle.

For the next few moments Devine stood listening with strained attention. At first he could hear nothing except a little breeze that sighed among the tops of the firs, but by and by he became sensible of a stealthy rustling somewhere in the shadows. Then a branch snapped with a sharp distinctness that set his heart beating a good deal faster than was comfortable. Making a sign to Saunders, he strode back to the tent and picked up the ax.

After that they set out together down the little trail that led past the willows to the lode, slipping as silently as possible through the shadows, though now and then a stone clinked beneath their feet, or a stick or twig snapped as they passed, with a sound that seemed startlingly loud. Nobody, however, seemed to hear them, and at last they sank down amidst a brake of tall fern near a little, neatly-squared stake which had been driven into the soil. The brake was in black shadow, but a broad patch of moonlight fell on the green carpet of wineberries a yard or two away. The rustling had ceased, and they could hear nothing for several anxious minutes; then it commenced again. A man floundering through that kind of bush makes considerable noise, even when it is daylight and he can see where he is going. Then one of the jumpers, who apparently had fallen into a clump of thorns, broke out into half-smothered expletives, and there was a soft laugh, evidently from a comrade.

"Looking for the stake," said Saunders with a rather grim chuckle. "They mean to put the work through before they come round to call on us. As far as I can figure, there can't be more than four of them."

That appeared to Devine quite enough, but he recognized the necessity for a determined opposition. He knew that he had framed his record before the Gold Commissioner, and that it would not be difficult for the men who pulled up that stake to swing his claim a little off the richest of the lead. This would give them an opportunity for staking off a good deal of the strip he meant to hold, and once they took possession it would be a case of proving them wrong; and when it came to testimony, they were two to one. He felt sincerely sorry that Saunders had not sent the boys word of his discovery a little earlier.

In the meanwhile the rustling had ceased once more, and Devine felt the silence react upon his nerves. What the strangers were doing he could not tell, but he fancied that they must be consulting together somewhere among the trees. He felt that it would be a vast relief if he could only see them; and he glanced around at Saunders. The latter crouched among the dewy fern, impassively still, a blurred, shadowy object, with the rifle across his knees.

Then the crackling of undergrowth commenced again, and Devine fancied that he could distinguish the movements of four men. He heard the fern rustle close behind him, and saw that his companion had raised himself a trifle. The latter appeared to be gazing into the bush, and looking around sharply the surveyor started as a figure materialized out of the gloom where the moonlight streamed down between the trees not far away. The man stood amidst the silvery radiance, and Devine was relieved to notice that he had nothing in his hand. Then he turned partly around, and his voice reached the pair who watched him.

"Have you struck it yet?" he asked.

An invisible man replied that he had not yet found whatever he was searching for; and in another moment a sharp snapping suggested that a third stranger was floundering through the bush. He came into sight close by the first and stopped.

"I can't strike that post," he said. "The bush down that way is black as pitch. Guess I'll have to look for a pine-knot and get a light."

"They'd hear you chopping," said the man who had appeared first. "The tent's just back there among the firs. We have got to have that post shifted before they know we are about."

There was no doubt as to who it was that he referred to, and Devine saw Saunders hitch himself forward a little.

"If I'd only three or four ca'tridges!" he said half aloud.

Devine sympathized with him. His comrade was a very indifferent shot, but it would have been a relief to feel that they had something besides the ax to fall back on as a last resort. Firearms, as he was aware, are seldom made use of in a dispute in British Columbia, but, for all that, men have now and then been rather badly injured during an altercation over a mineral claim. At close quarters a shovel or a big hammer is apt to prove an effective weapon.

Then, and neither was afterward quite sure how it happened, Saunders lost his balance and fell forward amidst the fern. He did not do it noiselessly, and one of the two jumpers sprang backward a pace.

"Somebody in that clump of fern," he said, and then apparently recovered a little from his alarm. "It's that blame fool Charley."

There was no longer any possibility of concealment, and Saunders suddenly stood up in the moonlight which had crept close up to the brake, a tall, gaunt figure with the rifle glinting at his hip.

"It's not," he said laconically. "It's going to be a funeral unless you light out of this."

The men did not stop to consider, but vanished on the instant, and Devine, breaking into a little laugh from sheer relief, fancied that they had jumped behind adjacent trees. Saunders, who stood gazing into the shadows, waved his hand.

"You'll stop right where you are, boys, if you're wise," he said. "There'll sure be trouble if you come out again."

The men did not come out, but there was a smashing of undergrowth as two more came running up. They were visible for a moment as they sprang out into the open space between the willows and the first of the firs, and then apparently they saw Saunders, for they plunged back among the trees. The storekeeper sank down behind the fern.

"It's quite a good light, and one of them might have a pistol," he explained half aloud.

Devine considered this very probable; and when there was no sign of their opponents during the next few minutes he once more became conscious that his heart was beating unpleasantly fast. The jumpers apparently had vanished altogether, but he fancied that they were considering some plan of attack. By and by, a voice came out of the shadows.

"There's the post close up against the fern," it said.

"That," remarked Saunders, dryly, "is going to put a hustle on to some of them."

He was right, for a moment later a man stepped out into the moon-light.

"Put down your gun. We want to talk," he said.

"Then," replied Saunders, who did not stand up, "go ahead; but you'll stop in the light; and if you feel like sending any of your partners to work a traverse round this bunch of fern, you can remember that I've got the forehead plumb on—you."

The man's gesture indicated that he understood the situation, and, though he had jumped for cover a little earlier, as most men in his place would have done, it was evident that he was a courageous rogue.

"I want to tell you that there are four of us, and we've come up quite a way to shift that post for you," he said. "There's no use making trouble, for it has to be done."

Saunders touched his companion's shoulder.

"Chip in," he said softly. "Talk like a land agent trying to sell a ranch. We've got to keep this crowd quiet. The boys can't be far off."

Devine agreed with his last statement. The moonlight was bright enough for one to travel by, at least in the brûlée, and he was suffi-ciently acquainted with western human nature to feel certain that every man in the settlement would have started when he heard of their dis-covery, and, what was more to the purpose, would not waste a moment on the journey. Men going up to a new gold strike do not, as a rule, trouble themselves about want of sleep or weariness. On the other hand, he did not think they could possibly arrive before morning, which meant that he must keep the jumpers talking for several hours. It appeared very doubtful whether their patience or his conversational powers would hold out, but he meant to do what he could.

"I'm not quite as sure that you're going to move that post as you seem to be; and, anyway, I don't quite see why you want to do it," he said. "You can't take possession of a duly recorded claim."

The jumper laughed.

"Your record won't hold. You should have made it clearer; given two-point bearings, or blazed your line on trees."

"Why?" asked Devine. "This post fixes the key boundary."

"Trouble is that we're going to move that post," said the other man.

He did not appear impatient, and Devine deduced two things from the fact that he was willing to discuss the matter. One was that the jumper, who evidently had not met the Indian, was unaware that the men from the settlement were then in all probability pushing on as fast as possible through the brûlée, and the other that the man had no desire to pro-ceed to extremities. This was reassuring as far as it went, but it must be admitted that the surveyor was afterward a little astonished at his collectedness and perspicacity.

"Why don't you want to move all the posts?" he asked.

"We couldn't square that with your record," was the candid answer. "Moving one will swing you across instead of along the lead, and will let in our new location. I'm telling you this, because you'll probably be reasonable now that you understand the thing. Light out and don't make trouble, and you'll still hold quite a strip on the lead."

"Give us a minute or two to think it over," said Devine.

"In the meanwhile you'll stop just where you are," Saunders broke in.

The man waved his hand as though he conceded that point, and Devine turned to his companion.

"I've only one excuse to make. When I staked off the claims, I was in a feverish hurry to prove the lead and get down and record," he said. "Now, that's not an educated man, but he's got the hang of this thing as clearly as a surveyor could have done. It's evident that the man who hired him has drilled it into him, and, what is more, has warned him that he's to make no unnecessary trouble. We're to be bounced out of rather more than half our claim, but it's to be done as quietly as possible. He explained the matter in the expectation that we'd pull out and leave the field to them."

"You've hit it," said Saunders. "Don't answer. Let him speak again. We've got to gain time."

They waited several minutes in tense anxiety, for, after all, it was conceivable that, diplomacy failing, the jumper would adopt more forcible means. Then the man waved his hand.

"You've got to decide what you're going to do," he said.

Devine proceeded to urge every reason he could think of, and held him in play a little longer, until finally the jumper lost his patience.

"Oh," he said, "you make me tired! Light out and be done with it! We're going to pull up that post."

Saunders thrust forward the rifle barrel so that the moonlight sparkled on it.

"Then," he said grimly, "come right along and shift it."

Instead of doing so, the man jumped back into the shadow, which was perhaps a very natural proceeding. Then there was oppressive silence for a few minutes. Devine, who could not hear anything, felt horribly anxious as to what their opponents might be doing. Suddenly there was a fresh rustling among the undergrowth, and Saunders thrust the rifle into his companion's hands.

"Crawling in at the back of us! Let them see you on the opposite side!" he said.

Devine wriggled through the fern, and, though he knew that this was rash, stood up where the moonlight fell upon him, with the long barrel glinting in front of him. He fancied, though he could not be certain, that he saw a shadowy figure flit back among the trees, and in any case the rustling died away again. After that he crawled back to Saunders, for, as he admitted afterward, he did not like standing on the other side of that thicket alone.

He subsequently repeated the maneuver several times, and Saunders once or twice answered the jumpers' warnings with a sardonic invitation to remove the post. Neither of them afterward was sure how long the horrible tension lasted, though they agreed that a very little more of it would probably have broken down their nerve; but at length a faint sound came out of the shadows down the valley. It rapidly grew louder, and when it resolved itself into such a smashing of undergrowth as might have been made by a body of men, Saunders sprang up and waved his rifle toward where he supposed the jumpers to be.

"You'd better git," he said. "The boys from the settlement will head you off inside five minutes."

There was no answer, and it appeared that the jumpers had already departed as silently as possible. A little later the men from the settlement came limping in, and the foremost of them clustered round Devine, who sat just outside the fern, while Saunders, whose face showed a trifle drawn in the moonlight, stood still clutching the rifle.

"What's the matter? You're not looking pert, the pair of you," said one of them.

"Give me a cigar, if you've got one," said Devine. "Saunders will tell you about the thing. I've done quite enough talking for one night."

Saunders told the story tersely, and afterward snapped the magazine of his rifle up and down with a dramatic gesture.

"Held them off with that, and not a blame ca'tridge in the thing," he said.

CHAPTER XXVII

SAUNDERS TAKES PRECAUTIONS

The men from the settlement had been three weeks in camp. Saunders sat with his back to a big fir and a little hammer in his hand. There was a pile of shattered quartz at one side of him and another smaller heap of fragments of the same material lying on an empty flour-bag at his feet. Devine, who had just announced that dinner was almost ready, leaned against a neighboring fir, looking on with a suggestive grin; and a big, gaunt, old-time prospector, with a grim, bronzed face, was carefully poising one of the quartz lumps in a horny hand. Saunders, who had been at work since daylight that morning, had paid the latter six dollars for his services, and admitted that he was highly satisfied with the result. He was then engaged in manufacturing specimens.

There was already a change in the forest surrounding the lonely camp. The willows had been hewn down, great firs lay in swaths, with some of their mighty branches burnt, and a track of ruin stretched back from Saunders' tent to the side of the range. The Grenfell Consolidated Mine, three separate claims, occupied what was supposed to be the richest of the land. It was certainly the most accessible portion, for payable milling ore was already being extracted from an open cut. It was not the fault of Saunders that the Consolidated did not occupy the whole of it, but the law allows each free miner only so many feet of frontage, and the Gold Commissioner had shown himself proof against the surveyor's reasoning that, as Grenfell had found the mine, a fourth location should be recorded in the name of his executors. A dead man, as the Commissioner pointed out, could not record a mineral claim.

The men from the settlement had, however, promptly staked off every remaining rod of ground along the lead, and, though the spot was remote from anywhere, another band was busily engaged in an attempt to trace it back across the dried-up lake. How they had heard of it at all was not very evident, but as the eagles gather round the carcass and the flies about the fallen deer, so men with shovels and axes appear as by enchantment when gold is struck. Distance counts as nothing, and neither thundering rivers nor waterless deserts can deter them.

Saunders listened with great contentment to the ringing of the axes and the sharp clink of the drills. Men who labor strenuously from dawn to dark in the invigorating mountain air consume provisions freely, and, as the storekeeper was quite aware, those engaged on that lode would be compelled to purchase their pork and tea and flour from him.

"It was quite a smart idea to give Jim a commission on the sales, though I was kind of wondering if he'd have the sense to stay where he is and run the store," he said. "If he hasn't been fool enough to outfit the boys on credit he must have been raking in money."

Then he took up the lump of stone the prospector handed him and knocked most of it to pieces with the hammer; after which he handed one or two of the fragments to Devine, who grinned more broadly.

"Since Weston wants more specimens I guess he's got to have them," he explained. "I don't know any reason why we shouldn't send him the best we can. This lot should assay out, anyway, several ounces to the ton."

The prospector made a little grave sign of agreement, for this was a game to which he was more or less accustomed. Lode ore now and then is of somewhat uniform quality, but at times it varies in richness in a rather striking manner; and the storekeeper had spent six or seven hours picking out the most promising specimens. From these he had trimmed off every fragment in which, as far as he could discern, the precious metal was not present, with the result that any mineralogist to whom they might be handed could certify to the richness of the Grenfell Consolidated. Saunders was a business man, and quite aware that the vendor of any kind of goods, when asked for samples, does not, as a rule, submit indifferent ones.

"I guess," he added, probably referring to prospective investors, "this lot ought to fetch them. You asked the boys to come along, Devine?"

Devine said he had done so, and in a few more minutes several little groups of men, in dilapidated long boots and somewhat ragged duck, who had ceased work for their mid-day meal, gathered round the fir. They waited mildly curious when Saunders rose and made a sign that he required their attention, which they were perhaps the more willing to give because they were all his customers, and bills are apt to run up in a bush ranching community.

"Boys," said Saunders, "I want to point out that instead of owning gold-mines most of you would now be shoveling on the railroads or humping fir trees at the sawmills, if it hadn't been for me."

Some of them laughed, and some of them admitted that there was a certain truth in this, for the bush rancher who buys uncleared land usually spends several years in very strenuous labor before it produces enough for him to live on, and in the meanwhile he must either go away and endeavor to earn a few dollars every now and then or else fall into the hands of the nearest storekeeper.

"Our friend is a philanthropist," said one of them, who spoke clean, colloquial English. "We all admit his favors, but he doesn't mention that he puts them in the bill."

"And he doesn't charge anything extra for insects in his flour," said another man.

There was a little laughter, but Saunders gazed at them reproachfully.

"If you think it's easy making money out of the kind of crowd you are, all you have to do is to start a store and see. But that wasn't quite what I meant to say," he explained. "Anyway, I put the whole of you right on to this lead."

"You were quite a long while doing it," interjected one of the audience.

Saunders waved his hand.

"Am I a blame fool?" he asked. "I've no use for an inquisitive, grasping crowd worrying round my gold-mine until I've got things securely fixed. Still, you drove off those jumpers, for which you have my thanks; and I want in due time to get back the money most of you owe me."

"You can count on that, boys," said another of them. "It's a dead sure thing."

The storekeeper disregarded this.

"Well," he continued, "we'll get to the point of it. It's kind of easy finding a gold-mine when you've a friend of my kind to put you on to it, but it's quite often a blame hard thing to keep it. Now, you'll have men from the cities wanting to buy you up, offering you a few hundred dollars for the claims you've struck, and if you're fools you'll take it. If not, you'll hold off until the Grenfell Consols go up on the market and then give us first call on buying the lot. If we can't take the deal you'll get six or eight times as much in Vancouver as you would if you let go now."

One of the men who had spoken broke in again.

"Boys," he said, "when Saunders makes a proposition of that kind it's because he sees how he's going to get something out of it. But for all that, I guess it's sound advice he's giving you."

There was a little consultation among the men, and then one of them asked a question that evidently met with the favor of his companions.

"How are we going to live in the meanwhile?"

"That's quite easy," said the storekeeper, with a smile. "I'll supply you with pork and flour, drills and giant-powder, at bed-rock figure, while you get in your assessment work, and while you live on your ranches afterward until you make a deal. All I ask is that you won't sell until the Grenfell's floated, and that you'll give us first call then. It's a cold fact that if I had the money I'd buy you all up now."

There was truth in his last assurance, which was at the same time a highly diplomatic one, for it occurred to most of the audience that if there was anything to be made by waiting they might as well have it as anybody else; and after a further consultation they gave him their promise. Then they trooped away to prepare their dinner, and Saunders turned to Devine with a contented smile.

"I guess," he said, "we've headed those company men right off this lode, and, what's most as much to the purpose, the boys will have to trade with me if anybody comes up and starts another store. Just now I'd feel quite happy if I knew how Jim was running things."

He was soon to learn, for he had scarcely risen from a meal of salt pork, somewhat blackened in the frying-pan, and grindstone bread indifferently baked by Devine, when Jim and several strangers plodded into camp. He was very ragged, and apparently very weary, but he displayed no diffidence in accounting for his presence.

"It was kind of lonesome down there, and I figured I'd come along," he said.

Saunders gazed at him for a moment in mute indignation before his feelings found relief in words.

"And you raking in money by the shovelful!" he gasped.

"No," said Jim, decisively, "I wasn't quite doing that. Anyway, it was your money. I got only a share of it; and you didn't figure I'd stay back there weighing out flour and sugar when there was a gold strike on?"

Saunders contrived to master his anger, and merely made a little gesture of resignation. He was acquainted with the restlessness which usually impels the average westerner to throw up ranch or business and strike into the bush when word of a new mineral find comes down, though much is demanded of those who take the gold trail, and, as a rule, their gains are remarkably small.

"Whom did you leave to run the store?" asked Saunders.

"Nobody," said Jim. "Except two Siwash, there was nobody in the settlement; and, anyway, the store was most empty when the boys came along." He indicated the strangers with a wave of his hand. "As they hadn't a dollar between them I told them I'd give them credit, and they could pack up with them anything they could find in the place."

Saunders appeared to find some difficulty in preserving a befitting self-restraint, but he accomplished it.

"What did you do with the money you'd taken already?" was his next question.

"Wrapped it up in a flour-bag," said the man from Okanagan, cheerfully. "Then I pitched the thing into an empty sugar-keg. Wrote up what the boys owed you, and put the book into the keg too. Anyway, I wrote up as much as I could remember."

Saunders looked at Devine, who stood by, and there was contempt beyond expression in his eyes.

"That," he said, "is just the kind of blamed fool he is."

Then he turned to Jim.

"If I were to talk until to-morrow I couldn't quite tell you what I think of you."

Jim only grinned, and, sitting down by the fire, set about preparing a meal, while Saunders, who appeared lost in reflection, presently turned again to Devine.

"I guess I'll go down this afternoon," he said. "We'll have a fresh crowd pouring in, and they'll want provisions. Anyway, I've headed off those company men, and if it's necessary I can go through to the railroad and get hold of Weston by the wires."

Devine admitted that this might be advisable, and Saunders, who was a man of action, took the back trail in the next half-hour. He had held his own in one phase of the conflict which it was evident must be fought before the Grenfell Consolidated could be floated, and it was necessary that somebody should go down to despatch the specimens to Weston.

They were duly delivered to the latter; and the day after he got them it happened that he sat with Ida on a balcony outside a room on the lower floor, at the rear of Stirling's house. It was about four o'clock in the afternoon and very hot, but a striped awning was stretched above their heads, and a broad-leafed maple growing close below flung its cool shadow across them. Looking out beneath the roof of greenery they could see the wooded slope of the mountain cutting against a sky of cloudless blue, while the stir of the city came up to them faintly. Weston had already, at one time or another, spent several pleasant hours on that balcony. They had been speaking of nothing in particular, when at length Ida turned to him.

"Have you ever heard anything further from Scarthwaite?" she asked.

Weston fumbled in his pocket.

"I had a letter only a few days ago."

He took it out and handed it to her, with a little smile which he could not help, though he rather blamed himself for indulging in it.

"As you know the place and met my sister, you may enjoy reading it. Julia's unusually communicative. It almost seems as if I were a person of some consequence to them now."

Ida took the letter, and her face hardened as she read. Then she looked at him with a suggestive straightening of her brows.

"Isn't that only natural? You have found a mine," she said.

"The same idea occurred to me," laughed Weston; "but, after all, perhaps I shouldn't have shown you the letter. It wasn't quite the thing."

"Still, you felt just a little hurt, and that I could respect a confidence?"

Ida looked at him as if she expected an answer, and it occurred to Weston that she was very alluring in her long white dress, though the same thought had been uppermost in his mind for the last half-hour.

"Yes," he admitted, "I suppose that was it."

He could have answered more explicitly, but he felt that it would not be safe, for it seemed very probable that if he once gave his feelings rein they would run away with him; and this attitude, as the girl naturally had noticed on other occasions, tended to make their conversation somewhat difficult.

"What are you going to do about one very tactfully-worded suggestion?" she asked.

"You mean the hint that I should make a few shares in the Grenfell Consolidated over to my English relatives? After all, considering everything, it's not an unnatural request. I shall endeavor to fall in with it."

Ida's face did not soften. The man was her lover, for, though he had not declared himself, she was quite aware of that, and she was his partisan and very jealous of his credit. It was difficult to forgive those who had injured him, and these people in England had shown him scant consideration, and had spoken of him slightingly to her, a stranger. He noticed her expression and changed the subject.

"I have fancied now and then that you must have said something remarkably in my favor that day at Scarthwaite," he said. "I never quite understood what brought up the subject, but Julia once referred to a picture."

Ida laughed softly.

"I'm afraid I wasn't very tactful, and I shouldn't be astonished if your people still regard me as a partly-civilized Colonial. Anyway, there was a picture—a rather striking one. Do you remember Arabella's' making a sketch of you with the ax?"

"I certainly do. She wasn't complimentary in some of her remarks.

She called me wooden. But the picture?"

"Would you like to see it before you go?"

Weston glanced at her sharply, and she nodded, while a faint trace of color crept into her face.

"Yes," she said. "I have it here. I made Arabella give it to me."

She saw the man set his lips, for it seemed scarcely probable to him that a young woman who begged for the picture of a man would do so merely because she desired to possess it as a work of art. Besides, he felt, and in this he was to some extent correct, that she had intended the admission to be provocative. He was, however, a man with a simple code which forbade his making any attempt to claim this woman's love while it was possible that in a few months he might once more become a wandering outcast. He sat still for a moment or two, and it seemed to Ida, who watched him quietly, that he had worn much the same look when he stood beside the helpless Grenfell, gripping the big ax. This was really the fact, though he now entered upon a sterner struggle than he had been ready to engage in then. Once more he was endeavoring to do what it seemed to him right.

"Miss Kinnaird would have been better employed if she had painted the big snow peak with the lake at its feet," he said at length.

Ida abandoned the attempt to move him. She had yielded to a momentary impulse, but she was too proud to persist.

"Well," she said, "that peak certainly was rather wonderful. You remember it?"

"Yes," said Weston with injudicious emphasis; "I remember everything about that camp. I can see the big black firs towering above the still water—and you were sitting where the light came slanting in between them. You wore that gray fishing suit with the belt round it, and you had your hat off. The light made little gold gleams in your hair that matched the warm red glow on the redwood behind you—and you had burst the strap of one little shoe."

"Haven't you overlooked Arabella?" suggested Ida, who realized that his memory was significantly clear.

"Miss Kinnaird?" said Weston. "Of course, she was with you—but it's rather curious that she's quite shadowy. I don't quite seem to fix her, though I have a notion that she didn't fit in. She was out of key."

"That," laughed Ida, "was probably the result of wearing a smart English skirt. Do you remember the day you fell down and broke her parasol, and what you said immediately afterward about women's fripperies?"

"I didn't know that I had an audience," explained Weston, with his eyes twinkling. "I certainly remember that when you fancied that I had hurt myself you would have carried half the things over the portage if I had let you. We went fishing that evening. There was one big trout that broke you in the pool beneath the rapid. The scent of the firs was wonderful."

She led him on with a few judicious questions and suggestions, and for half an hour they talked of thundering rivers, still lakes and shadowy bush. He remembered everything, and, without intending to do so, he made it clear that in every vivid memory she was the prominent figure. It was here she had hooked a big trout, and there she had, under his directions, run a canoe down an easy rapid. She had enjoyed all that the great cities had to offer, but as she listened to him she sighed for the silence of the pine-scented bush.

At last he rose with a deprecatory smile.

"I'm afraid I've rather abused your patience," he said; "and I have to call on Wannop about the mine."

"You have told me nothing about it," said Ida. "How is it getting on?"

A shadow crept into Weston's face.

"There isn't very much to tell, and it was a relief to get it out of my mind for an hour or so. As a matter of fact, it's by no means getting on as we should like it."

Then, after another word or two, he took up his hat and left her.

CHAPTER XXVIII

WESTON STANDS FAST

Business called Weston to Winnipeg a few days after his interview with Ida, and, as it happened, he met Stirling at the head of the companionway when the big lake steamer steamed out into Georgian Bay. Neither of them had any other acquaintance on board, and they sat together in the shade of a deckhouse as the steamer ploughed her way smoothly across Lake Huron a few hours later. Weston had arranged to meet a Chicago stock-jobber who had displayed some interest in the mine, and he had chosen to travel up the lakes because it was more comfortable than in the cars in the hot weather, besides being somewhat cheaper, which was a consideration with him. Stirling, it seemed, was going to inspect the route for a railroad which an iron-mining company contemplated building. He lay in a deck-chair, with a cigar in his hand, apparently looking out at the shining water which stretched away before them, a vast sheet of turquoise, to the far horizon.

"Well," he asked at length, "how's the Grenfell Consolidated progressing?"

"It seems to be making most progress backward," said Weston. "Still, I suppose the fact that somebody evidently considered it worth while to send up men to jump our claim might be considered encouraging."

He briefly related what had taken place at the mine, as far as Saunders' letter had acquainted him with the facts, and Stirling listened thoughtfully.

"It's a crude maneuver, so crude that, as you've nothing but suspicions to go upon, it would be wiser not to mention them to anybody else," he said. "After all, the jumpers may have been acting on their own account."

"You believe they were?"

Stirling smiled. "I naturally don't know enough about the matter to decide; but, in a general way, when I come across anything that seems to the discredit of any gentleman of importance, or big combine with which I may happen to be at variance, I keep it judiciously quiet until I have the proofs in hand. I find it an excellent rule." Then he added in a suggestive manner: "You probably have had another rather more favorable offer since those jumpers failed?"

Weston admitted that this was the case and said that he had ignored the offer. He further stated that, as he had found the mine, he meant to keep it until he could dispose of it on satisfactory terms.

"That," said Stirling, dryly, "is a very natural wish, but one now and then has some trouble in carrying out views of that kind. I've seen your prospectus. Any applications for your shares?"

"They're by no means numerous." And a flush of anger crept into Weston's face. "If that were the result of a depressed market or of investors' indifference I shouldn't mind so much, but we are evidently being subjected to almost every kind of unwarranted attack."

"Any mode of attack's legitimate in this kind of deal, and there's a rather effective one your friends don't seem to have tried yet. Quite sure it wouldn't be wiser to make what terms you can and let them have the mine?"

"I'm afraid I haven't considered the wisdom of the course I mean to adopt. Anyway, it's a simple one. If those people want that mine they must break us first."

"Well," Stirling said, "I guess if I were you I'd allot very few of those shares to what one might call general applicants. Locate them among your friends and Wannop's clerks."

"There are uncommonly few general applicants, and my friends are not the kind of men who have money to invest. The same thing probably applies to Wannop's clerks. It's quite certain that nobody connected with the Grenfell Consolidated could make them a present of the shares."

"Considering everything, that's unfortunate, for, as I once pointed out, the next move will probably be to sell your stock down. It's a game that contains a certain hazard in the case of a small concern, because the stock is generally in few hands; but I've no doubt your friends will try it."

"Then we're helpless," said Weston. "We must raise sufficient money among the general investors, or give up the mine."

"The situation," said Stirling, dryly, "seems unpleasant, but it's the kind of one in which a little man who will neither make terms with a big concern nor let his friends help him might expect to find himself."

Weston sat silent awhile, gazing at the steamer's smoke trail which stretched far back, a dingy smear on the blueness, across the shining lake; and the contractor watched him with a certain sympathy which, however, he carefully refrained from expressing. There had been a time in his career when it had seemed that every man of influence in his profession and all the powers of capital had been arrayed against him. He had been tricked into taking contracts the bigger men would not touch; his accounts had been held over until long after the convenanted settling day, and he had been compelled to submit to every deduction that perverted ingenuity could suggest. He had, however, hardened his heart, and toiled the more assiduously, planning half the night and driving machine or plying shovel himself by day, whenever a few dollars could be saved by doing so. He had lived on the plainest fare, but he had, without borrowing or soliciting favors from any man, borne the shrewd blows dealt him and struggled on inch by inch uphill in spite of them. Now it seemed to him that this young Englishman was bent on doing much the same. At length Weston turned to him with a wry smile.

"It's quite possible that you're right, and the thing is too big for me, but I have got to see it out," he said.

Stirling made a little sign of comprehension. His companion's quietness pleased him, and he felt that, though the man must fight with indifferent weapons and with formidable powers against him, he would not easily be beaten. What was more to the purpose, the contractor did not mean him to be beaten at all, if he could prevent it, though this was a point that he did not consider it advisable to mention.

"Well," he said reassuringly, "no one can tell exactly how a game of this kind will go. All you can do is to hold tight and keep your eyes open."

They changed the subject, and nothing more was said about the mine during the rest of the journey.

In due time Stirling went ashore at a way port, and Weston met the man from Chicago in Winnipeg a day or two later. The latter asked a good many questions about the mine, but he contented himself with stating that the matter would require investigation, and Weston, who gave him a small bag of specimens, spent another day in Winnipeg in a very dejected mood. He felt the hideous cruelty of the system which, within certain rather ample limits, made it a legitimate thing to crush the little man and rob him of his few possessions by any means available. There was, it seemed, no mercy shown to weaklings in the arena he had rashly entered with none of the weapons that the command of money supplied to those pitted against him; but in place of shrinking from the conflict a slow, smoldering rage crept into his heart.

He remembered the weary marches made in scorching heat and stinging frost, how his shoulders had been rubbed raw by the pack-straps, and how his burst boots had galled his bleeding feet. There had been long nights of misery when he had lain, half-fed and too cold to sleep, wrapped in dripping blankets beside a feeble, sputtering fire, while the deluge thrashed the roaring pines. The bustle of the city jarred on him that afternoon, and he wandered out of it, but the march, parched with thirst, through the feathery ashes of the brûlée, rose up in his memory as he walked aimlessly toward the prairie, and he recalled Grenfell lying beside the lode he had died to find. It became a grim duty to hold his own, and once more he determined that his enemies should crush him before they laid their grasping hands on the mine. He shrank, however, from going back to Montreal and waiting there in suspense, and by the time he retraced his steps to his hotel he had decided that this was out of the question. He wrote a few lines to Wannop and started for the bush with the next day's train.

It was dark when he reached the camp, after an arduous journey, and found Devine and Saunders sitting beside the fire. The latter, it transpired, had engaged a clerk in Vancouver to take charge of his store, and he smiled when Weston inquired whether he expected the man to remain at the settlement any longer than his predecessor had done when he heard that there was a new gold find in reach of him.

"I guess I've fixed that," he said. "I took some trouble to get one who was very lame."

Neither of the pair, however, appeared cheerful, and Weston's face grew hard when he heard what they had to say about the mine.

"As you'd see by the specimens, we were turning out high-grade milling ore a little while ago," Devine observed.

"Well?"

The surveyor's gesture was expressive. "We're not in it now. Ore's turned spotty, and it's running deeper. I think I remember your telling me that Grenfell figured that the lode takes an inclination?"

"He certainly did."

"It's another proof that you could count on what he said. There's no doubt about that inclination. We can't get out ore that will pay for crushing with an open cut much longer."

"Then," said Weston, "we can follow it with an adit."

He looked at Saunders, who smiled in a rather grim fashion.

"Adits cost money to drive," observed the latter. "You have brought some along?"

Weston said that this was not the case, and Saunders spread out his hands.

"Well," he said, "I'm broke. Half the men on this location are owing me quite a pile, and it's clear that I'll never get a dollar out of them unless they strike it rich, or the Grenfell Consols go up with a bang. That's how Jim from Okanagan fixed the thing. Now I've got credit from a Vancouver wholesaler who takes a share in the store, and that will keep us in pork and flour, but the giant-powder and detonators in the shack yonder represent this syndicate's available capital. I bought a big supply when I was in Vancouver, but there'll be no more to be had when they run out."

"We'll go on until they do," said Weston, doggedly.

The next morning he laid his city clothes carefully aside, and borrowed from his comrades garments more adapted to the bush. They certainly did not fit him, but that was a matter of no account, and when he had put them on he commenced work in very grim earnest. He was hard pressed—up against it, as they say in that country—and every crashing blow he struck upon the drill was a relief to him. Indeed, he worked with curious cold-blooded fury that wore out his comrades long before night came. Saunders had invested the proceeds of several years of Spartan self-denial in the precarious venture, but that was as nothing compared with Weston's stake. He must succeed or relinquish all idea of winning the woman, who, he ventured to think, might listen to him when he had accomplished his task; and when he desisted at sunset his hands were bleeding and he had partly lamed Devine by an incautious stroke of the pick. That, however, was a matter about which the surveyor protested less than the hazards his comrade quietly took. He rammed the giant-powder into the holes with reckless haste, and, though the cheapest fuses are seldom to be relied on, he allowed his companions scanty time to get out of the mine when he lighted them.

It was the same the next day, and for most of the next three weeks. Indeed, Saunders and Devine were never sure how they contrived to keep pace with him; but they did it for the credit of their manhood, which would not allow them to be beaten by a Britisher. At nights their hands and backs were distressfully sore, but the adit they drove crept on steadily along the dip of the lode. Though they had worked reasonably hard already, their faces grew gaunter and harder under the strain, and as yet they had come upon little sign of any richer ore. In the meanwhile it was very hot, and all day the withering sprays of the fallen firs emitted heavy, honey-like odors under the scorching sun.

Then it occurred to some of the others that, as there had been several weeks of fierce dry weather, it would be a favorable opportunity to burn off the slashing, or clear away the branches of the felled trees, which is usually done before the great logs, which do not readily burn, are attacked with the saw; and one day, when the wind promised to drive the conflagration away from the camp, fires were kindled here and there among the tindery undergrowth. The attempt proved successful, and in a few hours the fire had spread into the surrounding forest. It crept on through the latter steadily, springing up the towering trunks from spray to spray, until the dark firs were garlanded with climbing flame. Beneath them the brushwood crackled furiously, and every now and then a mighty limb fell amidst a shower of sparks, while half-charred logs and rows of blackened stumps marked out the lode. The smoke obscured the sun until the workings were wrapped in a haze, and it crept into the adit where Weston and his comrades toiled; but they held on with their fish-oil lamps burning until the light outside grew dim, and then, crawling back, sore all over, to the wooden shack which had now replaced the tent, they lay down outside it when supper was over.

It was an impressive spectacle that they gazed upon. The conflagration was still not far from them, for, as a rule, a forest fire does not move very rapidly. Across the valley hung a dusky pall of smoke, and beneath it all trunks stripped to bare spires stood out black against a sea of flame. The latter, however, was of no very great extent from wing to wing, and, now that the wind had almost dropped, it made very little progress, though it crept on down the valley in a confined belt, rising and falling in pulsations with the sharp crackle of licked-up undergrowth breaking through the deep-toned roar. Saunders, lying propped up on one elbow, watched it meditatively.

"It's a high-class burn," he said. "Going to save somebody quite a lot of chopping. But if that breeze whipped round there'd sure be trouble."

As the men at work on the lode lived either in tents or rude shelters of bark and logs, this seemed very probable; but Weston was not in the mood to concern himself about the matter then.

"How much giant-powder have we got in hand?" he asked.

"Almost enough to last another three weeks with fuse and detonators to match. You'll have to find the next lot when that runs out."

Weston laughed.

"I've just sufficient money to take me back to Montreal, traveling Colonist, and I must go back to see how Wannop's getting on before very long. What are you going to do then?"

Devine looked at Saunders, who smiled at him.

"Push the adit right on, if we have to cut every foot of it with the drill," he said. "Before we let up, we'll rip the rock out with our naked hands."

It was a characteristic answer, but Weston was satisfied with it. He had discovered that if the men of the Pacific Slope were occasionally a trifle assertive and what he called flamboyant in their conversation, they nevertheless, as a rule, meant just what they said. It is, of course, not unusual for an imaginative person to describe what he intends to do in dramatic periods, but while some people are wisely content with that, the western bushman generally can be depended on to carry out the purpose.

They said nothing further, and presently went to sleep, with the crackle of the undergrowth through which the fire crawled ringing in their ears.

CHAPTER XXIX

THE FIRE

The shack was full of smoke when Weston awakened, coughing, and drowsily looked about him. Somebody else was spluttering close by, and in a moment or two he heard Devine relieve himself with a few expletives. Then Weston got up from his lair of spruce twigs fully dressed, for the night was chilly and the shack had only three sides to it, while the men who live in such places not infrequently take off their clothes to work and put them on when they go to bed.

"The wind has evidently dropped, and the smoke's drifting back. I can't stand much more of this," said Weston.

Devine, it seemed, had lost his temper.

"Then why don't you get out, instead of worrying people?" he asked. "Anyway, it's only one of the little luxuries that Saunders and I are quite accustomed to. I've been eaten by mosquitoes, sandflies, and other insects of various kinds. You've 'most smashed my ankle, besides sticking a grub-hoe into me, and Saunders must work out a big stone just when I was under it. We've been living most of two months on his rancid pork and grindstone bread, and now you make a circus about a little smoke!"

He broke off in another fit of spluttering, and the storekeeper's voice rose out of the vapor which seemed to be rapidly thickening.

"The wind's not dropped. It's shifted, and the fire's working back," he said.

In another moment Weston stood gasping in the doorway. A little chilly breeze, such as often draws down from the ranges in early morning, met him in the face, and the air was thick with drifting smoke. Hoarse shouts rose out of it and a patter of running feet, and it became evident that most of the men were departing hastily for the range or the remoter forest. Weston, however, could not see them, and it was, indeed, a few seconds before he saw anything except a confused glimmering behind a dusky pall of vapor. Then, as the smoke thinned, a bewildering glare shot up, and ranks of trees were silhouetted against a sea of fire that flung itself upon the rearmost of them and ran aloft from spray to spray, while the snapping of the smaller branches resembled volleys of riflery. After that the smoke drove down again and blotted out everything.

Weston, however, was not unduly alarmed. He concerned himself most about the possibility of their work being delayed during the next day or two. As a rule, an active man has little difficulty in avoiding a forest fire, unless it is of unusual extent, or is driven by a strong wind, and there was a wide space already burned clear to which they could remove their possessions. It appeared advisable to set about the latter task at once, for the conflagration was by this time uncomfortably close to them.

"Hand me the big flour-bag," he said.

Saunders hoisted it on his shoulders, and he stumbled away with it, coughing in the smoke, until he could deposit it in the cleared track where the fire had passed the previous afternoon. Then he went back for another load, and had some difficulty in reaching the shack, for the vapor filled his eyes and almost suffocated him. He fell down once or twice among the half-burned branches as he retraced his steps with his burden; but pork and flour and picks and drills were precious commodities in the bush, and he made a third journey, upsetting Saunders as he plunged into the shack. In the meanwhile, the other also had been busy, and at length they sat down gasping beside the pile of blankets, clothing, tools and provisions, with several other men who had hastily removed their possessions from adjacent claims.

"Where are the rest of the boys?" Saunders asked one of them.

"Some of them are in the workings, some of them on the range, but I guess it was for Vancouver the Fraser crowd started out. Seemed to me they meant to get there before they stopped."

Just then a shower of sparks fell about them and charred a hole or two in Devine's clothes, while they had a momentary vision of the front of the conflagration. It was not a reassuring spectacle, for the rolling sea of fire flung itself aloft in glittering spray to the tops of the highest firs, and the valley rang with the roar it made.

"Well," said Saunders, reflectively, "I don't know that I blame the Fraser crowd, and one of the boys was telling me not long ago that the settlement he came from was burned out. A thing of that kind makes a man cautious. Anyway, it's quite hot enough here, and we'll hump this truck along to the adit."

The others agreed that it would be advisable, but most of the things were heavy, and it was some little time later when Weston lighted a fish-oil lamp in the heading and held it up. The narrow tunnel seemed half-full of rolled-up blankets, flour-bags and slabs of pork, and a group of men, some of whose faces were blackened, sat among them.

"Our lot came in first. Have you got it all?" Weston asked.

They found the flour and pork, the tea and Saunders' rifle, as well as a couple of hammers and several drills; but Weston did not seem satisfied.

"Where are my clothes?" he asked.

None of them seemed to know, though it became evident that his city garments were, at least, not in the adit.

"Guess they'll be frizzled quite out of fashion if you left them in the shack," said one of the men. "A miner has no use for getting himself up like a bank clerk anyway."

Weston held up the lamp so the rest could see him. His face was black, and the sleeve of his duck jacket had several big holes in it. His trousers were rent in places, and one of his long boots was burst, while Devine's hat, which was too big for him, hung shapeless and dotted with charred holes on his head.

"I'm going back to Montreal in a day or two. Can I call on big stock-jobbers and company floaters like this?"

"Guess you can buy new ones in Montreal," said the miner.

"You can," agreed Weston, "when you have the money. The trouble is, I haven't. Saunders, I'm going back for those clothes."

They went with him to the mouth of the adit and saw the shack outlined against a dazzling blaze. It did not seem to be burning yet, but none of Weston's companions believed that it would be possible for him to reach it. The smoke had risen, and now rolled among the tops of the firs, but, though they stood at some distance from the fire, the air scorched their faces. Weston's showed up in the lurid radiance worn and very grim, and it was evident to Devine that the curious moodiness which had troubled him since he came back from the city was at least as strong as it had been.

"You can't get them now," he expostulated.

"Give me your jacket," said Weston, sharply. "It's thicker than the thing I have on."

The surveyor hesitated. He could see the sparks and blazing fragments stream past the shack, and he had no wish to encourage his comrade in the rashness he contemplated.

"Well," said Weston, "I'll go as I am."

Then Saunders remembered something, and seized him by the shoulder.

"Hold on!" he cried. "Did either of you bring the giant-powder and detonators along?"

Weston glanced at Devine, who shook his head.

"I didn't, anyway," he said.

For a moment or two there was a silence that was expressive of dismay, as they realized that in the haste and confusion they had saved only the things that could be replaced. The result of this might prove disastrous, for giant-powder and detonators are comparatively dear in that country, and in any case are not obtainable in the bush. To hire labor was in the meanwhile out of the question, and the progress two men could make cutting through hard rock with only the pick and drill was, as they were quite aware, likely to be remarkably small. Saunders made a little dejected gesture.

"Then," he said, "they're still in the lean-to behind the shack; and it would be kind of wiser to crawl back into the adit. The case of detonators was lying bang up against the giant-powder."

This was a significant statement, for it must be explained that although giant-powder, as dynamite is generally called in the west, as a rule merely burns more or less violently when ignited by a flame, it is still a somewhat unstable product, and now and then explodes with appalling results on apparently quite insufficient provocation. In use it is fired with a detonator, a big copper cap charged with a fulminate of the highest power, and when lighted in this fashion the energies unloosed by the explosion, though limited in their area, are stupendous. The detonator is almost as dangerous, for a few grains of the fulminate contained in it are sufficient to reduce a man to his component gases. At least, this was the case a few years ago.

Several men besides its owners had sought shelter from the heat and sparks in the adit, and they evidently agreed with Saunders that it was advisable to crawl back into shelter as soon as possible; but Weston stood still. He had for the past few weeks been looking disaster in the face, and this had produced in him a certain savage desperation which is not altogether unusual in the case of hard-pressed men who feel that they have everything against them. In his mood, which was not a pleasant one, each fresh blow stirred him to a grimmer effort, made with a curious quiet fury from which his comrades now and then almost shrank. Turning abruptly, he shook himself free from Saunders' grip.

"Well," he said, "I'm going to bring out that powder."

In a moment he had scrambled up the pile of shattered rock, and was running across the open space like a deer. It was strewn with half-burned branches, and here and there with little piles of glowing fragments, but he went straight through them without a stumble; and it must be admitted that his comrades stood still and watched him with consternation before it dawned on them that it was scarcely fitting to let him go alone. Then Saunders climbed up to the level ground somewhat deliberately.

"I guess," he said, "we've got to go after the blame fool!"

They set out; but Saunders, who had been keeping store for some years, was not remarkably agile; and one could hardly blame Devine for proceeding with a certain caution. However, they reached the outside of the shack soon after Weston had disappeared in it, and they stopped gasping. The air which scorched their faces seemed to frizzle their hair, and the smoke, which once more had descended, whirled about them. They could hear nothing but the roar of the fire.

Then a half-seen figure reeled out of the shack, and Devine, who was nearest it, laughed discordantly when his comrade thrust upon him a bundle of clothes. The thing seemed altogether incongruous, but he turned and set off toward the adit with his arms full of the garments, which got loose and flopped about him, until he flung them to another man who had ventured part of the distance.

"General Jackson!" exclaimed the miner. "He went back for his clothes!"

Devine did not stop to sympathize with his astonishment, but ran back to the shack, and Weston flung him a partly-filled flour-bag as he approached it. It fell close beside a glowing fragment, and the surveyor felt a little shiver run through him as he whipped it up, for he had some knowledge of the vagaries of giant-powder. He flung the bag over his shoulder as gently as possible, and once more started for the adit, though he proceeded with caution. He was desperately anxious to get rid of his burden, but he had no desire to shake it up unduly. Giant-powder will now and then go off without any very apparent cause.

In the meanwhile Saunders clutched at Weston as he turned back toward the hut. One had to enter it before gaining admission to the smaller shed in which they kept the giant-powder.

"You're not going in again? We've got one bag," he said.

"The other one is still inside," was the hoarse reply.

Saunders did not waste his breath in expostulation, but grappled with him, and he had rent part of Weston's jacket off his back in the effort to detain him when Devine came running up. Then Weston, wriggling around, struck the storekeeper in the face, and plunged back into the smoke as the latter dropped his hand.

They lost sight of him for almost a minute, and then he reeled out of the shack as the smoke drove away. A stream of sparks whirled past it, and close above him the roof was blazing, but he held another flour-bag in his hands, and his comrades, who had reasonably steady nerves, were almost appalled when he poised himself to throw it. There was only a thin strip of cotton fabric between the flying sparks and the plastic yellow rolls of powder. Still, the bag was thrown, and Saunders set off with it, while Weston stood gasping a moment and looked at Devine.

"There's the bag of detonators yet," he said, and, swinging around, disappeared again.

Devine remembered that there was no lid to the iron box in which they kept the detonators, and that they were intended to be ignited by the sparking of a fuse. He stood some little distance from the shack, and it did not occur to him that, as one person could carry the box readily, he was serving no purpose in waiting. Indeed, he was only conscious of a suspense that made it impossible for him to go away. He did not know how long he waited, but in the meanwhile the smoke whirled lower, and he could see nothing for a moment or two. Then it lifted, and the shack stood out in the midst of a lurid blaze. There was a horrible crackling, and Weston suddenly sprang into sight, black against the brightness, with the iron box, which had deer-hide straps attached to it, slung upon his back. The sparks rained about him, but he plunged through the midst of them, while the box banged against him. Then Devine turned and ran.

They reached the mouth of the adit safely, and when they crawled into it, Weston sat down and gasped heavily for a while before he turned to the others and pointed to the two bags of giant-powder lying on the floor. His duck jacket was burned in patches, and there were several red spots, apparently where sparks had fallen, on his blackened face and hands.

"Haven't you sense enough to take that open lamp farther away from those bags?" he asked.

There was a roar of hoarse laughter as his companions recognized the incongruity of the question; and Weston blinked at them, as though puzzled by it, until a light broke in on him.

"Perhaps it wasn't quite in keeping with the other thing, boys," he admitted. "Give me some tobacco, one of you. Mine seems to have gone, and I feel I'd like to sit quiet a minute or two."

The hand he thrust into his pocket came out through the bottom of it, for the lower part of the jacket was torn and burned; but one of the others produced a plug of tobacco, and when he had lighted his pipe Weston leaned back somewhat limply against the side of the adit.

"Well," he said, "I suppose it was rather a crazy trick, but if we'd been sensible we'd certainly have let the Grenfell Consolidated fall into the hands of those city men."

Then he turned to the storekeeper with a deprecatory gesture.

"I'm sorry, Saunders, but you would try to hold me. You ought to have known that you can't reason with a man in the mood that I was in then."

Saunders grinned. "I wouldn't worry about the thing. If there isn't a club handy the next time you feel like doing anything of that kind I'm going to leave you severely alone."

Then, through the roar and crackle of the fire, they heard a heavy crash, and one of the men nearest the mouth of the adit glanced at Weston significantly.

"It's kind of fortunate you got through when you did," he said. "A big branch has fallen right across your shack and broken it up."

CHAPTER XXX

DEFEAT

There had been trouble at the Board Meeting, and, now that it was almost over, the directors of the Grenfell Consolidated sat in dejected silence, listening to the animadversions of one of their comrades. They did not agree with everything he said, but it scarcely seemed worth while to raise minor objections, for they were willing to admit that the situation was desperate.

"We should never have proceeded to allotment," he said. "I warned you that the applications for our stock were quite insufficient to warrant the flotation of the concern at the time, but you apparently lost your heads over those specimens, and you overruled me. Now it's unpleasantly evident that we cannot expect to go on much longer, and I venture to predict a voluntary liquidation during the next few months."

"It certainly looks like that," said one of the others, gloomily. "Still, you might give us your reasons for counting on the thing, if you have any."

The man laughed—a little harsh laugh that had in it a hint of contempt for the intelligence of his colleagues.

"Will you let me have those estimates again, Mr. Weston?" he asked.

Weston, who sat with a set face gazing at the papers in front of him, handed several of them across the table. It was now some time since he had left the mine, and in the meanwhile trouble after trouble had crowded thick upon him. He realized also that he was rapidly losing the confidence of his companions. They were not men of any great account in that city, and it was significant that the Board Meeting was held in Wannop's little back office, where there was scarcely room for all of them.

"You have discussed those estimates at length already," he said. "I should, however, like to point out that I consider them absurdly high. In fact, I'd undertake to do the work at not more than two-thirds of the cost."

"This company," said the first speaker, severely, "has no intention of taking up road-making and the building of flumes and dams. It has, as I think you will admit, gentlemen, quite enough already on its hands."

There was some show of agreement from all but Wannop, and Weston set his lips. There had been a time when they had listened to his suggestions, but now it was becoming evident that they regarded him with suspicion.

"This," said his colleague, "is a little list of our requirements and expenditures before we can expect to get to work. Tools, drilling-machines and labor on the heading." He read out the cost of each item. "Then we have to provide a stamp-mill, turbines, flumes and dam; and, though Mr. Weston suggests a wood-burning engine to supply the crushing power, the saving effected would be no great matter. The point is that we now discover that the cost of these things will in one way or another be nearly double what we stated in our prospectus."

"That," said Wannop, dryly, "isn't altogether unusual."

"What is more to the purpose is that it will approximately absorb our whole available capital," said the first speaker, who took up another paper. "Then we have as an alternative scheme several leagues of road and trail cutting, including wooden bridges and a strip that must be dug out of an impassable mountainside. You have to add to it the cost and maintenance of pack-horses and the rates you'd have to pay the owners of the nearest crushing-plant to do your reducing. Gentlemen, I can only move that these estimates stand over, and that in the meanwhile we merely proceed with the heading."

They agreed to this. Then another of them spoke.

"It seems to me that there's a way in which we could save something as well as our credit," he said. "I've had a hint that another big concern might be willing to take us over."

They looked at one another in a manner which suggested that this was not altogether a new idea. Weston straightened himself suddenly.

"It will never be done with my consent," he said.

"Then," remarked the first speaker, "it is quite likely that you will find yourself in a minority of one."

"Mr. Weston can count on at least one supporter," said Wannop, shortly.

Then there was an awkward silence, until one of the others thrust back his chair.

"It's becoming quite clear that we can't go on," he said. "This concern was started wrong. We should have spent more money, taken first-class offices, and turned out floods of illustrated pamphlets."

"I just want to ask how you're going to spend money that you haven't got?" said Wannop. "I was quite willing to take the money. You wouldn't put it up."

There was a little laughter, and the meeting broke up; but Weston stayed behind with Wannop when the others went down the stairway. The broker, who sat down again, made a little dejected gesture.

"I guess the game is up. They're going back on us," he said. "In a way, I don't blame them. The Hogarth people have scared them off. They're not big enough."

"Have you any idea as to what they'll do?" Weston asked.

Wannop nodded. "Oh, yes," he said. "They'll hold out a month or two, and piffle away at the adit to save appearances. Then they'll call the stockholders together, and suggest turning the mine over to the Hogarth people on such terms as they can get. There are just two things that could save us—a strike of extra high-grade ore, or a sudden whim of investors to purchase western mining stock." He smiled in a wry fashion. "I don't expect either of them."

Weston sat still a moment, and then rose with an air of weariness.

"Well," he said, "I'm going back to the mine tomorrow. We'll hold on as long as possible."

He left; and a few minutes later Stirling came in. He sat down and handed Wannop a cigar.

"Now," he said, "we have got to talk."

"If you'd come a little earlier you'd have met Weston."

"Yes," said Stirling, "that's just why I didn't. Now, where's the trouble?"

"I'll tell you—though to some extent it's a breach of confidence. It's the shortage of money, and the fact that our stock is tumbling down."

"Tumbling down?"

Wannop smiled. "I might have said being clubbed down."

"I want to get the thing quite straight," said Stirling. "What made you take up this mine?"

"Mr. Weston's representations. I think I attached as much weight to them as I did to the specimens. I felt that was a man that I could put my money on."

"You feel that now?"

"I do," Wannop admitted. "In fact, it's hard to believe he will be beaten, though the rest of us are going back on him."

Stirling nodded in a manner which might have meant anything.

"So your stock is being sold down?" he said. "As I pointed out to Mr. Weston, considering that you haven't a great deal of it, that's rather a dangerous game. Are any actual holders parting?"

They had spoken without reticence, in terse, sharp sentences, as men who recognized the advisability of coming straight to the point, which is, after all, a custom that usually saves trouble for everybody concerned. The men who shrink from candor, lest they should give themselves away, not infrequently waste a good deal of time wondering what the other person means, and then decide incorrectly.

"They are," said Wannop. "Besides several small lots, one parcel of six hundred shares held in England changed hands, though that was when we stood near par and the stock was only beginning to break away. What we want is such a strike of ore as will startle mining investors."

"Anything else?" Stirling asked suggestively.

"Well," said Wannop, "we're not likely to get it. If a good strong buyer, who could wait, were to take hold, it would help us as much as anything."

"Quite sure?" asked Stirling very dryly.

"Isn't it evident? It would stiffen prices and scare off the Hogarth brokers. What's more, it would steady my colleagues' nerves."

"Yes," admitted Stirling, "it would do all that. However, I want to suggest that that isn't quite enough. Anyway, that's my view of it."

They looked at each other steadily for a moment or two, and then Stirling made a little forceful gesture.

"Now," he said, "I'm going to take hold of this thing; and in the first place I'll give you an order on my bank for all the money that seems necessary. You will take up some of that stock for me; and, as the Hogarth men will offer more freely as soon as they strike an actual buyer, in case prices stiffen you'll follow their lead and pitch the stock you bought on to the market."

"Some men would consider that was playing the other people's game," commented Wannop, with a chuckle.

"It would be, in the meanwhile," said Stirling. "Well, you won't let your sales—if you make any—get out of hand. You'll have to put on one or two smart men, and cover or sell at a lower price through different ones when it appears advisable. I shall naturally lose a little on every deal of that kind, but the only real trouble will be when you quietly gather in as much as possible of the stock the other people are offering. It will have to be done without raising suspicions, and before their broker can report and ask for instructions."

Wannop struck the table. "There's some hazard in it—but it's a great idea," he said. "They'll club the Grenfell Consols down quite flat."

"Until settling day. Then, when the other people have to deliver, they can't get the stock. We'll shove the prices up on them to anything we like."

Wannop gazed at him in exultation, but presently he asked a disconnected question.

"Why are you doing all this?"

"For money, for one thing," said Stirling, with a little flush in his face. "For another, because I've been sweated and bluffed and bullied by people of the kind you're up against, and now I feel it's 'most a duty to strike back." He clenched a big, hard hand. "I've watched my wife scrubbing and baking and patching my clothes in the old black days when I lived in a three-roomed shack because I was bluffed out of half my earnings by people who sent their daughters to Europe every year. I've nothing to say against legitimate dealing, but it's another thing when these soft-handed, over-fed-men suck the blood out of every minor industry and make their pile by the grinding down of a host of struggling toilers. By next settling day one or two of them are going to feel my hand."

He reached out for his hat, rather red in face.

"If I've any other reasons, they don't concern you," he added in a different tone. "All I expect from you is to do your part judiciously, and, as a matter of fact, it will have to be done that way."

He went out, and left Wannop sitting with the light of a somewhat grim satisfaction in his eyes.

In the meanwhile, Weston went moodily back to his hotel, and spent an unpleasant hour or two before he proceeded irresolutely toward Stirling's house. He realized that this was in some respects most unwise of him, but he was going away on the morrow and he felt that he could not go without a word with Ida.

She was sitting near the fire, which burned upon the open hearth, when he was shown into a daintily-furnished room. After a swift glance at him she rose and followed the maid to the door.

"I cannot receive anybody else just now," she said.

Then she came back and sat down not far from him, feeling that there was a crisis on hand, for, though the man's manner was quiet, there was trouble in his face.

"You have something to tell me. About your meeting, perhaps?"

"Yes," said Weston. "I don't, however, wish to trouble you much about the meeting. I merely want to thank you for your sympathy before I go away. You see, I'm going west to-morrow."

"Will you be long away?"

"Yes," said Weston, with a strained quietness that jarred on her. "In fact, it's scarcely probable that I shall come back here at all. The game's up. My directors have lost their nerve. The Grenfell Consolidated must go down in the next few months."

It was evident to Ida that whatever could be done must be done by her, or the man would go away again without a word, and this time he would, as he had said, not come back at all. For a moment or two she sat very still.

"Ah," she murmured, "I needn't tell you that I'm sorry."

"No," said Weston, simply. "I know you are."

Then there was, for a minute or two, a silence that both found almost intolerable and that seemed emphasized by the snapping of the fire. There was before the girl a task from which she shrank, but it was clear to her that, since she could not let him go, one of them must speak.

"What are you going to do in the west?" she asked.

"Push on the heading until we have to let the mine go."

"And then?"

Weston spread out his hands.

"I don't know. Act as somebody's camp-packer. Shovel on the railroads. Work on the ranches."

It was very evident to Ida that his quietness was the result of a strenuous effort. The barrier of reticence between them was very frail just then, and she meant to break it down. She leaned forward in her chair with her eyes fixed on him, and now the signs of tension in his face grew plainer.

"You speak as if that would be easy for you," she said.

Weston shut his eyes to one aspect of the question. He had not the courage to face it, and he confined himself to the more prosaic one.

"As a matter of fact, I'm afraid it won't be," he admitted. "The life I've led here, and the few weeks I spent at Kinnaird's camp, have rather spoiled me for the bush. Some of the customs prevalent in the trail-choppers' shanties and the logging-camps are a little primitive, and one can't quite overcome a certain distaste for them."

"That was not quite what I meant," said Ida.

Weston was startled, but she saw that he would not allow himself to wonder what she really did mean.

"Anyway," he answered doggedly, "I suppose I can bear any unpleasantness of that kind, which is fortunate, because there's apparently no way out of it. After all, it's one consolation to feel that I'm only going back to what I was accustomed to before I found the mine."

"Ah," said Ida, "you are very wrong in one respect. You speak as if you could bear the trouble alone. Don't you think it would hurt anybody else as much to let you go?" Then, while the blood crept into her face, she fixed her eyes on him. "Yes," she added simply, "I mean myself."

Weston rose, and stood leaning on the back of his chair, with one hand tightly closed. He had struggled stubbornly, but it was evident that his strength had suddenly deserted him and that he was beaten now.

"It would hurt you as much?" he said, with a curious harshness. "That's quite impossible. The hardest, bitterest thing I could ever have to face would be to go away from you."

He flung out the closed hand.

"Now," he said, "you know. I've thrown away common sense and prudence, all sense of what is fitting and all that is due to you. None of those things seem to count just now."

He drew a little nearer.

"I fell in love with you at Kinnaird's camp, and tried hard to crush that folly. Then I found the mine, and for a few mad weeks I almost ventured to believe that I might win you. After that, the fight to drive your memory out of my heart had to be made again."

"It was hard?" asked Ida very softly.

"It was relentlessly cruel." Weston's voice grew sharper. "Still, I tried to make it. I gave way in only one point—I came to see you now and then. Now it's so hard that I'm beaten. I've failed in this thing as I've failed in the other."

He straightened himself suddenly, with a little forceful gesture.

"I'm beaten all round, beaten to my knees; but I don't seem ashamed. Even if you can't forgive me, I'm glad I've told you."

"I think," said Ida, "I could forgive you for one offense—the one you seem to think most important—rather easily. It would have been ever so much harder to do that had you gone away without telling me."

"You mean that?" cried Weston, and, stooping over her, he caught one hand and gripped it almost cruelly.

"Can't you take anything for granted?" Ida asked demurely. "Must one always explain in full to you?"

She felt the man's arms close about her, and his lips hot on her cheek; but in another moment he drew away from her.

"But this is madness," he said. "I have nothing. In a few more weeks I shall be an outcast."

"Ah," said Ida, "you have given me all that counts for anything, and"—she looked up at him with shining eyes and burning cheeks—"you belong to me."

He stood silent for several moments, with trouble in his face, apparently struggling with himself.

"What are you thinking of?" she asked,

Weston raised his head.

"I dare not think," he said. "I've won you by unfair means—and yet, knowing that, I'm only filled with the exultation of it. Still, this thing has to be faced and decided now. You know I love you—but is it right that you should be bound to a man who may never be able to marry you?"

"Is that any great obstacle," asked Ida, "if I don't object?"

"It is," said Weston, hoarsely. "I want you now."

The girl was almost startled by the change in him. His restraint had broken down once for all, at last, and she saw by the tension in his face and the glow in his eyes that his nature was stirred to its depths. In a moment or two, however, he seemed to succeed in imposing a partial control upon himself.

"I had meant to come to you only when we had made the mine a success," he said.

"To save your pride!—you could think of that?"

Weston laughed harshly.

"My pride—there isn't a shred of it left. But now, at least, the situation has to be faced."

"Is it so very dreadful?" asked Ida, with a smile. "You have told me that you love me. Is that a thing to be ashamed of? Must I tell you that I am glad you came to me when you were beaten, and not when you had won? Is there anything that I should trouble myself about?"

"Your friends' opinion, your father's opposition——"

He broke off, and Ida, who turned in her chair, looked around suddenly with her cheeks flushed.

"My father," she said, "is able to speak for himself."

Weston started, for he saw Stirling standing just inside the doorway looking at them gravely. Their attitude and the girl's expression would, he realized, be significant to a man of the contractor's intelligence. Then Ida rose and faced the elder man.

"I think I would better tell you that I have promised to marry Mr. Weston when things are propitious," she said. She looked around at Weston with a smile. "At least, I suppose I have."

"Ah!" said Stirling, dryly, "the situation rather suggested it. Mr. Weston has, no doubt, something to say to me."

Ida glanced at Weston and slipped out of the room.

CHAPTER XXXI

HIGH-GRADE ORE

Stirling waited until the door closed before he turned to Weston.

"Sit down. We've got to have a straight talk," he said.

Weston complied, feeling that he had to face the most unpleasant few minutes he had ever spent in his life. He had given way to his passion in a moment of desperation, and he fancied that he could make no defense which would appear reasonable to such a man as his companion. In spite of this, he was filled with a certain reckless exultation. Ida Stirling loved him.

"What Miss Stirling told you was correct," he said. "At least, I intend to marry her if ever—things are propitious; but, as far as I can remember, she did not bind herself."

"There are occasions when one's memory gets a little confused," said Stirling, dryly. "You have made the situation quite clear; but there are one or two points to consider, and, so far, you haven't troubled to ascertain my views on the matter."

"That remark," said Weston, "is quite warranted. I have only this to say. When I entered your house half an hour ago I hadn't the faintest notion that I should permit my feelings to run away with me."

"Then this thing has been going on for quite a time?"

Stirling's tone was coldly even, but Weston did not like the question. The form of it rather jarred on him. He realized, however, that he was on his defense, and would probably have to put up with a good deal more than that.

"I have had a strong regard for Miss Stirling since I first met her in British Columbia," he said. "That, however, is all I can admit. I do not know how she thought of me, and I have, at least, never knowingly, until this evening, spoken a word which could show her what my feelings were."

"Oh," said Stirling, "you've lived in the woods. If you hadn't, you'd have found out by now that young women possess a certain faculty of putting things together. Anyway," he added enigmatically, "I don't know that the bush isn't as good a place to raise a man in as the hothouse Susan Frisingham talked about."

Weston gazed at him in some astonishment, but the contractor made a little gesture with his hand.

"Well," he said, "you meant to keep the thing to yourself?"

"Until I had made the Grenfell Consolidated a success, when I should have come to you."

"Quite the proper course," commented Stirling. "It's kind of a pity you didn't stick to it. When you had arrived at that wise decision, why did you come here to talk to my daughter?"

It was a shrewd question, and perfectly warranted, but Weston answered it candidly.

"I think I came because I could not stay away," he said.

"Then it never occurred to you that my daughter might fall in love with you?"

A flush crept into Weston's face.

"At least," he said, "I never came here with the intention of profiting by that possibility."

Stirling laughed in a rather dry fashion.

"Then she was to do it all at once, when you intimated that she had permission to?"

"It almost looks like that," Weston admitted, with an embarrassment that surpassed anything he had expected. "I'm afraid," and he made a deprecatory gesture, "that I've made a deplorable mess of the whole affair."

"You have," said Stirling. "As it happens, however, that's in your favor. If you'd shown yourself a cleverer man in this matter, it might have occurred to me that it was Miss Stirling's money that you had your eyes on."

Weston turned and gazed at him with the blood in his forehead.

"I wish with all my heart that Miss Stirling's money were at the bottom of the sea!" he said passionately. "There's just another thing I have to say. I came to your house in a fit of desperation a little while ago, so shaken by what I had just had to face that I was off my guard. When I told Miss Stirling what I felt for her it was a folly—but I did it—and I have no excuse to make."

Then, to Weston's astonishment, the contractor's manner changed suddenly, and he leaned forward with a smile.

"Well," he said, "it's possible that she could find one or two for you. But we have to face the situation. It seems that you love my daughter, and there is reason for believing that she is fond of you. Now, Ida has been accustomed to every luxury, and the only thing you count on is a share in the Grenfell mine, which I guess you will admit may go under at any time. What do you propose to do?"

"I don't know," replied Weston, simply. "It's a question that has been driving me to desperation lately."

"Well," said Stirling, "I could find a way out of the difficulty. Are you open to place yourself in my hands, do what I tell you, and take what I may think fit to offer you?"

"No," answered Weston. "I'm sorry—but I can't do that."

"Then, if the Grenfell goes under, you'd rather go back to the bush and chop trees for the ranchers or shovel on the railroads?"

Weston sat very still a moment, with his face awry. Then he looked up resolutely.

"Yes," he said. "I think that, by and by, Miss Stirling would be glad I did it. She would not have her husband her father's pensioner. After all," he added, "one meets with sudden changes of fortune in the west."

Then Stirling suddenly stretched out his hand and laid it on his companion's shoulder.

"I've been twice warned by short-sighted women that my daughter might make an injudicious marriage, and on each occasion I pointed out that when she chose her husband she would choose just right," he said. "Now it seems that she has done it, and I'm satisfied."

He let his hand fall, and, while Weston gazed at him in bewilderment, smiled reassuringly.

"Go back to the mine when you like," he added. "You admitted that you would take advice from me, and all I suggest now is that you hold fast to every share you hold, and make no arrangements of any kind until after next settling day. In the meanwhile, if you'll go along to the first room in the corridor it's quite likely that you'll find Ida there. I've no doubt that she'll be anxious to hear what I've said to you."

Weston could never remember what answer he made, but he went out with his heart beating furiously and a light in his eyes; and when he entered the other room Ida stretched out her hands to him when she saw his face.

"Then it isn't disaster?" she said. "You will stay with me?"

Weston drew her toward him.

"Dear, I must still go away to-morrow, but we have, at least, this evening."

It was all too short for them, but Weston left in a state of exultation, with fresh courage in his heart, and it was in an optimistic frame of mind that he started west the next day. For several weeks he toiled strenuously under the blinking fish-oil lamps in the shadowy adit, but there was now, as his companions noticed, a change in his mood. The grimness which had characterized him had vanished. In place of toiling in savage silence he laughed cheerfully when there was any cause for it, and showed some consideration for his personal safety. He handled the sticks of giant-powder with due circumspection, and no longer exposed himself to any unnecessary hazard from falling stones. The man was softer, more human, and on occasion whimsical.

For all that, the work was pushed on as determinedly as before, and both Saunders and Devine experienced the same difficulty in keeping pace with their comrade's efforts, though they had grown hard and lean and their hands were deeply scarred. Yard by yard the adit crept on along the dipping lode, and one evening they stood watching Weston, who was carefully tamping a stick of giant-powder in a hole drilled in the stone. The ore had shown signs of getting richer the last few days, but their powder was rapidly running out, and they had not decided yet where they were to obtain a fresh supply. His directors had sent him neither the promised machines nor the money with which to hire labor, and he chafed at the fact that, as it was a long and arduous journey to the nearest station where he could reach the wires, he could not ascertain the cause of the delay.

The storekeeper nodded when at length Weston carefully clamped down a big copper cap on a length of snaky fuse and inserted it in another hole.

"Well," he said, "I guess this shot will settle whether there's high-grade ore in front of us."

He struck a sputtering sulphur match and touched the fuses.

"Now," he said, "we'll get out just as quickly as possible."

They ran down the adit, with Devine in front swinging a blinking lamp, and crawled out, gasping, into the cold evening air as dusk was closing down. Then they sat around and waited until there was a crash and a muffled rumbling. Weston stood up, but Saunders made a sign of expostulation.

"You just sit down again and take a smoke," he said. "We've got to give her quite a while yet."

There was a reason for this. The fumes of giant-powder are apt to prove overpowering in a confined space, and in case of some men the distressful effects they produce last for several hours; but when Weston filled his pipe he scattered a good deal of the tobacco he had shredded upon the ground. A strike of really rich ore would, he knew, send the Grenfell Consolidated up, and he had worked since morning in a state of tense anticipation, for the signs had been propitious. He contrived to sit still for some minutes, and then stood up resolutely.

"You may wait as long as you like," he said. "I'm going back to the adit now."

They went with him, Saunders expostulating and Devine carrying the lamp. Thin vapor that turned them dizzy met them as they floundered into the dark tunnel. The lamp burned uncertainly, but they crept on by the feeble ray of light over masses of fallen rock, until they reached a spot where the adit was blocked with the debris. Weston, dropping on hands and knees, tore out several smaller fragments, and held up one of them; but as he did it there was a faint, hoarse cry, and sudden darkness, as Devine fell forward upon the lamp.

"Get me out! Quick!" he gasped.

Weston felt for the lamp, and contrived to light it, though he wasted several matches in the attempt; but he felt greatly tempted to disregard the dictates of humanity when he hooked it in his hat.

"Well," he said reluctantly, "I suppose we'll have to take him out."

They did it with some difficulty, and left him unceremoniously when they had deposited him, limp and almost helpless, in the open air; for miners who meet with unpleasantness of that kind recover, and one does not make a discovery that promises to put thousands of dollars into one's pockets very frequently. They went back, and, though Weston felt faint and dizzy, he flung himself down among the smaller stones, and thrust one or two of them into Saunders' hands.

"Feel them—and look at the break!" he exclaimed.

Saunders poised one of the stones carefully, and then glanced at the rent where it had been torn from the rock.

"Yes," he said, "we've struck it this time, sure. Guess we'll get out of this and make supper."

"Make supper!" Weston gazed at him incredulously. "I don't stir out of here until sun-up!"

Then he tore off his tattered shirt and stood up, stripped to the waist.

"Get hold of the drill," he said, hoarsely. "You've got to work to-night."

Saunders remembered that night long afterward. For the first half-hour he was troubled by a distressful faintness; and when that passed off, as the air grew clearer, his back and arms commenced to ache unpleasantly. He already had toiled since soon after sunrise; but Weston, too, had done so, and he, at least, seemed impervious to fatigue. So intent was he that every now and then he swung the heavy hammer long after his turn had run out, without asking for relief; and Saunders judiciously permitted him to undertake the more arduous task. By and by, however, Devine crept back to join them, and, when at length morning broke and the mouth of the adit glimmered faintly, Weston glanced at his bleeding hands as he flung down the hammer.

"I suppose we'll have to let up for an hour or two," he said reluctantly.

Saunders staggered when they reached the open air, and Weston seemed to have some difficulty in straightening himself, but they got breakfast, and afterward lay smoking beside the fire, almost too stiff to move. It was getting cold among the ranges now, and they were glad of the warmth from the blaze.

"We'll go on for two or three days," said Weston. "Then we'll pack every load of ore out to the New Passage smelter and get them to reduce it. Devine and I will take it down to the railroad over the Dead Pine trail. The freighter from the settlement should be in with his pack-train by the time we're ready."

"Nobody ever brought a pack-beast in or out by Dead Pine, and there'll be deep snow in the pass," Saunders expostulated.

"Then," said Weston, curtly, "I'm going to do it now. If we can't raise a stamp and reducing plant, we have got to prove that we can make a trail to the railroad by which we can get our ore out without spending a small fortune on packing. If we can get over Dead Pine divide it should shorten the present trail by half; and I'm under the impression that if we spend a few thousand dollars on making a road up the big gully it could be done."

Saunders looked at Devine, who made a little sign.

"Oh," he said, "he means to try it. I guess we've got to let him."

They went back to work by and by; and a few days later Weston and Devine and a grizzled freighter breakfasted in haste beside a sputtering fire. A row of loaded pack-horses stood close by in the rain, and a cluster of dripping men gathered round when at length Weston rose to his feet. The freighter waved his hand to them with a little, dry smile.

"We're going to blaze you out a new road, boys, and it will save me some in horses if it can be done," He said. "Guess you'll be sorry when you see what the next man strikes you for, if we don't come back again."

There was some laughter; and rude good wishes followed the three wet men as they plodded away beside the loaded beasts into the rain.

CHAPTER XXXII

GRENFELL'S GIFT

It was snowing hard, and, though it was still two hours before sunset, the light was growing dim when Weston pulled the foremost pack-horse up on the edge of the gully. He and Devine had each a beast in his charge, and the freighter had started with two, but one of these had been left behind with a broken leg and a merciful bullet in its brain. That country is a difficult one, even to the Cayuse horses, which are used to its forest-choked valleys and perilous defiles.

In front of them a rugged peak rose above the high white ridge of Dead Pine. They could see the latter cutting against a lowering sky some twelve hundred feet above, though the peak showed only a ghostly shape through its wrappings of drifting mist. In altitude alone the ridge was difficult to reach, but, while that would not have troubled any of the men greatly, the ascent was made more arduous by the fact that the unmarked trail followed the slope of an awful gully. The latter fell almost sheer from close beside their feet, running down into the creeping obscurity out of which the hoarse thunder of a torrent rose. Here and there they could catch a glimpse of a ragged pine clinging far down among the stones, and that seemed only to emphasize the depth of the gloomy pit. On the other hand, the hillside rose like a slightly slanted wall, and the sharp stones of the talus lay thinly covered with snow between it and the gully.

The freighter glanced dubiously up the hollow.

"I've struck places that looked nicer; but we can't stop here and freeze," he said. "We'll either have to take the back trail and camp among that last clump of pines or get on a hustle and get up."

"I'm certainly not going back," said Weston. "We have come out to see in just what time we can make the journey to the railroad over the new trail. When we have done it, we'll try to spread the information to everybody likely to find it interesting."

"You're not going to worry about how many horses you leave behind, I suppose?"

"That," said Devine, with a little laugh, "is one of the facts they never do mention in a report of the kind. We've lost only one so far, and two bags of rather high-grade ore."

"If you've one altogether when you fetch the head of this gully you'll be blame lucky," said the freighter. "Give that beast a whack to start him. Get up there!"

They went on, with the snow in their faces, and the stones they could not see slipping beneath their feet; and the light grew dimmer as they proceeded. A bitter wind swept down the gully and drove their wet clothing against their chilled bodies, while the hillside, growing steeper, pushed them nearer the brink of the awful hollow. The slope of the latter, as far down as they could see, was apparently too steep to afford a foothold, and every now and then there was a roar and a rattle as the stones they dislodged plunged into the depths of it. Weston, plodding along behind the freighter, however, kept his eyes fixed for the most part on the face of the hill, for it seemed to him that the cost of changing that perilous passage into a reasonably safe trail would not be excessive.

When they had climbed for an hour, the snow grew thicker, and it became evident that the light was dying out rapidly. The freighter announced that he could scarcely see a dozen yards ahead, and Weston could discern no more than the blurred shape of the horse that floundered over the slippery stones a few paces in front of him. He could, however, hear Devine encouraging the one he led, and occasionally breaking out into hoarse expletives.

"It's gluey feet they want," said the latter, when they stopped for a minute or two. "You can't expect horses to crawl up a wall."

"They've managed about half of it," Weston declared. "We could make this quite an easy trail with a little grading. It's the only really difficult spot."

"Well," said Devine, dryly, "I guess you could. In this country they call any trail easy that you can crawl up on your hands and knees. Still, that little grading's going to cost you about two thousand dollars a mile."

They could scarcely see one another when they went on again, and the sound of their footsteps was muffled by the sliding snow. Weston could dimly make out something that moved on in front of him, but it had no certain shape, and he stumbled heavily every now and then as the stones rolled round beneath him. He gripped the pack-horse's bridle in a half-numbed hand, but, as he admitted afterward, he made no attempt to lead the beast. He said he rather clung to it for company, for the others vanished now and then for minutes amidst the whirling snow.

Suddenly there was a crash and a cry behind him. For a moment he stood half-dazed, with his hand on the bridle, while the jaded horse plunged. Then he let it go as the freighter appeared, and together they stumbled back to where Devine was clinging to the bridle of another horse which lay close at his feet amidst a wreath of snow. He staggered back just as they reached him; there was a frantic scrambling in the snow, and then the half-seen horse rolled over and slid away down the white slope of the gully.

They watched it, horrified, for a moment or two; and said nothing for a brief space when it vanished altogether into the obscurity. The sight was more unpleasant because they knew that they had seen only the commencement of that awful journey. Then Devine, who was white and gasping, made a deprecatory gesture.

"I don't know whether it was my fault," he said. "The beast stumbled and almost jerked me over. Then I guess the bridle either broke or pulled out."

"Two horses and four bags of ore, and we're not through yet," commented the freighter. "Guess it's going to cost you something if you pack much pay-dirt out over Dead Pine trail. Anyway, you'll have to get that grading done before I come back here again."

"Get on," said Weston, quietly.

They struggled on; and in another half-hour the gully died out and lost itself in the hillside, after which they made a rather faster pace over the thinning talus. Still, it was snowing hard, and none of them was capable of much further exertion when, soaked through and white all over, they limped into the lee of a ridge of rock on the crest of the divide. A bitter wind wailed above them, but there was a little shelter beneath the wall of ragged stone, and, picketing the jaded horses, they lay down in their wet blankets, packed close together in a hollow, when their frugal meal was over. There was nothing they might make a fire with on that empty wind-swept plateau.

Any one unused to the gold trail would have lain awake shivering that night, and in all probability would have found it very difficult to set out again the next morning, for a horrible ache in the hip is, as a rule, not the least unpleasant result of such experiences; but these men slept, and took up the trail almost fresh with the first of the daylight. It was by no means the first time they had slept out in the open in the frost or rain, and fed on wet, unwarmed food.

In due time they reached the settlement on the railroad; and, after delivering the remaining bags of ore to the station-agent and leaving the freighter with his horses, Weston went back along the trail with Devine. Descending the gully in clear daylight, they reached the Grenfell camp without misadventure.

It was some time later when the freighter, coming up by the other route, with provisions, brought them a letter. It was from the manager of the reducing plant, who stated that the yield of the ore sent him for treatment was eminently satisfactory, and he enclosed a certificate with particulars, as they had requested. Probably with a view to further business he also offered to purchase any of the Grenfell shares they might have to dispose of.

Saunders' eyes gleamed as he handed the certificate around.

"I guess that's going to send our stock up with a bang," he said. "We'll put it right into Wannop's hands, so he can get a notice of the new mineral field into the papers. The smelter man doesn't seem to know that the last news we had was that the Grenfell stock was tumbling down, but when he's open to buy it's a sure thing that he figures it will soon stand at a big premium."

Then he waved his hand impressively.

"After what Weston has told us, boys, you want to get hold of the significance of that. People have been selling our stock way down, on the notion that before they had to deliver they could cover at a still lower figure. Now, they can't buy it. We're going to smash them flat."

They celebrated the occasion that night with the most elaborate meal Devine could prepare, and invited as many as possible of their neighbors, who also had struck what promised to be payable milling ore. As it happened, their satisfaction was fully warranted, for a few days after Weston's letter arrived in Montreal two gentlemen connected with western mines called on Wannop. Stirling was sitting in the latter's office at the time, and he made no sign of retiring when they entered.

"We should like a few minutes' conversation with you about the Grenfell stock," said one of the strangers. "Naturally, we'd prefer to have it alone."

Wannop looked at Stirling, who smiled and answered the man.

"I'm afraid you'll have to put up with my presence," he said. "In fact, this is a pleasure that I've been expecting for the last few days."

"What standing has Mr. Stirling in this matter?" the stranger asked.

"I hold most of the Grenfell stock that's likely to be salable," said Stirling, dryly. "You can't pick up much on the market, which is presumably why you have come to Wannop. Seems to me you have been selling rather heavily."

"If we'd known you were in it, we might have let the thing alone," one of the men admitted.

"You're going to realize that it's quite a pity you didn't."

The men looked at each other, and one of them turned to Stirling.

"I'll get to the point," he said. "We have certainly been selling, and now that settling day is almost on us we find that we can't buy in. Now, of course, if you hold most of the available stock you have the whip hand of us. We'll admit that right away, and we're quite prepared to face any reasonable tax you and Wannop may think fit to exact. Still, it might be wiser to be reasonable."

"How much do you want?" Stirling asked.

They told him how many shares, and Stirling appeared to consider.

"Well," he said, "what are you going to offer?"

One wrote something on a strip of paper and handed it to the other, who nodded, and made an offer.

"That's our idea," he said. "I don't mind admitting that it will cost us twenty cents on the dollar."

"No," said Stirling, "it's going to cost you just whatever I like to call it. I can swing every dollar that stock stands for up to two or three. Will you do me the favor to glance at that certificate?"

Wannop handed it to the nearest man, and the latter's face fell.

"Now," said Stirling, "at the moment, you're the only people anxious to buy; but I've only to send that certificate and a nicely worked-up account of the rich new find around to the press, and everybody with a dollar to spare will be wanting Grenfell stock. Still, there'll be no shares available—I've made sure of that. I'll ask you, as men with some knowledge of these matters, where's the price going to?"

One of the men sat down limply.

"What'll you take to hold the thing over until after settling day?" he asked.

"In money?" inquired Stirling, whose face grew hard. "If you put it that way, we'll call it half your personal estate."

The second man, who saw that his companion had been injudicious, hastily broke in.

"No," he said; "in the shape of mutual accommodation. Perhaps there's some little arrangement you might like us to make."

Stirling laughed, "Anyway, why should you want to make an offer of that kind? Suppose I held the certificate over, it wouldn't straighten things out for you. You have to deliver to the people who acted on my behalf so much Grenfell stock, and you can't get it—now."

"That's true," was the dejected answer. "What are you going to do?"

"That," said Stirling, grimly, "is a matter that must stand over until I can send for the man who found the Grenfell mine. I can't tell you what course he's likely to adopt, but in the meantime I'd like to point out just how you stand. You set in motion the laws of supply and demand to break a struggling man. They're the only ones you recognize; but, as it happens, they're immutable laws that work both ways, and you're hard up against them now. It's not a pleasant situation, but I can't say how far we may be disposed to let you off it until I've had a talk with Mr. Weston. After that, I'll send for you."

There was nothing more to be said; and when the two men went out, Stirling turned to Wannop.

"If you can get a wire to Mr. Weston, tell him to come back at once."

"I'll have it done," said Wannop. "He said he had sent an Indian to wait for letters or messages at the nearest railroad settlement. You have those men in your clutches. You could break them if you wanted to."

"Well," laughed Stirling, "on the whole I'm more disposed to make them hand over a moderate sum, and to let them off after that, on condition that in the future they keep their hands off the Grenfell Consolidated."

"You'd take their word?" Wannop asked.

"Yes," said Stirling, with an air of whimsical reflection; "in this case, anyway, I 'most think I could. They've had about enough of the Grenfell Consols. I guess they found them prickly."

Then he went out, and Wannop despatched a telegram to Weston, who left the mine immediately after it reached him. Somewhat to his astonishment, he, found Stirling awaiting him when he sprang down from the car platform in the station at Montreal, and the latter smiled benevolently as he grasped his hand.

"Ida would have come along if I'd let her," he explained. "I felt, however, I'd better make things clear to you before you saw her. We'll go straight to Wannop's office and have a little talk."

It did not take Wannop long to explain the situation; and when he judiciously left Weston and Stirling alone together, the latter smiled at his companion.

"Well," he said, "as the specimens we have just been handling seem quite as rich as the last lot, it's evident that your share in the Grenfell will keep you comfortable, and, as far as I'm concerned, there's no reason why you and Ida should not set up housekeeping as soon as you like. Now, it's my intention to hand her a block of the Grenfell stock as part of her wedding present, on condition that she takes your advice as to what she does with it. I'd just like to suggest that you make the people who want that stock subscribe quite smartly, and then let them off. It's not wise to push a beaten enemy too far."

Weston, who agreed with this, expressed his thanks and then asked a question.

"Wannop mentioned one lot of six hundred shares. Where did you get those?"

"They were thrown on the market by an English holder. I believe you gave some stock to friends over there?"

"I did. On condition that they didn't sell without consulting me."

"Then it seems that somebody must have gone back on you."

Weston's face grew a trifle flushed.

"I think," he said, "we'll let that subject drop altogether. It's a rather painful one."

Stirling made a sign of comprehension.

"Well," he said, "I've other business on hand, and I guess Ida is expecting you."

Weston took the hint; and not long afterward Ida was smiling up at him with shining eyes. They had a good deal to tell each other, and some time had passed when Ida said:

"We'll go back to the bush again as soon as the snow melts, if only for a week or two." Then she flashed a quick glance at him. "That is, unless you are longing for a trip to England."

A shadow crept into Weston's face as he remembered the six hundred shares, but he smiled a moment later.

"No," he said. "We'll go over there together by and by—but not just now. We'll camp beside the lake where I met you first, instead."

After a while Ida lifted his right hand gently, and glanced down at the battered knuckles and broken nails.

"I'm glad it's hard and strong—strong enough to keep me safe. And those scars will wear off, dear," she said. "There are scars of another kind that don't—but with those you and I have nothing to do."

Then she looked up at him.

"Do you know what first made me think of you?"

"I don't," replied Weston, smiling. "In fact, I have often wondered."

"Then," said Ida, "I'll show you. I mentioned the picture once before, but you didn't think it worth while to look at it. That was left to me. I looked at it very often while you were away."

She led him across the room, and Weston started and flushed when she took out the picture Arabella Kinnaird had made.

"No," said Ida, "I really don't think you have any reason to regret your conduct that eventful evening."

"I never fancied that you or Miss Kinnaird saw me," laughed Weston. "I'm afraid it was a remarkably foolish action."

"It was one of the little actions that have big results," said Ida. And in this she was correct, for one must reap as one has sown. Then she looked up at him.

"If you hadn't taken Grenfell's part that night you would not have found the mine."

Weston smiled, and gripped the hand he held in a tightening clasp.

"The mine!" he said. "Grenfell gave me you!"

THE END